LIBYRINTH

LIBYRINTH

PEARL NORTH

TOR®

A TOM DOHERTY ASSOCIATES BOOK
NEW YORK

LIBYRINTH

Edited by James Frenkel

A Tor Teen Book
Published by Tom Doherty Associates, LLC
175 Fifth Avenue
New York, NY 10010

www.tor-forge.com

Tor® is a registered trademark of Tom Doherty Associates, LLC.

Library of Congress Cataloging-in-Publication Data

North, Pearl.
    Libyrinth / Pearl North. — 1st ed.
        p. cm.
    "A Tom Doherty Associates book."
    Summary: In a distant future where Libyrarians preserve and protect the ancient books that are housed in the fortress-like Libyrinth, Haly is imprisoned by Eradicants, who believe that the written word is evil, and she must try to mend the rift between the two groups before their war for knowledge destroys them all.
    ISBN-13: 978-0-7653-2096-4
    ISBN-10: 0-7653-2096-7
    [1. Books—Fiction. 2. Fantasy.] I. Title.
    PZ7.N815Li 2009
    [Fic]—dc22
                                                                    2009001514

First Edition: July 2009

Printed in the United States of America

0 9 8 7 6 5 4 3 2 1

For my sister Betsy,
who read Charlotte's Web *to me*
every night when I was four.

ACKNOWLEDGMENTS

I would like to thank my husband, Steve, for his untiring support and tactical advice; my editor, James Frenkel, for his helpful insights; and my agent, Jenny Rappaport, for her enthusiasm. Special thanks go to the Untitled Writer's Group for their encouragement and critiques. In particular, Jonathan opened up a whole culture to my imagination with the suggestion that "they would call themselves Singers." I read much of this novel to Sharon, Diana, Susan, Dominique, and Sandy of the Women Writers and their responses were helpful and invigorating.

Finally, my thanks to those writers whose books populate the pages you are about to read, as well as to all writers past, present, and future. Words are the carriers of ideas, and our world is continually enriched and refreshed by those who ply them.

LIBYRINTH

1

Griome's Letter

The wind howled and the flames roared, but the books, as they died, merely fell silent.

The Eradicants had arrived before dawn, erecting their bonfire outside of the Libyrinth's main entrance, as they did every year. For weeks the Libyrarians and their clerks had been collecting books for the annual sacrifice.

Now Haly, clerk to the Libyrarian Selene, stood with her people in a ring around the bonfire, watching the black-robed, masked Eradicants file out from the vaulting, ornate archway of the Ancient library to feed the fire with words. Dead words, according to the song the Eradicants sang.

When a word is spoken, it is born, when it is written, it dies. Sacred fire of life, free the shackled dead. The meaning of the murdered word, by Yammon may it be said.

The low, sonorous chant droned on as the smoke from the burning books grew thicker, spreading an acrid cloud across the flat, rocky Plain of Ayor. The rising sun painted the Libyrinth's great central dome, towering spires, and massive curved walls with flames of its own. The structure was one of the greatest sites the Ancients had left behind; a library so vast that even after generations, Haly's people had yet to catalogue all the books it held.

And it was built to last. When the Eradicants had first begun migrating into the southern part of the Plain of Ayor over two hundred years before, they had tried to seize the Libyrinth, but even their advanced weaponry could not breach its thick stone walls. Unfortunately the nearby city-states of Ilysies and Thesia were more vulnerable, and since most of the people of the Libyrinth were connected with those nations by blood or allegiance, the Eradicants soon extracted a treaty that included this yearly ritual of destruction.

Haly shivered in the chill wind and pulled her brown clerk's robes closer about her. The Eradicants said the books were dead, but she knew different. For as long as she could remember, she'd heard their voices. She heard them now, uttering their last words to her as the flames consumed them.

"Wilbur liked Charlotte better and better each day. Her campaign against insects seemed sensible and useful," said the book in the hands of the Eradicant at the front of the procession. As he neared the fire, its flickering glow reflected off the black metal of the gun half-hidden among his robes. Haly knew well the book he held; *Charlotte's Web*, one of her oldest companions. As he tossed it into the fire, Haly's throat clenched and the bitter, salt taste of sorrow filled her mouth.

She glanced up at Selene, who stood next to her with an expression of blank, stony endurance. On her other side, her friend Clauda, a kitchen servant, glared at the Eradicants with sullen anger. All the faces of the Libyrarians, the clerks, and the servants were set and hard, immobile. They did not cry. They would not give the Eradicants the satisfaction of seeing them cry. Briefly, fiercely, Haly envied them their inability to hear the books. They knew these tomes, sure, with their eyes and their minds, even with their hearts. But they did not have to hear the voices of Wilbur and Templeton and Charlotte grow faint and drift away in the smoke of the fire. The wind shifted, flinging sparks to sting and sizzle at Haly's tear-streaked cheeks.

After the burning, Haly fled to the maze of bookshelves beneath the Libyrinth, to the books that had not been burned. "Two houses, both alike in dignity"; "He was just a country boy"; "In a hole in the ground there lived a hobbit." The multitude of familiar voices comforted her even as she grieved those she'd lost.

It was dark down here, the towering metal shelves spaced so closely that they brushed her shoulders on either side. Apart from the ever-present book voices, the stacks were silent. Incidental noises were quickly absorbed by the books, which gave off a dry, peppery smell, and in some cases, when the books were very, very old, a fragrance like marigolds.

The trails the Libyrarians used were marked out in palm-glow; luminescent handprints and fingerprints giving directions in a language of the Libyrarians' own devising. At a glance Haly could tell that *Anna Karenina, Uncle Tom's Cabin,* and *101 Things to Do with a Potato* lay to the right, while one hundred volumes of the *Intergalactic Encyclopedia* lay to the left.

Of course, *she* had other markers as well. "The heart of the young Gascon throbbed violently, not with fear, but with eagerness," said a book to her left. Haly stopped, leaned against one of the metal struts of the shelves, and allowed herself to become lost in the adventures of d'Artagnan, Athos, Porthos, and Aramis.

Haly's earliest memories were of wandering these stacks for hours against the warnings of her elders; cautionary tales of overzealous Libyrarians who lost their way in the endless maze and never returned. But even as a child, Haly had liked the tales the books told better, and in forgotten corridors she discovered worlds of adventure and majesty, and secrets. Tiny things like the thoughts of ants, vast things like the language of stars, and all the in-between things, like what happened to her food when she swallowed it and the financial difficulties of mid–nineteenth century French philosophers.

Often the things she said when she got back were cause for punishment as well—like the time she told Peliac that a creature called the lungfish was the first being to walk on dry land.

"Lungfish? Lungfish?" she had cried, her long, thin face stretched even longer in horror. "There never was such a thing as a lungfish! Don't spout lies, or deign to teach your elders, child. Now off with you! A night without supper will teach you not to mock the wise."

Before long, Haly learned to keep the voices of the books and the things they said to herself. Now, at fifteen, she knew a good deal more than a clerk should, but most importantly she knew how to keep her mouth shut. The other clerks and Libyrarians had forgotten that she was once that odd child who spouted stories and facts before she could read.

Nod, of course, being an imp, never forgot anything. As Haly approached the stairs that led out of the stacks, carrying an armload of books for Selene, he popped his bald, fist-sized head out from a shelf. "What do they say? What do they say?" he cried, leaping to the floor and tugging at the hem of Haly's robes. Nod was a foot tall, with long, wiry arms and legs and pebbly red skin. He grinned at her, his eyes nearly disappearing in his tiny, wizened face.

"I can't read to you now, Nod," Haly told him. "I have to get these books to Selene."

"Wicked beastie!" shouted Nod, shaking his tiny fist at her and hopping up and down in fury. Haly stepped around him, adjusting the stack of books in her arms.

"The world is made of stories. Their variation is without number, but every tale that was ever told belongs to one of these sacred seven: Birth, Peril, Hunger, Balance, Love, Death, and Mystery," said *Theselaides*, which spoke the loudest. It wasn't the one she would choose to listen to. There was one at the bottom, for instance, that had a woman's voice—a calm, quiet voice saying something about rivers, and a snake, and a sacred tree, but *Theselaides* was closer, and a bully. "Each of the Seven Tales has its own guardian and its own science, but beyond them all is Time," it said adamantly as she climbed the stairs to the Great Hall.

The door to the stacks stood in the alcove of the Fish, opposite the pointed arch of the hall's main entrance. Haly blinked in the light that streamed into the vast round room from the skylights in the dome far above. Spaced at even intervals about the Great Hall were the alcoves of the Seven Tales, each with a carving of its guardian—Mouse, Goat, Lion, Fish, Cow, Dog, and Fly—over the archway. Above the carvings, a balcony ran all the way around the room.

Between the alcoves, the walls of the Great Hall were lined with shelves that in turn were lined with books; but here, human voices could be heard as well. Black-robed Libyrarians and their brown-garbed clerks browsed the shelves and stood about the large, round console in the center of the room, studying, gossiping, and debating. Not far from where she stood, Peliac ran a group of children through their lessons. "A-B-C-D-E-F-G, H-I-J-K-L-M-N-O-P, Q-R-S, T-U-V, W-X, Y, and Z. Now I know my ABCs, all the books are mine to read."

"Birth is the first tale and Literature is its science, for without imagination nothing would exist," said *Theselaides*.

Haly skirted the lesson group and crossed the Great Hall, passing through the archway to the pillared entrance hall. Ahead of her were the massive, ironclad outer doors. On either side was the passageway that ran around the Libyrinth in a great circle, connecting the kitchen, dining hall, stables, and towers.

As Haly neared the kitchen, the smell of roasting quail beckoned to her in its own language, and her stomach rumbled in answer. "Hunger is the third of the Seven Tales. The Lion is its guardian, and biology is its science," said *Theselaides*. She glanced at the stairs that led to Selene's quarters. If she took these books to her now, the Libyrarian might have another errand for her right away, and then who knew how long it would be until she got something to eat. Maybe not until after the Eradicants' feast.

Haly found Clauda in the laundry yard, hanging tablecloths up to dry. "You missed lunch," her friend said, taking Haly's hand and dragging her between the rows of damp, white fabric. Like most of the servants at the Libyrinth, Clauda was an Ayorite. She was shorter than Haly, with a broader build and paler skin. She had shoulder-length coppery brown hair, blue eyes, and freckles. Haly was part Thesian, dusky and slender by comparison.

Clauda plopped on the ground and pulled a small bundle wrapped in leaves from her apron pocket, proffering it to Haly. "Sit down," she said. "I saved this for you."

Haly sat beside her friend and unwrapped the parcel with eager fingers. It was still warm, and after she'd removed the first few layers, steam rose up to greet her with its delicious aroma. Quail. "Clauda, this is for the feast tonight. . . ."

"Aw, they'll never miss one, or two." Grease glistened at

the corners of Clauda's mouth. She shrugged. "I was hungry, and I knew you would be, too. Besides, better we should have them than those book-burning bastards. Here, I've got bread, too." She pulled a white, fluffy slab from that same all-giving pocket. Haly stopped arguing and feasted.

"A Thesian showed up this morning after the burning; an envoy from the prince," said Clauda as Haly concentrated on picking the steaming, fragrant flesh from the quail without burning her fingers. Clauda was an accomplished gossip. "The Eradicants have conquered Thesia, and the royal family is in prison. They'll probably be executed."

The quail suddenly turned dry and tasteless in Haly's mouth. Until now, the city-states of Thesia and Ilysies had protected the Libyrinth from the Eradicants, had sold them food in exchange for information, and generally supported them. Now, with one of them gone, the Libyrinth was more vulnerable than ever. Not to mention the fact that many of the Libyrarians were from noble Thesian families, including Head Libyrarian Griome, uncle of the ruling prince of Thesia. "That's bad news," she said, feeling numb. "Poor Griome."

Clauda nodded. "I never thought I'd feel sorry for that old sour melon, but I do. Having to entertain these monsters when they're about to put his own nephew to death? He must be beside himself. I bet he'd do anything to save him, if he could."

"The second Tale is Peril. Peril is the Goat," said *Theselaides*.

"Clauda!" Kitchenmaster Sakal's harsh voice lashed out at them from the kitchen doorway. "I know you're hiding out there again, avoiding work. Get back in here right now! We have a feast to put on!"

The feast was one of the most bizarre formalities of the Eradicants' annual visit. As if to show their indifference to the rite of Eradication, or perhaps to prove the bounty of their storehouse to enemies who someday might wish to starve them by siege, the Libyrarians always prepared a lavish meal for their unwelcome guests.

As Clauda scrambled to answer the kitchenmaster's summons, Haly gathered up the books she'd collected for Selene and headed back to the seventh tower.

"Every book is a door into someone's soul," said *Theselaides*.

The room she shared with her mistress was at the top. It was small and round, with a hearth across from the door, and two windows, one facing east and the other facing west. In the winters (and it was only barely spring now) it was drafty, but they kept the fire burning, and at night pushed Selene's bed and Haly's cot closer to the fire.

Selene now stood at the fire, bending over to poke at the flames with a stick. As Haly came in she straightened and turned around, flinging her long, dark hair behind her. Her pale face was drawn and grave. Though only three years older than Haly herself, Selene was always serious. When Haly first became her clerk, she'd been afraid of the severe young Ilysian, the daughter of Queen Thela Tadamos herself. But in the three years that she had served Selene, she'd found her to be kind and patient, if somewhat humorless. Now Selene's eyes burned with dark anger and she looked back at the hearth. "One of these days the Eradicants are going to start burning Libyrarians as well as books," she muttered, casting the stick into the newly sprung flames.

At that *Theselaides* started up again. "None but the Ancients understand the secret of the fire that does not burn. They encased this miracle of light and power within the objects we know as Eggs, but though I have long sought the method, I have never discovered it. In the days of my youth I believed kolfusion to be the answer, but I was proven wrong—"

"Put them on my desk, Haly," said Selene, gesturing to the

cluttered table between the east window and the door. Haly searched the table for a clear spot, and finally settled them on top of a hand-drawn map, ringed and spotted with tea. The books quieted down as she turned away from them, but not before *Theselaides* fairly shouted, "At the cost of many lives!" at her retreating back.

She went to stand beside her mistress at the hearth. "The Eradicants have conquered Thesia," said Haly.

"I know," said Selene. "We must act on my discovery soon, or it will be too late." Selene reached atop the mantelpiece and from beneath the yellowed skull of a rabbit she pulled a parchment, folded and sealed with red wax. "Take this to Griome, would you?"

"Yes, mistress," she said, and took the letter in her hand.

"To Head Libyrarian Griome," the letter said. "Accept the salutations and solicitations of your servant, most learned scholar. I must once again raise the subject of the underground vault, which I believe to contain many valuable books, and one in particular that is of great significance."

"Shh," Haly told the letter under her breath, hurrying toward the door. She knew a great deal more about goings-on in the Libyrinth than she or anyone else would like.

"Until now, you have refused to send an expedition in search of the vault on the grounds that its precise location is unclear. I am privileged to say that I can now satisfy your concerns on that account. My recent discovery of a mention of the vault in the personal journals of Othalia of Ayor has allowed me to pinpoint the location exactly. In fact, I have prepared a map, which I will be delighted to display to you at your earliest convenience," the letter said on the stairway.

"In closing, allow me to say once more that I would be honored to lead the expedition to the site in order to secure *The Book of the Night* for the greater glory of the Libyrinth and the furtherance of our sacred calling."

The Book of the Night! Haly nearly tripped and fell down the stairs. So that was why Selene had been so tireless in her efforts to locate the vault.

As she rounded the final curve of the staircase, Haly nearly ran into Arche, Frise, and Breal, who stood under the archway in close conversation. They were all clerks and all a year older than her. Arche drew herself up as Haly came to an abrupt halt in front of her. Frise and Breal, who were in the bloom of first love, moved to one side and leaned upon each other, waiting to see what she would do.

Arche was Griome's clerk, and as such, she ruled over the other clerks, rewarding those she liked with the prestige of her friendship, and heaping scorn upon the rest. Like her master, she was a pureblood Thesian, with dark skin and tightly curled hair. She looked down her classical Thesian nose at Haly and said, "What's your hurry, Hallucination? Does your little cook friend need your help in the kitchen?" Frise and Breal exchanged sly, knowing smiles.

Haly didn't have many friends among the clerks. Not being able to talk about what the books told her somehow made it hard to talk about anything else. She was always examining her words before she spoke them, afraid she was about to give something away. The whole process made her shy and withdrawn among her peers. But it was Clauda, a servant and not a proper companion for a Libyrarian-born child, who had always and without hesitation believed in Haly's ability to hear the books, and though they never spoke of it anymore, Clauda's belief somehow made Haly feel free to say whatever might be on her mind.

"We'll all be helping in the kitchen this afternoon," Haly noted. The three clerks frowned at her. Griome's insistence that the clerks serve the Eradicants at the feast was a sore spot. Haly wondered if they'd heard about the fall of Thesia yet. If not, she wasn't going to tell them. "I have a letter for your master," she said, holding out the folded parchment in hopes that Arche would take it off her hands.

But she only sneered at her and said, "Take it to him yourself."

Without another word, Haly hurried past them and up the steps of the fourth tower. The letter Selene had given her wouldn't shut up. It kept repeating itself, and if it kept this up she was going to start thinking about what it said. She hated that. Things always got so complicated, and she worried. Except this time excitement made her hands tremble. No book was more sought after—by Libyrarian, Thesian, Ilysian, or Eradicant—than *The Book of the Night*. The tome held the secrets of the Ancients, all of their machines and miracles, and most importantly, the method for making the Eggs that powered them.

Rare and prized above all else, one Egg could light and heat the Libyrinth for generations—no more palm-glow, no more pneumonia in the wintertime. And no more Eradicants. Whoever possessed a Maker of Eggs would rule over the others. And now she understood Selene's sense of urgency. According to her findings, the vault was located on the border of—

"Shh," she said again, this time to herself, and then took up humming in her head a little ditty Clauda had taught her: *One makes two, three makes four, we'll come knocking on your door, with a six-pack Cadillac, give that god a phone, this cold hand is—*

Thesia.

Grunting in exasperation, Haly slammed her hands against the door of Griome's chamber with somewhat more force than was necessary. It swung open wildly, crashing into the wall behind it.

Griome looked up from his table, squinting at her from behind the thick lenses of his glasses. Lines etched his sagging jowls with bitterness, and a fringe of sparse white hair stuck out around the edges of his bald brown head. Haly bowed hastily and approached him with the letter outstretched in her hand. "Libyrarian Selene sent me with this," she said.

With agonizing slowness, Griome wiped the ink from his quill with a black-streaked cloth, and set it down on the table. He reached out and took the letter from her.

Haly nearly sighed with relief. They didn't understand how much these little errands of theirs cost her. She swung around again and headed for the door.

"Did I give you leave?"

She stopped short. Still facing the door, she hung her head. "No, sir. I beg your pardon, sir."

"Begging is of little use, and stop hanging your head like a whipped mule, girl. Turn around!"

Haly did so. Griome glowered at her over his desk. "A fine excuse for a clerk you are. Dashing off without a by-your-leave." He opened Selene's letter and read it quickly. His face betrayed little, but when he finished, there was a note of barely suppressed excitement in his voice as he said, "Tell your mistress I will be happy to meet with her tomorrow, as soon as the Eradicants depart. Now, I happen to have another errand for you, if you're not too busy."

She wouldn't point out that his own clerk loitered downstairs with nothing to do. "Of course, sir. I'm sorry, sir."

Griome grumbled but berated her no further. He dipped his quill in his pot of ink, and began to write. "Dearest Nephew." The words, their ink still wet, sounded raw with emotion, a level of anxiety and affection that Griome would never permit himself to show. Haly felt her cheeks go red and she stared out the window behind Griome, trying not to hear his words, but it was no use. "Do not despair," the letter went on. "Even now, in your darkest hour, there is hope. A new development has arisen. One of my Libyrarians has uncovered the location of *The Book of the Night*. It may be the

Eradicants can be persuaded to spare you in exchange for such information. Take heart; all that can be done is being done. Your affectionate uncle, Griome, Head Libyrarian."

Shock and dread filled Haly. How could Griome do such a thing?

He scattered powdered bone upon the ink to dry it, folded the letter, and sealed it with black wax. He handed it to Haly, saying, "Take this to the envoy from Thesia, and be quick about it. He is in the stable yard, preparing to depart."

She didn't dare meet Griome's eyes as she took the letter from him. Her hand shook, but he didn't notice. Should she destroy this letter, or deliver it as she was told? It didn't matter. Griome would go forward with his plan regardless.

Haly hurried to the dim, cavernous stable. The overwhelming smell of hay and dung coated the back of her throat. Sunlight from the large archway at the end of the double row of stalls lit the dusty air with millions of tiny particles of brilliance. She ran out into the yard, past the goat shed and the chicken coop, to where the Thesian envoy, resplendent in his green and black livery, prodded his horse toward the gate with his heel. The boar of Thesia fluttered on the banner above his head.

"Wait," cried Haly, waving the letter in her hand. When she handed it over to him he glanced at the seal. He gave her a curt nod and was off, Griome's desperate words fading as he went.

It's bad enough they come here and burn our books, but we have to cook for them, too," Clauda growled as Haly approached her. She stood with Jan and Bessa at the worktable that ran the length of the steamy, clattering kitchen. "All our best stores, too." Clauda nodded at the steaming pot of asparagus soup in front of her.

Beside her, ten-year-old Jan shrugged his shoulders and arranged bowls on a tray. "What can we do?"

Clauda spat into the soup pot. "Not much," she said, stirring vigorously.

Haly leaned in and whispered in her ear, "I have to talk to you, right now." By the time she'd returned from the stable yard, Selene and the other Libyrarians were in Griome's quarters with the Eradicants, working out the details of next year's quota. They'd be there until the feast began. There was no opportunity to warn her mistress of Griome's plan.

Clauda looked up at her, curiosity gleaming in her eyes. "But the feast will start soon."

"I know."

Clauda's eyes widened further. She knew Haly wouldn't risk getting in trouble unless it was something really important. She turned to Jan. "We're going to need more flour. I'll fetch it."

"So do you think Griome will steal Selene's map?" Clauda asked when Haly finished. They were in the storeroom, surrounded by sacks of flour and barrels of preserved goat meat.

"I don't know. Maybe he'll have Arche do it. Maybe he already has. But I still can't believe Griome would really give the location of *The Book of the Night* to the Eradicants."

"To save his family?" Clauda shrugged. "Put yourself in his place, what would you do?"

Haly didn't know. When she was a very tiny baby, her own parents had ventured deep into the stacks and never returned. But Clauda's mother, Hepsebah, was the Libyrinth hearthmistress, her father was the stablemaster, and her uncle was Sakal, the kitchenmaster. She had numerous siblings and cousins among the Libyrinth servants. She would know. "What are we going to do? If the Eradicants get *The Book of the Night*, they'll destroy it."

"Or worse, what if they don't destroy it?" said Clauda. "What if they find someone to read it for them? Then we'll really be up Calamity Mountain without a rope."

The door to the storeroom opened. Sakal stood there, glowering at them. "There you two are. Shirking again! The Eradicants are waiting for their soup. You." He grabbed Haly by the arm. "Just because you're Libyrarian-born doesn't mean you can do as you please. You'll serve that soup, girl, along with the rest of your snot-nosed kind." He dragged her from the storeroom and shoved her toward the row of clerks awaiting the serving trays that were being laden by the kitchen staff. Frise and Breal were there, smirking, but where was Arche?

"And you!" bellowed Sakal, rounding on Clauda. "Don't think I won't tell your mother and father about this!" Clauda yelped as the kitchenmaster cuffed the side of her head. "Help Jan with the salads!"

Haly took her laden tray out into the dining hall. Like a row of dark birds, the Eradicants sat at the senior table that ran the length of the room and stood on a raised platform. Griome, one of the few senior Libyrarians who was not displaced by the guests, bore their company with stony cheer.

The Eradicants had taken off their masks. As Haly served the soup, she glanced once or twice at their faces, surprised, as always, at how ordinary they looked. She always expected yellow eyes and sharp teeth. That was how they'd been described to her as a child, and that was how she still thought of them, even though she knew better. Hastily she placed the brimming bowls before them.

As she served the last Eradicant, a tall, lean man with a deeply lined face, Arche entered from the corridor with a folded piece of paper in her hand. She handed it to Griome. It looked like a letter, but it was no letter. Even before Haly glimpsed its tea stains, she knew what it was. The only words it spoke were the names of places: the Plain of Ayor, the Tumbles, the Pit of Glass. Selene's map. Haly stood, frozen to the spot, watching in horror and helplessness as Griome glanced at it, then refolded it and handed it to the Eradicant at his right, a hawk-nosed man with closely set, piercing gray eyes.

Forcing herself to move, Haly turned, stepped off the plat-form, and walked swiftly back to the kitchen. She found Clauda licking all the salad plates before piling lettuce and watercress upon them. Haly gripped her friend's shoulder with such force that Clauda gave a start of panic. "Sakal, I was just—Oh. Hi." She took in Haly's expression and frowned. "What is it?"

Haly leaned close and spoke quietly. "You know what we talked about just now? It's happened."

2

The Devouring Silence

It's gone," said Selene, after she and Haly had searched their chamber for her map, leaving no book, blanket, table, or chair unturned. "Whosoever neglects the Tales neglects salvation," muttered *Theselaides* peevishly, from the corner where it lay amid a heap of papers and quills.

Selene ran one hand through her hair, slowly turning in place, gazing about the disheveled room as if the map might suddenly appear out of nowhere. At last she stopped and her hand fell to her side. The setting sun threw a broad bar of gold into the room, casting her face in shadow, but something of the sun remained in her eyes, burning. "Are you sure, are you absolutely positive that it was my map Griome gave to the Eradicants?"

Haly nodded. "I recognized the rings from your tea," she said, silently adding, *Please, don't ask me more. Just let me help.*

Selene bowed her head, righted the overturned chair, and set it in its place beside the hearth. She sank into it and stared at the glowing embers of the fire. The room grew dark as the sky outside turned purple with dusk. Selene looked at Haly, her face filled with self-recrimination. "I told Griome about the map in the letter you took to him."

Haly barely stopped herself from saying, *I know.*

"Silence is the habit of the fearful," said *Theselaides.*

Abruptly Selene stood up. She dredged a pair of saddlebags from beneath her bed and started packing.

"What are you doing?" asked Haly.

"I am going to attempt to reach the vault before the Eradicants," said Selene, continuing to toss clothes and papers and books into the saddlebags. "There is something in it that they must not have. Something they desire more than all the heads of the Thesian ruling family together in a basket with a bow upon it. And Griome has all but given it to them."

"*The Book of the Night.*" The words came unbidden from Haly's lips. She fell silent, too late.

Selene turned to stare at her. "You know, then."

Haly did not like to lie, but she knew the truth would not be believed. "I saw, in your notes one day. I didn't mean to, but—"

Selene shook her head impatiently. "They must not possess it. Ilysies is no more than four days' ride from the vault. Perhaps if I can reach my mother's palace in time, it can be hidden."

"I will go with you," said Haly.

Selene shook her head again. "You have served me well. It is worse than ingratitude for me even to speak of this with you, much less ask—"

"You are not asking," said Haly.

"When Peril joins Mystery, the Dog eats well," said *Theselaides.*

* * *

They went down the tower stairs to the ground floor. The feast was still underway, so it was only a matter of nerves for a Libyrarian and her clerk to pass unnoticed through the hallway and into the stables.

As they neared the stalls where the horses were kept, Haly heard footsteps behind them. She tensed and shrank against a stall door, inching for the darkness, but the figure she saw hurrying toward them was not the tall, robed form of an Eradicant. It was Clauda, struggling under the weight of a basket tied to her back.

"What are you doing?" she whispered as Clauda reached her.

"What does it look like? You're not leaving me behind. Bet you didn't think to pack any food, did you?" She hitched her shoulders, making the basket wiggle. "This was supposed to be for the Eradicants' trip back, but they can forage for bitter berries for all I care."

"How did you know?" said Selene, the blade of her knife winking silver as she returned it to her belt.

"Who do you think slipped that note into your salad?" said Clauda.

Selene glared at Haly. "How much does she know?"

"I know enough," said Clauda. "I know where we're going and I know—"

"Where do we go? Where do we go?" came a voice from the top of the stall door, and the tiny, grizzled form of Nod the imp leaped down and landed on top of Clauda's basket, making her stagger.

Selene stared at Clauda and Nod in silent anger. "We don't have time to argue about it," she said. "Come on. If you know of this, it's better you not stay here anyway."

Dawn found them on the ragged plain, the cold wind whipping their cheeks with dust. The Libyrinth was nothing but a memory beyond the edge of the horizon, and for Haly the sky rang with the absence of its voices like a great blue bell struck by the rising sun.

Selene's horse stopped to nibble at the leaves of a wind-bitten shrub and she prodded its flank with her heel. The beast dug its broad, split-toed hooves into the dirt and bellowed in protest. Haly and Clauda's mounts joined it and the three horses set about steadfastly denuding the shrub with their mobile lips and yellow, slablike teeth.

"I guess we'll take a break," said Selene with a nervous glance at the horizon behind them. "But only a short one."

Grasping the long, woolly locks of her horse's pelt, Haly lowered herself to the ground and stretched, trying to ease the aching in her butt. Clauda rummaged in her basket and passed out salted rolls.

Haly bit hungrily into the roll. She stayed close to her mount, taking what comfort she could from its bulk. The vast horizon and flat landscape unnerved her. "How much farther is it?" she asked around a mouthful of roll.

"Another three days," said Selene. "We'd better keep moving."

When they remounted, Nod, who had been exploring a nearby rock, clambered up the shaggy pelt of Haly's horse, which grunted in protest. As he topped the creature's flank, his little hands grasped Haly's cloak and then her hair.

"Hey, what are you doing?" she cried, trying to disengage him, and succeeding only in tangling him further in her hair. "Hey, get off. Ow!"

"He's trying to get a better view," Clauda observed as Nod scrambled to the top of Haly's head. "Hey Nod, can you see anything, are we pursued?"

"Are we pursued, are we pursued?" said Nod unhelpfully.

"Aw, he wouldn't know an Eradicant from a wallow rat,"

said Haly, snatching him from her skull and plunking him down on the horse's rump.

Toward nightfall they came to the edge of a wood, the trunks of the trees like black fingers raised against the glow of the setting sun. Their horses stumbled as they rode them into the shadows of the branches.

"Can't we stop?" asked Clauda. "Don't Eradicants sleep, too?"

"I think I heard somewhere that they do," grumbled Haly.

Selene nodded, her face lined with weariness. "We'll make camp in the cover of the trees, but no fire."

They spread their saddle blankets in a clearing, and Clauda brought bread, fruit, and dried sausage out of her basket. With a large, sharp cleaver, she sliced the sausage and handed each of them a palm-sized piece. They ate in silence, and afterward Haly fed apples to the horses. When she returned, Clauda was already snoring. "Get some sleep," said Selene. "I'll stay up and watch."

"Beasties sleep, beasties sleep, Nod watches," said the imp from somewhere in the branches above them.

Selene glanced at Haly, and she shrugged. "I guess he doesn't want to be caught by the Eradicants either," she said.

Selene tilted her head doubtfully, but her eyes were already closing. "He sounds more alert than the rest of us anyway," she murmured, lying down.

Haly shifted on the hard ground, trying to find a comfortable way to support her head on her arm. They'd ridden all night and day; she should be too tired to care about the sticks and rocks beneath her, but she twisted and turned, and got up several times to rearrange her blanket.

It was the silence, she realized. All her life she'd been surrounded by the voices of the books—muted at times, but ever present. Now that they'd stopped riding, the silence pressed in upon her, impenetrable as the thick walls of the Libyrinth.

"Selene," she whispered to the dark form beside her.

"What is it?" Selene's voice was muffled with weariness.

"After we get *The Book of the Night*, we'll go to your mother's palace in Ilysies."

"Yes."

"Is it a very beautiful palace? Are there soft beds? Will there be wine, and a fire?"

"Most certainly, and the bounty of her lands on the table."

"Olives?"

"Olives and cheese, and a goat slaughtered for the return of the daughter. Now get some sleep, we travel again in a few hours."

The wind rustling the leaves slowly died away, and darkest silence crept in among the trees. Haly lay on her back, exhausted, waiting for sleep to take her. But it would not come. She heard Selene drop into the deep, steady breathing of sleep, and still she lay awake.

The night was cloudless, and she could see through the branches of the trees the stars shining in a multitude of light. She searched among them for the constellations she knew, and found the Mouse. Palla, the crèche nurse, used to tell her a Mouse story when she was small: There had once been seven blind scholars who set out to conquer Time. But they were struck down for their folly and turned into mice who, though they no longer knew what Time was, were even more at its mercy than they'd been as humans.

Living creatures were at the mercy of other things besides time, Haly thought. With a sigh she got up and walked a short distance from their camp to squat among the bushes.

When she returned, not even the deep, soft breathing of Clauda and Selene or the snorts of the horses broke the stillness. As Haly groped her way toward her blanket, she saw a deeper darkness curled around Selene's motionless form like a tentacle of the night.

Haly squeezed her eyes shut, and then opened them, staring harder, but the apparition did not dissolve. In fact, it appeared more solid than ever, its curving shape defined by a vivid absence of light. She glanced around the camp and saw more tentacles. Clauda was almost completely enveloped in them. Her entwined form shifted across the ground in a series of rapid jerks. The tentacles were dragging her away.

Nightmare horror welled up in Haly's throat and burst past her lips, but her scream made no sound. She lurched forward in dreamlike disorientation, fighting against a sudden lethargy, trying to reach Clauda to pull her free. Before she could take a step, her left foot went numb. Haly looked down and saw a tentacle slithering up her leg. Her calf went numb, and then her knee. She tried to drag herself away from it, but sleepiness overwhelmed her, and she found herself lying down without consciously deciding to do so.

Tentacles slid up her body, destroying sensation as they went. Silence enveloped her; she could not even hear the rush of her own blood. Accustomed all her life to hearing things, this absence of sound sent a wave of terror rolling through her to disturb her imminent slumber. In a surge of panic she stood, whipping her torso from side to side and shaking her legs to dislodge the darkness. Despite her efforts, a tendril still spiraled up her leg, and with fingers stinging with the return of sensation, she gripped it and tried to pry it off.

It was a mistake. As soon as she touched it, her hands went numb again, and again the wave of sleepy nonfeeling rose up to engulf her. Haly bit her tongue. Faintly she felt the spark of pain, and she bore down, using it to anchor herself in wakefulness.

She released the tentacle and forced her nerveless legs to back her farther away from the thing. She stumbled and fell, her shoulder crunching against a fallen branch. She rolled, both her legs now entangled in numbing blackness, and groped for the branch. Grasping it awkwardly, her teeth still bearing down on the tip of her tongue to prevent herself from losing consciousness, Haly beat at the thing entwining her legs. Doubtless she struck herself as often as the tentacle, but she couldn't feel the difference.

Over and over again she flailed at it with the stick; the absence of sound, of feeling, and the near invisibility of her opponent made it difficult to gauge her success, but eventually the tentacle slipped away like a receding shadow, leaving in its wake the pain of her bruised and gouged legs. She stood up, her tongue awash with agony and the taste of blood.

The tentacles dragged Selene from the clearing now, too, and Clauda had already disappeared among the trees. What had become of Nod she did not know, but the horses were also entangled. As she watched, one of them lurched to the ground. The tentacles around it slowly dragged it across the ground in spasmodic jerks. Haly trembled. She knew what this was now. A Devouring Silence. She had thought it no more than a tale Palla told to frighten the children, but no. It was real. One of the most dreaded machines of the Ancients, it would devour her friends if she did not stop it.

Using her branch to fend off tentacles, Haly frantically searched the clearing until she found Clauda's basket. She rummaged through it and her hand closed around the wooden handle of the cleaver. With her stick in one hand and the cleaver in the other, she ran from the clearing, taking a path perpendicular to the direction in which the tentacles dragged Clauda and Selene. She gave the tentacles as wide a berth as she dared, and then she turned and headed toward their source.

As she ran she slashed out at shadows with the cleaver, and she continued to bite down on her aching tongue, fearful that every branch and leaf that touched her was a nerve-deadening tendril. Twice she had to stop to hack away a real tentacle. She ran until her lungs burned. A terror that she had overshot her target seized her. But there, just ahead in a clearing not much smaller than the one they'd camped in, she saw the profile of an enormous face lying flush with the ground.

It was twice as wide across as Haly was tall. Its monstrous tongue thrust from its lips and split, and split again and again and again, to form hundreds of tendrils of unlight with which to stun its victims and drag them back to its waiting maw. But here, at the mouth, the tongue was only one massive thickness.

Haly circled around the clearing until she was above the thing's forehead. She crept closer. There were lines carved in the ancient steel face, lines curving and spiraling across the brow and cheeks. She reached the ring of soil that the Devouring Silence had turned up when it had tunneled there from underneath the ground to strike at them.

Beyond the chin of the monster, she saw two human-sized coils of tentacle and a smaller third one lurching ever more rapidly toward the mouth. She didn't have much time. Clutching the hatchet, she ran across the forehead, leaped over the left eye, and planted her feet on the cheek. She lifted the cleaver up and swung it down on the tongue. It felt like chopping through tough muscle, like the stag she'd helped Clauda butcher once. A metallic shriek pierced the silence of the night and Haly gripped the cleaver tighter, chopping at the monster's tongue until at last she severed it. It flew apart into thousands upon thousands of tattered rags of blackness, which fluttered away into the sky and took the night with them.

Clauda, Selene, and Nod sat up, blearily looking around in the dawning light. From the woods Haly heard the horses snorting and brush rustling as they righted themselves. With an odd, detached clarity, she watched Selene take in the

Devouring Silence and herself standing on it with the cleaver in her hand. Selene's eyes went wide with shock and her mouth drew back. She let out a long, low murmur, "Bountiful Mother . . ."

Haly opened her mouth to tell them what happened, but her swollen tongue stopped her words. Blood ran down her chin. She staggered to the chin of the monster and stood swaying, suddenly finding it difficult to work out how to move her arms and her legs in order to climb down. The pain in her tongue was very bad. The cleaver slipped from her fingers. She heard it hit the iron face as if from a distance, and wondered what had become of her stick. The trees wheeled against the lightening sky above and she realized she was falling.

Clauda caught her. "Come on, come on," she muttered, getting her shoulder under Haly's arm and helping her take a few steps away from the face. "You're okay. Come on. By the Seven Tales, a Devouring Silence . . ."

Then Selene, too, was at her side, with Nod perched upon her shoulder. "What happened to you?" she said, her voice tense with fear.

"She cut off the tongue, the tongue," chirped Nod. "It flew away."

"Open your mouth," ordered Selene. "Let me see."

Squeezing her eyes shut against the pain, Haly unlocked her jaw. More blood poured from her mouth. The taste of it made her nauseous. When Selene probed carefully at her tongue she cried out but managed not to pull away. "You've bitten it," said the Libyrarian. "Not quite clean through, by the looks of it. It's bad enough, but it could be worse. A poultice of accar leaves will stop the bleeding and stave off infection."

Her swollen tongue wrapped in accar leaves, Haly sat on the ground and watched as Clauda and Selene dug up the Devouring Silence. The bitterness of the leaves made her want to gag, and her tongue seemed to fill her whole mouth; a feeling like suffocation.

When Clauda and Selene at last unearthed the Ancient machine, they used branches cut from the trees to prop it up and flip it over onto its face, revealing the ridged, flexible underbelly with which it propelled itself underground. Squatting in the middle of it, Selene sliced through the underbelly with her knife. She reached in, felt around for tense moments, and then, with a grin, withdrew her black-streaked arm and held up the glowing amber ovoid of the machine-monster's power source.

An Egg. Wonder washed over Haly and she almost forgot the pain of her tongue. She had never thought she would see a real Egg. Her face radiant, Selene jumped from the carcass and came toward her, holding it out to show her. It was about the size of Haly's two hands clasped together. Selene handed it to her. It was warm. A tracery of copper or bronze or perhaps something else entirely wound around its smooth, glowing surface. It was beautiful, and it could power the Libyrinth's defunct heating system for generations to come.

3

The Vault

As they traveled, the plain grew rockier. Three days after their encounter with the Devouring Silence, they came to a place where large slabs of red stone jutted up out of the ground at all angles. "We must be close," said Selene. "This is the Tumbles. We're on the western edge of the plain." For most of the day they wound their way through the maze of striated, wind-scoured rocks.

Weary atop her horse, Haly let the wind's voice lull her. Her enforced muteness compounded the lonely silence of the plain. Her tongue was healing, but Selene had advised her not to try to talk, and in any case, the accar leaves prevented it.

As the wind blew through the jumbled, tilting slabs, it took on a voice of its own, sometimes whispering, sometimes singing, sometimes howling. When the wordless murmuring became muted, comprehensible language, she thought at first that she was asleep and dreaming. "Everyone celebrates but for myself, who must work. But I can hear their songs from my window and they strengthen my resolve." "Heat to the boiling point in a double boiler over, not in, boiling water, one-half cup dark molasses." " 'How is he?' 'Weak. They are quite pitiless.' "

The voices were faint but discernable. Haly sat up in her saddle, eagerly looking around. They were at the far side of the Tumbles. On either side of them a large slab of rock jutted up, slanting, to form a rude archway above their heads. Beyond stretched the flat, pebbly plain once more. Haly squinted against the afternoon sun. A circular mound rose from the ground not far away. She might have mistaken it for a low hill, but when she looked at it, the voices became more distinct. "I was awakened by the waves dragging at my feet."

She nudged her horse up alongside Selene's mount and tugged at her mistress's sleeve. When Selene turned to face her, Haly pointed. Without a word, Selene spurred her horse on toward the circle. "What?" said Clauda, riding up alongside Haly. "What is it?" She glanced at Haly and then caught herself. "Oh, never mind," she said, and took off after Selene.

N ow, how do we open it?" asked Clauda. They had cleared away the dust and rocks to reveal a shallow dome of brass, its rim divided into seven sections. In each section was engraved a different pattern of dots. Selene shook her head. "I haven't got the first idea. None of my research mentioned anything like this. I hope we're in the right place."

Haly listened to them with only part of her attention. While they were clearing the hatch of debris, a book had started talking to her. She had noticed before that sometimes when she was very wrapped up in her thoughts, the books that spoke to her offered relevant passages, and so she paid attention. "It is sound that made the Ancients what they are," this book said to her now, "and sound that is the key to most of their works."

"This has to be it," protested Clauda. "What else could it be?"

"This is it, is it," chanted Nod.

"Do you know how to open it?" Clauda asked him. He'd been very helpful in cleaning the dome, unusually so.

But apparently that was the limit of his contribution for the day. "Nod only cleans. Nod knows not the minds of the Makers."

The Makers, Haly thought, and then the book said, "But what is sound but a vibration—a wave? Sometimes light, too, is a wave."

"Maybe it's a kind of clock," said Clauda. "There are seven sections, like the seven hours. Maybe to open it we have to press the correct hour." She peered at the sky, taking in the angle of the sun.

"A clock? That's absurd. Who would seal a vault with a clock?" scoffed Selene.

Clauda shrugged. "Well, who knows what the Ancients would do? I mean, who would make a thing that burrows underground, pops up, and puts people to sleep with its tongue? I don't know. I think this looks like a clock."

"No." Selene shook her head adamantly. "Do you see these?" She pointed at the sequence of dots along the rim. "These are constellations. They correspond to the Tales. See?" She pointed to one that had a single dot in the center and a ring of six dots around it. "This is the Fly. And this one is the Goat." She indicated one with two dots close together.

"I've never understood why that's supposed to be the Goat," complained Clauda. "It doesn't look anything like a goat."

"It represents the horns," Selene told her.

"Well, the constellations are the Seven Tales and the Tales are the hours, so maybe it *is* a clock."

"It's not a clock, Clauda."

Seven tales, seven hours, seven notes, thought Haly, and
the book interjected, "To explore the works of the Ancients
one must align oneself with the vibrations of the world, and
this world loves music like a flower loves the sun, and opens
to it." Seven notes. She raised a hand, trying to get Selene and
Clauda's attention, but they were too busy arguing.

"What if it is constellations, then," said Clauda. "What
then?"

"It's a matter of figuring out the correct sequence."

"And how are we supposed to do that?"

"According to Theselaides, he unsealed the doors of the
Libyrinth by humming the descant chorus of the Losian con-
certo," said Selene.

Yes! Music! Haly grabbed Selene's sleeve and yanked on it.
"Mmm! Mmm!"

"Yes, I brought my copy of *Theselaides* with me. It's in my
saddlebag," Selene told her. "Will you fetch it?"

Haly shook her head but Selene had already turned back to
Clauda, who stood with her hands on her hips. "So how did
Theselaides figure all that out?" she demanded.

"The declension of Arcturius Sirius to the second moon,
divided by the circumference of a chuckle bird's egg," said
Selene.

"Huh," scoffed Clauda. "The black science of math. You
know, some say Theselaides never existed."

"Then how do you explain the book he wrote?"

In frustration, Haly jumped on top of the dome and lifted
her face, opening her mouth and holding her arms out as if in
song.

"Yes, we need to understand the stars, the sequence of the
constellations, in order to open it. I know, but how do we know
which is the right sequence?" said Selene.

Haly shook her head again.

"What are you doing up there?" said Clauda.

Haly pleaded to Clauda with her eyes. She opened her mouth again and with her hands, pretended to be drawing out sound.

"If you're going to be sick, don't throw up on the dome," said her friend. "We just cleaned it." She turned back to Selene. "I still say it's a clock. Like an old Earth alarm clock. Maybe it's set to open at a special hour. Do you know what time it was when Theselaides discovered the Libyrinth?"

Selene cocked her head to one side. "I thought you didn't believe in Theselaides."

Haly threw up her hands, moaned, and then spat out the poultice of accar leaves. "They're notes. Musical notes," she said. "I'm pretty sure all we have to do is sing them, in order."

Clauda and Selene both stared at her. "That's all?" asked Clauda.

"How do you know?" asked Selene.

Haly gaped. "I learned it from a book," she said.

Selene gave her a puzzled frown. "What book?"

Haly shook her head. "I don't know." A twinge stabbed her tongue. Was that blood she tasted? "Please don't ask me anything more. It hurts to talk. Let's just try it and see if it works, okay?"

The three of them stood evenly spaced around the dome, while Nod perched upon the rump of one of the horses and watched. They cleared their throats. They began at the bottom of the scale, their untrained voices scratchy at first, then smoother as they held the note.

The segment engraved with the constellation of the Mouse, the Tale of Birth, flared into golden light and lines appeared, emanating from its single dot like petals from a flower. Clauda, who stood nearest to it, broke off in a gasp and the light faded. She quickly took the note up again, and the light strengthened.

By unspoken accord, Clauda stayed with that first note when

Selene and Haly moved up the scale. The segment for Peril, the Goat, lit up, and this time, the lines emanating from its dots connected, both to one another and to those that flowed out now from Birth like rays from the sun.

Selene stayed with Peril and Haly alone sang Hunger, the Lion. Its three points gave forth lines of golden light that interconnected with all of the others in a pulsing, glowing web. Haly could hardly believe what she was seeing. She was so captivated by it that she barely heard the book that had helped her say, "The one thing they never failed at was beauty."

Now, supported by the other two notes, Birth maintained its light as Clauda sang Balance, the Fish.

They worked their way up the scale until every segment around the dome was alight and the carvings were no longer visible beneath the intricate web of interconnection between the Seven Tales. Haly glanced at the faces of her friends. Did she look like that, too—transported with wonder? Did they feel like she did—that no matter what occurred in the rest of her life she was one of the fortunate, just to witness this?

The lines of light arced up in great loops like a flower—like the very first note had looked when they sang it. A hole appeared in the center of the dome and grew bigger, and Haly realized that what had appeared to be solid brass was in fact a series of interlocking panels so well fit as to be invisible. The hatch opened and the light went away.

They stopped singing. Haly tasted blood and realized that her wound had reopened without her knowing it. And her throat was raw. It was dark now. How long had they been singing? It had only seemed like a few minutes. Against all rationality, Haly wanted the dome to close, so they could sing and see the wonderful light again. She heard Clauda take a deep breath and sigh, and Selene made a small, wistful sound somewhere between a moan and a laugh. Maybe they felt that way, too. Silently, they stepped over the rim of the hatch.

Panels of soft white light illuminated the steps as they descended them. It was spare, functional light compared to what they had just witnessed, but welcome all the same. "The Egg must still be intact," said Selene in a low, wondering whisper. "Of course, I should have realized that before."

The stairs opened out into a round room about twenty-five feet in diameter, lined with empty shelves. The floor was white tile. Panels of light in the ceiling added their illumination to the lights on the stairs, so much brighter than firelight and palm-glow. In the center of the room stood a round desk, a smaller, more utilitarian version of the console in the Great Hall at the Libyrinth. It was made of a smooth, white material that was neither stone, wood, nor metal.

Haly walked along the perimeter of the room. Behind the empty shelves was a blank wall, but she could hear books on the other side, clamoring for her attention. "All that is told here happened some time before Mowgli was turned out of the Seeonee Wolf Pack"; "Route the wiring from the front light along the frame members to the area of the generator-mounting bracket"; "When tweetle beetles fight it's called a tweetle beetle battle."

Just as in the Libyrinth, there were stacks hidden from view behind the façade of the room they were in—shelves upon shelves of books. But unlike the Libyrinth, there was no door providing access to these stacks. She knelt to peer beneath the lowest of the visible, empty shelves, and discovered that they continued down through a hole in the floor. She just made out the tops of a few books. She reached for them, but the space was too narrow for more than her forearm. As she pulled her hand back out she saw a pair of eyes looked back at her. "Nod? What are you doing there?"

"How clean it is! How clean!"

Haly blinked. The voice was coming from behind her. Tiny hands grasped the back of her robe, and she felt the imp clamber up to her shoulder. Then who was staring at her? Haly gasped and straightened. Panicking, she grasped Nod around the middle and tore him off her back. She held him in her hand, and glanced back beneath the shelves, but there was nothing there.

"She must put Nod down, she must put him down!" Nod struggled violently in her grip.

Haly looked at him and, shaking her head, set him down. He scrambled beneath the shelves and disappeared.

"How do we turn it on?" Selene wondered aloud, still staring at the desk.

At her words a panel, which they had not known was a panel, rose from the top of the desk to reveal a smooth, white face roughly the size of a cart's wheel. "Welcome to the Southwest Visitor Overflow Station," the face said through unmoving lips. Its voice was a mellow contralto. "Please state your desired title, author, or subject matter."

They looked at one another. After a moment's hesitation, Selene said *"The Book of the Night."* There was a pause, and then the console said, "One volume entitled *The Book of the Night* found. Please stand by."

Selene turned to Haly, her face filled with barely suppressed excitement. Haly felt queasy with nerves and she looked over and saw Clauda's tense expression. For generations the Libyrarians had been searching for *The Book of the Night*, so often referred to by Theselaides and other early Libyrinth scholars who concerned themselves with Ancient technology, but so far, never found. Selene looked back at the face and they all watched it expectantly. The face was silent, immobile, and peaceful. "What happens now?" Selene wondered aloud.

Across the room, movement caught Haly's eye. A set of shelves was moving. She blinked. Yes, definitely moving. Like a waterwheel, the shelves cascaded down the wall and disappeared at the level of the floor, replaced at the top by new shelves. Shelves with books on them. "Um . . ."

"Do you think our desk in the Great Hall does this, too? Or would, if it had an Egg?" asked Selene, still staring at the face in the desk.

"Hey, I'm a cook, how should I know? But, maybe . . ." said Clauda.

"Uh . . . folks," said Haly.

"What?" said Selene and Clauda in unison, staring at her.

"Look!" Haly pointed at the moving shelves.

"Oh," gasped Clauda softly, in awe.

"Oh," said Selene, with a note of surprise.

Eventually, the shelves stopped moving, and they stood staring at a wall of books.

Haly went to the shelves, reached out, and took a book off the shelf. *"The Book of Night,"* it told her, and its green cover bore the mark of the seven-pointed star, just as described by Theselaides. "I am the Literate Iscarion, and these are my words," it said, and its voice was the same one that had told Haly about sound and light. Her hands shook. Wordlessly, she handed the book to Selene.

Selene's hands trembled, too, as she took the book from Haly. She ran her fingers across its cover. A frown marred her reverence as she caressed the hand-lettered title. "What language is this? I've never seen it before." There was a pause as she went very still, staring at the cover. She opened the book and flipped through the pages. "It's not one of the known alphabets." Her voice was faint. Haly heard hope dying in it.

"Selene, I . . ." she started. Selene turned toward her and the look in her eyes silenced Haly.

While Haly struggled to speak, the book told her, "The great Liberation is accomplished and it falls to me to interrogate my former master. Endymion is sick and mad and dying, as she's been for many years, but now she's the last Ancient; all the others are gone."

Selene turned from them and put the book carefully back

on the shelf. "All this time, and now, it's in an unknown language," she murmured. "Indecipherable. Useless . . ." She gave a short, hysterical bark of laughter, but when she turned around again, her face was carefully composed. "I'm going to feed the horses and settle them for the night in the shelter of the Tumbles." She turned and headed for the stairs.

"Selene!" Haly cried, at last overcoming her silence. "Wait!"

But Selene did not stop. She put one hand over her mouth, and she ran up the stairs and out.

Haly turned to see Clauda looking almost as stricken as Selene. Cook or Libyrarian, the promise of *The Book of the Night* was a long-cherished dream. "Do you believe me when I say the books talk to me?"

Clauda tore her wistful gaze from the book and looked at Haly. She nodded. "I always did," she whispered.

Haly took *The Book of the Night* from the shelf again. "This one talks to me like all the others. It doesn't matter what language it's written in. I can still hear it."

Clauda's eyes widened. "Tell me. Tell me what it tells you."

Her tongue hurt, but she would speak sharp shards of glass to share this with her friend. She thought of going after Selene, but she would be back soon enough, and then both she and Clauda would convince her. Haly sat down on the lowest step of the stairs with the book unopened in her lap. Clauda sat beside her and Haly recited again from the beginning.

"Unraveling her secrets is the very last task I ever wished for, now or ever, but Yammon says I must and I know that he's right. I don't know what I'll be able to understand now, when so little has ever been clear in all this time, but I will try."

There was a noise from above, from the open door of the vault. She looked up, expecting Selene, but instead saw three masked figures descending the steps, their black robes swirling about them. Haly stood and the book fell from her lap, landing with a loud smack on the floor. Clutching each other, she and

Clauda backed up until they were huddled against the console, watching as the Eradicants advanced upon them. The Eradicants carried tall staves, each topped with a glowing blue orb. As they reached the floor of the vault, they pointed the orbs at Haly and Clauda.

"Mind lancets," whispered Clauda.

4

The Blade and the Jar

The three Eradicants that faced them wore masks with long, pointed noses like birds' beaks. The masks were black, and they covered their faces from the mouth up, but she could see their glittering eyes. Their hoods were off. The Eradicant in the middle, the tallest, said, "Where is the third one?"

Haly looked at Clauda, who returned her confused gaze with one of tightly controlled fear. They both looked up at the Eradicant who had spoken.

"Three of you fled the Tomb of Dead Words," he went on. "Where is she?" He jerked his mind lancet forward and twisted his hand on the shaft. Tendrils of blue light danced around the glowing orb.

"W-we don't know," said Haly, realizing that by the Tomb of Dead Words he meant the Libyrinth. She looked closer at their faces, trying to see if she could recognize them from the burning. But the beaks distorted their appearance so much it was hard to tell anything about what they really looked like.

The one who spoke stepped closer. "Put your hands on your heads," he said.

With her heart sinking into her stomach, Haly raised her arms and felt the brush of Clauda's wrist as she did the same. The vault suddenly seemed very small.

The Eradicant turned to the thinner of his two cohorts. "Vinnais, you and Soth go back outside. Secure the ammunition and check for her." He looked back at Haly and Clauda and waved the sparking mind lancet at them. "I can fry you both before you reach me," he said.

Haly believed it. As the other two Eradicants went back up the stairs, she stared, mesmerized, at the blue fire crackling over the surface of the mind lancet's orb. She'd heard about these weapons, how they could paralyze, kill, or drive one insane. She thought she could smell the electricity—a smell like snow and ashes.

Time crawled by as they sat there under the watchful gaze of the Eradicant, whose blue eyes were like smaller versions of the mind-lancet orb, gleaming behind his long-beaked mask. Haly tried to listen to *The Book of the Night*, which still lay on the floor beside the stairs, but it was difficult to concentrate on anything except the arcing fire of the mind lancet and the gleam in the Eradicant's eyes. She got only a few fragments: "the breath of the tides," "corrupting influence of power," and "harness the wind."

At last Vinnais and Soth returned without Selene. That was something, at least.

"Their mounts are gone, too," said Vinnais. "She must have seen us coming and abandoned these two, to save herself."

Could that be true? Haly wondered, and decided she didn't care. She was just glad Selene was safe.

"We might as well tie these two up," said Soth, the shortest and heaviest of the three. "When Michander gets here, he might want to talk to them."

The third Eradicant, the one who had stayed below, shook his head slowly. "We can do better than that," he said. "These two are Libyrarians as well. Lits." The way he spat that last word, there was no mistaking it as an epithet. They all read. They can *tell* us which one of these is *The Book of the Night*. Then, when Michander arrives, we can present it to him. Such initiative will surely be noted." Beneath the mask, his mouth spread open in a smile.

Soth frowned. "But Ithaster, how can we be sure they aren't lying to us? They could make us look like fools in front of Michander."

Ithaster's hands flexed on his mind lancet. "We can be sure," he said. "Look how they huddle together. They are fast friends, just as that fat fool Griome said. The dark one is the clerk, the other one a servant, a slave in all but name, yet worse—a willing slave. Still, they care for each other. You can see it. Soth, take the servant and tie her up."

"No," Haly protested, wrapping her arms around Clauda and gripping her tightly as Soth came forward and seized her friend by the wrists. Clauda jerked her head forward and bit Soth on the arm. He gasped in pain and drew back a moment, enough to give Clauda a chance to kick him in the knee. Haly rushed forward, trying to grab him around the waist and bring him down, but instead she wound up tangled in his robes at his feet. He kicked her in the stomach and by then Ithaster and Vinnais had come to his aid. Ithaster held her as the other two tied the still-struggling Clauda to one of the vertical support beams of the shelves.

When Clauda was secured, Ithaster whirled Haly around and tapped the end of his mind lancet against her shoulder. Sudden fire raced through her body—agonizing, paralyzing. She screamed. That one brief touch left her trembling and sweating.

"Stop it!" shouted Clauda. "We'll give you the book!"

Ithaster gripped Haly's shoulder, both steadying and restraining her. "I know you will. That was just a small demonstration, the mildest of the lancet's capabilities." He lowered his head to Haly's ear. "We will do far worse to her if you don't cooperate. Do you understand?"

Her head still ringing from the attack, Haly nodded. It was useless. They were going to burn every book here anyway, regardless of whether or not *The Book of the Night* was identified. And in the meantime . . .

"Good," said Ithaster. "Now, we will go through every book in this vault until we find it, and if you lie, or fail to identify it, your friend will suffer unspeakable pain. Don't think you can trick us. We have our own ways of identifying *The Book of the Night*, and if we find you have been false, well . . . Vinnais."

Vinnais struck Clauda in the stomach with his mind lancet. Blue fire burst across her body and she convulsed, her raw scream shredding what was left of Haly's nerves.

Haly's mouth filled with sweet-tasting saliva, and she doubled over and threw up at Ithaster's feet. When she stopped retching, she straightened up shakily and drew the back of her hand over her mouth. "Here," she croaked, and taking Ithaster's arm she pointed to *The Book of the Night*, which was lying on the floor by the steps. "This is it," she said, drawing him after her as she crossed to pick it up. "This is *The Book of the Night*. I swear it. By all the books of the Libyrinth, I swear it." She held it out to him.

It was silent in the vault but for the murmuring of books and Clauda gasping to recover her breath. Haly didn't dare look at her. She kept her eyes on Ithaster, who stared at her a long moment. "That is the book you were reading from, when we found you," he said.

Haly hadn't thought she could be more frightened, but now

she knew she'd been wrong. If they thought she and Clauda had learned anything of use, they'd kill them, but it was too late now. Helplessly, she nodded her head. "Yes."

"When I was a child, she tormented me," said *The Book of the Night*.

"She wasn't reading, Ithaster," said Soth.

Ithaster jerked his head to glance at him and then looked back at Haly, glaring. "What? You mean she's lying?" He grabbed her by the neck of her robe and jerked her forward, raising his mind lancet in his other hand.

"No!" Haly cried out, squeezing her eyes shut.

Behind her she heard Soth say, "I saw the book in her lap when we descended. It was shut."

"I saw it, too," said Vinnais.

The grip on her robe loosened. Haly opened one eye and saw that the mind lancet had been lowered. Ithaster eyed her closely. "But you said you were reading it, when you know that means we have to kill you both."

Haly's mouth opened and shut.

Ithaster cocked his head to one side. "Why would you do that?" He leaned forward slowly, his beaked mask poking her in the cheek. "Unless it was to cover up something even worse. . . ."

"Witchcraft," murmured Vinnais.

Ithaster nodded his head in agreement. He glanced at the book in his hands. "Now I must torment her," it said as he set it down on top of the console.

"Michander will be very impressed with us," said Ithaster, returning his attention to Haly, "when we present him with both *The Book of the Night* and a confessed witch." Tucking his lancet under his arm, he seized Haly's wrists and dragged her to the bookshelves, about a quarter of the way around the vault from where Clauda hung in her bonds, her eyes closed, her pale skin shining with sweat.

Haly tried to wrench her hands free from Ithaster's grip, but he thrust them up over her head and kneed her in the stomach. If she hadn't thrown up already, she would have now. Instead she hung in his grip, gasping, as Vinnais left Clauda's side and came to assist Ithaster. Vinnais untied the cord at his waist and wrapped it around Haly's pinned wrists, binding her firmly to the strut.

Ithaster stepped back and regarded her with satisfaction. Beside him Vinnais was expressionless. Haly felt her heart beating very hard. In her mouth, her injured tongue pulsed in unison, like a fat, wet frog. With a desperate effort of will, she kept from gagging again as the metallic tang of blood overcame the bitter taste of bile. She took a deep breath and tried, somehow, to steel herself for what was to come.

"But I find the task brings me no joy," said *The Book of the Night*.

Ithaster lifted it from the console and ran his hand over the ancient green cover. "It bears the mark of Iscarion. There is no doubt, then," said Ithaster.

He looked back at Haly again. For a moment there was a look of uncertainty in his eyes, and then it was replaced by skepticism. "You had already read it, and were reciting it from memory."

"Yes!" agreed Haly eagerly.

Too eagerly, she realized as Ithaster grinned and brought his face close to hers. "You lie!"

Speechless, she shook her head.

Ithaster's breath was stale in her face. "Yes you do. You are a witch, and I will have your confession. But it must be done properly, as Censor Siblea has taught me. Soth, fetch my kit."

Soth went up the stairs and returned a few minutes later with a carved wooden box with a handle on the top and a latch on one side. He handed it to Ithaster, who set it down on the console beside *The Book of the Night* and opened it.

He took out a short, curved dagger with a black blade, and a small earthen jar capped with a wax plug. "Now," he said, holding the knife to her cheek, "how did you know the words of the book without reading them?"

Haly didn't answer.

"That will never do," he said. "Vinnais." As Clauda shrieked under the blow of the mind lancet, Ithaster slashed Haly across the cheek with the knife. Its blade left a trail of fire, and her hands convulsed against their bonds to reach it.

"Oh, it's bad enough," Ithaster assured her. "It'll scar. But it'll be the least of your woes if you do not tell us everything now."

She had kept her ability a secret for so long. For so long she had feared discovery and punishment, and now, here they were, staring at her through the eyes of her inquisitor. But it would only be worse if she did not confess. Worse not just for her, but for Clauda, too. She glanced at her friend and the terror and pain on her sweat-streaked face made up Haly's mind for her. Just the same, the forbidden words came slowly, catching in her throat like jagged bones. "I . . . I can hear—"

"Haly, don't—" croaked Clauda, her words cut short by another burst from the mind lancet. She went limp and silent.

"I can hear the books," said Haly, refocusing on Ithaster. "They speak to me. That's why the book was closed. I was speaking what the book told me."

The Eradicant stepped back warily. "You *are* a witch. By what sorcery do you cause dead words to speak? What evil deeds do you bend them to? Plague? Fire? Famine? Flood? Well?" He poked her burning cheek with the knife.

"I—no, I'm not a witch, there was no spell. I was just reading, I mean listening, telling. That's all."

"You *are* a witch." He emphasized his words by prodding Haly's swollen cheek with the knife. "How else do you hear a book without opening it?"

"I don't know. I always have."

"That's no excuse." Ithaster grasped her head with one hand and held her still as his knife bit into her flesh, a throbbing pain that grew as the Eradicant slowly carved a curve around her temple.

"Please don't. I didn't mean to do anything. I'm sorry, I really am," Haly whimpered.

"Not good enough," the Eradicant murmured lightly. With an air of distraction he extended the new cut downward until it met with the slash on her cheek. He sat back and surveyed his work. "Now. You are a witch, that is not in dispute. But for the salvation of your soul you must admit your crimes." He produced a small jar, and uncapped it. "Lye. It will cauterize the wound, which will prevent infection. It is most unpleasant, but it is for your own good. You'll see."

The first touch of the powder was like a searing brand burning through her flesh, through her bones, wiping away thought and wrenching a babbling scream from her lips. As she squeezed her eyes shut against the acrid fumes, all hope of somehow withstanding the Eradicants fled. As soon as she could speak she said, "No more, no more, whatever you want, I'll do it, I'll say it. I did it. I'm a witch. I'll do whatever you want."

Ithaster grinned at her. "Indeed you will," he said, and lifted the knife to her face once more.

A wordless sob tore from Haly's lips as she desperately tried to back away. But there was nowhere to go. From above ground came the sound of an explosion, and the vault shook. Ithaster stumbled and dropped his knife. Dust sifted down between the cracks in the ceiling tiles, a few of which fell to the floor with a clatter.

"Yammon's tonsils," cried Vinnais, "what was that?"

"It came from outside," said Soth, picking himself up off the floor. The three Eradicants exchanged glances. "Our wagon! The ammunition!" yelled Ithaster, and they ran up the stairs.

Haly looked to Clauda, who had awakened. Her friend returned her gaze steadily and worked her hands, trying to twist them free of the ropes. Haly tested her own hands as well, but there was no give in her bonds. Neither of them needed to speak. They both knew this was the only chance they'd have.

Frustration and panic bubbled inside Haly and she jerked her hands uselessly, uttering a steady stream of profanity.

"Be still, be still, she must be still," muttered a voice at her ear. Nod. Desperate hope rose inside Haly, and she forced herself to be still as she felt tiny fingers plucking at the ropes that bound her hands. Looking over to Clauda, her jaw dropped at the sight of Nod untying her bonds as well. Another Nod. There were two Nods. Sudden, stinging circulation returned to her hands as her Nod at last loosened the final knot and she was free. Clauda, too, stumbled forward, rubbing her wrists and shaking all over. Haly went to steady her. "Are you all right?"

Clauda gave her a look full of pain and rage. "I'm alive. Come on, let's get out of here."

Haly grabbed *The Book of the Night* from the console and held it against her chest with her right hand, while she snaked her left arm under Clauda's shoulders and helped her friend up the stairs. One of the Nods scrambled ahead of them. She thought she caught a glimpse of the other one disappearing behind the shelves. "There are more dimensions then the ones we know," said the book.

Night had fallen, making the open hatch above them a black portal filled with stars. As they peered over the edge of the hatch the air was cool against Haly's face, welcome despite the sting of her wound. The Eradicants' wagon was on fire. She saw their frenzied forms, silhouetted against orange flames as they ran to and fro, trying to put out the blaze. Above the crackle of the fire and the cries of the Eradicants, Haly heard a growing rumble. She felt it through her hands, which gripped the rim of the hatch, and then out of the darkness came Selene, riding at the head of eight galloping horses, her hair streaming out behind her. She must have stolen the Eradicants' horses, Haly thought fleetingly as she watched the panicked herd thundering toward them. As the Eradicants broke away from their efforts to quell the fire and ran for their rifles, she rode them down. Haly saw Vinnais fall with a strangled cry beneath the hoofs of one wild-eyed beast. Ithaster managed to reach his gun, and took a shot at her but missed.

Clauda jumped up and waved her arms. "We're over here!" she cried, and then ducked down as a bullet whizzed past. Haly peeked over the edge of the hatch and saw Selene, her black robes painted orange by the light of the fire, wheeling on her horse. Ithaster and Soth, both now armed, stood between her and the vault. Selene reached inside her cloak, drew out the glowing Egg from the Devouring Silence, and held it aloft. As Ithaster raised his rifle again, she heaved the Egg into the burning cart.

"No!" cried Haly, Soth, and Ithaster in unison as the Egg arced across the night sky like a falling sun, and fell into the fire. And then Selene was charging toward the vault, scattering the two Eradicants in her wake. Haly caught a glimpse of Soth attempting to retrieve the Egg from the burning wreckage of the cart, and then Selene was there before her, towering upon her mount. She held the reins of their two horses in her hands. The other beasts had scattered in panic.

"Come on," she shouted. "Mount up. When the Egg explodes . . ." She didn't finish. She didn't need to. Haly looked about for some sign of the Nods but found nothing. There was no time. She hauled Clauda up and they both scrambled onto their horses and galloped after her.

Haly concentrated every fiber of her being on getting as far away as possible from the fire and its time bomb. When it came, the detonation made the explosion of the ammunition seem like a sneeze. It was a sound and a quake like the earth splitting in half. It nearly unhorsed Haly. Her horse uttered a bellow of terror and redoubled its speed. All three of them tore into the darkness, galloping under the pitiless stars.

A wild joy filled Haly at the cold night air whipping through her sweat-damp hair and stinging against her face. They were getting away. They were actually getting away.

There was a distant crack, and then a sudden jolt and a scream from Haly's mount broke her rejoicing. Groaning, her horse stumbled and fell to its knees, breathing heavily. Selene, who had been riding just behind her, wheeled her horse around and came back. "Get on!" she shouted.

"No," said Haly, realizing all at once that the best chance for Clauda and Selene to escape was for her to give herself up. "I'll slow you down and we'll both be caught, plus they'll have the book. Here." She shoved *The Book of the Night* at Selene. "Take it."

Selene hesitated. Beyond her, Haly saw Clauda getting smaller and smaller. She knew what she was running from. Nothing, not even their friendship, would stop her. Good. Another rifle shot pierced the night, but went wide.

Haly pushed the book at Selene again. "Take it!" she shouted.

"But it's useless," Selene protested.

There was no time to explain to Selene that she could hear the book, and it wouldn't do any good in any case. "You're the best scholar in the Libyrinth. You'll find a way to translate it. Besides, the Eradicants don't know we can't read it. We can't let them destroy it. Take it and ride to Ilysies."

Selene took the book from her, but otherwise she didn't move. Her lips worked, but no sound came out. "Fire heralds

the end, but leaves cold in its wake; cold and silence," said
The Book of the Night.

"Go!" roared Haly, and she yanked down hard on the
horse's tail. The beast snorted its indignation and sprang into
a ground-eating gallop. Haly watched Selene's face recede, a
dwindling moon in the night, and then she turned to face the
Eradicants.

5

The Last Wind of the World

Clauda fell through thundering blackness lit with flashes of fire and lightning into a thicket of glass brambles. Tiny slivers of bright pain stabbed at her every time she moved. She lay still at last and, staring up, saw a great black bird wheeling across the red sky, a bolt of blue lightning clutched in its talons. The bird banked, and with a horrible scream, dove for her.

She sat up and opened her eyes, the harsh echoes of her own scream ringing in her ears. Her hands, outstretched to fend off the terrible bird, brushed cool rock, and she realized she was in a cave. A vent hole above let in a little light, but not as much as the brilliance that blazed from the cave opening, making her eyes sting. Her hands shook and she lowered them to the woolly blanket that covered her lower body. She frowned and tried to quell the shaking, only succeeding when she trapped them between her draped legs. And then her legs started shaking.

The cave abruptly darkened, and for a moment she thought she was losing consciousness. But it was only Selene, blocking off the light as she entered the cave mouth. She came to Clauda's side, a shocking look of concern on her face.

Clauda remembered the scream. "It was a dream," she said, heat rising to her face. In her lap, her hands jerked back and forth like her grandma Sulie's had done the year before she died. She pulled them up and held them against her chest.

Selene stared intently into her eyes. She held up one finger and ran it back and forth across Clauda's field of vision. "How do you feel?"

Clauda watched Selene's finger track back and forth in front of her eyes, realizing fully that she in fact felt horrible. The harsh light and the movement of her eyes made her queasy. Her tongue tasted like she'd spent the night licking the hearth in the Libyrinth kitchen. Her heart still hammered from her dream and she felt so tired, she could barely get enough breath. Then there was that trembling business in her arms and legs. And not only there. Deep inside her, too, in some mysterious place between her heart and her stomach was an unsteadiness, like she was somehow not put together as tightly as she'd once been. "I'm okay," she said.

Suddenly Selene's finger was gone and the Libyrarian pressed her head against Clauda's chest. Deeply shocked, Clauda braced herself for tears, but there were none.

"Your heartbeat is rapid," said Selene, sitting back again. She took each of Clauda's hands in one of hers. "Try to grip my hands," she said, frowning at Clauda's spastic response. Selene released her hands and turned to reach for Clauda's food basket. Clauda watched in frustration as Selene pawed through her carefully packed basket and at last drew out a flask of water. She uncorked it and held it to Clauda's lips. "Drink," she told her.

Clauda swallowed the water. It helped a little with the bitter, ashen taste in her mouth.

Selene gave her more water, putting a hand behind Clauda's head to steady her as she drank. When the Libyrarian pulled the flask away, Clauda drew a trembling hand across her dripping chin and glanced around the small cave, which was littered with saddlebags and bedding. "Where's Haly?"

Selene's eyes widened, and then she looked down at her lap. "They shot her horse. She wouldn't ride with me. . . ."

A chill settled over Clauda as Selene related the details of Haly's recapture in a flat, expressionless voice. She barely remembered anything about their flight; just an impression of wind and night, her own overwhelming urgency to flee as fast as her horse could carry her, and the feel of the animal's coarse pelt as she clung to its neck and rode, rode, rode, never once looking back. "We have to go back for her," she said, pushing off the blanket and struggling to her feet.

Selene shook her head and said something about it being impossible, but Clauda didn't pay any attention. Instead she concentrated all her effort in getting to her feet. It was hard to control the movements of her legs and her balance was off, but she managed to stagger to the cave mouth, her head spinning at the motion. She gripped the rock and looked out, gasping as she saw the vast Plain of Ayor spread out three hundred feet below them. "Seven Tales," she whispered.

They were already high up in the mountains. Obviously Selene had decided against going back for Haly. Had decided for both of them. Clauda turned to Selene, an accusation on her lips. The cave and its dizzying view wobbled and dimmed and she found herself on her hands and knees, scant feet from the rim of the rock ledge outside the cave mouth.

Nothing but a narrow band of stone stood between her and empty air.

The trail widened past the cave mouth, and there the horses stood tethered in a shallow curve in the mountainside. Before she could even try to crawl toward them, or back up into the cave again, strong arms hauled her back from the edge of the cliff. Selene lifted her and carried her into the cave again, dumping her unceremoniously onto the nest of blankets where she had awakened, then more gently positioning her so that her back rested against the cave wall. Selene rummaged through the food basket again and produced a dried-up chunk of cheese. "Here," she said, carving off a small piece and holding it before Clauda's lips. "Eat this."

Clauda wrinkled her nose at the desiccated crumb. Humiliation mixed with the anger that was already warming her face. To be tended to by a Libyrarian, of all things. People like Clauda were supposed to take care of people like Selene, not the other way around. "I can feed myself. Give me that," she said petulantly, motioning to the basket. Her hand trembled and she quickly lowered it.

Selene gave her a skeptical look and placed the basket in her lap. She sat back on her haunches and watched as Clauda reached in, searching for an apple and spilling most of the contents of the basket before finally finding one and managing, with both hands, to draw it out. Clauda wedged it between her knees and reached for her cleaver.

Selene drew a breath and opened her mouth as if to protest, but she caught Clauda's glare and stopped, a raised eyebrow her only commentary.

"Why did you bring us all the way up here when we just have to go back down again?" Clauda said obstinately, gripping the handle of the cleaver as hard as she could and lifting it to the apple.

Selene grimaced bitterly. "We're not going back down, we're going up—"

"Suck a goat!" Clauda swore as she fumbled the cleaver and nicked herself.

"Here," said Selene, taking the cleaver away from her. "Why don't you let me do this?"

"Because I'm the cook, that's why."

Selene gave her her best wry look. Clauda frowned and stuck her bleeding finger in her mouth.

With infuriating ease, Selene carved off a slice of apple and paired it with the cheese. She held out the morsel. "How many times did you get hit with the mind lancet?" she asked.

"Three, I think." Clauda reached for the food and got it about halfway to her mouth before dropping it. "Crap."

"You're lucky," said Selene.

"You don't say," said Clauda, pawing at the pieces of apple and cheese in her lap and only managing to turn them into smaller pieces of apple and cheese, now fuzzy from the blanket. She *was* hungry.

"I mean it," said Selene, carving another slice of apple and cheese. "Your eyes track. Your mind seems to be intact. You certainly aren't having any difficulty speaking."

Clauda opened her mouth to comment and Selene, with a grin of triumph, shoved the food in.

"Urgh!" Clauda protested, chewing angrily.

Selene shrugged. "These tremors are the mildest of the possible effects of a mind-lancet attack, and don't worry, they're temporary. Unless . . ."

Clauda swallowed. "Unless what?"

Selene shrugged again. "Unless they're not."

Glumly Clauda let Selene feed her the rest of the apple and about half of the remaining cheese. Finally she said, "You never answered my question. Why did you bring us all the way up here?"

Selene sighed. "There's a pass through the mountains ten miles from here. Once we cross it, we'll be in Ilysies."

"Ilysies! Why would we go to Ilysies? Haly is down there!" She raised her hand and pointed outside the cave mouth. It shook and she quickly lowered it again.

Selene glared at her. "We can't go back for her and you know it. Our only hope is to convince my mother the queen to help us." She waved a hand at Clauda. "You can't even walk. Last night"—her voice grew higher in pitch, a near hysteria that frightened Clauda almost as much as the Eradicants did—"you were unconscious by the time your horse collapsed! I had to pry your arms from around its neck." Selene looked down at her hands, which were folded in her lap. They gripped each other, their knuckles white. She released them and stood, pacing the small confines of the cave. "What was I supposed to do?" the lean, dark Libyrarian demanded. "I couldn't go back then, with you like that. I didn't know if . . . I couldn't wake you up. Why did you have to come along anyway? Why did you have to poke into business that has nothing, *absolutely nothing,* to do with you?" Selene stared at her, her eyes accusing. "You shouldn't even be here."

"Oh, so it's my fault," said Clauda bitterly, because really, it was. It would have been too late to do anything about Griome's treachery if Clauda hadn't put that note in Selene's salad. It had seemed so exciting, at the time, to be part of an adventure.

"No!" shouted Selene. "It's my fault! You're my responsibility. Haly is my responsibility." She bent and snatched *The Book of the Night* from her saddlebag and waved it at Clauda. "I was so obsessed with this stupid book that I thought it was worth any risk to save it. Now look what's happened! My clerk has been taken by the Eradicants, the Egg we found is destroyed, and this? This invaluable text that would save the world? It's useless." She threw it and it fluttered across the cave and landed in a corner.

"Not useless," said Clauda, and then, suddenly remembering an explosion last night as she fled, "Did you say you destroyed the Egg?"

"Don't you remember?" Selene's eyebrows drew together. "What do you mean, not useless?"

"Haly can understand it." Clauda leaned forward. "You mean you really burned an Egg?"

Selene's jaw tightened. "I had no choice."

Clauda sat back again. "No choice? Cowshit. You did, too. Leave us there. I mean it's an Egg, for Tale's sake. You can't just burn it, even to save someone. Think what that Egg could have meant to the rest of our people. They could use it to power the heating system—no more wood smoke and pneumonia. Or to light the stacks. Maybe even both. Nobody's that important."

Selene gave her a look unlike any Clauda had seen from anyone before. "Remind me of that the *next* time I'm sitting in the dark listening to you scream."

Clauda pressed herself back against the wall, wishing that for once she'd kept her mouth shut. The food Selene had fed her sat hard in her stomach.

Selene turned away and picked up *The Book of the Night* again. She opened it and stared at the pages for a while. With her back still turned, she said, "What did you mean that Haly can understand it?"

Relieved at the change of topic and the opportunity to be right, Clauda said, "Maybe you heard some rumors, back home, about how she used to pretend that the books talked to her?"

Selene gave her a tight nod.

"She wasn't pretending. It's true. It's always been true.

That's how she knew Griome was making a deal with the Eradicants. She heard it from his letter to his nephew."

Selene thought about that for a moment. "And how she knew how to open the vault. She said she learned it from a book. . . ."

"Probably the maintenance manual that was sealed inside the vault at the time," said Clauda. "And it's how she can understand *The Book of the Night* even though it's in a language nobody knows."

Selene's shoulders drooped and she came and sat down across from Clauda. "Are you sure?"

Clauda nodded. "She recited it to me. Just the introduction. Something about it being the words of the last Ancients. That's what really got us in trouble—or Haly, anyway. They made her tell them about the books talking to her." Clauda suddenly felt very much the kitchen scrub speaking to a Libyrarian, idiotically trying to keep her friend out of trouble, out of sheer reflex. "She had to, Mistress Selene. She didn't want to." She found that she could no longer take Selene's steady, understanding gaze, and looked down at her twitching hands. "They think she's a witch."

She heard Selene's slow, deep sigh, whistling out like the last wind of the world.

"Do you know what they do to witches?" Clauda blurted, looking up.

Selene looked at her with utter stillness, no longer patient, but detached. "No."

"Well neither do I, but we know what they have done, what they might be doing now. . . ." Crap, she was babbling like a stripling. She might be a lowly pot girl, but she was in this situation. Haly was captured and there was no taking anything back. She couldn't afford to be afraid. Haly couldn't afford it. She straightened up and looked at Selene. "How do we get your mother to help us?"

6

Iscarion's Folly

Haly sat on the ground a little distance from the blasted remains of the vault, her hands tied behind her back. Her feet were tied, too, but just the same, Vinnais sat watching her, a rifle in his hands and his splinted leg stretched out before him. "It wouldn't take much," he'd told her after Ithaster had put the rifle in his hands, "just the littlest move, and I'd have all the excuse I need to shoot you dead. It's my leg that's broken, not my hand."

She believed him. Soth was dead, killed in the blast that Selene caused when she threw the Egg into the burning cart. Now Ithaster searched the wreckage of the vault for *The Book of the Night*. The knowledge that he would not find it was all that warmed her in the chilly dawn.

Ithaster emerged from the shattered hatch of the vault, covered with dust and streaked with soot. He sat down heavily beside Vinnais and glowered at her. She had told him the book would not be there, but he hadn't believed her.

"No luck?" asked Vinnais.

Ithaster spoke while still staring at Haly. "No. But it's a shambles in there. Shelves have fallen over. The control station is completely obstructed. We'll have to wait until Michander gets here to clear the wreckage, extract the Egg, and start burning the tomes. Quite likely it is as the witch says, and her cohorts got away with Iscarion's tome, but we won't know until every book has been checked." Ithaster's expression was grim. "Michander will be displeased with us."

Was this why they burned the books one by one at the Eradications, Haly wondered, instead of simply slaughtering the Libyrarians and setting the whole place on fire? Was there one book the Eradicants wished to spare from the flames?

Vinnais nodded. "Just the same, I hope he arrives soon. If we have to go the day without water . . ."

Haly swallowed. Already she was as parched as the dry land around them. She was hungry, too, and her left cheek was one big pulse of pain, steadily throbbing in time with her heart.

Ithaster gave Vinnais a look of concern. "At least I can get you some shade."

Ithaster built a shelter out of struts from the wreckage of the vault and his and Vinnais's robes—beneath them they wore leggings and close-fitting shirts knitted from nubbly, undyed yarn. After that he began removing books from the vault, making little piles of them on the ground. "It is far better to be feared than loved if you cannot be both"; "Little boys squash ants in fun, but the ants die in earnest"; "Samuel Spade's jaw was long and bony."

When the day grew too hot, Ithaster stopped and sat with them in the meager shade. They were silent in mutual thirst and hunger. Haly constantly watched Ithaster, but he barely acknowledged her presence. It seemed he was too preoccupied with survival to bother torturing her again. She tried not to think about what would happen when the other Eradicants arrived.

Heat and thirst overwhelmed her, and she dozed in spite of herself. She was awakened again by Ithaster singing in a bass voice pitched to carry, "Children of the Word, Singers of the Song, voices from afar chant praises to Yammon." She opened her eyes and saw him standing on a nearby rock, waving his arms.

Across the sun-struck plain came the reply, faint yet clearly audible, "Holy are the chords, sacred is the Song, weaving through the world the blessing of Yammon." Haly could just make out tiny figures in the distance, wavering and winking in the shimmering air. One of them appeared to have a cone-shaped instrument through which he sang.

Haly watched with mixed feelings as the Eradicants approached. They had two wagons, and they would have water and food, and she was horribly thirsty and hungry. But there was no guarantee they would give her any of what they had. And then, of course, there might be more "questioning"—more horrible pain—and she didn't think she could bear that.

She recognized Michander as the Eradicant who'd received Selene's map from Griome. He had a long, high-bridged nose and close-set gray eyes that took in the smoking ruins of the cart and the twisted hatchway of the vault before turning their penetrating stare to Ithaster. "Subaltern Ithaster, what has happened here?" he demanded.

As Ithaster drew breath, two other Eradicants left their wagons and came to stand beside Michander, listening intently.

"Ithaster, Soth, Vinnais we, Singer subalterns of Michander three, traveled to small Ayor grave for thee, Iscarion's *Book of the Night* to seek. Found we Libyrarian and servant these, come to enact Griome's treachery. To steal the book and sneak away, but in the tomb we made them stay. The Libyrarian gave us Iscarion's tome, and revealed herself a witch of—" Here Ithaster faltered and fell silent, obviously searching for an appropriate rhyme.

"Come, come," clucked Michander. "Quickly."

Ithaster nodded and resumed his chant. "The Libyrarian revealed herself a witch to be, when she knew the book with no need to read. It was Soth and Vinnais heard the passage . . ."

As Ithaster sang his briefing, the two Eradicants accompanying Michander whispered his words to themselves, and when he had done, they turned away, each reciting the entire account over again from the beginning.

They continued their recitation as they set about dealing with the immediate necessities of burying Soth and setting Vinnais's leg. She thought she might take some satisfaction in his screams, but she didn't. But then, he wasn't Ithaster. Ithaster's scream she was pretty sure she could have relished.

They passed around water skins, and one of the Eradicants, a man of middle years called Hephaestus, knelt beside her and helped her to drink. Haly gulped frantically at the sweet water, afraid she wouldn't get enough, but he held the skin for her until she'd had her fill. They had food, too, and Hephaestus fed her. All of which meant only that they wished to keep her alive, she warned herself, meeting Hephaestus's impassive gaze.

Michander declared that Groil, Basmuth, and Tirran would remain at the vault, burning the books and extracting the Egg, while the rest would return to the Corvariate Citadel. She assumed she was included in "the rest," and she wondered what would happen to her after they got there, but she didn't dare ask, or do anything else that might draw attention to herself. She tried to be very small, as if she could hide inside herself. So far the new batch of Eradicants seemed barely to have noticed her, but that could change.

The cadences of Ithaster's report continued as Hephaestus and Forvane put her in the back of one of the wagons, still with bound hands and feet. As the wagon pulled away Haly smelled smoke. She craned her neck around to see Basmuth feeding books to a fire one by one. If she concentrated, she could hear the book voices beneath the relentless drone of the Eradicant doggerel: "Simon was inside the mouth"; "I saw death rising from the earth"; "Never live in the village again." The voices were but fragmentary whispers, soon swallowed by distance and fire.

As they traveled north and west, the country became marginally more habitable, and in the middle of the second day, they reached a village, a small collection of rough stone huts huddling in the midst of dusty fields and goat pens. A girl who was breaking clods of dirt in one of the outlying fields spotted them. She turned toward the village and put her hands to each side of her mouth. "Singers!" she cried out in a high, carrying note, then tossed aside her mallet, hopped the stone wall, and ran alongside the wagon, grinning.

Haly thought the people would flee, but no. Instead they came pouring out of houses and barns, shouting with joy. Some of them sang, too. Haly heard the word "Singers" spoken again and again, always in tones of happy awe. She also heard the word "witch," with accompanying glares and fingers pointed her way.

By the time they reached the village, there was a crowd of at least one hundred waiting for them. The dirtiest person Haly had ever seen pushed to the front of the crowd and took Michander by the hand, her mouth gaping in a wide grin. Haly, still tied in the back of the wagon, watched in stunned amazement as Michander allowed her to lead him through the throng and into what was surely one of the most impoverished of the meager dwellings. As his back disappeared through the doorway, Haly looked to Ithaster and Vinnais, but they were busily engaged with a man who was worried about a sick cow.

"Remember the song?" said Ithaster. "The one I taught you last time we passed this way?" He broke into his rich bass, "Mares get bloat and cows get bloat if too much pulse you feed them. Hay for a day or two, good as new."

"How are the windmills coming?" Hephaestus asked one middle-aged couple. The pair seemed marginally more well-fed than the rest of the villagers—the head man and woman, no doubt.

"We've built five more since you were here last. But it's hard to get the people to work on them. Song or no, they don't believe that they'll create holyfire."

Hephaestus nodded. "They'll believe when their homes are aglow with light and warmth this winter. After the blessing, we'll teach you how to build the generator."

Haly felt disbelief and outrage at the thought of peasants such as these with electricity while the venerated scholars of the Libyrinth shivered by their hearth fires.

Her thoughts were interrupted when Michander reappeared in the doorway of the hovel with a baby in his arms. A loud cheer erupted from the crowd and women scrambled to spread a newly woven wool blanket on the ground in the center of the village clearing. Hephaestus stood beside Michander holding a case identical to the one Ithaster had in the vault—the one that held the knife she'd been cut with. Haly's heart hammered and her cheek throbbed. But this was only an infant. What could it possibly have done wrong?

The crowd drew back to give everyone a view as Michander knelt and placed the child facedown on the blanket. As he opened the case, Haly muttered, "No." And then louder as panic rose up inside her: "No, no. Stop him!" Why was everyone just standing around watching?

An angry villager leaped onto the cart, slapped her across the face, and plastered a hand firmly over Haly's mouth. "Shut up, you crazy witch," she said. "You'll ruin the blessing!"

The pain of the blow on her injured cheek brought tears to her eyes. Haly blinked them away and watched as Michander took from the case a small, square patch of material. She could just make out a symbol on it: two winged serpents twined about a staff. She'd heard about these from some of the late-period Earth texts; dermal patches used to deliver medicine.

"Behold the mark of Yammon," said Michander. "In the name of our holy prophet, who delivered us from evil, I place upon this child, Isabel daughter of Giselle, the mark and ward of his protection." He peeled a piece of white paper from the patch and then pressed the patch to the child's back, where it adhered. "May Yammon protect you and sustain you and make you strong. By the word of our savior and his song eternal."

It was a vaccination of some sort. It made sense. A child who received the mark of Yammon would survive common childhood illnesses like spotted fever and wasting sickness that would kill a child who had not received the blessing. By making the inoculation a baptism rite, the Eradicants ensured that these simple people would become ardent followers of their cult.

Michander lifted the infant, who had not uttered so much as a whimper, and handed her to a woman who might have been the daughter of the crone who had greeted him. As one, the villagers broke into song, "Children of the Word, Singers of the Song, accept our humble welcome, good servants of Yammon. Sacred mark of truth, make our children strong, protect the blameless babe, and deliver us from wrong. . . ."

After the song, tables were erected in the village clearing, and a feast was held. A goat was slaughtered and roasted, and steaming platters of pulse and oats were brought forth. Haly was seated between the villager who had struck her and Vinnais, her hands untied so she could feed herself. The food was simple but filling, and she ate gratefully.

As she shoveled buttered oats into her mouth, Vinnais turned and eyed her. "You don't mind taking what they have to offer, then, even if you Libyrarians won't share your knowledge with them," he observed.

Haly blinked. She'd never even considered that before. Clearly the Eradicants, who possessed knowledge only dreamed of by the Libyrarians, shared it freely with the common folk.

Vinnais lifted an eyebrow and nodded at the expression on her face. "That's why we're going to win," he said.

In the afternoon of the day after they left the village, Michander called a halt at the edge of a vast crater. It had been the site of some great explosion, the heat of which had turned the sand to glass. Haly, sitting in her usual spot in the back of the wagon, still with hands and feet tied, blinked in the bright glare of the reflected sun. Michander, Ithaster, Vinnais, and the others stood in solemn silence, staring out at the great bowl of glass. "Iscarion's folly," muttered Michander before ordering them to resume their march.

The following evening they finally reached the Corvariate Citadel; a vast collection of domes and arches rising up from the plain. It was far larger than the Libyrinth, at least the above-ground portion of the Libyrinth, but built along similar lines: nested domes and tall spires, the latter of which were connected by delicate archways. Where the Libyrinth was cast in tan sandstone, the Citadel was gray. And it glowed. It seemed infused by its own constellation of light, emanating from behind walls, winking through windows. She turned to Vinnais and said, "What makes all that light?"

"These," he said, holding up the Egg from the vault. "The Corvariate Citadel has twenty Eggs."

"Twenty-one, now," added Ithaster.

It was not until they approached the vaulting steel gates that the true size of the place bore in upon her. The outer walls stretched up past the limits of her vision, and the iron doors of the main gate, which groaned open after a brief exchange between Michander and the guards at the outer guardhouse, were taller than the dome of the Libyrinth's Great Hall.

Seeing the grandeur in which her enemies lived, fresh despair washed over her. How could the Libyrinth ever withstand them? All they had was the Libyrinth's walls and the goodwill of Ilysies and Thesia—goodwill bought with the coin of knowledge—and now that frail garment was tearing. Maybe they would have been better off to do as the Eradicants did—ally with the peasantry. Thesia no longer existed to protect anything. How long would Ilysies stand?

The great iron doors clanged shut behind them and the stillness of the plain was replaced by thrumming activity. Thousands of people and beasts, hauling carts of lumber, stone, grain, and vegetables, passed up and down the broad avenue and smaller side streets, as well as across the bridges that spanned the distances between buildings. The air was filled with the competing melodies of countless songs, combining to form a discordant symphony. Haly smelled smoke and sweat, dust and dung. The streets were paved with gray slabs of stone.

The domed buildings on either side—some no larger than the huts of the village, others rivaling the the Libyrinth in size—were decorated with carven spirals, lines curving, undulating, lending everything an aqueous, shifting appearance.

Haly wondered at all the people who were abroad at this hour. She said to Vinnais, "It must be at least the hour of the Fly by now, and yet the streets are filled with people. When do they sleep?"

"They sleep when their shift is over," he said. "When we were slaves, we worked in shifts. When the Holy Prophet Yammon freed us, we kept the custom, because it is more efficient. But now everyone has adequate off-shift time for sleeping, eating, praying, singing . . ."

Haly lost track of his words as the building at the end of the avenue came into view. Surrounded by a large plaza, a collection of domed towers rose up, higher even than the city walls. There were seven of them, the one in the center the tallest of all. And they were interlaced with connecting archways. As they neared it, Haly saw that a great face was carved into the tower nearest to them in such a way that the arched entranceway formed a gaping mouth. "What is that place?" she asked.

"Your destination," he replied. "The Temple of Yammon."

The cart lurched through the gates of the temple into a courtyard that was practically a city unto itself. Everywhere she looked there was activity, all going on by the light of the brilliant white lamps set in the walls of the courtyard and strung overhead on wires. They pulled past a group of men and women unloading lumber from a sledge under the supervision of a black-clad priest and came to a halt before the broad steps that led up to the temple proper.

"Ithaster, see to the wagon," said Michander. "Hephaestus and I will take her to the dungeon."

They ushered her up the steps and across a vast echoing hall. She caught a glimpse of tall pillars and an intricately carved dome before being bundled through a doorway to a narrow passage that led to a staircase leading down. The sparse light here was just enough to guide them down the stone steps to an even narrower passage, damp and rank and lined with iron doors.

Hephaestus produced a key and unlocked one of those doors to reveal a cell. Without ceremony, or explanation, Michander shoved her through the door and shut and locked it behind her.

7

Clauda in Ilysies

Clauda shivered in the cold mountain mist and pointed her horse's head to follow Selene's beast. Sheer rock walls jutted up around them. She could see little of the narrow pass down which they crept, for the clouds were low this morning, cloaking them in an icy vapor that found its way into her bones no matter how many blankets Selene heaped upon her.

At least she could sit her own mount today. Just as Selene had said, the tremors were lessening. Her grip on the horse's reins was strong, if a bit rigid from the cold.

They were on the far side of the pass, having spent the last two days negotiating a narrow, icy trail through the snowbound heights. Just as well that she'd had to ride with Selene—warmer, and less chance of her inexperience causing a misstep that could send her and her mount plunging down the mountainside. She wanted to get to Ilysies, sure, but not that fast.

By midafternoon, they reached the foothills and began following a little stream that splashed and burbled merrily among boulders now liberally scattered with scrub and wildflowers. The clouds lifted and the bright sun grew warm on Clauda's face. The air smelled sweet. Clauda caught sight of a small green lizard sunning itself on a nearby rock. The lizard saw her, too, and with a swish of its tail it disappeared.

"Clauda, come here," called Selene, who sat her horse on a rise where rock gave way at last to earth. "Look," she said, pointing as Clauda came up beside her. "Ilysies."

The land gently sloped away below them; a long, gentle expanse of green, threaded through by their companion the stream, which wound down the valley to meet a mighty river. All along the river were fields and dwellings, more and more as the river made its way to the blank blue vastness of the ocean, and then, just before the sea, hazy in the distance but picked out by the bright hot sunlight, the graceful spires and brilliant white walls of Ilysies, like the cake Clauda's mother Hepsebah had made for Griome's sixtieth birthday—the grandest thing Clauda had ever seen, until now.

She wanted to stay there forever, just drinking in the sight. There was so much of it, and all of it miraculous. The green land, green as she'd never known land could be; the fantastical city like something out of a hummingbird's dream; and beyond all of it, the ineffable ocean, hiding all of its secrets in its depths. Her heart pounded with a wildness somewhere between fear and elation, and she would have sat her horse until the sun went down, taking in her first sight of the sea, but beside her, Selene gave a wild whoop and charged her mount down the slope, howling joyously and lifting her arms up to the sky. Clauda, her heart leaping, spurred her mount after her and the two of them galloped down the gentle land, the moist heat of the sun-warmed grass embracing them as they laughed and lifted hearts and hands to the glorious all-giving sun.

If her first sight of Ilysies took Clauda's breath away, the smells and sounds of the city, once they were within its walls, threatened to rob her of her wits. The numerous winding streets were thronged with people dressed in every form of garb imaginable, from the fitted waistcoats and trousers of Thesia to the flowing tunics sported by a ruddy-skinned people whom Selene informed her came from across the sea.

The abundance of goods for sale in the teeming marketplace was enough to break her heart, thinking of the winter months when the Libyrinth must subsist on turnips, onions, and pulse. Selene took the reins of Clauda's horse and led her along, after she'd blocked traffic twice and inadvertently knocked over a watermelon stand. Watermelons, she marveled, craning her neck to peer regretfully behind her as they left the marketplace and started down a broad avenue lined with white walls and ornate gates. She'd only seen a watermelon once before in her whole life.

At the end of the grand street stood the palace, an enormous complex of buildings surrounded by high, whitewashed walls that glowed pink in the setting sun. Before the gilded gates stood a phalanx of scowling guards dressed in white tunics and pantaloons, heavy rifles in their hands.

"Vorain!" Selene called out as she dismounted and approached the formation. "Is your father still selling himself in the marketplace? I could use a good lick and I don't want to spend too much."

"Princess Pointy-head!" The biggest woman Clauda had ever seen hurtled toward Selene and enveloped her in a bear hug. Clauda blinked and looked at the rest of the guards.

They were all women. She looked back at Vorain, who had released Selene and now held her at arm's length, beaming. "Bountiful Mother, it's good to see you. I didn't know you were visiting. What's the Libyrinth like?" A slight frown replaced the grin and a line of worry formed across Vorain's broad forehead. "You look thin."

Selene laughed off her old friend's concern. "I see you've made captain. Congratulations."

"Ah, I've been in charge of this bunch of sag-bottomed walruses for well on five years." She turned and saw the other guards shifting restlessly and craning their necks to get a look at Selene. "Corliss, Beatrice, stop standing there like a couple of sunstruck gooney birds and open the gate for Princess Selene!" She signaled the elegantly slender watchtower that stood just behind the outer wall.

"Vorain," said Selene shaking her head, "don't announce—"

But Vorain was already bellowing, her hands to her mouth. "Lieutenant Patakis, sound the trumpets for the arrival of her gracious majesty, daughter of our magnificent queen . . ." Clauda didn't think it possible, but as the gates opened, Vorain's voice grew even louder. "The Libyrarian Selene!"

From that moment on, Clauda was caught in a whirl of ceremony and solicitude. As trumpets skirled from atop the inner wall, grooms in white leather breeches ran across an open yard the size of the Great Hall back home. They were bare-chested, both the men and the women. She looked down from the dizzying sight of the trumpets gleaming red in the setting sun, into the equally dizzying depths of a pair of brown eyes. A girl about her own age, fine-boned like Selene and athletically slender, took the reins of her horse from her hands, and smiling, led her toward the inner gate.

When Clauda stumbled dismounting, Selene told the inner gatekeeper she'd been injured by a mind lancet. Clauda was immediately swept up in a flurry of gauze-draped attendants.

Selene disappeared behind a froth of sleeves as they whisked
Clauda to a small but sumptuously appointed room, with a
soft bed draped with red and purple silks, and a glow warmer
on a small pedestal in the center of the room.

Here the blinding white of the outer palace gave way to a
comforting stonework gray, warmed with voluptuous wall
hangings and cushions. At the doorway her entourage abated
somewhat, leaving Clauda in the company of a boy and girl
who could have been the brother and sister of the groom
who'd taken her horse. Before she could protest that she
needed to be with Selene, that they both sought an audience
with the queen on a matter of the utmost urgency, these lithe
and elegant creatures had her undressed and sitting in a
steaming tub of sage-scented water. They scrubbed her clean
and then installed her in the bed, which was warm and soft,
and without doubt the loveliest bed Clauda had ever met.
Smiling, her doe eyes slanting with amusement at Clauda's
dumbstruck expression, the girl handed her a cup of steaming something, which Clauda sniffed and discovered was
mint tea.

She was thirsty, and it would be rude to reject such determined and well-wrought hospitality—a poor beginning to her
acquaintance with these Ilysians.

She'd drunk about half the cup when a woman entered the
chamber and bowed low. "With your permission, Clauda of
Ayor, valued servant of the princess Selene," she said, "the
House of Tadamos has great skill in the art of kinesiology. I,
Adept Ymin Ykobos, have learned from childhood at the
hand of my grandmother, herself the heir of a tradition going
back to the time of the Ancients themselves. Will you permit
this servant to treat you?"

Clauda blinked and looked uncertainly from the two attendants to Ymin, who was much older and, unlike everyone else

she had seen so far, was dressed in a skirt and shawl of blue picked out with green flecks. The effect of the clothing was such that she seemed to blend into the background, while the others, in their whites, with their tan skin and gazelle necks and limbs, stood out vividly in the dimness. Kinesiology—that was massage, she was pretty sure. "Uh. Okay," she said.

If she had known what would be involved, she would have taken her chances with the occasional tremor, she reflected an hour later, her face mashed into the bed as the gazellelike attendants held her arms and legs in grips of iron, stretching her lengthwise while Ymin played up and down her spine with what she could only assume was a spiked mallet.

"The mind-lancet attack destabilized your core. We have begun reunifying your energy pathways, but it's an ongoing process," said Ymin when at last they were done. The adept smelled faintly of camphor and lavender. "You can help that process along with certain breathing and meditation techniques I will teach you."

Clauda lay on her back, sweating beneath a velvet comforter. In the wake of Ymin's ministrations, a wave of warm lassitude swept over her. The attendants propped her up with pillows, and gave her more mint tea.

When she had drained the cup, Ymin took it from her. "Close your eyes," she instructed, "and visualize yourself as a tree. Your spinal column is the trunk of the tree, and all your nerves stemming out from it are branches and roots."

A tree? Clauda opened her eyes and raised a skeptical eyebrow at the adept, who frowned. "Kinesiology is most effective when the patient is an active participant in her recovery. Close your eyes, please."

Clauda obeyed her.

"Imagine your roots spreading all the way down through your feet and beyond them, through the floor and down into the ground—deep into the ground. Take a deep breath and imagine that you are drawing warm, golden, healing energy up through your roots, all the way up and through your spinal column trunk, and up, up, into the branches spreading out through your arms and neck. Exhale and release the energy through the leaves and twigs at the crown of your head and the tips of your fingers. Release the energy into the sky."

Maybe there was something in the tea they had given her. Clauda actually felt as if she had roots and branches.

"Now breathe in again and draw the warm, healing light of the sun down through your leaves and branches. Draw it down to your trunk and exhale, releasing the energy through your roots, deep in the earth. You are a circuit, connecting earth and sky. With each breath you reinforce your connection with the above and the below, and you solidify your own internal energy pathways, which are a part of that great circuit."

Within the space of a few breaths, Clauda felt a deep sense of calm and well-being all through her body. Maybe it wasn't just the tea.

"How do you feel?" asked Ymin.

Clauda opened her eyes, almost surprised to find herself still sitting in the bed in her chamber and not atop the green hillside she'd been imagining. "Good. Um. I don't know . . . more solid than before?"

The adept grinned. "That is good news. Despite some initial resistance, it would seem that you have a natural talent for this kind of energy visualization." She stood. "I'll return tomorrow morning, and we'll see what has held through the night."

Clauda, sinking back into the wonderful bed, nodded vaguely and watched as the attendants trailed out after their mistress. There was something she should be doing, she thought, but exhaustion overrode her tired brain, forcing her eyes closed, and she slept.

* * *

Clauda awoke and was halfway across the chamber to light the ovens before she realized this was not the Libyrinth kitchen. The events of the past eight days came back to her in one crashing instant, and she wobbled a little on her feet. Haly. The Seven Tales. She had to find Selene; they had to speak to Queen Tadamos. She glanced around the dim chamber, trying to work out what they'd done with her clothes. Hurriedly she lifted the grate from the glow warmer, but even with this improved light, the most she could find was a luxurious quilted brocade dressing gown draped carefully across a chair. She had a grave suspicion that her clothes had been permanently discarded.

With shaking hands she threw on the robe and dashed out into the hallway, where she encountered a servant bearing a tray with tea and round, golden pastries of a kind Clauda did not recognize. "Mistress . . . ," the girl murmured, taken aback at Clauda's disheveled and quite likely half-crazed appearance.

"What is your name?" said Clauda, cinching the dressing gown closed.

"Scio Mnassis."

"Scio, where is the princess Selene?" Clauda took a pastry from the tray and bit into it. Very good. Flaky yet substantial.

"Mistress, I would be pleased to serve you in your chamber," replied Scio, looking every bit as mortified as she should.

"I'm sure it would be the thrill of your day." Clauda took the tray from her hands and set it gently on the floor beside the doorway. After an instant's hesitation, she plucked another pastry from the tray and straightened. Her head swam. She decided to just keep talking. "But don't be fooled by the high-brow company I keep. I'm just a servant like you, and my mistress, the princess Selene, needs me. Right now. Please, Scio, take me to her." Clauda put a hand on the Ilysian's forearm, as much to steady herself as to convey her sincerity.

Scio cast a wistful look at the carefully arranged tray, and then back to Clauda's pleading face. Clauda thought she saw curiosity in her eyes, as well as pity. "Very well, mistress. Her chamber is this way."

But when they reached Selene's chamber after a hurried walk down several hallways and two courtyards, they found it empty but for a stout woman who was changing the bedding. "Corazol, where is the princess?" asked Scio.

Corazol turned and studied Clauda with frank curiosity. Clauda looked right back at her. So there were a few fat Ilysians. That was good to know. "Princess Selene is my mistress," Clauda added. "I must attend upon her."

Corazol scowled. "She said she had urgent business with her mother, that's all I know."

Clauda gritted her teeth. So Selene was going off to talk to Thela Tadamos on her own, leaving Clauda behind to languish in uselessness. Well, they'd just see about that, wouldn't they? "Where is the audience chamber?" Clauda demanded.

Both Corazol and Scio gasped. "You cannot appear before the queen in your dressing gown!" breathed the girl.

"Let her," said Corazol with an insolent smirk. "Let the rest of the court see what barbarians these Ayorites are. Let her go before the queen in a bathrobe and humiliate her mistress." Corazol finished making up the bed and took Clauda by the arm, steering her back out into the hallway. "You go that way past three courtyards," she said, pointing. "It's just past the double doors." Corazol stood back and folded her arms, watching her expectantly.

It was a dare, Clauda could see that. Neither Corazol nor Scio thought she'd dare to appear dressed as she was, with her hair uncombed and sleep crust around her eyes. Corazol clearly thought she was an uppity foreign servant pulling rank.

They didn't know. "Thank you," Clauda told them, and took off at a run.

In the pillared courtyard outside the audience chamber there were already several people waiting, seated on white marble benches spaced far apart in the large, open room. In the center of the courtyard stood a statue of a woman, over ten feet tall, also in white marble. This was the Ilysian god. They just had the one—well, there was a son or a lover or something, but he didn't seem to be in charge so much. It was interesting, she thought, how at the Libyrinth everyone believed in the Seven Tales, even those like her who didn't quite understand them, and the Eradicants had their prophet, and the Ilysians their goddess. So someone had to be wrong, right? She pushed the thought aside.

Selene sat facing a set of large double doors that were decorated with a marble frieze depicting vineyards. Her back was to Clauda, and a gleaming brass bowl sat at her side. As Clauda strode across the arcade toward her, Selene's hand dipped into it and withdrew to her mouth. Her fingers were red.

"How dare you!" said Clauda, coming up behind her. "You were going to talk to her without me!" She stood behind and to the side of Selene, so the Libyrarian had to twist and crane her neck to look at her.

But Selene did so with a look of blank and innocent composure. Clauda saw that the bowl held berries, and Selene had already eaten quite a few—her lips and fingers were red with the juice. "Clauda. How are you feeling?"

"I'm fine, except that I woke up and found you sneaking off to talk to the queen alone."

One corner of Selene's mouth quirked up. "She *is* my mother, you know. And what on earth are you wearing, by the way? That has to be the most ornate bathrobe I've ever seen in my life."

Clauda blushed, and then cursed herself for letting Selene embarrass her. "I couldn't find my clothes."

"Mmm. They probably burned them." Selene wore her customary black Libyrarian's robes.

"Oh, and after eight days on the road your linen smelled like honey butter, I suppose."

Selene pursed her lips and shook her head. "No. They burned mine, too, but I had an extra set. I fear you have fallen victim to the Ilysian notion of Ayorite finery," Selene said, indicating the robe. She suppressed a smile and picked up the bowl at her side, proffering it to Clauda. "Here, try these. They're not raspberries, but they're something very like them." She nodded her head. "They're quite good. Have you ever had raspberries?"

Clauda's own guilt fueled her anger and she charged around the bench to face Selene full on, her hands on her hips, her head cocked forward accusingly. "I can't believe you. Haly's been captured by the Eradicants and all you can think about is raspberries."

Selene gazed at her steadily. "Not raspberries, but raspberries are probably the only safe subject of conversation in the Courtyard of Petitioners." Selene glanced at the others who were awaiting audience with the queen. Several were staring openly at them. "Don't confuse it with thought. Now sit down, and for the Mother's sake, be quiet."

Clauda gritted her teeth and sat down beside Selene. She took a handful of berries from the large, engraved bowl, and chewed anxiously. "I still can't believe you were going to leave me out of it."

Selene shrugged, impassive as always. "There is no need for you to be here. And you need to rest. Adept Ykobos says the mind-lancet attack destabilized your core quite badly. You're supposed to have another session with her. Why don't you go back to your chamber and relax until then?"

Tales, how Clauda hated the way Selene treated her like a child. Back home she'd steered clear of her; for one thing she was a Libyrarian and an authority figure, and for another, she was a lousy source of gossip. In any case, at home Clauda would never dare speak to her so bluntly, but they weren't at the Libyrinth anymore. Selene was all she had and she was terrified of what might be happening to Haly even as they sat here eating berries and gazing past marble columns at rolling green vistas of lush, Ilysian farmland. She couldn't afford to give Selene the dignity of her position, even in the house of her mother, the queen. "You'd better know what you're doing," she told her.

This won her a sharp, shocked glare from Selene. She didn't permit herself to take satisfaction from it, but decided she would once they'd gotten Haly back and everything was all right again. She blinked and thrust her head forward, speaking quietly. "They think she's a witch, Selene. They've already tortured her. Who knows what may be happening to her right—"

"Look!" Suddenly Selene grabbed Clauda by the arm and pulled her in so close she could smell the berries on her breath—their red juice looked like traces of blood on her lips. "I know. I know how bad it is. I wish we could run around Ilysies shouting out our disaster at the top of our lungs until we raise the whole country and take the Corvariate Citadel by storm. But that won't work. I may not be the spinner of threads my mother is, but I was raised by her. Now shut up and let me think."

Abruptly released, Clauda sat back, blinking. She dropped the berries she still held back into the bowl.

Moments later they both heard two sets of footsteps behind them, and a pair of youths with garlands of blue flowers in their hair padded across the arcade and opened the doors to the queen's reception room.

Selene stood. "You are going to appear before the queen of

Ilysies dressed in a bathrobe," she observed sadly. Clauda nodded firmly and followed her into a large room made of marble. White gauze curtains hung from seven arches on the far wall. Brilliant sunshine filtered through them, bringing a diffuse radiance to the airy chamber. A sunken area in the center of the room held a rectangular reflecting pool, its waters catching the light and casting spangles upon the high ceiling. On either side of the pool was a lounging area, and beyond it, centered between two of the arches, stood a delicately wrought writing desk—carven wood inlaid with mother-of-pearl. The room was unoccupied.

Clauda looked up at Selene nervously. The daughter of the queen of Ilysies held her head high, her face a mask of serenity.

A soft rustle from across the room caught Clauda's attention and she looked up to see Queen Thela Tadamos standing beside an archway, the sky beyond her briefly, brilliantly blue as she let the curtain fall back.

Thela Tadamos was tall like her daughter, with the same arching dark eyebrows, bold cheekbones, and prominent nose. The skin at the corners of her mouth and eyes had softened, but those gentle creases only served to deepen her vibrant beauty. She wore a floor-length tunic and a diaphanous shawl, both a brilliant white that set off her tan skin. Her dark, sleek hair was swept up in intricate braids dressed with black pearls that echoed the gleam of her gray-blue eyes. Clauda's mouth went dry and her wits fled as those piercing eyes swept her briefly and then focused on Selene.

The queen crossed in front of her desk and stood facing them across the reflecting pool. She raised her hands to either side. "The walls of Ilysies smile to have their daughter within them once again," she said in a mellow contralto.

"In their nurture do I thrive," replied Selene, who then descended the steps to the reflecting pool, knelt, and dipped her fingers into the water. "As clear as the waters of the Ilysi River, so are my intentions this day," she said. Uncertain, Clauda moved to kneel beside her, but a short shake of Selene's head stopped her.

"Then rise, and we will put minds and hearts together for the good of all," said the queen.

Selene stood, walked around the pool, and climbed the few steps to where her mother stood waiting. Thela broke into a smile and took her daughter in her arms. "My sweet Selene," she murmured, "it is good to see you again."

Clauda watched from the opposite side of the pool, suddenly aware that, in truth, she did not belong here. This was the meeting of a mother and daughter who had not seen each other in a very long time.

When they parted, Thela looked at Clauda and then tilted her head inquiringly at her daughter. Amusement brightened her eyes as she said, "My dear, did you not give the poor thing time to dress? Really, you must learn temperance."

Selene rolled her eyes and it dawned on Clauda what Thela was implying. She blushed to her toes and was rooted to the spot, too embarrassed to move. "Mother, this is Clauda of Ayor, my servant. She has survived a mind-lancet attack and is still somewhat . . . impaired." Selene shot her a look so intense Clauda flinched. "Kneel!" she whispered out of the corner of her mouth. Clauda collapsed to the floor and touched her forehead against the cool tile. "I beg your forgiveness for her unfortunate appearance," Selene continued, "but she is loyal and true, and it pleases me to keep her near at hand, with your leave, Majesty."

Clauda peeked up between her arms to see Thela gazing beatifically at her daughter. "It is a salve to my heart that you have a servant you value so highly, my dear."

It was clear to Clauda that Thela thought she and Selene

were lovers. Clauda was mortified. A Libyrarian and an Ayorite servant—it just wasn't done, not by self-respecting people of either group. Clearly, given Thela's delighted reaction, things were done differently in Ilysies.

"Rise, Clauda of Ayor," commanded Thela. "Ilysies welcomes you, and hopes that you find here the healing you require."

Clauda rose. She moved hesitantly toward the pool, but Selene shook her head and Clauda walked around it instead and climbed the stairs, pleased beyond all measure that she didn't stumble or shake. She stopped before Thela and bowed deeply in the Ayorite manner, with both legs straight and her hands clasped behind her back, the way she'd seen her parents do toward Griome so many times. "Your Majesty," she murmured.

Clauda followed Selene and Thela Tadamos, who settled themselves on a low couch in one of the sitting areas. After a nod from Selene, she perched on the edge of a green velvet chaise. A servant bearing a tray of food and drink entered from a side door Clauda had not noticed, so artfully was it painted to blend in with the walls.

Clauda observed the servant as she set the tray on the low table and poured rich, dark, steaming coffee into three delicate little cups. She looked much as the other Ilysians she'd met so far—dark hair and fair skin, but of course they didn't really look exactly alike. Clauda noted her snub nose and the faint sprinkle of freckles across her cheeks.

"So," said Queen Tadamos, accepting a tiny cup from the servant. "How fares the Libyrinth?"

Selene stirred sugar into her cup with a tiny silver spoon. "Much as it did when last I wrote you, Mother." Though the queen's manner had softened after the formal greetings, Selene retained her rigid politeness.

"Which was over a year ago," Thela observed. "Really, my dear, it is fortunate I have a great nation to occupy my mind, else I might pine and waste away for want of attention."

Selene glanced at her lap. "I apologize. I have been busy."

The queen smiled, clearly enjoying baiting her daughter. She paused, watching as the servant retreated through the camouflaged door, then she sat forward with eagerness. "And what news of Griome?"

Selene's mouth quirked. "I'm sure you know that much better than I."

Thela ignored this jibe and shook her head sadly. "It was a terrible thing the Singers did, executing the entire Thesian royal family. There was a moment eight days ago when it seemed their hand might be stayed, but no. They beheaded them all in the capital square while the masses cheered." She took a deep breath through her nose and fixed her daughter with a piercing look. "The same thing may happen here before long."

"I'm sure you've taken steps to avoid a similar fate." Selene's cold, uncaring tone shocked Clauda. This was her mother's life they were talking about, not to mention the fate of an entire kingdom—the land of Selene's birth.

Thela tilted her head and took a sip of coffee. "Steps, yes, surely . . . and yet, what steps can one take to avoid a tidal wave? These Singers outnumber us, and they have better weapons and the support of the Ayorite peasantry. True, we have an army of our own, and the Lian Mountains make our conquest inconvenient, but with Thesia fallen, what else is there for them to do?"

Hope and fear seemed to strain Selene's reserve. "You have no other recourse?"

"What recourse? We will fight until the last of us is dead and our blood poisons the Ilysi River."

Silently Selene shook her head. "But it may not come to that, Mother. I . . . I offer an alternative." Selene withdrew *The Book of the Night* from her robes.

"A book? Ah, Selene, my dear . . ." Thela trailed off, an expression of fondness and disappointment on her face.

"Not just any book, mother. Look . . ." Selene indicated the design on the cover.

The queen of Ilysies bent toward the tome and drew in a long, slow breath. "Bountiful Mother," she whispered. She bit her lips and her eyes were bright with tears.

"The secrets of the Ancients can be yours for the protection of Ilysies, if only . . ."

Her mother, half reaching for the book in Selene's lap, looked up sharply. "If?"

Selene nodded, and handed the tome to her mother. "Open it."

Her mother eagerly wrapped her hands about *The Book of the Night* and settled it in her lap. With one long finger she reverently traced the seven-pointed star that was engraved on the cover before opening the book and peering at the text. She looked up at Selene. "What language is this?"

"No known language, Mother."

"Are you sure?"

"Who would know better than I?"

The queen gazed at her for a long time through narrowed eyes. "What is this web you spin, my daughter?"

"There is one who can decipher the book."

"One."

"Yes, and one only, for she need not read these words to know them. My clerk, Halcyon, is blessed. Every word ever written speaks itself to her. Thus she has been since she was born. I know it of a certainty, for she learned that Griome planned to disclose the location of this book to the Eradicants from a sealed letter that he wrote to his nephew." Selene nodded at the book in her mother's lap. "And before she was taken by the Eradicants, she read the opening passage of *The Book of the Night* to our servant, Clauda."

Clauda nodded eagerly. "It said, 'I am the Literate Iscarion, and these are my words.'"

Thela tilted her head thoughtfully and then narrowed her brow. "If your clerk was the recipient of such a miraculous power, why is this the first I've heard of it, Selene?"

"She revealed it to no one, for fear of persecution, which indeed has come to pass."

"They think she's a witch," blurted Clauda.

Selene gave her a stern look and told Thela of what had occurred at the vault. When she was done, Thela turned to Clauda. "But the Singers witnessed her reading from a closed book."

Clauda nodded.

"Then surely they realized . . ." Her shoulders sank. "Were they very young?"

Selene and Thela were both looking at her, waiting for her to answer. She looked to Selene, who gazed back at her with an expression that seemed to say, *You wanted to be here.* "I don't know. Maybe three years older than Haly and me. About Selene's age."

Thela nodded. "When they take her to the Citadel, and the censors hear their report, they will realize . . ." She turned to Selene. "Do you know the prophecy of Yammon?"

Selene shook her head.

"Ah, my daughter. It is always well to know the dreams of your enemies. These Eradicants, as you call them, believe that one day a Redeemer will come and liberate the written word; most especially the words contained in *The Book of the Night*, so that it can be understood by those who cannot read. They call the blessed event the Redemption, and it is to them as the Tale Time Will Tell is to you, my dear."

"Or the return of the son," said Selene.

Thela tilted her head in half acknowledgment. "But we Ilysians are wise enough to sample transcendence on a yearly basis. Saving it all up for one big day makes people . . . well . . . a bit unbalanced, in my opinion."

Selene frowned, but didn't say anything to contradict her.

"The point is, your clerk matches their description of the Redeemer. What you have brought me is Ilysia's doom."

"What?" said Selene.

Thela spread her hands on top of the book. "They covet this knowledge, as we all do. And through the Redemption it can be theirs. Since they now know that *The Book of the Night* is in Ilysies—"

"How will they know that?" Clauda bit her lip. She'd just interrupted the queen of Ilysies.

But Thela smiled sadly at her. "She will tell them, my dear."

Oh. Of course.

"Now that they have their Redeemer, they will not rest until they possess *The Book of the Night* as well. Ilysies will be invaded within a fortnight if we do not act quickly."

Clauda didn't like how this was going. They'd come to Thela for help in rescuing Haly. So far the subject had barely been mentioned. Instead, Thela had succeeded in turning the gift of the book into a curse and focusing the conversation on the survival of Ilysies, which Selene might consider more important than saving Haly. Which was more important, of course, to anyone but Clauda. But she was here for Haly. She was perhaps the only one who was here solely for Haly, and she had to do something. "Your Majesty. If you can bring Haly safely to Ilysies, then you need fear no one ever again. All that is written there"—Clauda held her hand out to the book— "will be yours, and the Eradicants will tremble before you." Her heart pounded as if it would explode. She watched the queen carefully.

Maybe it hadn't been such a good idea to speak. Thela lifted her chin and eyed her coldly. "And how would you propose I do that, child? Ride my chariot into the Corvariate Citadel and simply say, Hand over to me the most important person in your religion?"

Selene stared at Clauda with a closed, tense expression. Why, why had she felt she needed to be here? She was messing everything up. She licked her lips, and to buy time, asked, "This Redemption of theirs—is there a particular place where it's supposed to happen?"

Thela lifted one eyebrow. "At the Libyrinth. When it is concluded they will destroy it."

Selene breathed in sharply. Clauda swallowed. That gave her an idea. "Then they have to move her. And they have to go through the Tumbles to get there. Your army can ambush them and take her back."

Thela studied her closely. One corner of her mouth lifted ever so slightly. In amusement? Approval? "It's not bad," she allowed. "Except that they won't move her until they have the book." She paused.

Clauda opened her mouth, and at the same time, she and Thela both said, "Unless the book is already at the Libyrinth."

Clauda blinked. Thela grinned at her.

"Are you both mad?" said Selene. She turned to her mother. "Didn't you just say that they'll destroy the Libyrinth after their Reclamation—"

"Redemption," corrected Thela.

"Whatever. They'll destroy the Libyrinth. And you're going to make it easy for them, by taking *The Book of the Night* to the Libyrinth."

Clauda, inspired by the queen's grin, had another idea. "Do the Eradicant leaders have to go inside the Libyrinth in order to perform the Redemption?"

Thela nodded slowly. "Instead of ambushing them in the

Tumbles, a contingent of Ilysians could get to the Libyrinth before the Singers and hide in the stacks. . . ."

"We could take out their leaders," continued Clauda, "get Haly and the book back, and hide them in the stacks where no Singer will ever find them. And in the meantime the rest of the Ilysian army can come up behind the Singer forces outside. . . ."

". . . and they'll be pinned there and no one need ever fear the great Singer army again," concluded Thela with a nod of approval. "I like the way this servant of yours thinks, Selene," she added, never taking her eyes off Clauda. "Be careful or I may take her from you."

Selene stood. Her dark eyes raked Clauda with a look of unfathomable betrayal. "You can have her." She turned to her mother and bowed stiffly. "Your Majesty," she said, and swept out of the chamber.

8

The Horn of Yammon

Haly crossed her arms and rubbed her hands up and down her upper arms. It was cold down here. The cell was carpeted with straw, and dark. It smelled like the Libyrinth stable, with an added hint of sickly sweet fear. Movement in the darkest corner of the cell made her start back, staring. She just barely made out a bent, shrouded figure, huddled where the stone walls met.

"What kind of witch are you?" It was an old woman's voice, breathy and soft but perfectly distinct; like a wisp of smoke floating through the darkness to her ear.

Haly pressed herself back against the door. "I'm not a witch."

A low, dry cackle emanated from the darkness. "Same kind as everyone else here, then."

Haly took a deep breath and sidled to the corner opposite

the other prisoner. She sank to the floor and pulled her knees up to her chest.

The old woman leaned forward, and Haly saw her eyes gleaming with the faint light from the tiny window in the cell door. "Oh, but you *are* a child," she said. "And not one of Yammon's chorus, I think." She edged closer and the square of light from the window fell across her face. Haly gasped. Her face was covered with spiraling scars. They were like the lines she'd seen on the buildings outside, like the lines on the face of the Devouring Silence, too.

The old woman beckoned to her. "Come into the light, child; let Mab see you."

Afraid of what might happen if she didn't obey, Haly stood and slowly shuffled to the center of the cell, where the light could reach her.

The old woman came so close, Haly could smell her stale breath. "Ah," she whispered, and raised a long-nailed finger to Haly's injured cheek. Without touching the swollen flesh, that finger traced the curving line Ithaster had engraved upon her face. "They've just begun with you."

Haly bit her lip and shrank back. "Please," she whispered.

Mab made a sympathetic sound and tilted her head inquiringly. "Poor thing. Please what?"

Haly shook her head. She didn't know.

"Here," said Mab, turning back to her corner and returning with the remains of a loaf of bread smeared with some kind of brown paste. "I still have some of my dinner left. You must be hungry." She shoved the food into Haly's hands.

Haly crept back to her corner and sat down again. She regarded the food a moment, grateful for the kind gesture, though she couldn't imagine eating anything now. She heard Mab sigh and return to her corner.

Resting her chin on her knees, Haly stared into the shadows, but could see nothing of her cellmate in the darkness. It was as if she wasn't there. No, not true—Haly could hear her breathing. Slow and steady, like sand blowing back and forth across the Plain of Ayor, the sound lulled Haly into an exhausted sleep.

The wind whipped up sandstorms around the caravans of books that were being brought to the vast face in the center of the desert. Selene and Clauda tossed books into the monster's maw. They looked like Vinnais and Soth, but she knew they were really Selene and Clauda.

"You know some people say she never existed," said Clauda.

"Then how do you explain all these books?" answered Selene.

"I know what kind of witch you are," said the book in Clauda's hands.

Haly opened her eyes and pushed herself up. She brushed the straw from her cheek and rubbed her eyes. It was still dark in the cell, but now she could hear a voice down the hall singing. Well, shouting, more like, the sound softened only by distance, and getting louder all the time. "Miscreants, witches, criminals rise, you'll work this day or I'll have your hide."

She heard a rustling of straw and Mab was at her side. "Here," she said, her chin dripping. She held out the water bucket. "Drink your fill now, for you'll get no more until midday. And if you know what's good for you you'll eat that bread and peabea I gave you last night."

"What?" Haly shook the fragments of her dream from her mind and took the bucket from Mab. "Work? What?"

Mab gave a harsh laugh. "You don't think they feed us for nothing, do you?"

Haly hoisted the bucket to her mouth and drank. When she was finished she rummaged in the straw until she found the remains of Mab's dinner. She picked a few pieces of straw off it and took a bite. It was terrible—the bread was burned around the edges and the peabea was dry and cracked. She managed no more than a couple of mouthfuls before the door to their cell was flung open and a harsh voice cried out, "Rise! You'll work this day or pay with your lives!"

Haly followed Mab out into the hallway, which was already crowded with prisoners. They looked uniformly old, though some were Haly's own age. They all had dirty, exhausted faces and dull eyes. They stank, and Haly shrank into herself, trying not to touch anyone, but they were packed body to body in the narrow hallway. She saw a louse crawl down the neck of the prisoner in front of her and she began to itch. They all shuffled down the hallway together, herded through a doorway by the two largest Eradicants Haly had ever seen.

Haly stepped through the doorway at the end of the hallway and suddenly the smell of her fellow prisoners, the horror of them brushing against her with their soiled garments, even her fear and despair, fell away as she gazed upon a vast chamber, the ceiling arching into dimness far above. And into that vast indeterminance soared a great iron funnel, its flared opening facing them like a devouring maw. Massive steel beams supported the structure, which tapered down into a spiraling tube and ended in a rounded bulb approximately the size of Haly's head. The entire construction stood upon a wheeled platform held stationary with heavy blocks of stone.

"The Horn of Yammon," whispered Mab beside her.

One wall of the chamber was lined with ovens. Even from here, she could feel the heat radiating from them. A long line of people, looking even more exhausted and dirty than Haly's group, shoveled fuel into those ovens, while others worked bellows to keep those fires hot. Guards patrolled up and down the line, shouting out orders and prodding the weary with metal rods that appeared to be more primitive versions of the mind lancets.

Haly heard a rhythmic metallic clang and saw people in goggles and leather aprons hammering red-hot pieces of metal into shape. She took another look at the horn. Gaps in its surface revealed the framework beneath. A team on a catwalk riveted a panel in place, while nearby another pair examined an unclad section. One of these men held a small device in his hand. It looked like a tiny stringed instrument of some sort. He plucked the strings, listened, plucked some more, and turned and spoke to his partner, who ran to the nearest metalworker and shouted, "Make this piece two and a half octaves wide by five and three fourths octaves long." The burly man nodded and resumed hammering.

Judging by raggedness of clothing and gauntness of faces, it appeared that those maintaining the fires were prisoners.

"Feed the fire! Heat the steel! This day of breath you earn by zeal!" cried one of the guards on Haly's group, confirming her suspicions. Her group formed into a line, as did the group at the ovens. As they filed past each other, each departing prisoner handed their shovel to one of those arriving. When Haly took the shovel from a short, heavily scarred man who somehow had the strength to leer at her, it was so heavy she nearly dropped it.

It was exhausting work, becoming more agonizing as time and the heat of the fires took their toll. As they labored, the prisoners sang, their voices low and harsh with fatigue:

Feed the fire, heat the steel, the mark of Yammon will
  reveal,
Feed the fire, heat the steel, the evil which my heart con-
  ceals.

Feed the fire, heat the steel, my sins by labor I must heal,
Feed the fire, heat the steel, or in my soul wear sorrow's
*   weal.*

Haly wondered how they could spare the breath. It was all she could do to keep her grip on her shovel and concentrate on getting the coal into the oven instead of spilling it on the floor.

"Faster, lit filth, that plodding won't keep the fire hot!" cried one of the guards, and he touched his prod to the back of her calf, making her jump. The pain was not so debilitating as that of a mind lancet, but it was bad enough. "Speed up or the rest of your cohorts will get the same," said the guard. The other prisoners snarled at her, and with a sob Haly forced her quivering muscles to greater speed. Beside her, Mab winked and cackled. "It's not just your soul that wears sorrow's weal!"

After what seemed like days, they were given a break. Haly collapsed on the floor not far from the ovens and watched distractedly as a team of Eradicants attached another panel to the horn. What was the purpose of such a thing, beyond providing backbreaking work for "evildoers" such as herself? She lacked the will to pursue the question, just as she lacked the strength to join the other prisoners, who fought one another to get at the water trough. Her muscles felt flayed, and her joints ached. She wasn't sure she could stand again, or lift her arms, even if she tried.

She couldn't do this, she thought. She wasn't brave like Clauda, or strong like Selene. She was afraid. All her life she'd been afraid—of discovery, of punishment. Well now she'd been discovered; now she was being punished. And just as she'd always suspected, she couldn't bear it.

When the call to return to work came, her muscles trembled so badly she could barely stand, barely lift her shovel. The other prisoners glared at her—all but Mab, who looked amused. One of them, a tall, rangy man too thin for his frame, stuck his face in hers and snarled, "You'll keep up, or you'll have more than Quorl's prod to worry about!"

Haly became insensible to anything but the burning of her muscles and the breath laboring in and out of her lungs. She tried hard to go as fast as she could, but it wasn't enough. True to his word, Quorl shocked the whole row of prisoners, and the tall man would have shoved her into one of the ovens if Mab hadn't pulled her out of harm's way and given him her own post at the bellows, the easier of the two jobs.

Ignoring the glares and curses thrown at her by the others, Haly stared fixedly at the shovel in her hands as she turned from coal pile to oven and back again, over and over. She drew breath and found, in some deep place within herself, the strength to be angry. With a will, she swallowed her pain, her terror and despair. She plunged her shovel into the pile of coal and sang, "Feed the fire, heat the steel, the mark of Yammon will reveal!"

By the time their shift was through, she was barely conscious anymore. She was awake, yes, and in great pain, but her mind felt as if it were stuffed with cotton, and only the most abrupt and startling sensations broke through the numbness. She followed Mab back to their cell on legs she could no longer feel, fell gratefully onto the dirty straw, and instantly fell asleep.

To be awakened what seemed like seconds later, by Mab shaking her. "No," she muttered. "No, I can't. I can't." She tried to burrow deeper in the straw, but Mab hauled her up bodily. "They're from Censor Siblea, you fool! He wants to see you. When Censor Siblea wants to see you, you go. Get up!"

Blinking, Haly became aware that light streamed into the cell from the open door. A pair of robed figures stood there, one of them holding a lantern that glowed brighter than any she had ever seen before. "Are you the Libyrarian Halcyon?" demanded the other.

"I'm just a clerk," Haly muttered, rubbing her eyes.

"It's her. Take her," said Mab, hauling Haly up and shoving her at the figures.

"You will come with us," they said. They took her by the arms and marched her out of the cell and down the hallway, in the opposite direction from the workroom.

She stumbled on the stairs and they hoisted her up the stone steps. They hurried through the large chamber she'd seen before, and up several more flights of stairs until at last they opened a door and ushered her into a room that was carpeted in red.

Haly's feet sank into the rich pile as she was brought to a wooden chair and made to sit. It was warm in here, though there was no fireplace. She heard the door shut behind her.

Glowing orbs set into the ceiling lit the room, which was paneled with golden brown wood. Red curtains obscured a window across from her, and between her and the window stood another chair, larger than hers and upholstered in leather. Beside that chair was a small, marble-topped table, and on the table sat a knife with a curved black blade and a small stone jar. *No*, she thought, and looked behind her in panic, but the guards were gone and the door had been shut.

She was about to leap up and try to open it, though she was sure it was locked, when another door, paneled like the room and invisible until now, opened. Through it stepped a very tall, very bony man in the black robes of an Eradicant, but with a ribbon of red running around the edge of the hood that was pushed back over his bald pate. He sat in the chair across from her and crossed his legs, interlacing his fingers and resting his hands on his raised knee. For several minutes he simply sat there, regarding her with what seemed to be friendly curiosity. His eyes were almost colorless, like shards of glass faintly reflecting the light in the room. She had the feeling that despite his kindly expression, he could carve into her soul with them.

Her gaze slid unwillingly to the knife and jar on the table, and he caught her glance. "Oh, I'm sorry," he said. "These were left out from my last interview. It must distress you to see them here." He stood and picked up the knife and the jar and crossed to a wall, where a touch of his hand sent a panel swinging out to reveal a cupboard. He put away the articles and shut the door. Turning around, he gave her a gentle smile. "I don't think I'll need them with you."

He turned to another section of the wall and opened another cupboard door, from which he drew a flask and two glasses. Haly wondered just how many of these walls were actually walls. He returned to his chair and set the glasses down on the table. "I am Censor Siblea," he said, uncorking the flask and pouring a ruby red liquid into the glasses. He turned to face her, holding out one of the glasses.

Though her body cried out with thirst, she shrank from the proffered beverage.

Siblea shook his head. "Don't worry, I do not mean to poison you. It is only currant wine, infused with some healing herbs." He took a drink from his own glass, then came closer and held her glass to her lips. "It's very restorative."

Haly didn't see how she had much choice. She let the liquid slip past her lips. It filled her mouth with bursting deliciousness, and she eagerly drank more. If it was a drug, then he was taking it, too. And it couldn't be poison for the same reason. Besides, why go to all this trouble and then just kill her?

Siblea resumed his seat and set the empty glasses on the table. "Halcyon the Libyrarian," he said.

Haly shook her head, then found herself afraid to contradict him.

Siblea raised an eyebrow. "What is it, child?"

She licked her lips. "I'm only a clerk."

Siblea's eyes narrowed and he gave her a puzzled little shake of his head. He was still smiling.

"I'm not a Libyrarian, only a clerk."

Siblea's smile twisted with wry humor and he lifted his hands out in a magnanimous gesture. "Oh, well, it's all the same to us *Eradicants*, you know." He leaned forward. "Tell me, how long have you heard books talking to you?"

She decided right then that she would tell him anything he wanted to know. "As long as I can remember."

Siblea nodded. "So as far as you know, you were born this way."

"Yes."

"Do you hear all books, or only certain kinds?"

"All of them."

"What about other forms of writing"—he waved one hand vaguely—"letters and so forth."

Haly nodded. "Those, too."

"Pictures?"

She shook her head. "No."

Siblea sat back in his chair and steepled his fingers. "Maps?"

"Only the words on them."

"How old are you, my dear? What do they call you at home—Halcyon, or—"

"Haly."

"How old are you, Haly?"

"I'm fifteen years old."

"When were you born?"

"In the hour of the Fly on the seventh day of the seventh month of the forty-ninth year of the Goat."

Siblea stood and paced about behind his chair, chanting softly under his breath. He was setting her answers to rhyme, she realized. She wondered why he didn't have attendants to do this for him, and then thought that perhaps he preferred to be the sole witness to his subject's confession.

A warm glow suffused Haly, and despite herself, she relaxed. It was the wine, she realized. She was filled with a sense of well-being, a warm drowsiness in her body that nonetheless left her mind clear and free of anxiety. She found she welcomed his questions. She became eager to share all she knew of her ability. And perhaps that last part was not just the wine at work. No one but Clauda had ever believed her before. No one had ever shown curiosity about how she heard the books or why. It was its own kind of drug, this interest of his.

Siblea stopped pacing and murmuring and returned to his chair, looking at her closely. "Do you love your books very much?" he asked.

She gaped at him. How could an Eradicant ask such a question?

"I have thought a great deal about you Libyrarians and your books," he said, acknowledging her surprise. "It seems to me that perhaps they are to you as cherished as our songs are to us. I've been to many a liberation. You are not the first to cry as the dead words are burned."

By the Seven Tales, yes. She recognized him. He'd been the Eradicant at the far end of the table at the feast. The one she'd just finished serving when she saw Griome give Selene's map to Michander. And he recognized her. A chill went up her spine.

Siblea pursed his lips. "But it is so foolish of you to put all your faith in a thing that can be destroyed. Perhaps your people have forgotten that they were once enslaved. Slaves know this. Rely on nothing that can be taken from you. A song, once learned, can never be taken, you see."

Unless only one person knew the song, and that person died, thought Haly, but she kept silent.

Siblea stood again and paced behind his chair. He was warming to his lesson. Haly was reminded of Peliac, and a sudden knife-sharp homesickness—even for Peliac's irritable pomposity—swept over her. But Siblea was not Peliac. He was kinder and more interesting.

"I've often wondered why those who read consider themselves superior to those who don't, when it is the Song that is eternal, and the singers of the Song who wield the power of its teachings. But arrogance is the folly of the literate. It was Iscarion's principal sin, of course—the failing that destroyed him and his followers; that nearly destroyed us all." He paused and looked at her with his pale eyes, his expression unreadable. "Do you know the story of Iscarion and *The Book of the Night*?"

Enraptured, Haly shook her head. It had been days since she'd heard a story.

"I could sing it to you," he said, "but I doubt you'd understand much of the verse, so I'll tell you instead. When Yammon was yet a child, a slave right here in the Corvariate Citadel, he had a best friend, and that was Iscarion. The two grew up together, and in all that Yammon did, Iscarion was at his side. When Yammon led the Liberation, Iscarion was his second. And Iscarion, in defiance of the Ancients' law, had learned to read.

"This was not entirely unknown. Despite the most barbarous oppression, some slaves always managed to learn, and sometimes they taught others. At the time of the Liberation, there was a sizeable population of Literate among us, and most of them were early followers of Yammon. They fought side by side with us to gain freedom, but once freedom was gained, things changed.

"The valiant warriors of the Liberation kept one Ancient alive. The Literate said that the knowledge confessed by this being—who was put to the question just as you have been, my dear—was too precious to leave to song. After all, Iscarion said, songs change, but writing is permanent. Yammon, beguiled by his love for his friend, put Iscarion in charge of the interrogation.

"Iscarion compiled all that he learned in a book, and he called it *The Book of the Night*, in reference to the long darkness of slavery and the new promise of freedom brought by Yammon. But when Yammon said, 'Come, brother, share with us what you have learned,' he would not tell him. Iscarion said, 'You are illiterate. I risked everything you have risked, and I have risked more, for I learned to read. Let to all come the benefit of their efforts. Let the Literates, who have risked more than those who sing, reap the benefit of their effort. The Singers are not worthy; it is we, the Literate, who conquered the masters.'

"And Yammon said, 'Then let us all be Literate. If you learned, so can I. Teach us all.'

"But Iscarion refused, saying that those who learned in slavery had risked their lives, but those who would learn now risked nothing. 'Let the Singer sing and the Literate rule,' he said.

"At last Yammon saw the error of his love. He had thought Iscarion was a brother, but Iscarion held himself above Yammon. These two who had fought side by side for liberation now fought each other, and the followers of Yammon fought the Literate and defeated them. Many called for Iscarion's execution, for the execution of all the Literate, who would make themselves masters. But Yammon knew mercy, and in remembrance of the bond Iscarion betrayed, he allowed his former friend to leave the Corvariate Citadel and take his people with him.

"The Literate left the citadel with their book. They went to the city of Chaldoa, and to prove their superiority they built a Maker of Eggs. 'Soon we will have all the power in the world,' they said, 'and we will go back to the Corvariate Citadel and we will take what is ours, and we will enslave the Singers.'

"But by their pride were they damned. They built the Maker of Eggs, and it exploded and all were killed but for Iscarion, who fled with his cursed book of stolen knowledge, and was never seen again.

"Yammon saw the fire that purified the Literates' sin, and he wept for Iscarion's betrayal and the knowledge lost through pride. In his sorrow the Song sent him a prophecy, that one day *The Book of the Night* would be found and a Redeemer would come, a child of Iscarion for whom text is song. This Redeemer would revive the murdered Word and restore to the Singers what had been stolen from them."

So the Eradicants did want *The Book of the Night*, and not just to destroy it. They wanted what was inside it, just like everybody else. "Is that why you haven't destroyed the Libyrinth yet?" she asked. "Because it might hold *The Book of the Night*? That's why you burn the books one by one, isn't it?"

Siblea smiled, and Haly's stomach turned. "Of course," agreed Siblea. "But thanks to you, we will not need to tolerate the Tomb of Dead Words much longer."

She thought she'd throw up, but there was little enough in her stomach. All she could do was cough and retch.

"There now, my dear," Siblea said, and patted her on the shoulder. "All will be well, you will see. The Redemption is for everyone, and once you have accomplished it, you and your brethren will rejoice in your liberation."

Her?

A child of Iscarion, for whom text is song.

Siblea knelt at her side so that his eyes were level with hers. "You are a very important person, Haly."

9

The Ayorite in the Bathrobe

The queen of Ilysies sighed.

Clauda stared hard at her own hands. She was afraid to move. Selene had abandoned her in a foreign land. What was she going to do now?

"Oh, go after her, child," said Queen Thela. Clauda looked up at her, and Thela nodded. "Maybe you can make her see reason. Goddess knows I never could."

Clauda caught a glimpse of Selene leaving the pillared courtyard. She followed her to a large yard that was surrounded by barracks. Soldiers practiced drills in the yard, marching in formation, each wielding a weapon that looked like a cross between a rifle and a mind lancet. She spotted Vorain at the far end of the yard, conducting target practice. A row of soldiers aimed their weapons at piles of gourds stacked upon the ground, and at Vorain's word, twisting rays of white-blue holyfire sprouted from the weapons, reducing the gourds to smoking fragments. The air filled with crackling noise and the smell of holyfire drifted across the yard.

Selene stood beside a gate to a smaller practice yard, watching the drill. Clauda walked up to her and grabbed her by the sleeve. "What in the Seven Tales was that all about?" she demanded.

Selene glared at her and wrenched her arm out of Clauda's grasp. "I could ask you the same. What do you think you're doing?"

"It's a good plan," protested Clauda.

Selene sneered. "It's her plan. And if you believe everything she tells you, then you're even more naive than I am." Selene nodded at the soldiers practicing in the yard. "See those weapons? It's because of my research that she has them. She assured me she'd use the knowledge to heat homesteads in the uplands—the winters there are harsh. But she lied. She does that very well." Selene spun around again and stalked off, her black robes billowing out behind her.

Clenching her jaw, Clauda followed Selene. Out of the corner of her eye she saw Vorain take notice of their passage and call to one of her lieutenants. "Take over for me, Galatea," she said.

This one, a fraction of the size of the yard they'd just left, sported a low ring of stone filled with sand. A rack against the barracks wall held knives and other things that Clauda could only identify as oddly shaped strips of padded leather with buckles. As Clauda closed the distance between them, Selene removed her robe, depositing it on a nearby bench. Her small-clothes soon followed.

"What's wrong with you?" Clauda demanded, coming to a halt beside her. The smell of the holyfire had made her dizzy. At least, she *thought* it was the holyfire. Selene was naked.

Clauda stared. How could someone look so regal without a stitch on?

Selene ignored her and began taking items from the rack and buckling them on. It was armor, Clauda realized. Leather coverings for the neck, the wrists, the belly, and groin—anyplace where a knife wound might prove fatal.

"If we don't work together, Haly is doomed," Clauda whispered.

Selene shot her a look full of daggers. She secured bracers to her forearms with quick, brutal movements. Staring over Clauda's head, she said, "Fancy a match?"

"Not when you have that look in your eyes," said Vorain, who stood behind Clauda.

"I'll take you on," said another voice. They all turned to see a woman standing beside the rack of knives. She was a few years older than Selene, her dark Ilysian hair tied back severely. She was fully as tall as Selene, but of a broader build. Her chin was blunt rather than pointed, and her eyes were light hazel in color.

"Uh-oh," murmured Vorain, but Selene stepped toward the newcomer. "Jolaz," she said in a tightly controlled neutral tone. "It's been a long time."

"And I've been practicing," the other woman replied, eyeing Selene with amused disdain. "What about you? There can't be much call for knife-fighting at the Libyrinth."

Selene fastened the last catch on her leather armor. "Some things you don't forget," she said. "Suit up. Vorain will referee for us."

As Jolaz changed into her armor, Vorain took Selene aside. "This is reckless, Selene, even for you. What's happened?"

Clauda couldn't make out Selene's murmured reply, but evidently Vorain's words had little effect, for as soon as Jolaz was ready, the two combatants went to the sandpit, where they slowly circled each other, both of them holding short, curve-bladed knives at their sides. Reluctantly, Clauda and Vorain walked to the edge of the arena to watch.

"Who is that?" Clauda whispered to Vorain.

"Jolaz. The heir." There was a troubled note in the soldier's deep voice.

"Is she . . . Selene's sister?"

"No. The queen appoints her successor as she chooses. Often it is a family member, but not always. In this case . . . Jolaz has been a servant in the palace from birth. As a little girl she served the queen as a scribe. At twelve she was appointed heir."

"Is that why Selene is mad at her mother?"

In the ring, Jolaz lunged at Selene, who danced backward and made several short, slashing movements with her blade.

Vorain looked at Clauda and raised an eyebrow. "Not much gets past you, does it?"

"I don't know about that," muttered Clauda, "but you'd have to be blind, deaf, and witless not to figure out that *something* is wrong between them."

"Your mistress is jealous of Jolaz, but not over the throne. It's just—" Vorain hissed as Jolaz's sweeping slash missed Selene's rib cage by about three inches.

"Shouldn't you break this up?" said Clauda. "Someone could get hurt."

Vorain nodded. "I would if I could, little Ayorite. You ever try telling needle-noggin what to do?"

She had a good point. "So why is Selene jealous of Jolaz, then?"

Vorain sighed. "The heir learns statecraft at the monarch's side. From the time that the choice for an heir is made, the two are nearly inseparable. When Selene was preparing for her initiation into womanhood, it was Mother Papilos who taught her the mysteries, because Thela had no time to spare. When Selene was ill with goose-spot fever, Thela only visited her once. But Jolaz spent every day with the queen. Of course Selene understood why, but . . ."

"She still couldn't help feeling that Jolaz had stolen her mother," Clauda finished.

Vorain nodded.

In the ring, Selene blocked Jolaz's blade with an armored forearm, and swung her own blade out to carve a shallow furrow across the other woman's bicep. "First blood," said Vorain.

"Two out of three," said Jolaz.

"Agreed," said Selene. The combatants circled each other again. Jolaz lunged and Selene dropped and rolled into a somersault, coming back to her feet behind Jolaz, who turned and cast a handful of sand in Selene's eyes.

Selene backed up reflexively. Her heel connected with the outer wall and she stopped, blinking.

Jolaz closed in and raked Selene's ribs with an arcing slash. Selene gasped and whirled, grasping Jolaz's knife arm. She kicked Jolaz's legs out from under her. Jolaz fell, but on the way down she did something with her left leg and her free arm and suddenly, Selene was on her back in the sand with Jolaz's knife at her throat.

"End of match," called Vorain.

Jolaz stood and sheathed her knife. She looked down at Selene with a faint smile, and offered her hand to help her up.

Selene, her eyes bright and her cheeks flushed, glared back, ignored the hand, and got to her feet on her own. They shook hands. "Another match?" said Selene.

Jolaz shook her head. "I must attend upon Her Majesty," she said. Clauda tried to discern disdain or smugness in her tone, but could detect neither.

Selene clearly did, however. Her hands clenched into fists as she watched Jolaz walk placidly to her pile of clothes and start dressing.

Blood dripped from the slash across Selene's ribs. Clauda started toward her, but Vorain held her back. "You'd better let me see to her. She seems upset with you for some reason." Vorain's look was both bland and penetrating. "There's a feast this afternoon and you'll want to get ready for that. . . ." She wrinkled her brow. "Why are you in a bathrobe, anyway?"

Clauda returned to her room, where she was fitted for garments—a knee-length, belted tunic of moss green trimmed with brown—and then Adept Ykobos arrived with her assistants. The kinesiologist frowned and clucked her tongue as she examined Clauda. "You need to practice your meditation and avoid stress," she said. "There is ample opportunity for you to meet our gracious monarch at the feast this afternoon. No need to go gallivanting about the palace in your bathrobe at the crack of dawn. Now much of the work we did yesterday has been undone."

"I feel fine," said Clauda.

Ymin nodded. "You do now. But here . . ." She took Clauda's elbow between her index finger and thumb, lifted it to shoulder height, and then reached down and brushed her fingertips over the top of Clauda's opposite knee. Hot pain flared up, shooting from the elbow, up her shoulder, down her spine, and into the knee. "Ow!" Clauda gasped.

"You see," said Ymin. "You are out of balance. The goal of kinesiology is integration. That is what we must all strive for, but you more than most."

"Integration?" said Clauda.

Ymin nodded. "The state of harmony between body and

mind, when all energy pathways flow without restriction to and from the core, thus making communication between the mind, the heart, and body instantaneous. It is a state few achieve and almost none maintain on a permanent basis—"

"Then what's the point?"

"The point is, the closer we come to it, the more in balance we become and the better our bodies and minds function. For someone like you, who has experienced a severe interference of the energy pathways, such training is essential. Now, lie on your stomach and close your eyes. Helene, Po, take her arms."

After Ykobos left Clauda sweating and sore, the chamber servant Scio came to prepare her bath. "You don't have to do this, you know," said Clauda, sitting waist deep in steaming water. The round tub was hammered copper, and almost twice her length in diameter. Clauda took the sponge, foaming with lavender-scented soap, from the girl's hands. "I can wash myself. Honest."

Scio shrugged and put another pitcher of water on the glow warmer. "Steward Sopopholis has assigned me to be your body servant for the duration of your stay. I'm to attend you in all things."

And watch her, and keep her out of trouble. Anger threatened to stiffen Clauda's jaw, and she deliberately hid it. This was Selene's doing, no doubt, to prevent any further embarrassing incidents—or to keep her from upstaging Selene in front of her mother. What a selfish brat! The plan she and Queen Thela had come up with together was a good one.

Pleasure warmed her as she remembered Queen Thela Tadamos smiling at *her*, Clauda the pot girl, because she'd matched wits with her. Why couldn't Selene see that Clauda had talents to offer the situation? At home, she'd been both reviled and courted as an inveterate gossip. She always knew who was mad at whom, who was sleeping with whom, who owed whom a favor and why. She loved knowing. People were interesting—people and the things they did and their reasons for doing them, both true and convenient.

She'd always thought of it as sort of a hobby, but now she had a chance to really do something with it. She couldn't just let herself be shepherded around enjoying luxuries while Haly was in trouble. And even though Selene was a hothead with no appreciation for Clauda as anything other than an unwanted burden, she was right about one thing: Queen Thela was, well, a queen, and they could trust her about as much as the Goat trusts the Lion. No matter how good a plan they had, there was no guarantee that Thela would adhere to it.

"Are you well, mistress? Shall I call Adept Ykobos back?"

Clauda realized she'd been standing stock-still, staring at the sponge in her hand as her thoughts ran their course. "No. I feel fine, thank you. But there's been a mistake. I'm a servant myself. A servant can't have a servant," said Clauda, hoping to appeal to Scio's sense of status.

Scio perched on the edge of the bath and dipped her feet in. "Fine, then. I could use a bath, too," she said. She removed her tunic, slid into the water, and submerged herself.

Lifelong communal living had somehow failed to inure Clauda to this sight. The flush on her skin deepened, although it was already warm and pink from the heat of the bath. Clauda leaned back and slitted her eyes, pretending to be in deep contemplation of her toes while in fact observing Scio in the water.

She was beautiful. Like Selene, she had dark hair and pale skin. Her hair fanned out around her in the water and her smooth skin gleamed like moonlight. She had a waist like the curve of a swan's neck and small breasts with dark rose tips that reminded Clauda of those berries Selene had been eating.

This wasn't the first time she'd felt this way. Since she was twelve she'd had a pretty good idea what Libyrarian Lital had been trying to teach them in biology. The idea of kissing someone other than her mother or father no longer seemed weird and outlandish to her, and she was glad that she lived at the Libyrinth, where the fact that she liked girls was a matter of no consequence to anyone but herself.

But somehow the whole thing had taken on a new significance since she'd arrived in Ilysies. First the groom girl and now Scio . . . What was it that was so distracting about the women here?

Resurfacing, blowing water, Scio said, "But I have to stay by you just the same. This is my big chance to prove to Steward Sopopholis that I can handle responsibility. I don't want to spend the rest of my life carrying trays and changing bedding. I want to be a steward myself one day—either here, or maybe at the summer palace. When you're the steward, you hear all the best gossip. Nobody ever tells me anything good because I'm just a chamber servant."

Scio's other charms were forgotten as Clauda studied the gleam in the girl's eyes. Could it be that she'd found her Ilysian counterpart—an ambitious servant with a taste for gossip? Clauda thought about that. Maybe she shouldn't get rid of her. Maybe she could use her.

Scio soaped up her hair and piled it in snaky ringlets on top of her head. "For instance, I bet the steward knows why your mistress has come home. Nobody else does." Scio lifted her eyes to Clauda's and blinked slowly, boldly, and falsely guileless.

Clauda could not suppress a grin. "I'm sure a great many people would like to know that," she admitted. "But I would never do anything to put my mistress at a disadvantage, even if she is a stubborn fool."

"She was angry with you this morning, wasn't she?" asked Scio.

Clauda shrugged and nodded.

"Don't you hate it when the people you work for don't appreciate you?" said Scio.

Clauda looked at her. Scio gazed at her matter-of-factly. Clauda hesitated, then gave Scio a small smile and a nod.

"I know," said Scio, leaning her head back against the tub in exasperation. "I'm always trying to convince Steward Sopopholis that I'm ready to be one of the queen's personal servants, but she just ignores me. She thinks I'm too young." She stuck out her tongue.

Clauda sank lower in the water. "Selene thinks I'm totally useless," she complained. It felt good to complain. "I could help her, but she won't let me."

Scio nodded. "The only good thing about being disregarded," she said, getting out of the tub, "is that people tend not to pay much attention to what you're doing." She dried herself off and then held up a towel for Clauda. Their eyes met. Neither said another word, but Clauda knew she had found an ally.

The feast for the return of the daughter was held in the Arena of the Bull. Couches and low tables provided seating on the deep, shallow steps surrounding the playing field. Clauda sat at Selene's side, to the left of the queen, on the uppermost step. Behind them a pillared colonnade led to the Court of the Mother, where she and Selene had waited that morning. The stately figure of the Ilysian goddess gazed enigmatically at the queen's back.

Jolaz sat on Thela Tadamos's other side, placidly nibbling sugared almonds and making casual observations to the queen. When they first sat down, Jolaz had offered Selene warm greetings and polite comments on the delight of having Ilysia's daughter among them once more. Selene accepted her civilities with tightly held formality, and now sat stiffly beside her mother, responding to the queen's remarks with strained goodwill.

Jolaz made no further attempt to converse with Selene, and Selene said nothing to her. And Selene's conversation with the queen was on the order of, "Have you seen the rose garden?" and "The new barracks yard is most impressive."

It was like sitting on the other side of a brick wall. If Selene would just swallow her pride and make conversation with Jolaz, they might learn something useful. But no, of course not. Any awkwardness Clauda might have felt at being among such exalted company was swallowed by her frustration at seeing this opportunity squandered.

The feast, however, was like something out of a dream—new lambs roast with spices, quail served with apricots and mushrooms, asparagus with pine nuts, mint and lemon ices, pitchers of wine, breads so light they felt like a cloud upon the tongue—and it went on and on for hours, it seemed. People ate leisurely, distracted by conversation and by the entertainers who performed on the lawn. Acrobats and dancers and musicians followed one after another, so that the whole was a succession of increasingly improbable miracles, starting with the sugared almonds and culminating in the bull dance.

This last was heralded by skirling trumpets and a lull in the talk. Young men and women dressed in tight-fitting white breeches—the same grooms who had greeted their arrival in the palace yard the day before—trotted out and took up stations at the four corners of the lawn. Among them Clauda spotted the girl who had taken her horse. The trumpets rose to a crescendo, and two little girls no more than six years old, with garlands of flowers around their necks and in their hair, came out of a set of large double doors directly opposite the queen. They led a roan red bull, which also wore flowers about its neck and horns. One of the children untied the length of silk with which it was tethered, and then she and her cohort disappeared through the doors once more.

From somewhere, drums beat. The grooms stamped their feet in anticipation. The bull pawed the ground and lowered its head. Its horns, tipped with silver, gleamed in the sunlight. The whole courtyard was silent now, breathless.

One of the grooms ran from his station straight at the bull, which snorted and sprang to meet him, hooves flinging sod in its wake. Still the youth ran at the bull and Clauda was wondering what sort of deluded barbarity this was, when the boy grasped the beast's horns and executed a flip over the animal's back, landing unscathed behind it.

This incredible feat was greeted only by polite applause. Outraged on behalf of this amazing athlete, Clauda clapped loudly, and was just raising her fingers to whistle when Selene stayed her with a cool hand. "They're just getting started," she said.

Over the course of the next hour Clauda saw those dancers repeat the youth's feat over and over again, each time embellishing it with some added bit of daring, such as leaping back on the animal's rump after landing, or two grooms leaping over the bull's back crosswise. It all culminated when the groom who had taken her horse—her groom of the almond eyes—won the day by riding the bull standing between its shoulders, then leaning forward and plucking the garland from its horns. The girl straightened and executed a backflip to land, sure-footed and beaming, on the green field of glory.

Clauda forgot to clap. She stared witless at the shining figure on the field, and it struck her that she beheld a god—a shining example of youth and exuberance, beauty and daring. All too quickly, this new-formed deity received her reward— a silver circlet for her hair—gave her salute to the queen, and exited through the double doors.

Clauda sighed and took a sip of watered wine, then looked around. The feast was breaking up at last. Selene, nodding at her mother's parting words, stood up and hailed Vorain. "How about a game of father's bluff?"

The big soldier nodded and grinned. " 'Bout time I got to win back some of what I lost to you at your farewell party."

Selene, suddenly full of solicitude, put a hand to Clauda's shoulder and leaned over her. "Are you tired? Would you like to retire? Scio could escort you back to your chamber, or," she added as Clauda began to shake her head, "you can come and play cards with Vorain and me. I'll lend you some coins."

Well, there was no way Clauda was going straight to bed. At the same time, saddling herself with a gossip wasteland like Selene would be criminally perverse and negligent. Just as she was mulling this over, Scio appeared at the top of the steps. Clauda gave a feeble sigh and let her head droop. "I do need some sleep," she pretended to admit. "If my sore muscles will allow it. We must hope for Haly's sake that the Eradicants do not possess the art of kinesiology."

Selene nodded and gave her an awkward pat on the shoulder. "Rest well, then. With the Mother's blessing, you will mend soon."

Once they left the Arena of the Bull, Scio grabbed Clauda's hand and pulled her into an alcove graced with a small statue of an extremely distracting nature. "Do you truly wish to retire?" asked Scio.

Clauda, trying not to stare at the tiny clay figures with their vivid paint and delighted expressions, shook her head. "No, of course not."

Scio smiled and arched her neck, her chin bent down coyly. "Good. 'Cause I can show you something that would impress your mistress." Her voice fell to a whisper and she squeezed both of Clauda's hands. "Hardly anybody knows about it."

Clauda forgot all about the statue in the thrill that went though her at those words. "What is it?"

Scio raised her head and stood back, releasing Clauda's hands. "That, you'll have to see for yourself."

10

The Song

After her interview with Siblea, Haly was escorted by a youth in brown robes to a luxuriously appointed chamber with a large canopied bed. The floor was covered with fine rugs and the walls were hung with tapestries. There were lights like the ones in Siblea's office, and like Siblea's office, it was warm here, though there was no fire. The youth showed her how to turn the lights on and off by a switch near the door, then left her and locked the door behind him.

She stumbled to the bed and fell upon it, welcoming the black tide of exhaustion that overwhelmed her and obliterated all thought.

She awoke to light streaming in through the windows of the room. She stretched experimentally and winced. Her body ached everywhere. Lying still and staring up at the red-and-yellow spiral pattern in the canopy above the bed seemed like a good thing to do. She thought over her interview with

Siblea. So he thought she was this Redeemer of theirs, and evidently that had won her release from the prison.

Good so far, and yet, if the Eradicants ever came into possession of *The Book of the Night*, they would force her to translate it for them, and then there would be nothing to stop them from destroying the Libyrinth. But they didn't have *The Book of the Night*. Selene had it. Perhaps it was already safe in Ilysies. She clung to that thought.

When she at last roused herself, she discovered a basin of steaming water on a table in the center of the room. Beside it sat a washcloth, soap, fresh smallclothes, and a neatly folded clean brown robe. She had just finished washing and dressing when a key turned in the lock on her door and the same brown-robed boy from the night before entered with a tray. Breakfast. The smells issuing from the tray awakened her hunger. She sat down in a chair on the other side of the table.

As the youth approached her with the tray she eyed his robes. They were brown, like her clerk's robes. The Eradicants wore black, like the Libyrarians did. She thought of Siblea's tale about Iscarion, but by then the tray had been set before her: smoked fish, bread, barley porridge with honey and cream, a steaming mug of coffee, and a dish of sliced . . . oranges? Yes, oranges. She'd seen them only once before, among the tribute sent from Ilysies in return for the invention of palm-glow.

"Thank you," she murmured, poised to devour it all. She glanced up. "What's your name?"

The boy, who couldn't be much older than her, blinked in surprise, and then said, "Gyneth."

"Thank you, Gyneth," she said. It couldn't be too soon to establish good relations with what appeared to be her principal jailer.

Of course she knew what they were trying to do, with first the harsh treatment and then the reprieve. Many a book had told her of it. "Good cop, bad cop" was what the late period

Old Earth crime novels had called it. It was a way to soften her up, to get her to do what they wanted. Just then, her mouth gloriously full of smoked fish, she didn't care.

Gyneth waited politely in a chair by the door until she'd consumed every last scrap of food. Then he took the tray and the used wash water, set them on a small marble-topped table, and returned to her, a jar like the one Ithaster had used in his hand.

At the sight of it Haly started back and frantically kicked the chair out from under her. A low moan escaped her lips, "No . . ."

"It's only salve," said Gyneth. "For your cut—it's infected."

The lye Ithaster had put on her cut had been in a jar like that, and it was supposed to stave off infection, too. She remembered vividly the burning pain of it. She managed at last to free herself from table and chair, and she sprang to the windows, which were barred.

She spun around, facing Gyneth. He still stood beside the table, the jar in his hand, looking nonplussed. Haly searched the room for a weapon of some kind. The food tray had come with nothing more lethal than a spoon for the porridge. There was no fireplace, and therefore no fire irons. There was nothing.

Gyneth edged slowly toward her. "Listen. Censor Siblea told me to treat the cut on your face. If I don't, I'll be in trouble."

She sneered at him even as she pressed herself back against the windows. Perhaps she could break one and use the broken glass . . . "What will he do, send you to the dungeon?"

Gyneth, still looking perplexed, gave a little shake of his head. He cleared the table and came around toward her, the jar in his outstretched hand.

Haly gripped the window ledge. "No? No prison for you? No peabea? No mind lancets? But then, you're not a witch, are you? But I am. I'm a witch, and if you take one step closer, I'll curse you."

He hesitated. "Censor Siblea says you're the Redeemer."

"That's right. So who are you going to obey—him or your Redeemer? I'm your Redeemer and I say put the jar down and get out of here."

Gyneth gnawed his lower lip. "He hasn't tested you yet. He says he has to test you first, before he can be sure. . . ."

A test? Seven Tales, was there no end to their ordeals? She felt stronger from the good food, and was suddenly filled with reckless, desperate energy. She eyed this Gyneth closely. This was no Ithaster. He was barely taller than she was, and slight of build. Why not, she thought. What difference did it make? They would do with her whatever they wanted, no matter what she did. She might as well give a little back, while she could, to whom she could. Without another word she launched herself at Gyneth.

She grabbed him around the waist and took him down. He gave a soft grunt of surprise as he landed on his back. She scrambled on top of him, straddling his chest, pinning his hands to the floor. He still clutched the jar and she lifted that hand and slammed it back onto the floor. He cried out and the jar rolled out of his loosened fingers and away across the floor. He struggled, trying to free himself, but she hung on tight. "You want to hurt me?" she panted. "I'm going to hurt you."

"No. Please," he said. His eyes were very wide, his chest heaving. Was this what she had looked like in the vault? She stared down at his sweating, fearful face, and suddenly her grand breakfast turned in her stomach. She scrambled off of him and dove for the jar, which had come to rest just beneath the bed.

Gyneth sat up, but made no move to approach her. "It's just salve," he said, rubbing his scraped knuckles. "See for yourself."

She unscrewed the jar and took a quick glance inside. It looked innocuous enough. She lifted the jar and sniffed it. It smelled like the camphor with which Palla the crèche nurse had dressed her childhood wounds. She touched it experimentally with her left pinkie. It felt cool, that was all. She walked cautiously toward Gyneth. "Don't get up," she told him. "Just give me your hand."

Calmly, Gyneth lifted the hand she'd bashed against the floor. The skin on his middle two knuckles was split and bleeding slightly. She watched his face as she spread a generous dollop of the salve on his wound. He smiled encouragingly. His hand never trembled.

Experimentally, she put a tiny dab of the stuff on the cut on her face. It didn't hurt. It felt good; cooling, soothing. She took a solid dollop and ran it along the cut. It eased the tightness and burning that had been so constant for the past five days, she almost didn't notice it anymore.

"You should apply it every four hours," said Gyneth, sitting back on his haunches. He cocked his head, peering at her. "You missed a spot, up by your temple."

Haly was suddenly overtaken by trembling. She thought it was exhaustion catching up with her again, but then why was the room blurred and the heat that had been in her cut now in her eyes and nose? Don't cry, she told herself, not now, not in front of this Eradicant. She tried to put more salve on her wound but got it in her hair instead, and then the first, humiliating sob burst forth. She sank to the floor and lowered her head to her knees, hiding her face with her arms. It was all she could do—that, and shake.

At last she mastered herself and sat back, wiping her nose on the sleeve of her robe. Gyneth was still there, staring at her with curiosity. "I didn't think the Redeemer would cry."

She gave him a bitter grimace. "Maybe I'm not the Redeemer. I haven't been tested yet, right?"

"True," said Gyneth.

Haly hesitated, then blurted, "What is the test? What are they going to do to me?"

Gyneth shook his head. "They're not going to *do* anything to you. It's just to verify that you can hear text as if it were song."

Frustration and fear made her words sharp. "And how are you going to do that? You people don't have any books."

Gyneth looked down, biting his lip. "Not the Righteous Chorus, no, of course not, but some criminals do." He glanced at the door. "Last night Censor Siblea received information that a family was harboring a book beneath the floor of their house. They were arrested and the book was seized. One of them will recite it for a chorus. Then the book will be brought to you, but you won't be permitted to read it. You'll be asked to recite it while it's in a locked box. That's all."

So she wasn't going to be tortured again. She swallowed against the relief that threatened to undo her again. Then another thing occurred to her. "What if the prisoner lies in their recitation?"

Gyneth gave her a reassuring smile. "People don't lie to Censor Siblea."

She stared at him. He had a good point. "When?"

"The day after tomorrow."

It was too soon. She was too tired. She needed to think about all this, but she felt as if she was going to drop where she sat. "I need to rest," she told him.

Gyneth nodded. He helped her to stand, and guided her to the bed in case she should falter. Sliding between the clean bedsheets was a luxury past all description. Just as she was about to rest her head on the soft pillow, she smelled camphor. Gyneth stood beside the bed, the jar of salve in his hand. "You missed a spot," he said.

With a sigh, Haly nodded.

His fingers were deft and cool. There was apparently a whole section of the cut, extending across her temple, which she'd not been aware of—or had forgotten, in the midst of everything else. When he was finished, Gyneth stepped back, his eyes downcast, a blush rising on his cheeks. "I'm sorry Ithaster did that to you. He's in a lot of trouble now. He should have known. He should have recognized the signs. And they shouldn't have put you in the dungeon." He looked up at her. "That's only for the wicked."

Haly thought about Mab and the family that had hidden the book. She stared into Gyneth's clear, pale eyes and realized that he really believed it. "How long have you lived in the temple?" she asked him.

"Since my sixth year."

And she had been born in the Libyrinth, and lived there all her life until now. How much choice did either of them have in what they believed?

Gyneth closed the door behind him as he left. The soft click of the lock turning was the last thing she heard.

Until she awoke again sometime in the early afternoon to the smell of roast pork and the sight of Gyneth standing at the foot of her bed with a laden tray.

The meal was roast pork loin with apricot sauce, braised greens, and millet cake. It wasn't going to work, she resolved. All this wonderful food and luxurious treatment was not going to make her forget that these people were her enemies. But there was no reason *they* had to know that. She ate everything and silently relished every bite, while Gyneth waited patiently beside the door. When he collected the tray, he hesitated at her bedside. "Holy One . . ."

"You shouldn't call me that. It hasn't been proven yet," she pointed out.

Gyneth nodded. "I would ask a favor of you, miss."

Haly arched her eyebrows. "A favor? Of me? What could
I possibly do for you?"

Gyneth bit his lip and then looked at her, his silver-blue
eyes earnest and intense. "Let me attend you at the test. I
wish—I wish to be present."

"You want to be there."

Gyneth nodded, his cheeks coloring. He looked at her from
beneath his very straight, flat brow, his eyes shining. "Yes. To
be one of those present at the Confirmation of the Redeemer.
To be witness to the opening moment of the Redemption
of the Word. The Redemption is all we dream of, we devout of
the Chorus."

Something in the gleam of his eyes made her very uncomfortable. She frowned and blew out her breath. "There's more
to this than the Maker of Eggs, isn't there?"

Gyneth looked surprised at first, then nodded. "You know
about the Maker of Eggs." He shrugged in admission. "That is
the most worldly benefit of the Redemption, but there is so
much more to the Liberation of the Word." He began to sing
in a clear, liquid tenor, "When the Song and the Word are reunited, the Song will be heard by all the multitudes, and each
in his own voice will Sing."

He looked at her penetratingly, and with what she could
only describe as love. Not love for her personally, but for a
savior. Seven Tales, she was an object of religious devotion.
Haly sighed. "What's that supposed to mean?"

Gyneth was confounded. "Mean?"

"Yeah. Mean. The song will be heard by the multitudes.
What song? Each in his own voice will sing? I'd like to know
how else they'd do it. So everybody sings the same song all
over the world at once. So what?"

Gyneth was stricken. "But it is the Song."

"Oh, the Song, I see. What's the Song?"

He looked utterly amazed and dismayed. "Oh, you don't—of

course—you . . ." He tilted his head to one side and leaned toward her, peering at her like she was a wounded bird. "You don't know the Song."

"Does it go, 'Oh Susanna, oh don't you hide from me, I've come from old Ilysies with a ten-pound block of cheese'?"

He smiled and shook his head. "It doesn't have words— at least, not yet." He nodded at her knowingly. "But it's the voice of the world. The . . . song that is in everything. It is what makes us alive. It moves through us, and through everything around us. The Song is what makes everything happen."

"Oh, no, sorry—that's Time."

Gyneth screwed up his face and leaned back, eyeing her with skeptical derision. While he had all the regard in the world for her holiness, he apparently had none for her opinions.

"You know," she insisted, "Time is what keeps everything from happening at once. Oh, right, I guess you don't know. See, there are the Seven Tales: Birth, Peril, Hunger, Balance, Love, Death, and Mystery. They combine together to make bigger tales, and Time determines what order they go in. It makes a big difference: If you have Love and then Peril, that's bad, but if it's Peril first and then Love, that's good, see? The Tale of Tales, now, that's the story of everything that has ever happened or will happen. We'll never know how that story goes, because that is the one that only Time can tell."

Gyneth still had that scrunched-up look on his face, like he'd bitten into a green apple. "I thought you people worshipped animals."

Haly shrugged nonchalantly, thrilled at being able to shock this earnest, devout soul. "Oh, we don't really worship anything, you see. We acknowledge Time as a force beyond ourselves, and revere it, I guess you'd say, but it's not like you with your prophet and your song. The animals are the characters in the Tales, and when you're old enough to um . . . you know, get your first blood, the healer consults the signs and determines which Tale you're under. The animal for that Tale is your guardian."

Gyneth narrowed his eyes. "What about the boys, then?"

Haly blinked. "What about them?"

"Well, boys don't bleed. So does that mean they don't get a guardian?"

"They bleed when they get initiated. Didn't you?" she challenged. What was he talking about, boys don't bleed?

Gyneth looked alarmed. "Initiated?"

"Yeah, to become men." She shook her head. "You don't do this? Get an operation so you can't accidentally father children? How do you keep from overpopulating the temple here?"

Gyneth gave her a blank look. "We don't have women priests."

"Well, that's stupid."

Gyneth's eyes flashed. "It's a lot better than mutilating half the population."

"Oh for Time's sake, it's not mutilation! It's a tiny little incision in the base of . . . um. Anyway, the point is, everyone has a guardian. Mine is the Fly."

Gyneth looked like he was as relieved as she was to change the subject. "The fly?" He snorted. "The Redeemer should have something better than that." He stopped short, suddenly looking worried. "I think this is blasphemy."

Haly shrugged, noncommittal. "The Fly is for Mystery. Mystery is a two-way story, which means it can be good or bad. The Fly spots a drop of honey, lands in it, and gets stuck. That's bad. But then when the Fly is on the Cow's rump, the Cow swats it with its tail and the Fly lands on a pile of dung." Her voice faltered a bit. "That's . . . good."

Gyneth stared at her in appalled silence. Haly's cheeks

became hot. She'd never thought before how disgusting that was. "Well, Mystery really isn't the best one to start with," she blustered. "Peril is better. Peril is the Goat. My friend Clauda has the Goat for her guardian. The Goat is grazing in tall grass. The Lion is hiding in the grass, stalking it. See, even though Peril is bad, it doesn't always turn out bad. The Goat is brave, and if the Goat is brave and smart, it might get away."

He was still unmoved.

Haly closed her mouth on further justification. That's what she was doing, she realized—trying to justify her faith to this Eradicant. Because she was embarrassed, all of a sudden, to be a Libyrarian. The Seven Tales and the Tale Time Will Tell felt threadbare and homely in the glare of this Yammon and his Song.

At last Gyneth gave her a conciliatory smile and said, "Once you pass the test, you will set aside such ideas."

Anger sparked in her heart. "I don't care what happens with the test. I'm not going to become an Eradicant."

He frowned. "Singer."

She bared her teeth. "Book burner, torturer, ignorant, illiterate savage!"

Gyneth jumped up. "You're going to fail the test! You can't be the Redeemer!"

"Maybe I don't want to be your stupid Redeemer, you ever think of that? Maybe I'll fail the test on purpose."

Gyneth's chest heaved and he stalked to the door. "Go ahead then, if you miss the dungeon so much." He paused at the door and looked over his shoulder at her. "You should fail," he said. "How can you be the Redeemer when you don't know the Song? When you don't even want to know the Song?" He opened the door and turned to face her. "And we're not ignorant, in case you haven't noticed." He toggled the switch by the door, making the lights flicker on and off, and then he left.

Dinner was roast squab, bean shoots, and barley bread. Haly ate it in determined silence as Gyneth waited sullenly by the door. Breakfast was much the same, but at lunch, Gyneth entered with Siblea behind him, and the censor stood with his hand on the back of Gyneth's neck as the boy told Haly that he was sorry for raising his voice to her, for wishing ill of her, and for presuming to instruct her in holy doctrine.

Siblea beamed at both of them and patted Gyneth on the shoulder. He turned to Haly. "The boy was right about one thing, my dear. It is the shame of the world that you don't know the Song. It would give you a better appreciation of your exalted role. But we can do something about that right now." He cocked an ear. "Services are just starting." He held out his hand to her. "Come along, now."

Haly, who had sat silent in her chair all this time, shrank back from that hand, but she did stand. She would go with them. Why not? Why not hear this stupid song of theirs? If nothing else, it was a chance to get out of her comfortably appointed cell.

They walked side by side down the broad stone corridor— Haly in the middle, of course. Siblea held her elbow gently as if he were guiding her, which of course he wasn't—he was making sure she didn't try to run for it.

The temple halls were built out of slabs of the same gray stone she'd seen elsewhere in the Citadel, the high, arching ceiling supported intermittently by buttresses. Occasionally they passed a slab that was larger than the others, and decorated with flowing lines and spirals. "What are those?" she asked, pointing at one.

"Songlines," Siblea explained. "They represent the flow of the Song through all things."

"Is that why you carve them in the faces of your prisoners?" she asked.

"Of course," said Siblea placidly. "All disease, physical, mental, and social, results from being out of harmony with the Song. It is a way to remind people of their eternal connection."

They arrived at a small door, which slid open when Gyneth touched a panel beside it. Inside was a small room, and all three of them went in, Haly more hesitantly than the other two. She didn't see another door. Siblea's grip tightened on her elbow and he said, "Come, my dear, it is only an elevator."

She got in, very unhappy about being in such a confined space with the two of them. Gyneth pressed another button, the door closed, and then she felt the room moving upward. Siblea smiled indulgently at her involuntary gasp, and she flushed. These people were illiterate and they were supposed to be uncivilized, ignorant, and backward, but time and again, she was the one who felt as if she sported a bone through her nose like a savage in a Victorian adventure novel.

The room came to a halt and the door opened out into a long, curving hallway lined with archways. Siblea and Gyneth escorted her through one of these and she caught her breath. They were on a small balcony, one of many lining a cavernous amphitheater, its floor two hundred feet below. Directly ahead loomed the massive figure of a man wrought in steel, his chin roughly level with their balcony. His mouth was open, lined with white teeth that were . . . moving. With a start of relief Haly realized the mouth was a platform, and the teeth were people in white robes.

Haly swallowed. "Is that—"

"Yammon, yes," said Siblea. "Please have a seat. In a moment you will hear the Song."

Haly saw the other balconies filling up rapidly. She leaned over the balcony to spy people gathering in rows on the floor below, and regretted it. They were so small down there. It was such a long drop. A little voice in her head said, "Jump."

She backed away and sat down in the chair beside Siblea's.

Gyneth stood behind them. Haly smelled incense and saw faint wisps of smoke rising from Yammon's upraised palms.

Soon the murmuring of voices in the amphitheater became silent and a voice, which was many voices together, boomed from the statue of Yammon. "Welcome, My children. Take your places and be glad, for each of you is a beloved member of My Righteous Chorus, and as the Song revealed Itself to Me and delivered us all from slavery, so it will aid you in your own time of need."

Then Haly heard a sound unlike any she had ever heard before—a low hum, so deep it reverberated in her bones. Siblea and Gyneth opened their mouths and joined in, and she could hear that throughout the amphitheater, others were doing the same. It went on and on, thrumming through her body, growing louder and louder, until she feared its bass reverberations would shake apart the very stones upon which she sat. And then a single voice soared up above the hum, a voice of such singular, crystalline clarity that it brought tears to her eyes. Soon this voice was joined by others and they interwove with one another like birds in flight.

Despite everything, Haly felt her heart lifted by these voices, felt her body merge with the thrum that her own throat echoed. Her hands and feet tingled and her heart raced as if she herself were a winged creature, climbing ramparts of air and scudding across vistas of sea and mountain. The Song intensified in volume and tempo and pitch, carrying her higher and higher until she felt as if the whole world lay before her. She could feel all of it, every stone and every heartbeat, and it was all part of the Song. This was like what she had felt at the vault, when she and Clauda and Selene sang together and the light came out and opened the door for them. Only this was so much more—not a pretty light show, but more something she felt inside, like a realization. They were all together: she, Siblea, this multitude of Eradicants, the stone beneath her feet, and the creatures in the ocean far away. All things were united in the Song, and since she was part of it, they were part of her. She could never really be alone, and the concept of "enemy" was meaningless.

At least for as long as the Song lasted. When it was done, Haly sat stunned, her heart aching with the loss of that all-connecting, all-encompassing sound. And in another moment she felt despair for herself and her home. The Seven Tales were untidy and diffuse, whereas the Song was unified and powerful. The Tales took years of study to appreciate. They weren't something you could explain to a stranger in a few minutes. Few enough of her own people had the dedication to seek their wisdom. But anybody could understand the Song. *She* understood the Song, and yearned for it.

11

The Wing of Tarsus

Clauda let Scio lead her by the hand through passages narrower and less adorned than those she'd seen in the rest of the palace: servants' passages. As they passed the laundry, Corazol emerged, her face red from the steaming vats, and offered an all-purpose rebuke: "You two are up to no good, I'm sure." Scio flashed her a broad, smug smile, and her hand tightened around Clauda's as they continued on their way.

They passed more people as they neared the familiar clatter and cooking smells that meant kitchen in any land. Some of the servants were friends of Scio's who either congratulated or chastised her for her good fortune in avoiding the postfeast chores. Others merely gave them suspicious looks, but everyone stared at Clauda. She was beginning to wonder if she had gravy smeared on her face when it struck her that most of them had probably never seen an Ayorite before. With her broad build and coppery hair, she looked nothing

like the Ilysians. She was exotic. Clauda grinned at the thought
and was almost disappointed when Scio steered her down an
even narrower passage that led away from the bustle of the
kitchen.

They came to a small door that opened onto a spiral staircase. Scio took a glow stick from its holder beside the door, and
with a conspiratorial smile, led her down into the darkness.

The walls around them changed from cut stone to sheer
rock, rough hewn and glistening with moisture. They were
far below the palace now. Clauda shivered in the damp. She
heard a distant crashing sound, and then heard it again. A
periodic, muted catastrophe—the ocean.

They came to the bottom of the staircase and made their
way along a small, winding tunnel. Clauda was grateful that
she didn't suffer from claustrophobia. All the same, her hand
sweated in Scio's grasp and she felt the tremor inside herself
that she associated with the effects of the mind-lancet attack.

They came to a shadowed alcove in the tunnel wall. Scio
showed her a crevice in the stone, through which a little light
shone. "It's a spy hole. The palace is full of them. This one—
there's a crack in the cave wall," said Scio. "Ages and ages
ago someone carved out a hole in it, so you can look through
it and see . . ." The hole was about the size of Clauda's fist.
Scio stepped back and gestured Clauda toward it.

Through the hole Clauda beheld a moderately sized and
well-lit cave, open on one end to the ocean, but dry. And in
the middle of the cave sat a large gold object in the shape of a
crescent moon, spanning roughly twenty feet from tip to tip.
But this crescent was gold and it was carved with the same
flowing lines she'd seen on the Devouring Silence. Unlike
that horror, this thing was beautiful, whatever it was. Clauda
took her face away from the spy hole and looked at Scio.
"What is it?" she whispered.

"None other than the Ancient flying machine," said Scio.

She leaned in so her face was right next to Clauda's and she whispered in her ear, "The legends are true. It's real."

"A flying machine?" Clauda leaned back, flushed and amazed—and suddenly a little skeptical. She tried to get a good look at the girl's face but failed in the dim light. "Have you seen it fly?"

"No, but come on. Doesn't it look familiar to you?"

"What?" Clauda was lost.

"A wing of gold, inscribed with the name of the ocean? Look at it. It's the Wing of Tarsus."

Oh, of course, the Wing of Tarsus. "What's the Wing of Tarsus?"

Scio gaped at her a moment, and then understanding dawned. "Oh, of course, you're an Ayorite. You don't know the legend of Queen Belrea and the Wing of Tarsus. It's an Ancient flying machine discovered by our founder."

"Does it really fly?"

Scio nodded slowly. "If you know how to operate it, it does, but not many have the skill to master it."

Clauda peered back through the hole in wonder. Behind her, Scio went on, "It slew the people of Piscea with a sword forged from the goddess's wrath."

This was a very big deal. A secret weapon. A flying machine. Clauda had a sudden vision of the wing sailing across the Plain of Ayor, smiting every Eradicant in sight. That, as much as her awareness of the great secret to which Scio had made her privy, brought tears to her eyes. Her view of the wing blurred and she blinked rapidly, turning her face back to the tunnel and to Scio. "Thank you," she said, clearing her throat. "But why are you showing me this?"

Scio's smile was little more than a glimmer in the darkness. She stood close, and she smelled of the lavender soap they'd both washed with. "We can help each other," she said. "I can help you impress your mistress by showing you things that might be useful for her to know, and you can help me by getting her to praise me to Steward Sopopholis. I mean, she is the princess. If she says I should be promoted . . ."

The next morning Clauda jumped out of bed as soon as she awoke and dressed herself in the clothes she'd worn the previous night. She splashed some water on her face, grimaced at her unkempt reflection in the mirror beside the washstand, and headed for the door. She needed to find Selene.

As if summoned, the princess of Ilysies appeared at her door, looking every bit as postfestive as Clauda did. "Oh, good," she said, "you're up. I told Scio you'd breakfast with me this morning. We need to talk."

With grave trepidation, Clauda followed Selene to her chamber, where a feast of braised hare, fresh asparagus, poached eggs, and the ever-popular pastries awaited them. Clauda forgot her fear in the rumbling of her stomach, and for a time no word was spoken. They ate with relish. At last, Selene wiped a smear of egg from her gently curving lips and poured the coffee. "My mother thinks there is a spy in the palace," she said, sitting back, her voice half muffled by the cup as she held it before her and inhaled the steam.

Clauda dropped her fork and it fell with a clang onto her plate. Her hands and feet tingled and she felt dizzy. She stared at the floor and forced herself to breathe slowly. She waited for Selene to tell her that she'd been found out, that all was lost. Selene didn't say anything. Clauda looked up.

Selene regarded at her over the rim of her coffee cup. Clauda could not quite decipher the expression lurking in her dark eyes. "So you *were* up to something last night. You should learn to school your reactions better. And relax. She thinks the spy is an Eradicant and she doesn't suspect Scio, because if she did, she would never have assigned her to you."

Clauda caught herself gaping and closed her mouth. "Why do you mention Scio?" she managed.

Selene gave a derisive little snort of laughter. "The two of you left the feast together. When I went to your chamber to check on you, it was empty. I can only assume you were with Scio, and from what Vorain tells me, her reputation as a busybody is much the same as yours was back home."

Busybody! Anger flashed through Clauda. "You checked up on me?"

Selene glared back at her. "I was worried about you."

That put a stop to the next bitter thing Clauda was about to say. She turned her attention to the pastries, bit into one, and chewed it a moment before saying, "Do you want to know what I found out?"

There was silence, and Clauda looked up to see Selene downing the rest of her coffee. The Libyrarian finished, set the cup down on its saucer with a clink, and said, "Yes."

"Have you heard of the Wing of Tarsus?"

"Of course I have. It's a national legend. Every Ilysian child over the age of three has heard the story of Queen Belrea and the Wing of Tarsus. What of it?"

Clauda ignored her contemptuous tone. "The wing is real. I saw it in a cavern beneath the palace."

Selene looked abashed for a moment, then skeptical. "Are you sure?"

Hiding her smile, Clauda described what she'd seen.

Selene stared off into the middle distance. "So that is Mother's secret weapon," she said at last. "I knew she had to have something."

"Scio told me it is a flying machine, and that it can slay enemies."

Selene nodded. "It is a powerful weapon for the defense of Ilysies . . . if Mother has found someone who can pilot it."

"Can't anyone fly it?"

Selene shook her head. All skepticism, all contempt was gone from her now. "It is a device of the Ancients, and they are notorious for being . . . tricky. Maybe one or two women in a generation have the aptitude to master it. It was supposedly lost at sea by Belrea's great-great-granddaughter, Ama. I wonder where it was found, and when? For all I know, it's been there all along." She paused and then gave Clauda one of her dark, intense looks. "What's almost as interesting is why Scio showed it to you."

Clauda found herself taken aback in the absence of Selene's arrogance. She didn't quite know what to do with this neutral regard she suddenly enjoyed. "She said we could help each other. She wants you to praise her and get her a promotion."

Selene pursed her lips. "Let's hope it's as simple as that. In the meantime, be careful." She drained her cup and stood. "I'm going to the library. Do you want to come along?"

Clauda nodded. As she followed Selene out of the room she chided herself for feeling proud to be asked. Yesterday she'd been furious with Selene; now she was gobbling up scraps of praise from her like a puppy. She should find Scio and talk her into showing her more spy holes. Then again, if she went to the library with Selene she could learn more about the Wing of Tarsus.

Selene led Clauda down the hallway, around a corner and down another hallway until they reached the Courtyard of the Petitioners. They took the low, broad steps to the right of the pillared hall, and Clauda found herself in a garden filled with rosebushes.

They followed a path through the roses to another set of steps on the other side, and took those up to another pillared hall. To their left, on the same side as the doors to the queen's chambers, stood a pair of doors carved with images of books and scrolls and quills. Selene opened them to reveal a large, rectangular room four stories tall, lined with shelves.

A gentle hush lay over the room and Clauda recognized the smell of old paper. She wondered what Haly would hear if she was here, and wished she could be here to tell her.

There were three other people already in the room, one a servant dusting the shelves, the others two elderly women seated on benches beneath the windows on the far wall, reading in silence. It was a far cry from the bustle of the Great Hall back home.

"Of course, it's not the Libyrinth," Selene said, as if reading her thoughts.

"No, but . . . it's impressive, all the same. How many books are there here?"

"Ten thousand," said Selene. "About three-quarters of them Ilysian, the rest Earth texts acquired from the Libyrinth."

Clauda looked at her. "I didn't know we sold books from our collection."

"Not often, but in times of famine, it's been known to happen."

And Ilysies the Fat would always have food to trade, thought Clauda, trying to decide how she felt about that. As an Ayorite servant of the Libyrinth, she'd been educated to read and she had access to the books of the Libyrinth—as long as the book in question was not needed by someone more important. But in practicality, her duties in the kitchen left little time for reading. In the evenings, when Palla told tales by the fire, she welcomed them, and seldom sought out the printed page.

Except for one book that she'd found on an afternoon when she'd snuck away to explore the stacks with Haly.

She'd read *The Cricket in Times Square* all through that night, though she felt groggy the following day. She hid it under the loose hearthstone in the kitchen, and when it was her turn to keep the fire burning through the night, she read it again and again and again.

She looked at Selene, gazing fondly at the shelves around her. "What's your favorite book?" she asked the Libyrarian.

A soft laugh crinkled the skin at the bridge of Selene's nose, and for a moment she was the spitting image of her mother. "Can't you guess?"

Clauda shrugged.

Selene drew herself up, a parody of her typically dignified posture, but the little smile at the corners of her mouth gave her away. "Why, *Theselaides*, of course."

Clauda wrinkled her nose. "*Theselaides*? That's not a story."

Selene shook her head. "But it is a story. It's the story of his life and all that he learned. A story is nothing more or less than a sequence of facts, or in the case of fiction, lies, that are imbued with meaning.

"Theselaides was a wealthy nobleman, and he left his comfortable home to seek knowledge of the world around him. And he discovered the Libyrinth. What could be a better story than that?"

Especially to an Ilysian princess who abandoned her own home for the sake of learning, thought Clauda, glimpsing for the first time how plain facts could be a story as stirring as the most fantastic fairy tale. "Is there a copy of it here?" she asked.

"Oh, yes. Over here." Selene led her to a shelf in the corner and reached down to retrieve a battered and obviously much-loved book. She cradled it gently for a moment, smiling fondly at it, and then handed it to Clauda.

The front cover was tenuously attached to the binding by a few worn threads. Opening it carefully, Clauda found its pages smudged, and here and there notes had been scribbled in the margins in a childish version of Selene's elegant scrawl. This was obviously Selene's childhood copy of the book.

"Why didn't you take this with you when you went to the Libyrinth?" she asked.

"Oh, my mother would sooner part with a daughter than a book," Selene said without rancor. "And the Libyrinth has two copies of its own." She took the book back from Clauda and replaced it on the shelf.

Clauda found herself with a half-formed question on her lips. It was something about why Selene resented Jolaz but not Theselaides, and which comforted her more—research or simply being away from the palace. And of course it was utterly unaskable. "Is there anything about the Wing of Tarsus here?" she said instead.

Selene smiled broadly and led her to a section of shelves along one wall. "From here to the floor," she said, holding her hand to the shelf at waist height.

Clauda whistled, and earned a glare of reproach from one of the women who were standing by the window.

"Well, it is the national legend of the founding of Ilysies," said Selene.

"So Belrea was the first queen?"

Selene nodded.

Clauda was about to ask her what Ilysies was before it was Ilysies when they both heard footsteps entering the library. They turned. It was Steward Sopopholis, with Scio trailing behind her.

"Your Grace," the steward addressed Selene, bowing low. "Her majesty Queen Thela requests your presence in the audience chamber."

"Of course," said Selene.

"Shall I accompany you, Your Grace?" asked Clauda.

Selene gave her an ironic smile at her hesitant use of the honorific. "No, Clauda. I will see my mother alone today. Perhaps you would like Scio to show you around the palace."

Good idea. As soon as Selene and Steward Sopopholis had

left, Scio steered Clauda to an empty corner of the library. "Was your mistress impressed?" she asked.

Clauda thought about that. *Perhaps you would like Scio to show you around the palace.* "Yes."

"That's good." Scio trailed one finger along the spines of the books on the shelf beside her. "And did you talk to her about helping me?"

After a fashion, Clauda thought, but only said, "Yes."

Scio grinned, then grabbed Clauda by the shoulders and squeezed them. "Do you think she's talking to Steward Sopopholis about me right now?"

"I don't know," said Clauda. *Probably not,* she thought.

Scio accepted this with a tilt of her head. "Well, we'll have to find some other way to impress her, then." She bit her lip and looked around them, then leaned forward and whispered in Clauda's ear, "Would you like to hear what the queen discusses in her audience chamber?"

Scio led Clauda to an alcove that butted up behind the part of the audience chamber where she had sat with Selene and Queen Thela the day before. Three-quarters of the way up to the domed and filigreed ceiling, the wall to her left sported a tiny, crescent-shaped opening like a winking eye. Through it she saw a slice of blue sky, and realized that on the other side lay the cliffs and the sea.

Though the alcove was ornate enough, it was clear no one ever came here. Light from the window slanted down through dusty air to strike an equally dusty niche on the opposite wall. There stood a small statue, its paint faded with age, of a girl with a fish tail and serpent hair rising out of the waves and brandishing a trident that was missing one prong. Scio pointed to the statue. "The Little Goddess of the Sea," Scio said by way of explanation. Like the statue Clauda had seen in the alcove outside the Court of the Bull, her face was rendered in great detail, with eyes that still held life, for all that age had blinded them, and lips no bigger than the tip of Clauda's thumb, parted in an expression of exultant joy. "Let her whisper in your ear," said Scio.

Clauda did as she was told. For a moment she heard nothing, and then she heard Selene's voice saying, "Does that matter?"

"I suppose not." It was Queen Thela. "Go. Get ready. I will speak to General Tadakis and put the plan into action. You will ride out tomorrow."

Clauda heard the faint sound of a door closing.

"What did you hear?" asked Scio. "Anything good?"

Clauda heard the door again. She shook her head and motioned for Scio to wait.

"General Tadakis, thank you for coming," said Thela.

"Your majesty," said a woman whose voice Clauda did not recognize. "I have begun mustering the army, as you asked. What will be our objective?"

"I want you to take the army over the mountains and into the Plain of Ayor. Wait there for the wing. When it arrives, follow it and attack what it attacks."

"We follow the wing," said the general.

"Yes," said Queen Thela.

"You give no further instructions?"

"No. And for now, you will not mention the wing. All your women need to know is that you are taking them into the plain, and that the heir herself will lead them to glory."

"The heir? Then I take it that the search for a pilot is finally over."

"Yes, no more of your women need be injured attempting to train on it. Jolaz will lead you."

"That is well, Your Majesty. The women will like that."

"I know," said the queen. "Now come with me, I want to show you the new rose garden."

At the sound of the door shutting, Clauda slid to the floor and sat slumped against the wall.

"What did you hear?" said Scio.

Clauda shook her head in an effort to clear it of a faint buzzing sound. She stood up and went to the opposite wall. She was shaking, but it wasn't entirely nerves. This was how she'd felt in the cave just before she collapsed on the ledge in the mountains. There was that same trembling feeling inside, in the place that Adept Ykobos referred to as her energy core. She was having a fit, right here in front of Scio.

Her hands and feet prickled with pins and needles, and the edges of her vision grew fuzzy as if gray flies hovered in the air all around her. She sat down on the floor abruptly, but it was either that or fall. She breathed, concentrating on fighting back the buzzing cloud that threatened to obliterate her awareness.

"What's wrong?" said Scio. She came and knelt at Clauda's side. "What is it—what did you hear?"

Clauda sank her head onto her hands and focused on taking slow, deep breaths and visualizing herself as a tree.

Scio put a tentative hand to her shoulder. "Are you ill?"

Clauda could not maintain her focus and lie at the same time. "It's because of the mind-lancet attack. Sometimes I get dizzy."

"Do you want me to help you back to your chamber?" she said, her voice wistful.

"No. Just . . . give me a moment."

A few more breaths, and the buzzing retreated. Clauda blinked. She could feel her extremities again. It had passed.

Scio still knelt beside her. "Better?" the girl asked.

Clauda nodded. Then without warning she grabbed Scio by the arm, holding her firmly. "Why are you showing me these things?" She kept her voice low.

Scio gave a little start and shook her head. "What? I told you already, so we can help each—"

"No," said Clauda. "There has to be more to it than that. The wing, what I just overheard, these are important things people aren't supposed to know about. This is dangerous. You're taking big risks. Why?"

Scio stared at her a moment, then seemed to make up her mind. "Okay, I'll answer your question, but it's best if we don't stay in any one place too long. Come with me." Scio led her down another servants' passage, this one leading behind the palace baths. As they went the passageway became increasingly dilapidated, until at last they came to a dead end littered with discarded tools and half-empty bags of mortar. The wall sealing the end of the passage was constructed of gray bricks and appeared to be newer than the surrounding stonework. "On the other side of that wall is the old queen's chambers," she said, sitting down on a sack of mortar.

Clauda sat down beside her.

"Not everyone likes the way Queen Thela does things," she said. "And some of us would like a different heir than the one she's chosen."

Oh. "And you're one of them."

Scio sniffed. "Queen Thela likes secrets, and so does her heir."

"And you like to know what's going on, don't you?"

Scio gave her a defiant look. "What's wrong with that? It hasn't always been this way. When the old queen reigned, the Ilysian people knew the mind of their queen. She trusted us." Scio put a hand on Clauda's shoulder. "Your mistress is much like her."

Comprehension dawned. "I see. So you would like Selene to be heir instead of Jolaz."

Scio nodded slowly. "Now you know," she said, and cast Clauda a sidelong glance. "Will you tell me why she has returned?"

Did she dare? Telling the truth might lose Clauda the help

Scio provided. But Scio had just told her that she prized honesty and hated secrets. Clauda hoped her instinct was correct. "For what you've already done, I owe you the truth. Selene is not here to challenge Jolaz for the throne."

Scio gave no reaction. "So why are you here?"

"My friend. My best friend, and Selene's clerk, a girl our age named Haly, is a prisoner of the Eradicants. We seek Queen Thela's help in rescuing her."

Scio gave her a rueful smile. "Then you will need help. Queen Thela does nothing out of mercy or charity."

"So I've been told."

Scio sank back on her haunches and looked at Clauda. "You told me the truth even though it might have cost you and your friend an ally."

"You said you don't like secrets. I judged that you would appreciate my honesty," said Clauda.

Scio smiled. "And you judged correctly."

12

The Book in the Iron Box

No knife or jar sat "forgotten" on the little table beside the chair in Siblea's office today. Instead there was a stout iron box, secured with padlocks. "I hope I shall be able to confide in you completely, as I have never been able to do in anyone before," said the book inside the box.

Haly hadn't realized how much she missed book voices. She ran to the table and ran her hands over the box, her fingers quickly tugging the padlocks in useless eagerness.

"Now, now, that would ruin the test, wouldn't it?" said Siblea, coming through the door at the back of the room.

Haly stood straight, her hands at her sides. "You have a book. Why haven't you burned it like all the others?"

Siblea was taken aback, but he quickly recovered, smiling. "Why, because of you, my dear. Because with this book we can determine with certainty whether or not you are our Redeemer. It was found two nights ago beneath the floorboards of a house right here in the citadel. Apparently the family has been hiding it for generations. Well-respected folk, too. Very disturbing."

They'd be in the dungeon now, Haly realized, wondering who they were and what had made them take such an enormous risk.

Siblea shrugged. "It is also fortuitous. We have received recitation of a portion of the text from the father of the house." Siblea waved Haly to her chair. "Now we will hear yours."

Haly tried not to think about how the father's recitation was obtained. She looked over her shoulder to where Gyneth stood holding the back of the chair. He nodded and smiled encouragingly.

"In spite of everything, I still believe that people are really good at heart," said the book.

With her heart beating very hard, high up in her chest, Haly sat down. Siblea seemed barely able to contain his excitement. He stared at her avidly and clasped his hands together. "You hear it, don't you?"

She nodded, frantically trying to think. She could fake it. She could recite something other than what the book told her—and go straight back to the dungeon. The muscles in her arms and back spasmed at the memory of what she'd endured there—and that had been only one day.

"There's no need to be frightened, my dear. What we're going to ask of you is very simple. Gyneth, bring our guest a glass of water."

Gyneth crossed to the hidden cupboard, poured a glass of water from a pitcher there, and handed it to Haly. Her hand shook. She grasped the glass with both hands and raised it to her lips. They didn't have *The Book of the Night*. And as long as they didn't have that, they wouldn't destroy the Libyrinth, Redeemer or no. She hoped.

She drained the glass before handing it back to Gyneth.

"When the others arrive, you will simply recite to us what the book tells you, starting from the beginning. Do you understand?" said Siblea.

"Others?"

There was a knock on the door.

Gyneth opened the door and Censor Michander entered, followed by the oldest man Haly had ever seen. He was older than ninety, she guessed, maybe even a great deal older. He was very thin, and he walked with the assistance of a brown-robed attendant. But once settled in Siblea's chair he lifted his head and fixed her with black eyes that were perfectly clear all the way down to the seventh hell.

"Welcome, High Censor Orrin," said Siblea, bowing low. "May your voice ring sweetly now and forever in the Song eternal."

Orrin's voice was reedy, his tone perfunctory. "May Yammon's melody bless your ears."

"High Censor, Brother Michander," said Siblea, "it is with unutterable joy that I greet you on this day, which will be the first new day. Allow me to present to you the Libyrarian Halcyon."

Clerk, thought Haly.

"Enough, Siblea," said Orrin. "You say the girl is our Redeemer. You have the means to prove this. I'm waiting."

Siblea turned to Haly. He knew, of course, that she could fail on purpose—spew a babble of nonsense that would send them both to the dungeon.

But she'd been to the dungeon. She nodded and focused her attention on the book in the chest, doing that thing where she sort of asked it to start at the beginning. "Anne Frank, the diary of a young girl," it said, and Haly repeated it.

"Sunday, 14 June, 1942. On Friday, June 12, I woke up at six o'clock and no wonder; it was my birthday." Behind her, she heard Gyneth gasp. Siblea's eyes seemed to glow. Orrin and Michander exchanged glances and turned toward her attentively.

She hadn't read to anyone since the vault. She had thought she might never read to anyone again. It felt wonderful. Anne's words came from another planet thousands of years ago and yet they held in them her spirit. She was a truth, sailing across a limitless ocean of nothingness, with no light to guide her, and yet reaching them just the same.

Here was something that song did not do: The very particular and precise record of another person's inner life. A person who confided to you that the very things that make you feel weak and foolish and frightened, frighten and embarrass and frustrate them as well. That they love as you love, that they faced even worse problems than yours, and their love triumphed in the end. *How do you measure the value of that?* she wondered, unable to repress a fierce grin as she recited, "There is a saying that paper is more patient than Man."

They all stared at her in open wonder now. "The same, exactly the same," murmured Orrin. Behind her she heard Gyneth utter something midway between a sob and a laugh. Michander and Siblea fell to their knees, as did Orrin's attendant. The high censor himself bowed low in his chair. And they all sang, "Redeemer oh Redeemer, raise your voice for us. Speak the murdered word and save us all from silence."

She had passed their test and lost her audience all at once. Frustrated, she cleared her throat and continued reciting, but it was clear they were no longer listening. Siblea cried openly. The gleam in Michander's eyes balanced on the knife edge of triumph and terror, and old Orrin stared at her with avid hunger. Her voice trailed off.

Gyneth came around from behind Haly's chair and clasped hands with Orrin's attendant, who said, "It was the same. All exactly the same! Did you hear?" Gyneth, his face red and wet, nodded his head. The light in his eyes was so bright it was hard to look at. His sob turned to a laugh, and both boys jumped up and down together, hugging and crying and laughing until with a start they remembered that they were in the presence of holiness. Subduing themselves, they got to their knees again and bowed to her. Their noses ran. They looked as unlike a pair of menacing Eradicant book burners as anything she could imagine. They looked like two people who would walk through fire for her.

Meanwhile, Siblea had joined Orrin and Michander in huddled conversation. Their voices were low and tense. She could make out but a few words: "But will She cooperate?" "If only we had the book." ". . . announced, but when?" "Not before the horn is completed." From time to time they glanced over at her speculatively. It gave her a very odd feeling to see these men she feared so much looking at her like that.

She tried to glean as much as she could from their conversation, but was constantly distracted by Anne's description of her birthday festivities. After so long away from the Libyrinth, the sound of a book voice was like cool water in the desert. She knew she should pay attention to the Singers; they were discussing her fate. But all she really wanted to hear was what Anne had to say: "Anti-Jewish decrees followed each other in quick succession."

All too soon, the Singers seemed to realize that she might be listening in on their conference, and they straightened. Their faces were formal and respectful, and they bowed to her.

"Gyneth, will you escort our Redeemer to Her rooms?" asked Siblea.

Reluctantly she got up and went to the door. Then she stopped and turned around. She was the Redeemer, damn it. "What about the book?" she asked them.

They all looked at her, at a loss.

"What is going to happen to the book?" she elaborated.

"It has served its purpose," said Michander. "It will be liberated."

Haly swallowed against the dryness in her mouth. "But what if you need it again, to prove to others . . ."

Orrin smiled, showing her two rows of small, square teeth. "Holy One, I am the high censor. If I say you are the Redeemer, then you are the Redeemer."

Haly did not know where her sudden courage came from, but thought perhaps it was the book in the iron box. "Then let me fulfill my purpose. Let this be the first book I redeem."

Orrin narrowed his eyes. Michander frowned and said, "*The Book of the Night* will be the first book you redeem."

Haly's heart clenched with panic at what she was about to say. "You don't have *The Book of the Night*."

Michander bared his teeth. "But we will have it, and soon! You think it's out of our reach in Ilysies? We will raze Ilysies to the ground. By the time we're done, that bitch-queen Tadamos will be begging to give it to us—"

"Brother Michander," admonished Siblea, "you must not speak so to our Redeemer."

Michander flushed and looked to Orrin, who shook his head disapprovingly.

"Honored fathers of the Righteous Chorus," said Haly, hoping she had the appropriate honorific. She needed to strike the right balance of authority and respect, just as *Seven Principles for Success in Sales* had always said, much as she'd tried to ignore it. She was a miraculous figure to these Singers, but she did not think Orrin would forget that she was also a helpless clerk. "There is something that has long puzzled your Redeemer. Now that you know who I am, and the new day is at hand, I would have you explain it to me."

They stared at her expectantly. Good. They were at least

willing to hear her question. "If I am to redeem the words that have been written, why do you burn books?"

Siblea answered her. "The fire liberates them, Holy One. They reside unspoken in the Song, until by your Redemption, they are given voice once more."

"Then it is your belief that only a book that has been burned can be redeemed." She knew that wasn't true. If it were, they would not be so careful to avoid burning *The Book of the Night.*

"No, Holy One. The Redemption is for all words, murdered and liberated alike. All will join with the Song, and the Song will speak."

"Then why bother burning them?"

"Because they are dangerous!" blurted Michander, whose eyes blazed with anger before he caught himself and dropped his gaze. "Holy One," he added.

Dangerous to whom? Haly suppressed the tiny smile that twitched at the edges of her lips. These men whom she had feared all her life were themselves afraid—afraid of losing technological supremacy. They burned the books so no one else could learn what they could not learn, and they used the concept of liberation to justify it.

"What Censor Michander means is that it is our duty to unite murdered words with the Song whenever we find them, by whatever means is available to us," said Orrin.

Haly drew herself up and gave them a smile she hoped was full of compassion. "Too long has the Song been wordless. Too long has the will of Yammon been open to interpretation by those less righteous than yourselves. But you have overcome centuries of darkness and error. Truly, the shining perfection of your love for the Song has brought me to you, of all the generations. The Redemption will be yours, but first you must cast off the errors of the past."

Michander's vivid gaze mellowed to pride, Siblea looked at her with dawning respect, and Orrin's flat, black eyes were flat, and black.

Haly spread her arms and boomed, "No word that has been burned can be redeemed!" Before they could say anything, before her heart stopped dead with terror, she moved to the iron box on the table and placed her hand upon it. "My covenant with you begins now, here, with these words. I can redeem them for everyone, but not if you burn them.

"As a Libyrarian, it was my job to preserve knowledge. The people of the Song understand the importance of preserving knowledge, and this knowledge is the most important of all because it concerns *people,* and their wisdom and beauty and folly transcend Time. Their words are here to teach us how to survive. I can bring you their teaching, but you must choose. Cast off the old way of false Liberation, or turn your back on Redemption and dwell in silence forevermore."

In the stillness that followed, she thought they must all hear the frantic pounding of her heart. All the religious phrasing was nothing but a cover. She had given them an ultimatum—if they wanted her to translate *The Book of the Night,* then they had to stop burning all the other books. How would they react to such a power play? She waited. They stared at her, and then at one another. At last, Orrin gave a fractional nod, and Haly breathed again.

That night she slept with the locked box in her arms, Anne's words lulling her to sleep. She'd saved one book . . . for now. Maybe somehow she'd save the rest.

In the morning Gyneth brought her breakfast as usual, but after she finished, he stood in front of her for long moments, his head bowed, his fingers twitching on the handles of the tray. At last she said, "Is there something you wish to say to me?"

Gyneth bowed, somehow bending his body over the tray

full of dishes without dropping anything. "Holy One, I—" He stopped, still bent over his tray, apparently numb with reverence.

Haly sighed. She got up, took the tray from him, set it down on the table beside the door, and said, "Sit down," indicating the bench at the foot of her bed.

Gyneth gaped at her.

"Oh, for the sake of the Seven Tales! Two days ago you were telling me I was an ignorant savage, remember?"

His face, already red, deepened in color and he began to kneel.

"No! Stop it! Look at me!"

With difficulty, Gyneth met her eyes.

"I promise I won't smite you. Now what did you want?"

Gyneth's eyes strayed to the locked box and he chewed the corner of his upper lip, apparently trying to gauge the peril of asking for whatever it was he wanted. At last he found the courage to say, "What happens to her?"

"To whom?"

"To Anne."

Ah. "Do you want to hear more?"

"Yes, Holy One."

Haly smiled.

After meals, Haly recited the diary of Anne Frank to Gyneth. And whenever she paused for a drink of water it was hardly a break at all, because he was full of questions. What was a Jew? What was a concentration camp? Were the Jews literate, and the others people of the Song? Was that why they were persecuted?

When Haly explained that reading and writing were part of the standard education of the time, Gyneth fell silent, looking very grave.

"It's not anything bad, you know, reading and writing."

Gyneth's eyes widened in shock, and he fixed his gaze on the floor at Haly's feet.

"It's just a skill. One anybody can learn."

Gyneth's hands clenched on his knees. His head shook almost imperceptibly.

"No?"

"I would not presume to correct the Redeemer," he said, his voice cold.

She'd liked him better when he was telling her she was damned. "But your Redeemer commands you to. And while we're at it, your Redeemer commands you to look at her when you speak. And stop bowing all the time."

Gyneth stared at her, anger and fear in his eyes. "Those who commune with the murdered words cannot hear the Song."

"But I hear the Song."

"That is different. You're the Redeemer."

"And what if I told you that what you've been taught about reading and writing is wrong?"

"You can say anything you want to me. You're—"

"The Redeemer." Argh. Frustrated, Haly tugged at the locks on the metal box. If only she could show him he had nothing to fear.

Gyneth stood. He began to bow, then caught himself and straightened again. "With the Holy One's pardon, I must go now. I have to prepare for my Circuits."

Haly blinked. It hadn't occurred to her what Gyneth did when he was not here. "Circuits?"

"The comprehensive exams every subaltern must pass in order to enter the priesthood. Electronics, mechanics, metallurgy, medicine, and agriculture. There are a lot of songs to learn. But Censor Siblea says I'm almost ready. I'll be one of the youngest in my generation to give recital."

"And Siblea is your teacher?"

"One of them. But he is my mentor. That is why I assist him with you."

Just as she had assisted Selene back at the Libyrinth. Again she thought about their identical brown robes and she wondered about Iscarion.

But first things first. After Gyneth left, Haly set about trying to get the metal box open. She set it on the bench beside the window where the light was good, and took a close look at the locks. They were key locks—nothing special, but also quite impassable unless she had the key or could pick them. No password or flash of book-borne inspiration could help her here. It was a simple mechanical problem.

"And I firmly believe that nature brings solace in all troubles," said the book.

She rummaged around the room for something with which she could attempt to pick the lock. There was nothing. She took another look at the locks. Perhaps they could be broken with brute force. As if she had that in plentiful supply. Still, it was worth a try.

Haly picked up the table beside the door and hefted it. It was small but the top was marble and she could barely lift it. She placed the box on the floor, lifted the table, and tried to drop it on the book so that it hit the hasp of one of the locks. She only succeeded in putting a dent in the wood floor, so she tried again.

There were twelve dents in the floor by the time she gave up, her arms trembling from the strain of lifting the heavy table. She sat down on the floor and stared at the box.

"Who besides me will ever read these letters?" asked the book.

She examined the hinges, which she discovered were covered by a protective metal housing, so she couldn't push out the pins.

"What does she say, what does she say?" she heard from a slight distance.

At first Haly thought it was the book, and some trick of acoustics or distraction. But then the voice came again, more insistently and from beneath the bed. "What does she say?"

Haly's heart leaped into her throat as she watched Nod crawl from beneath the bed and hop to the box. He laid his tiny hands upon the metal and put his ear to it, looking up at Haly plaintively. "Nod misses the stories."

She grabbed him and clutched him to her chest, kissing the top of his bald, red head. "Nod! Nod! I'm so glad to see you! What are you doing here? How long have you been here?" Her words tumbled out, one after the other.

Nod squeaked and struggled to free himself, finally pinching her sharply with two tweezers-sized fingers. "Nod didn't follow her all this way so she could strangle Nod!" he scolded bitterly, hopping away from her to crouch on top of the locked box again. "*Here* here—Nod just get here. Stuck in nasty dungeon place for days." He made a face.

Seeing Nod again made Haly realize how much she missed the Libyrinth. Tears welled in her eyes but she swallowed, blinked, and quelled them. "Did anybody see you?"

"Tsk. Beasties never see Nod. Beasties too big to notice little Nod in the corner, along the wall, among the curves of the Big Metal Noise Tube they build down there. What is that thing for, does she know?"

Haly shook her head.

"Nod neither," he muttered. "Don't like it, though."

Haly nodded and sighed. "I'm so glad to see you."

Nod snorted impatiently and put his fists to his hips. "Glad mean she tell Nod story now?"

"I'll tell you a story, but first you must do something for me."

Nod lifted his hands to his ears and pulled them. He hopped

up and down on the box. "Do something for her! Days and days in stinky dungeon and she says do something for her." He bared his teeth. "This Nod should have gone with the Clauda beastie. Fine. What does she want?"

"This box is broken, Nod. It won't open. See if you can fix it."

For half an hour Nod swarmed over the box. He investigated the locks and the hinges, at last succeeding in prying off the hinge covers with his tiny fingers and removing the pins.

Haly lifted the small, much-mended book from the box. It was paperbound, the picture on the cover faded to a ghostly image, barely discernible but for the eyes, which stared out at her with such intensity, it was as if they were alive. She was almost afraid to open the book for fear it would disintegrate, but the paper and ink used by the late-period Earth publishers was nearly indestructible. She opened it and ran her fingers over the words, and though her voice was raw, she recited to Nod for a full hour.

That night she slept with the book cradled against her chest, and Nod curled beside her head. She slept well.

*   *   *

From ancients before Ancients comes the adage;
Current times resistance equals voltage.

The Chorus of Electromagnetism sang with enthusiasm, their voices filling the small recital hall. The chamber was one of many just like it throughout the Temple of Yammon. At the far end of the room the floor rose up in a series of steps, each about two feet higher than the previous one. These steps curved in an arc facing a podium centered before them. The chorus stood upon the steps, and each row had a clear view of their conductor, who directed them from behind the podium.

Behind him, and closest to the door, benches provided seat-

ing for those who came to listen, though performance was by
no means the primary function of either the recital halls or the
numerous choruses that used them. Through practicing their
repertoire of songs, the Singers preserved their knowledge.

Siblea, Orrin, and Michander had decided that Haly needed
to develop an appreciation of their way of life, so in the three
days since the test, Haly had visited almost twenty different
choruses, each dedicated to a different area of knowledge. She'd
listened to the Chorus of Medicine, the Chorus of Mechanics,
the Chorus of Soldiers (of which Michander was the conductor),
even the Chorus of Cattle Breeding.

Positive charge, negative charge, these are the two kinds.
Like charges repel each other, opposites do bind.

The chorus finished singing. As the men on the steps bowed
deeply to Haly, the conductor turned around, beaming. "An
honor, Holy One," he said, and bowed also. Haly, flanked by
Siblea on one side and Michander on the other, stood along
with them and nodded her head stiffly.

The chorus members were all staring at her with identical
expressions of awe and reverence. It was like this everywhere
she went. It creeped her out. It wasn't so bad when they were
singing and she could concentrate on the music, but now,
with all of them just staring at her like they expected her to
perform some miraculous feat at any moment—like spout
wine from her ears, for instance—she just wanted to get out
of there.

But as usual, after the singing there was a little reception to
endure. Members of the Chorus of Electromagnetism produced
a small table that was a twin to the marble-topped one in Haly's
room. The conductor, Tifius, sat down on the bench behind
theirs, and the table was set between the two rows of benches.
Michander, Haly, and Siblea turned around on their bench so

they could face him, and members of the chorus served them tea and oatcakes. At least, sitting this way, she faced away from most of the chorus, though she could still feel their adoring gazes boring into her back.

"I tell you, Siblea, Michander, I never thought this would come in my lifetime," said Conductor Tifius, a shortish man in his early sixties with pale hair and eyebrows, and blue eyes that sparkled with excitement. He glanced at Haly and bowed his head. "Holy One."

Haly sighed and nibbled on an oatcake. That was pretty much the extent to which any of the conductors spoke to her.

"Just imagine, a Maker of Eggs! Tell me, Siblea," Tifius continued, "when will the presentation be made, have you decided?"

The presentation. Haly's stomach churned at the mention of it. She set the oatcake down on the edge of her plate with a soft clink. Siblea had informed her this morning that she was going to have to stand in the mouth of that enormous statue of Yammon and sing to the multitude of the Righteous Chorus. Not just the Singers in the temple, but almost all the people in the Corvariate Citadel would fill the enormous amphitheater for the event.

"That depends on how the work of the Chorus of Acoustical Engineers progresses, Tifius. We want to hold the presentation on the eve of our departure on the pilgrimage, and we won't be ready for that until their work is completed."

"Oh, of course, of course," said Tifius. "I understand completely."

Haly didn't. "What work?" she said.

Tifius looked at her in shock and bit his oatcake in half. Michander frowned and looked like he wanted to tell her to shut up, but Siblea merely smiled and said, "I believe you did your part to move things along when you first arrived here, Holy One."

"That horn thing in the dungeon?" she said. Conductor Tifius blushed visibly at the mention of her imprisonment. "What does it do?"

"You will see in time, Holy One," Siblea assured her.

Tifius swallowed the remainder of his oatcake and stood up, apparently unnerved by a Redeemer who actually spoke and asked questions and referred to grisly realities. "Well, this has been an honor, the honor of a lifetime." He bowed deeply to Haly again, and shook hands with Michander and Siblea, who also stood. "I suppose you have a busy schedule. I wouldn't want to make you late for your next appointment."

"Where are we going now?" Haly asked once they were in the hallway outside the recital hall.

"We're visiting Subaltern Chorus Five," said Siblea. "I think you'll enjoy this one. Its members are all your age. In fact, it is Gyneth's chorus."

"I don't understand," said Haly. "What is its subject matter?"

"It has no subject. It is an administrative chorus. I myself am a member of the Chorus of Censors, and there is also a Chorus of Conductors. The subalterns are organized in choruses by age and the rate at which they have advanced in their studies. Each chorus is educated as a group by attending the recitals of other choruses, and as individuals by being apprenticed to priests. I am very proud of Gyneth. He is only fifteen, and yet he is a member of Subaltern Chorus Five, the very last chorus before an initiate sings his circuits and becomes a priest."

As Siblea spoke, they proceeded down a wide hallway with floors and walls made of large, gray stone blocks. Some of the blocks were engraved with songlines, as she'd seen before. On her other side, Michander stalked, silent and, she suspected, a little bored.

Siblea took her elbow and steered her to the right, into a

large courtyard that was open to the sky and carpeted with grass. Numerous footpaths wound among the shrubbery, small ornamental trees and sculptures of vague, undulating forms that resembled the songlines in three dimensions. Priests wandered the pathways, humming and singing softly to themselves.

"What are they doing?" she asked Siblea.

"Most of them are memorizing. Some are composing." He pointed to a short, wiry priest who walked with his hands clasped behind his back. "That is Conductor Faravan of the Chorus of History. He is most likely composing. His chorus is by far the most active in composition, since history is always being made. When he completes his composition, he will sing it to the Chorus of Censors, and we will make any alterations we feel are advisable, before the song becomes a part of our overall body of knowledge."

Haly stopped and turned to face him. He was so matter-of-fact about it. He gazed at her with his customary faint smile, as if there could not possibly be anything objectionable about what he had just said. "And will you cut out the part where the Redeemer is imprisoned in the dungeon?" she demanded.

Michander huffed and crossed his arms in annoyance, but Siblea pursed his lips, considering. "No," he said. "I think it makes a better story if we leave that in."

Haly had no idea how to respond. Siblea's frank and unapologetic acknowledgment of censorship left her speechless. She turned and they continued to walk along the footpath, but not before she heard Michander mutter under his breath, "Of course you'd leave it in. It wasn't a member of your chorus who made the error."

As they neared the far end of the courtyard, they passed a priest who was playing one of the little handheld harps she'd seen used in the dungeon. He stood alone in a small alcove formed by dense hedges. Haly paused to watch him. He plucked the strings, listened, then plucked out a new sequence of notes, listened to those, and so on. "What is he doing?" she asked Siblea. "Is he composing, too?"

Siblea followed her gaze, put one finger to his lips, and tilted his head to the side, indicating that they should move on. When they had passed the opening to the alcove, Siblea said, "I did not wish our voices to disturb him. He is doing mathematics."

"What? But he was just playing music."

Michander snorted. "What do you think numbers are, Holy One?"

Siblea raised his hands. "Perhaps a better way to put it is to say that musical notes are the voice of numbers." At her still-puzzled look, he tried again. "Each number can be represented by a musical note. Manipulating notes in music is equivalent to manipulating numbers with mathematical operations like addition, multiplication, and so on." He raised his eyebrows, waiting to see if his words would sink in.

Haly didn't fully understand, but she could at least grasp the basic concept as he'd described it. It made her wonder, though. "Is there more information in the songs, then, than just what the words say?"

Siblea smiled at her. "For those whose ears have been trained to hear it, there is."

Despite tarrying in the garden, Haly, Siblea, and Michander arrived early at the recital hall used by Subaltern Chorus Five; that much was clear by the raucous shouts and laughter issuing from the doorway as they approached. From the far end of the hallway, which was much like the one they'd passed through on their way to the courtyard, a black-garbed priest was hurrying toward them. Siblea smirked and put his hand to Haly's elbow. "Let's get there before Conductor Cyncus," he murmured.

To Haly's surprise, Michander gave a snort of laughter and they all quickened their pace. As they neared the room, the voices from inside became clearer.

"Gyneth wants to kiss her! Don't you, Gynnie? You want to—" Haly recognized the voice as belonging to Orrin's attendant, Thale.

"No! I don't! Shut up!" That was Gyneth.

Haly, Siblea, and Michander reached the doorway to the recital hall. Inside, Gyneth and three other boys were rough-housing while ten or twelve more looked on and shouted occasional remarks and encouragement. All of them were Haly's age or a little older, and dressed in brown robes.

On the lowest step at the back of the room, Thale had Gyneth in a headlock, and a heavyset blond boy was trying to climb onto his back. "Gah! You're so fat, Baris, you're going to break my back," shouted Gyneth. He wrested himself free of Thale's grip and straightened, dumping Baris onto the floor.

A smaller, dark-haired boy tackled Gyneth and they both fell down. He and Baris pinned Gyneth to the floor and Thale stood over him. "Admit it, you want to kiss her!" said Thale. He lifted his robes and turned around. He flexed his legs, sticking his long-underwear-clad butt over Gyneth's face. "Admit it or I'll fart on you!"

Gyneth was laughing so hard he could hardly force the words out. "You're just jealous 'cause even though you're Orrin's attendant, I have the best job."

Thale scrunched up his face dramatically, and then a loud fart noise was heard. Everyone screamed and scrambled back to the corners of the room, yelling, "The green death! The green death!"

After days and days of somber reverence, Haly found it a relief to see people acting silly. Standing in the doorway with Michander and Siblea, she couldn't suppress a giggle.

At once the boys all turned their heads to the doorway and froze at the sight of her. Gyneth's hair stood up on one side of his head. His flushed face turned a deeper shade of red and the merry light in his eyes fled as he stared at her in horror. Beside him Thale tugged his sleeve and they both hastily got to their knees and bowed in supplication, the other boys following their lead. So much for silliness, then.

"My apologies, my apologies," said a voice behind Haly. She and the two priests turned to see Conductor Cyncus standing in the hallway, breathing hard. He was a middle-aged, plump, dark-haired man with a soft face and bright dark eyes. "I beg your pardon, Holy One, may you live now and forever in the Song eternal." He bowed to her. "I did not realize you would be so prompt. I—"

"Never mind, Conductor Cyncus," said Siblea. "We are early." Haly glanced at him and then at Michander. Both of them seemed amused to have caught the conductor and his chorus unawares. So despite all outward appearances of rigid order and obedience, it seemed that the Singers had a sense of humor, after all.

"Oh. Oh." Cyncus peered past them into the recital hall and saw the boys prostrating themselves from scattered positions about the room. "Boys," he said sharply, as Michander stepped to the side to let him pass. "Take your places at once!"

As the boys sang about the periodic table of the elements, Haly thought about what she had seen and heard. They had been teasing Gyneth about a girl. Was it her? Did she want it to be her?

So far as she'd seen, she was the only girl in the temple, outside the dungeon, that is. But there might be others she hadn't seen, or they might be talking about someone outside the temple. Why did that idea fill her with disappointment?

Maybe it was as Gyneth said, and he didn't want to kiss this girl anyway, whoever she was, and the boys were just teasing him because they were jealous.

She watched Gyneth as he sang, his eyes clear and warm, his voice rich and deep. She watched his lips move around the words, and she wondered what they would feel like on hers.

13

Peril is the Goat

Clauda stood in the open doorway of Selene's chamber, watching the tall, slender Libyraryian pack her saddle-bags with methodical grace. "You were right," she said. "We can't trust your mother."

Selene looked up. She opened her mouth to speak, then stopped herself and abandoned her packing. She went to Clauda, drew her inside by the arm, and shut the door. She turned, her back to it, her hand still gripping Clauda's arm. "What did you learn?"

Clauda licked her lips. Her mouth was dry. She was afraid, and it was making her stomach tremble. Or maybe that wasn't the fear. She heard flies buzzing. "I don't think you should go to the Libyrinth."

Selene looked more closely at her. "Are you ill?"

Clauda shook her head, though she could feel the shaking

now deep inside her—definitely more than fear—and it echoed in a numb tingling in her hands and feet.

"But you're shaking. Come now, come here." She led Clauda to the low couch and sat down beside her. Her hands gripped Clauda's tightly. "Breathe. Remember what Adept Ykobos taught you."

Clauda took several deep breaths, imagining that she was a tree; drawing energy up through the soles of her feet, releasing it through the top of her head and then drawing it down again through her head and releasing it into the ground below. It helped. The tingling in her hands and feet receded. She regarded Selene, who had taken care of her after the mind-lancet attack, who had thrown an Egg into a burning cart to save her and Haly. How could Clauda consider herself good with people when she had so completely missed Selene's true value, her loyalty, her bravery? Scio was right; she would make a fine queen. "You can't go," she croaked.

Selene's lips compressed with worry and stubbornness. "Tell me why. What's changed?"

Clauda nodded. "Not here," she said.

"You're right," said Selene. She looked at the door and then back at Clauda. "It's a fine day today, and you really musn't miss Ilysies in springtime. I know what we'll do."

They rode out beyond the palace and beyond the city, both of them together on a large black horse that Selene called Goliath. Selene did not think Clauda was fit to ride by herself, and Clauda didn't dispute it. It was a fine day, and Clauda tried not to let her anxiety overshadow the warmth of the sun and the strength of Selene's arms around her as the Libyrarian gripped the reins with competent hands. Clauda let herself lean back against the comforting solidity of Selene's chest and tried not to think at all.

They dismounted on a hillside bordered on one side by a

vineyard and on the other by the abrupt cliff and the blue sea. There was not another human being as far as the eye could see.

Selene spread a blanket on the ground and took food from a basket that she'd lashed to the back of Goliath's saddle. They ate soft cheese and honey, bread, cucumbers, and the little red berries that were not raspberries. At length Selene uncorked a flask of watered wine and poured them each a cup. "Well?" she said, handing Clauda her cup.

Clauda took a drink to forestall the inevitable. She cleared her throat. "Scio showed me another spy hole," she said.

Selene raised one eyebrow, but didn't comment.

"I heard Queen Thela talking with you, and then with General Tadakis."

Selene nodded.

Clauda swallowed. "She's not telling the general to attack the Libyrinth."

Selene's eyes widened.

"She's not telling her where to attack at all. She told her to take the army into the Plain of Ayor and await the wing. They are to follow it and attack what it attacks."

Selene took a deep breath and slowly nodded. "I'm not surprised. My mother loves secrets, and she suspects an Eradicant spy in the palace. She would not risk them discovering her plans."

"We can't count on her sending the army to support you."

"I tried to tell you that before," Selene observed without rancor. "It's even odds whether she'll save the Libyrinth and exact tribute from us, or conquer the Corvariate Citadel while it's all but abandoned."

Clauda swallowed, absorbing this. "You can't go," she said.

Selene smiled at her and shook her head. "But it's a good plan."

"A good plan? You didn't think so yesterday."

"That was before you discovered the wing, and eavesdropped on the queen's conversations. And have you found out why Scio is helping you yet?"

"She wants you to be heir."

"Oh, dear." Selene rolled her eyes and laughed. "Me, queen—can you imagine?"

"Yes. Maybe you should. Maybe you should stay and challenge them and—"

Selene shook her head. "And be poisoned or walled up or just disappear? And then what would happen to Haly? Even if I could succeed, and I can think of nothing I'd enjoy less than ruling a nation, we don't have that kind of time."

"But—"

"No. I'm going and you're staying and that's my final word as your senior ranking Libyrarian."

"I-I'm staying?"

"Yes. When I go to the Libyrinth with the book, I want you to stay here and keep up what you've been doing. It could be useful."

Useful. How typical that when the words she had longed for Selene to say finally came, they were unwelcome. Irritation overcame irony. "Are you insane? Don't you understand what that means? If she doesn't help us, the Eradicants will destroy the Libyrinth, and you'll be . . . You can't go."

Selene gave her a crooked grin. "Oh, but I have to go."

Clauda couldn't speak. All she could do was shake her head. There were tears in her eyes, and she didn't even care. Haly was lost, and Selene seemed determined to follow her right into the hands of the Eradicants.

Selene's grin faded and she leaned toward Clauda, putting a hand on her knee. "Don't you see? In the first place, if I don't go, Mother will know we suspect her, which means she'll suspect we've been spying on her, and that could be very dangerous for you. And in the second place, I took the opportunity of last night's card game to recruit my escort to the

Libyrinth—the best of Vorain's regiment. Women loyal to her, and by extension, to me.

"Even if Mother doesn't send the army to the Libyrinth, a well-trained fighting force, guided by those who know the Libyrinth well, can hold out in the stacks against a much larger force for a long time. And I'll be able to get Haly back. They'll have to bring her inside, you see, for their Redemption, and we'll be waiting for them."

The tingling was back in Clauda's hands and feet, and gray flies buzzed at the edges of her vision. "But then what? You'll be trapped there. It's only half a plan!"

Selene shrugged. "It's half of a good plan, Clauda. And in the meantime you'll be here, working on the other half."

"W-wh-what?"

The look of trust and affection Selene gave her pierced Clauda to her unsteady core. "You've gotten us this far, haven't you?"

Clauda's muscles started locking up.

Selene gripped Clauda hard by the forearms. "Remember what Adept Ykobos taught you."

Clauda tried to imagine she was a tree, but this time it didn't work. All she could think of was Selene bleeding to death on the marble floor of the Libyrinth's Great Hall. "I-I can't."

"Then focus on something else. Anything. Focus on me. Look into my eyes, Clauda. Concentrate."

Though the gray flies hovered everywhere around them, Clauda could just keep them away from Selene's eyes if she stared hard enough, and she fell into twin tunnels of night as her mind clung to the fact that Selene was counting on her.

After what seemed like a long time, the fit passed, leaving her muscles sore in its wake. She slumped to the ground and lay on her back. Selene hastily fetched her saddle blanket and folded it, lifting Clauda's head and easing it back down on the padding. "As soon as we get back to the palace you're seeing Adept Ykobos. And this time I want you to actually do what she tells you. Complete bed rest if she says so. These tremors should have gone away by now, but if anything, they're getting worse. You need to rest more."

"How am I going to come up with the other half of the plan if I do that?"

Selene frowned. "You'll just have to find a way. Here." She lifted Clauda's head and put the wine flask to her lips. "Drink some."

Clauda sipped the watered wine and said, "Are you sure you're not just leaving me here to keep me out of harm's way?"

"Yes. Clauda, I know you're scared. I wish I could take care of everything. But I learned a long time ago that different people are good at different things. I can't afford to protect you. Haly and I are going to need you here. And you won't be safe. I'm sorry."

"Well, as long as I'm not safe, either."

It's as I suspected," said Ymin Ykobos after a prolonged and painful examination of Clauda's energy pathways. She helped Clauda to sit up and pulled the comforter over her sweat-chilled skin. One of her assistants brought Clauda a cup of water, which she accepted gratefully. Selene sat in one corner of the room, looking grim as she paged through a copy of *Theselaides*. It wasn't her childhood copy. It was the one she'd brought with her from the Libyrinth, though it was nearly as worn as the other.

Ymin sighed, her lips compressed, and continued. "The disruption has worsened. It is most likely permanent. What you do now will determine how much of your muscular function you will retain."

Clauda shook her head in confusion and looked to Selene, who stared back at her wordlessly.

Ymin leaned forward, grasping Clauda's forearm and reclaiming her attention. "I'm talking about your ability to walk, Clauda of Ayor. Your ability to pick things up, to manipulate them. Feeding yourself, dressing yourself. You can lose it all if you keep on the way you've been, darting about the palace at all hours and fretting over . . . whatever it is that has brought you and your mistress here. You have got to relax, and rest, and practice the meditations I've taught you."

"I have practiced," Clauda mumbled. How was she supposed to relax when Haly was in trouble, when the Eradicants were going to destroy the Libyrinth, when Selene was blithely riding off to her own destruction? Just thinking about it made her tremble.

"Now see? It's happening again, isn't it?" said Ymin.

Clauda nodded.

"You've noticed that the attacks come when you're under stress. You need to avoid stress, and if you can't avoid it, you must learn to control your response to it. Take deep breaths and focus. Do the tree meditation, or develop in your mind a picture that relaxes you, and focus on that."

Oddly enough, the image that came to Clauda's mind was Selene in the palace library, smirking at her own parody of herself and saying, "Why, Theselaides, of course." Clauda nodded at Ymin. "Yes, Adept. I will."

Ymin sighed again and stood. "Well, you'd better, or you'd better find someone who will be willing to take care of you for the rest of your life. Now, I want you to drink this"—she motioned to a pot of tea brewing on a side table—"and sleep for as long as you can. When you awake, summon me. Do you understand?"

Clauda nodded.

After the adept and her assistants left, Selene came and crouched by Clauda's bed. "What she said"—clumsily, her hand sought Clauda's through the comforter—"if things don't go well . . . if you need . . . I'll take care of you. I promise."

"I don't want anyone to take care of me, Selene," said Clauda, already becoming drowsy from the tea. There was something in it to make her sleep, she was sure.

"Of course you don't. But if you need it, you don't have to worry. I'll take care of you."

Clauda couldn't help but smile at the earnest look on Selene's face. Dear Selene, she always took everything so seriously. "Then you'd better stay alive, in case I need you to keep your promise," Clauda said.

Clauda awoke in the middle of the night, the palace dark and silent all around her. She felt remarkably better after sleeping, whole and solid and strong again. It was hard to believe that Ymin's admonishments were anything more than scare tactics to keep her in line. All the same, she kicked off the comforter and did the stretching exercises she'd been taught, and meditated—or at least tried to. Selene would leave at dawn. She was depending on Clauda to stay behind and make sure the queen sent her army to the Libyrinth. How, precisely, was she supposed to do that? Clauda wondered.

Restless, she got up and put on the ornate padded robe they'd given her. She would walk just a little—to stretch her muscles and help her focus her mind. There was no harm in just walking a little, slowly, quietly. That's right, she thought, realizing that she'd been letting herself get upset about what was happening, and that she couldn't afford to do that anymore.

Clauda sighed. Uncertainty gnawed at the edges of her newfound calm. Her gaze landed on a book on her bedside table. It was Selene's copy of *Theselaides*, the one she'd brought from the Libyrinth. Clauda smiled and picked it up. It felt good in her hand. She thought of Selene in the library. She breathed slowly.

She decided to take a walk down the hall. Moving really seemed to help, and as long as she didn't run or otherwise exhaust herself, it would be all right. She took the book with her. Maybe, if she found a place open to the moonlight, she'd read.

The palace was silent, beautiful in the spare light from the third moon, and she could gawk at her leisure. She walked past pillared courtyards and alcoves, gardens and pools.

The thing to do, she thought, resting on a bench under a bower of fig trees and gazing into a rectangular reflecting pond, was to get Scio to help her spy on Jolaz. If Jolaz were flying the wing into battle, then sooner or later, the queen would have to tell her what the real target was.

Of course, it would be easier to spy on Jolaz and the queen if she did not remain lost in the Ilysian palace, never to be seen again, Clauda thought, two hours later as yet another pillared courtyard taunted her with its vague familiarity. How many of them were there? Surely one of the ones she had passed was the one that was just two left turns from her chamber—the one she passed through on her way to the audience chamber, the Arena of the Bull, and the library? But try as she might, she could not find her room. She even tried leafing through the book *Theselaides*. The author had been an Ilysian, but there was no help there, either. And she was getting tired. And she had to stop and meditate a lot.

Let the Lion gnaw it, she thought, sitting down on the bench in an arbor. She'd just wait here. The sky above the open courtyard was already starting to lighten. It would be dawn soon, and some servant would find her and take her back to her chamber.

As she sat down her shoulder brushed some of the fig leaves. They crumbled. She looked more closely at the bower. These trees were dead, their leaves shriveled and dry on their branches. She turned around. The water in the pool was at half level and it was murky and dark. This was an abandoned place.

She remembered what Scio had said about the previous queen's chambers. A mixture of excitement and dread quivered in her belly. She must have wandered in here when she'd hopped that broken-down wall in an effort to reach the hallway behind the baths and get her bearings. She breathed deeply to maintain her calm, and ventured into the passageway that opened at the opposite end of the pond.

It led to a large room that was probably the former queen's bedchamber. A raised platform stood in the center of the room. Broken bits of stone and masonry littered the floor, obscuring what looked like it once must have been quite beautiful mosaic of fish and winged women. A very few pieces of furniture stood shrouded in cloth. The walls were dust-streaked and there appeared to be water damage in the far corner of the ceiling. An archway to the right had been painted with a design of leaves or maybe birds, but the colors were so faded that they were barely discernible. Dust stung in Clauda's nose and throat and she stifled a cough. There was a faint, acrid smell in here that made Clauda wonder what had become of the old queen after all.

Her morbid speculations were cut short when she heard footsteps coming down the passage from the courtyard. Clauda barely had time to hide herself beneath a shrouded desk and peek back out through the folds of the cloth. She stared, breathless, as Thela Tadamos and Jolaz entered the room.

". . . impractical," Jolaz was saying.

"Of course I'm not going to attempt retrieving the girl," said Thela. The queen was dressed in her houserobe, a simple garment of thick blue cotton—fine quality but no match for the ornate richness of Clauda's own. Her hair was unbound. "That's ridiculous. Even if she is what Selene says she is, there is a bigger—and much more certain—opportunity in all of this." Thela walked to the sleeping platform and sat down on it. "General Tadakis and the army await you on the other side of the mountains. Her orders are to follow the wing and attack what it attacks, so you will fly the wing to the Corvariate Citadel. With most of the population on pilgrimage, the citadel will be more vulnerable than we can ever expect it to be again. It's an opportunity we can't afford to miss. Not if Ilsysies is to survive."

Jolaz, already dressed for the day, leaned against a shrouded object that appeared to be a harpsichord, and murmured her satisfaction. "If the attack succeeds, we will possess the citadel, all their weapons . . ."

"All their knowledge," added Thela. "And when they return from their holy quest they will find their own guns turned upon them. Plus, the destruction of the Libyrinth will put Ilysies permanently in the position of power, militarily, scientifically, and culturally."

"We'll have the largest library," noted Jolaz.

"Of course," said the queen, "and all those of the plain who would wish to learn will have to learn from us. I tell you, Jolaz, this means much more than ridding ourselves of the Singers."

Jolaz nodded her head. "Very wise, Your Majesty."

"Is my daughter ready to depart?" asked Thela.

"She is. She will be awaiting you on the parade ground in half an hour."

Thela nodded. "Leave me. I will retrieve the book, dress, and then bring it to her."

Jolaz turned away, then hesitated. She stood in the archway, looking over her shoulder at Thela.

"Yes?" inquired Thela.

Jolaz dropped her eyes, but turned to face her queen. "I just wondered . . . in light of what we've learned about the Singers' new weapon . . . must it be Selene who takes the book to the

Libyrinth? Why not send her servant instead, or perhaps one of our own trusted messengers?"

"I wouldn't trust that Ayorite farther than a fish can crawl," said Thela. "As for trusted messengers, we may *need* them."

Jolaz swallowed. "But according to Mab's report, the horn is perfectly capable of toppling the Libyrinth walls. Her situation will be hopeless."

Thela nodded. "A ruler must be prepared to make great sacrifices. If I spared her but let her beloved Libyrinth fall, she would become my enemy, and Selene may not be crafty, but she is bold. Sometimes that's enough."

Jolaz bowed deeply. "As always, your wisdom is a book of many pages, and I am only learning to read."

After she left, Thela stood staring after her for some time. Clauda saw her eyes shining, but could not divine what feelings the queen struggled with. At last, she turned and pulled the cloth from the object upon which Jolaz had been leaning.

It was, in fact, a harpsichord, ornate with ebony and gold inlay. The queen lifted the lid and withdrew a book from its interior. She set it down on top of the harpsichord. Its spine faced Clauda and she could just make out the mark of *The Book of the Night*.

Thela turned away and drew another book from the pocket of her robe. It was Selene's childhood copy of *Theselaides*. She paced the room, her head bent over the book in her hands, her unbound hair trailing in streams across her face. Thela could have been Selene, for the look of fond reverence with which she turned each page.

Thela sighed and straightened. She returned to the harpsichord and set the book down next to *The Book of the Night*. Her expression changed, as if she was mustering her determination, and again she looked like her daughter, only now it was the Selene who had thrown an Egg into a burning wagon. From the pocket of her robe she withdrew several items.

Clauda was puzzled as she saw Thela first take out a very small, sharp knife of a kind often used by Libyrarians to cut paper, and then a small jar, a brush, and four sheets of blank, sturdy paper. The queen flipped the book closed, all but its front cover, then pressed the knife to the crease between the binding and the endpaper.

Clauda barely stopped herself from crying out. Clutching the Libyrinth copy of *Theselaides* that Selene had left in her room, she forced herself to be still and watch as the queen of Ilysies removed the other book's binding. And then, when it lay dismembered, its spine sewing raw and frayed against the white cloth, Thela took up *The Book of the Night*, and did the same to it.

Shaking now, Clauda watched as the queen of Ilysies placed the text of Selene's childhood copy of *Theselaides* inside the binding of *The Book of the Night*. She brushed the inside of the cover and the front page of the book with glue from the little jar, and then she placed one of the blank sheets of paper over both. The sturdy sheet was just big enough to cover the blank front page and the inside of the cover, forming a new endpaper and sealing the book inside its new binding.

The queen did the same with the text of *The Book of the Night*, smoothed the cover of *Theselaides* down over it, and lifted the lid of the harpsichord upon which she worked, slipping the tome inside. She picked up the fake *Book of the Night*, put it into the pocket of her robe, and left.

By the time Clauda switched Selene's Libyrinth copy of *Theselaides* with the newly disguised *Book of the Night* and found her way out of the maze of passages and courtyards, Selene's chamber was empty, swept bare of all that might once have indicated the Libyrarian's presence. "Suck a goat," Clauda muttered and ran as fast as she could for the parade ground, that broad expanse of grass that they had crossed when first entering the palace. Panting, she came to a stop in the front entranceway.

On the parade ground, Selene stood facing her mother. Behind her, near the gate, was her mounted escort. Vorain held the reins of Selene's horse Goliath.

The queen kissed her daughter and murmured some words of farewell that Clauda could not make out. She took the fake *Book of the Night* from her sleeve and handed it to Selene.

As Selene strode across the parade ground to her escort, Clauda turned and ran down the outer passageway. If she could catch up with Selene outside the palace gates . . .

The trembling she had tried to ignore ever since she discovered the old queen's chambers grew worse as she ran, throwing off her stride. She was just past the servants' gate when she fell. She heard street noises, and distantly heard Selene's and Vorain's voices, but she saw nothing but the dust beneath her nose. She could not move, could not cry out.

14

Consorting with Demons

From the window of her room, Haly could see the practice yard of the Singer army. The stone courtyard was roughly five times the size of the Great Hall of the Libyrinth, but the mass of soldiers down there made it appear cramped.

Row upon row of black-garbed men marched in formation, wielding rifles and mind lancets. She tried to count them, but in the distance they quickly became an undifferentiated mass. What was undeniable was that there were an awful lot of them. Maybe thousands. She shuddered.

The door to her room opened and she turned to see Gyneth entering with her dinner. He kept his eyes down, and there was a pink tinge to his cheeks. He said nothing, simply set the tray down on the table before her and retreated to the doorway, where he stood, his hands folded in front of him, staring at the floor. Haly felt a little flutter of excitement. Maybe she was the girl the other boys in his chorus had teased him about. Why else would he be this embarrassed?

When she finished eating the meal of lentil cakes, noodle pudding, squash, and sweet potatoes, Gyneth collected the tray and turned toward the door. Apparently he wasn't going to ask to hear any more about Anne today. He was just going to leave. Suddenly she wasn't so sure she was right about the source of his embarrassment. Maybe he loathed her. Maybe he was embarrassed that anyone would think he could be interested in a Libyrarian, an enemy, a timid, plain girl nobody would ever like *that way*.

He was almost at the door. From somewhere inside her, very close to the place where she'd found the strength to speak up on behalf of Anne Frank's *The Diary of a Young Girl*, she found the nerve to say, "Where are all the women?" to his retreating back.

He stopped and turned around, surprised out of his mortification for the moment. "What do you mean?"

Haly had no idea where she was going with this, but she licked her lips and plunged on. "Outside, in the city, I saw women everywhere, working alongside men. But here in the temple, none. Except in the dungeon."

His face cleared. "Oh. I see what you mean. Oh, no. Women can't be priests."

"Why not?"

"Well, Yammon was a man," he said, as if that explained everything.

"So?"

Gyneth shrugged. "So, if women were supposed to be priests, then I guess the Song would have made Yammon a woman, but it didn't. So obviously only men are supposed to be priests." This seemed to make sense to him.

"But I'm the Redeemer, and I'm a"—she'd never thought of herself as a grown-up before—"woman."

"Yes." Gyneth sighed and set the tray down on the table beside the door. He came over and she pushed a chair out from the table and he sat down. "But that's different. The Redeemer . . . well, we don't get to pick the Redeemer. And it's always been known that the Redeemer would be a Libyrarian. So, I guess, you being female isn't all that much worse, and anyway, we have no choice."

How flattering. At least her annoyance was taking the edge off that pathetically heartsick feeling she'd had a moment ago. "So what do you do? Are you all celibate, or do you all like men, or . . ."

Gyneth blinked rapidly and he stared at the tabletop. The blush was back in his cheeks, and now she felt a certain satisfaction in making him uncomfortable. "We aren't allowed to marry," he said. "We are supposed to dedicate our lives to the preservation of knowledge and the worship of the Song."

"So you're celibate, then."

He picked up a crumb from the table and rolled it between his fingers, frowning, still not meeting her eyes. "We're supposed to be."

She was beginning to enjoy this. "What do you mean, 'supposed to be'?"

Gyneth shrugged and looked like he would avoid answering her if he could. But she was the Redeemer. "Everyone knows that Censor Michander visits the woman who runs the inn near the city gates, and she has six children. The three boys are subalterns here. They look exactly like him." A note of anger had crept into his voice.

"Everybody knows about it, but nobody says anything. And Conductor Tifius and Brother Ambro sleep together in the same bed and everybody knows about that, too." He paused and at last looked up at her. "And there are lots more. I think it's stupid to have a rule that nobody follows." He said it defiantly, as if he expected to be struck down or at least chastised for the criticism.

But Haly just nodded her head in agreement. "Libyrarians don't always get married, either, though we can. My parents were married, but a lot of people just . . . you know, do like what Michander and Tifius do." She sighed and eyed him carefully. She knew what she wanted to ask him next, but did she have the nerve?

"Did you have a boyfriend, back there?" he surprised her by asking.

"No," she said. "Have you, um, have you ever broken the rule?"

"No," he said.

She was sure she shouldn't be so pleased to hear this, but she was, and before she knew it, she was asking an even bolder question. "If . . . if you were going to break that rule, would you be like Michander or like Tifius?"

Gyneth gaped at her openly for a moment before turning his gaze resolutely back to the table. "I'd stay celibate," he said, and hurriedly stood up and turned away. He gathered the tray from beside the door and left.

By the next morning, Haly had come to her senses. What in the Seven Tales was she doing entertaining romantic notions about a Singer when her home and all her people were in jeopardy? She knew what it was. She'd heard about it years ago from the book *International Handbook of Traumatic Stress Syndromes*—Stockholm syndrome, where people come to sympathize and even fall in love with their captors. Well, she had a more important agenda to pursue with Gyneth than that.

As he cleared away the breakfast dishes, she went to where she had hidden *The Diary of a Young Girl* under her pillow. She slipped it into the sleeve of her robe and took her customary spot on the bench at the foot of the bed. "Do you want to hear more of Anne's story?" she asked Gyneth.

He turned to look at her. The tension that had hung between them since yesterday's recital seemed to evaporate, and he nodded his head and took his place at her side.

About fifteen minutes into the recitation, she slipped the book from her sleeve and opened it to the page from which she'd been reciting. She expected him to react immediately, perhaps to jump up and call for Michander and Siblea to throw her back into the dungeon, but instead he leaned over and glanced at the object in her hands. "What is that?" he asked her.

Of course. He'd never been out of the Corvariate Citadel. He'd never been to a "liberation." He'd never seen a book before. She didn't answer him right away. Instead she put her finger to the line of text she was reciting, and moved it along as she spoke the words, "I sat pressed closely against him."

Gyneth bent over closer, peering at the symbols above her finger. Suddenly he sprang up and dove beneath the bench, seizing the iron box from beneath it. He lifted it up and the lid fell off. He looked at the empty box and then, with a cry of rage, threw it across the room. It crashed against the wall beside the door.

"Yammon's tonsils! What have you done, you lit witch?" He pointed a shaking finger at the tome in her hands. "That's the book, isn't it?" Without waiting for her to answer, he put his hands to his eyes as if he would claw them from his face. He moaned and fell to his knees. "What have you done to me?"

Well, she'd expected him to be upset, but . . . "It's okay," she said lamely. "I haven't done anything to you. Just shown you some written words, that's all."

"That's all?" He lowered his hands and stared at her. He was crying. "That's all? I'll go blind now, thanks to you! Thanks to you I won't hear the Song anymore. Why?" He shook his head in bewilderment. "Why would you do that to me?"

"I-I'm sorry. But none of that is going to happen! You're not going to go blind! I'm not blind, am I? None of the other Libyrarians are blind. That's just stupid. And as for not hearing the Song, I can hear the Song and I read."

Gyneth simply shook his head and slumped back on his heels. He buried his face in his hands again. "It's different," he said. "You're the Redeemer."

"That's right, I'm your Redeemer. Do you doubt what I tell you?"

He was silent. Obviously he did. "All right, then," she said. "How soon do you lose your eyesight?"

He blinked up at her. "What?"

"You've seen written words. You said you would be struck blind by it. When?"

His mouth worked. "Ri-right . . ."

"Right away? Are you blind, then?"

He shook his head, but looked no less lost as he glanced around the room and then down at his hands. Haly set the book down on the bench and came and sat on the floor in front of him. She took his hands. "So that's one thing you've been taught about the written word that you now know to be wrong."

He took a deep breath and blinked rapidly, mastering himself with visible effort. "Y-yes, Holy One," he whispered.

"You wait, Gyneth. The Song will be sung the day after tomorrow. You go to services then, and you will hear it, I promise."

He didn't agree or disagree this time. He glanced at the iron box lying on the floor beside the door. "How did you get it open? It was supposed to be safe in there."

"I'm the Redeemer. I command powers you don't even know exist."

He took another deep breath. "Why did you show me?"

"Because I trust you."

He shook his head. "You shouldn't. I should tell Censor Siblea what you've done."

"Then he'll take the book away and you'll never know what happened to Anne."

Gyneth nodded and looked at her out of the corner of his eye. "And he might punish you, Redeemer or not."

Haly swallowed and remained silent. Gyneth rose but she stayed where she was, sitting on the floor, and watched as he collected the tray from beside the door and left.

All that night Haly waited for Siblea or Michander to show up, take Anne Frank's diary away from her, burn it, and then either haul her off to the dungeon or give her another curving scar on her face, but they didn't. In the morning when Gyneth arrived with her breakfast, he set it down on the table and retreated to his spot by the door, where he waited in grim silence. She tried to catch his eye but he stared straight forward and pretended she wasn't there.

She picked at her eggs and potatoes, not really hungry. At length she said, "I'm sorry I didn't warn you."

He swallowed but didn't reply, and he still wouldn't look at her.

"I'm finished," she said. "You can take the tray away now."

The following day she attended services with Siblea and Gyneth in the great amphitheater. She looked down at the hundreds of people on the floor far below, and in the balconies lining the walls, and tried to imagine there being even more of them, as she'd been assured there would be on the day of her presentation. She had that same woozy feeling she'd had the first time she'd looked over the edge of the balcony, and the same little voice inside urged her to jump. She turned around to face Gyneth, who stood in his customary spot near the door to the private balcony. He looked past her, just as he'd been doing since she'd shown him written words. In a few minutes, the truth of what she'd told him would be revealed, but it was obvious he did not believe that. He stood expressionless, like a person condemned. She wanted to say something, grab his hand, anything to reassure him that he wasn't damned, but she couldn't because Siblea was there. She turned around again and took her seat.

The Song swept over her, just as it had before, and she gave herself up to that soaring, swooping, unending sound that wrapped the whole world in its beauty, and brought all things together in harmony. When it was over, she turned around to find Gyneth standing quite as still as he had been before, only now, far from being blank, his face was suffused with wonder and relief. There was a fierce light in his eyes as they met hers, as of one who has seen the truth and will never bow to lies again.

The first thing to understand is that words are made of letters, and letters are . . . sounds," said Haly. It was the next day, and she and Gyneth sat on the bench at the foot of her bed, Anne Frank's diary open between them. "So each little group of letters is a word. And the words sound like the letters they're made of . . . mostly. Look." Haly pointed to a word on the page. "This word is 'cat.'"

"Cat," repeated Gyneth, peering at the letters on the page. "I don't know what I thought words would look like when they're murde— written," he said. "They look like they're broken. No wonder everyone thinks they're dead."

"But they're not. It's just that you're not used to looking at them. It'll take a little while for your eyes to learn how to see them so that they match up with the sounds they represent. But you'll learn, and then you'll hear them, too."

He looked at her, his eyes bright with hope. "Hear them?"

"Yes. You will see them *and* hear them, and they will live in you."

He was silent. His gaze slid from her back to the open book. Slowly, he nodded. "Is that a word?" he asked, pointing at the page. "It's just one letter."

"Yes. It is a single letter, but it is also a word. It is the word I. This word"—she moved her finger to the next one—"is 'sat.' Say them."

"I sat."

"Good. The next word is 'pressed.'"

"I sat pressed."

"And the next one is 'closely.'"

"I sat pressed closely."

She was very aware of the warmth of Gyneth's thigh against hers. Did he notice her? she wondered. She watched him carefully as they finished the phrase, "I sat pressed closely against him." His cheeks flushed bright pink, he breathed rapidly, erratically, but then, he was committing the cardinal sin of his religion. She studied the curve of his lips as he spoke the forbidden words, and she wished they were just a pair of clerks at the Libyrinth.

"You're doing really well," Haly told him when they took a break to stretch and drink some water.

Gyneth gave her a smile, then sighed. "You know, things were easier when all I had to do was obey my teachers and love the Song. Now I have all these questions, and they torment me." He crossed his arms and paced the room, his voice growing more agitated with every word. "I did not go blind, and I still hear the Song, but I wonder if your teaching has not cursed me all the same. Now I find myself questioning everything."

Haly leaned against the window seat. "Like what?"

He bit his lip and stared at her, as if trying to arrange the words in the proper order before speaking. "Have you noticed that the censors don't really seem to care about the Redemption?"

Haly laughed. "I'd say they're going to an awful lot of trouble over something they don't care about."

Gyneth shrugged. "I mean, they're excited because you're going to recite *The Book of the Night*, and then we'll have the secret for making Eggs—it's all they talk about. But they're not really talking about becoming one with the Song. I mean, if we're really all one with the Song, then I'm not sure why we'd need a maker of Eggs."

"Good point," said Haly, wondering how to guide Gyneth further down the path of reasoning that he'd started on. As it turned out, she didn't need to.

"I think they're using the Redemption for their own ends. I'm not sure they even believe in the Song. I think . . . they're using the Song to mesmerize us. To justify destroying the . . . Libyrinth and grabbing all the power for themselves. I-I-I want to be one with the Song, I do. But I'm not sure that's really what's going to happen."

"The Song is beautiful, Gyneth. No one could help but love it, no one could help but want to be immersed in it forever, but . . . the situation is like the potatoes in Anne Frank's diary."

He gave her a puzzled frown.

"Anne's ideas soared. And then eventually she'd come back to the state of the potatoes they were eating—rotten, fresh, plentiful, or sparse. See, you need both—the soaring and the potatoes."

A smile curled the corner of his mouth. "Holy One, this humble servant is incapable of following the purity of your logic."

She blushed. "What I mean is, you can't eat a miracle, but at the same time, people have needs beyond the material. There has to be both."

"So there isn't really going to be a Redemption, is there?"

Haly took his hands. "It won't be what you imagined, but that doesn't mean we have to let the censors turn it all into boiled potatoes, either." She paused. "Shall I tell you what I want the Redemption to be?"

He squeezed her hands. "Yes, tell me."

"All my life, I've had the books of the Libyrinth to guide and comfort and teach me. I want everyone to have that. I want everyone to be able to read. I *will* liberate the Word, but not through song. I will liberate one word at a time, one person at a time, and of all the devout chorus, you are the first. You are doing better all the time, Gyneth. Soon you will hear text as if it were song."

The next morning the bottom of the breakfast tray was covered with sand. Gyneth gave no indication that anything was out of the ordinary as he set the tray down and placed her dishes before her. It wasn't until they sat down for their lesson that he brought the tray with him, along with the fork. With the end of the fork he painstakingly wrote "I sat," in the sand. "I thought it might help me remember the words," he said, and the look he gave her was both nervous and exultant.

Nod had the sense to stay out of sight when Gyneth was there. Sometimes he crept out behind Gyneth, or through the window, and went who knew where for hours on end. Haly tried to get him to spy for her, but with only limited success.

"Ili sees? What does Nod care what Ili sees? Nod has enough with what Nod sees. Does she know these Singer beasties turn everything into music?"

"No, Nod. Not Ili sees. Ilysies. The country . . . ? Like where Libyrarian Selene comes from?"

He scampered up the bedpost and leaped from there to the

chandelier, and swung upside down from his knees, blowing raspberries at her.

The door burst open and Gyneth entered at a trot, his face bright. "Holy One, the censors are ready to present you to—" He stopped dead, staring at Nod. His pupils dilated and he took a step back before rallying. Grim-faced, he seized hold of the marble-topped table beside the door and leaped between Haly and Nod. "Get away from her, you demon!" he shouted, swinging the table at Nod, who sprang to the top of a bedpost, baring his teeth at Gyneth and shrieking inarticulately.

Gyneth screamed back, charging after him, climbing onto the bed and swinging the table.

"Gyneth! Stop!" cried Haly, running after him, trying to grab his arm.

She missed on the first swing, but fortunately, so did Gyneth. He left a large dent in the ceiling beam, and a few splinters of wood rained down on the bed.

"Gyneth! No!" Haly grabbed both his arms and hauled him down off the bed. "Stop it!" He stared at her, stunned, as she tried to wrest the table from him. "Nod's not a demon! He's an—" She stopped herself. Would "imp" be any more reassuring to him? "A friend," she finished.

Gyneth looked wildly from Haly to Nod, who scurried beneath the bed, muttering peevishly. "You consort with demons," he said. It wasn't a question. He turned from her. She watched his fists clench and unclench at his sides. "Oh, Holy One," he murmured. "You teach me to read, and I am not damned. Everything you teach me is the exact opposite of what the censors have taught me. In you my own faith is made unrecognizable to me. Now I wonder if it will survive the revelation of such a Redeemer as you."

"Nod is from the Libyrinth. He keeps it clean. He can be

annoying, but he won't hurt you," she said. The words were inadequate.

Censor Siblea appeared in the open doorway. "Gyneth, is our Redeemer ready? We must hurry. They are gathering in the—" He stared at Haly and Gyneth, frowning as he registered the expressions on their faces. "What is wrong?"

Haly looked at Gyneth. He could reveal Nod's existence to Siblea, and consign her to the dungeon for the rest of her days. Gyneth blinked and brushed his hands on his robes. "Nothing, Censor. There was a mouse in the room. It frightened our Redeemer, and I attempted to kill it, but it escaped."

Haly felt her heart start up again, swelling with every beat.

Drums echoed through the vast amphitheater. Haly resisted the urge to hide behind Siblea. They were in the mouth of the statue of Yammon, behind the platform where the chorus sang the Song. "There is nothing to fear, Holy One," he reassured her. "You know the song you are to sing. When the high censor introduces you, you will step forward and sing it. That's all."

That and travel to the Libyrinth to perform the Redemption, after which the Singers would destroy her home. There had been word that *The Book of the Night* was no longer in Ilysies. Gyneth told her they had it on good authority that the princess—it took her a moment to realize that must be Selene—was taking it to the Libyrinth.

But why would Selene do that? Haly had given herself up to the Singers so that Selene could get the book to Ilysies where it would be safe. Why would she jeopardize that now? All the previous night Haly had lain awake, beseeching the Seven Tales that it wasn't so, that this news was only a misdirection on Selene's part—a clever ruse like the Goat might perform, or perhaps simply a mistake, the province of her own guardian, the Fly.

"Members of the Righteous Chorus, the time of the Redemption has come." Orrin's voice floated back to them from the platform. "I present to you your Redeemer, Halcyon the Libyrarian."

The roar of the crowd was deafening, drowning out even the drums. Haly stepped out onto the platform. Hundreds of feet below, masses of Singers cheered and swayed, a human ocean of religious hysteria. She did not think anyone would hear her, but when she opened her mouth, the entire amphitheater fell silent, and her small, high voice rang out clear and true. "Now the time foretold has come, when Song and Word will be as one. Righteous chorus lift each voice. The Redemption is at hand—rejoice!"

When the last note faded the cheering burst forth again—a sound that was a song of its own sort, an unstoppable tidal wave of passion and longing.

That afternoon Haly sat at her window, watching the soldiers. When their practice was finished, the figures filed out through a gate into the city. The gate shut, and the small fraction of men who remained moved to a similar gate on the other side of the courtyard, which they slowly lifted to reveal a ramp descending into darkness. Other men appeared at the top of the ramp, hauling on ropes. Gradually, like the interminable rise of the seventh moon, a circular, gray shape emerged from the darkness.

It was the horn from the dungeon, now completed. At the end of its curving funnel, where the mouthpiece would be on a normal horn, was a small oval bulb no bigger than Haly's head. While the team of Singers with the ropes positioned the Horn of Yammon, those who had opened the gate wheeled a stone slab at least fifteen feet thick into position at the opposite side of the courtyard. The slab was at least as thick as the walls of the Libyrinth.

A Singer came forth holding a glowing Egg in his hands. Haly wondered if it was the same Egg that had been recovered from the vault. He climbed a scaffold up to the bulb at the tip of the horn, opened a panel on its surface, and placed the Egg inside. He closed the panel, turned a dial at the base of the bulb, and retreated back down the scaffold. The men hastened away from the horn and stood watching from the top of the ramp.

The sound began almost imperceptibly, as a minute vibration in the air. It grew, a low grating sort of whisper at the very limit of her hearing. Haly's fingertips and the soles of her feet tingled. The tingle spread to her spine and she rubbed at her face, which suddenly felt like it had little bugs crawling all over it.

As the sound grew, the crawling feeling intensified, and then suddenly it was gone. Now the horn was truly audible, a deep bellow like a mountain heaving itself up from a continental rift. The stone slab before it shook. Haly's breath caught in her throat as she saw a fine mist of sand lifting off of the block like steam from a pot of boiling water. And yes, that was exactly what the horn was doing to the stone: boiling it. The opposite wall of the courtyard became visible through the slab as the force of the horn's sound wave agitated and dispersed its particles, turning it into a slab-shaped cloud of dust.

Abruptly the horn fell silent and the dust fell, forming a gently sloping pile in the center of the courtyard. Haly's ears rang in the sudden silence. She stared at the dust pile that moments ago had been a wall as thick as any the Libyrinth had.

Her home, her people, the books that had taught and entertained and comforted her; they would all be reduced to a pile of dust, dispersed by the winds of the plain.

It would be done in her name. And there was nothing she or anyone else could do about it.

She was watching them sweep up the powdered debris when

the door to her room opened. It was Siblea, a look of happy anticipation on his face. "All is ready for the Redemption, Holy One," he said, bowing low. "We will depart tomorrow morning."

.

15

Po

The blood in Clauda's veins felt like it was full of stinging nettles. The pain was everywhere, racing in burning arcs through her arms and legs, her torso, even her face. It had been three days since Selene's departure, and she'd just this morning recovered the ability to speak. She was desperate to speak to Scio, but she'd had no opportunity.

"Concentrate," admonished Adept Ykobos, who ran stiff fingers down the inside of Clauda's left arm while her attendant stretched the limb out to the side. The adept looked haggard. She'd been working with Clauda almost nonstop since her collapse. "Use the visualization I taught you, and keep breathing."

Clauda did as she was told, picturing in her mind's eye a network of pathways, like the roots of a tree, branching out throughout her body. But these pathways were tangled and inflamed. As she inhaled, she tried to gently coax cool green energy through them, untangling and soothing as it went. But her energy hit a knot of deep crimson and splintered, forcing a hoarse cry from her throat. "Please," she whispered. "Can we stop?"

Ykobos sighed. "We might as well. This isn't doing any good." She waved off her attendants and sat down wearily on the edge of the bed. Her eyes were bleak as they scanned Clauda's face. "You have a very fluid energy system, Clauda of Ayor. Normally that's a good thing, but when it's been disrupted as badly as yours was, it presents a problem. Any imbalance spreads very rapidly, and when we do equalize one area, it soon goes out of balance again, trying to compensate for the discrepencies in other areas."

Clauda swallowed. Suddenly she wanted to beg Ykobos to continue the treatment. She couldn't stay this way. She had to talk to Scio, but she had not seen the chambermaid since her collapse. She needed to somehow get word to Selene, to warn her, but she couldn't even walk and other than Scio, there was no one she could trust. What was she going to do? The very thought unleashed another seizure, her rigid muscles jerking until she thought the bed would break apart. Ykobos came quickly, holding her down, her attendant Po slipping the padded bit between her teeth so she wouldn't bite her tongue or crack her teeth. When it passed Clauda lay limp and exhausted, and her caretakers looked little better.

"Adept Ykobos," came a voice at the door. It was a woman in a soldier's uniform. "Captain Athene needs you in the barracks; Sergeant Bilos has had a relapse."

Ymin drew her hand across her brow. "Yes, Bathir, tell her I'll be there directly." She looked back at Clauda. "Try to get some rest, and try, please try, to stay calm."

Clauda managed a nod, and then Ykobos was gone, Helene accompanying her. The boy Po remained behind. He sat beside her bed, holding the bit in readiness should Clauda have another seizure. Clauda looked at him, really noticing him for the first time. He was about fourteen, and still on the child-hood side of adolescence, though from the lankiness of his arms and legs, it wouldn't be long before he came of age. He had lighter hair than most Ilysians and his nose was smaller, the bridge of it flatter than those of most of his people. His eyes were a striking gray-green—though he usually kept them low-ered and she seldom got a glimpse of them. "Po," said Clauda, "can you fetch Scio for me, please?"

He shook his head. "I can't leave you. The adept said."

Clauda sighed. "Well, when you see Scio next, tell her I wish her to attend upon me."

The boy's eyes were wide. He nodded.

She needed to think about something other than her and Selene's and Haly's situations. She looked at Po again. "A relapse?"

The boy nodded. "Sergeant Bilos is very ill. Almost as bad as you."

"How was she injured?"

The boy blinked. "I'm not supposed to say."

Oh. A secret. Clauda welcomed the distraction. "Was it a mind-lancet attack?"

He shook his head. "I can't say." He stood up, as if putting distance between them would curb her curiosity.

Clauda remembered something from the queen's conversa-tion with her general. Something about soldiers being injured training on the wing. And both Scio and Selene had mentioned that few people had the ability to control the wing, and that it was dangerous to try. Curiosity was a welcome respite from worry, but she didn't dare press Po too much. "So, you're a boy," said Clauda, wanting to keep him in conversation and blurting the first thing she could think of.

He blushed, then nodded.

"I haven't seen many boys here," she observed, "just a few among the bull dancers."

Po swallowed and stared at his feet. He said nothing.

Clauda realized she had her work cut out for her. "Why are there so few of you?"

Po looked like he wanted to crawl under her bed and die, rather than speak. Still, he didn't seem to be able to ignore a direct question. "There are more females than males among us, on the whole. And of course it is a great honor to work in the palace. Naturally, the jobs go to women. The adept is my cousin. My mother went to a great deal of trouble to arrange this apprenticeship for me." He paused. "I apologize if I am doing a bad job."

Clauda tried to shake her head but decided against it when dizziness threatened to overwhelm her. "No. Not at all. You're doing a great job, Po. I appreciate how hard you've worked to help me. It's been difficult for everyone."

Po's face turned bright red. For a moment Clauda thought he'd collapse from apoplexy. Then he managed to say, "You're very kind to say that. I'm sorry you're so ill."

Clauda took a deep breath. "Me, too. So, what about the bull dancers? Why are there males among them?"

"They are the queen's consorts."

"Oh. That's very interesting. You know, at the Libyrinth, people don't care so much if you're a male or a female."

He said nothing, just stared at the floor at the base of her bed.

"Do you want to become an adept?" she asked.

His shoulders lifted. "I suppose," he said. His voice was little more than a whisper.

"Is there something else you'd rather do?"

That seemed to startle him and he looked at her, green eyes wide. "I—" He caught himself and looked at the floor again. "I am extremely fortunate to be here and to have the opportunity to study with the adept."

"You don't sound particularly thrilled about it."

He didn't answer.

"I'm sorry. I don't mean to pry. It's none of my business."

Po bit his lip and cast her a speculative look, and then glanced at the doorway. He seemed to be nerving himself up for something. Clauda waited patiently and focused on her breath.

"I'm no different than other boys," said Po at last. "I just want to be a good consort and sire daughters."

Clauda felt the corners of her mouth twitch and she forced herself not to smile. "Why can't you do that, then?"

Po looked sad. "Because of my appearance."

"Your appearance?"

He nodded. "My small nose and my light hair. I have a . . . please, I mean no offense . . . a look of the plain about me, is the way my mother puts it. Only a very broad-minded woman would accept me as a sire for her daughters, and my mother feared what would become of me if I became a Billy—an unattached male."

Clauda sighed and rolled onto her back, staring at the ceiling. "It's funny. Everybody here is fascinated with the way I look, because I'm an Ayorite. But with you they treat it as a bad thing, because you're Ilysian. And you don't even look all that much like an Ayorite, frankly. It all seems so stupid."

Po said nothing, but when Clauda turned her head to look, she saw him smiling. Her eyes strayed to her bedside table, reassuring herself that *The Book of the Night* was still there, sitting unnoticed in its *Theselaides* disguise, beneath Volume I of *Queen Belrea and the Wing of Tarsus*. "Po? Would you read to me?"

Po's company, the tale of Queen Belrea and the wing, and speculation about what had injured Sergeant Bilos provided Clauda with enough distractions to keep her free from seizures for the rest of that day. After dinner Adept Ykobos returned to her chamber, looking even more haggard. She and Helene and Po worked on Clauda for another hour, with middling results.

"Your mind is more settled this evening, so your body's response is improved, but I won't hide *this* from you; what we're doing now is palliative. We're making no real progress with your core."

The words sent a chill through Clauda, but before she had another fit, she focused on the adept's phrasing. *I won't hide this from you.* With a slight emphasis on the word "this"—which implied that she would, or perhaps already was, hiding *something* from her. The adept was tired, so there might be an opportunity here. "It is good of the queen to allow you to treat me."

Ymin could not hide the sour look that crossed her face. "Treat you." She sighed heavily and stared at her hands. Her muttering was swift and barely audible. Clauda only caught part of it: "If one can call it that . . . could heal . . . as it has the soldiers."

"Pardon?" said Clauda.

Ymin stood swiftly and straightened her shoulders. "Well. I will see you tomorrow morning. Try to sleep. Helene will stay with you and prepare you some tea to help with that."

As she and Po headed for the door, Clauda spoke up. "Po," she said.

He turned, and Ymin raised one eyebrow in surprise.

"Thank you for reading to me, and don't forget to talk to Scio for me."

At the mention of the chambermaid's name, Po startled. He glanced at Ymin and a look passed between them. He didn't really answer Clauda, just bowed and followed the adept out of the room. The door shut behind them.

Po, Helene, and Adept Ykobos never left her alone. The

three of them sat with her in shifts. When next it was Po's turn, Clauda said to him, "Has something happened to Scio?"

He was just bringing her a cup of tea, and at her words, he dropped it. The cup shattered and sprayed them both with hot water. Po bowed low. "I'm so sorry. I will bring you another cup."

"Please answer my question instead." Her stomach was tight. She already knew the answer, if not the specifics. She forced herself to take long, deep breaths. She'd never get anywhere if she kept having fits every time she was upset.

He gave her a stricken look and sank to the floor and began gathering the shards of broken porcelain.

"They've forbidden you to discuss it, is that it?"

Po didn't answer.

"I know they have. And I know something has happened to her."

Po paused in his cleaning. "Will you promise not to tell anyone I told you?"

"Yes, of course."

He looked up. "She was transferred to the summer palace."

She stared at him, taking in his grave, drawn expression. "Transferred? Really?" she asked.

He swallowed. "I don't know."

"If she was truly transferred, why all the secrecy?"

The boy shrugged and looked uneasily at the door. "We're not supposed to tell you anything."

Clauda breathed. She tried to imagine Selene in the library but the image was blotted out by Scio's face. Their spying had been discovered. That's why Clauda was under constant watch and her caretakers were forbidden to tell her anything. Scio was probably dead. Her breath broke into sharp taloned birds that flew away and left her in darkness.

When she awoke again Po was with her, though whether it was his next shift or only a few hours later she couldn't know.

Her body hurt. She feared for a moment that she had lost the ability to speak again, but managed to force out a hoarse whisper. "Read to me?"

Po nodded. He gave her a drink of water, some of which she managed to swallow and some of which dampened the coverlet and her neck. He took Volume I of *Queen Belrea and the Wing of Tarsus* from the bedside table and began to read: "Belrea and her sisters Talea and Nalea argued over who would fly the wing. Talea was the oldest, and headstrong, and she won the argument. When she took on the mantle of the goddess and became one with the wing, all was well, at first. But when she tried to exert her will and make the wing rise, the flow lines rejected her. They lashed her with fire and threw her from the goddess's embrace. Talea was ill then with the shaking sickness. Nalea, who was a healer, tried to give her sister relief, but all her arts failed."

"The shaking sickness?" said Clauda.

Po nodded. "Seizures."

"Like mine?"

He nodded again, and read on. "At last, in desperation, hoping that what had harmed might also heal, Nalea put Talea back into the wing again. This time, Talea did not attempt to control the wing. The flow lines forgave her, and they healed her."

Clauda kept very still and quiet. Po did not realize that she knew the wing existed, and she wanted him to keep reading. She was now more certain than ever that Sergeant Bilos had been injured training on the wing. Had the adept's slip the other day been a reference to using the wing to heal her?

"Belrea next attempted to fly the wing. Her subtle mind was able to invite the flow lines to follow their own inclination, and thus guide them to her will. She flew, and manifested the Sword of the Mother, and smote the enemies of Ilysies."

Po paused and took a drink of water.

"It's too bad the wing isn't real," said Clauda. "I bet it could heal even me."

By the light of the glow warmer, Clauda saw ripples appear on the surface of the water in Po's cup. He set it down. He stared at his hands for a long moment and Clauda got the impression he was making up his mind about something. "If it were real, it might be forbidden to you," he said at length.

Affection for Po filled her. "Then it's just as well it's not. I imagine it would be difficult for the adept to deny a patient a cure."

Po gave her a piercing look. "Difficult for us all." He broke off and stood. He came to her bedside, and under the pretext of adjusting her pillow brought his mouth to her ear. "We are not normally jailers, or spies," he whispered.

Clauda felt tears gathering behind her eyes. Po withdrew and she nodded. "Thank you," she said. "That's much more comfortable."

So Thela was keeping her alive in the hopes that she might reveal something useful, Clauda mused. She'd wondered about that. And Adept Ykobos resented it. And if Clauda could turn the adept, just enough to try using the wing to heal her . . . Excitement made her heart race and she remembered to breathe deeply, in and out, in and out. She closed her eyes and there was Selene, smiling at her in the palace library. And then she imagined herself in the wing, soaring across the Plain of Ayor, the Ilysian army following behind.

16

Miracles

Haly stood in the entranceway of the Temple of Yammon, clutching the metal box that contained Anne Frank's diary. Before leaving she'd had Nod replace the pins in the hinges, sealing the book inside once more. She told Nod of their leaving, told him to try to find a way to come with them, but she had not seen him since.

Siblea stood on her right, Michander on her left, a phalanx of soldiers in a wedge before her, and Gyneth and the rest of Subaltern Chorus Five behind her. Even through the thick steel doors of the temple she could hear the roar of the crowd outside.

That roar became deafening as two subalterns opened the tall, arching doors to reveal a cordon of soldiers holding back a screaming, waving sea of people from the elephant that stood before the steps of the temple. The beast was about six feet tall at the shoulder, with a long jaw, protruding brow bones, and a low, sloping forehead. Above its mouth hung a prehensile snout about four feet long. It had large, fan-shaped ears and a thick gray hide. It was covered in spirals drawn on its hide with white chalk. A barred, covered palanquin sat upon its back. It was an unseasonably mild day, the cloud cover low and the air laden with moisture.

With her mouth dry and her heart pounding, Haly stepped out from the shelter of the archway and allowed Siblea to guide her down the steps with a hand at her elbow.

As she reached the bottom step, a woman broke through the cordon and threw herself at Haly's feet.

"Thank you, Holy One, thank you!" she cried, reaching a hand out grasp at Haly's hem. "Your Redemption will heal my child. The Song will heal her, thanks to you!"

Haly realized that the bundle on the woman's back was a child—a child with a face as wizened as Nod's. A child that looked *old*. Haly had no idea what was wrong with her.

Swiftly yet gently, the soldiers gathered mother and child up and swept them back into the crowd that was straining the barricades. Haly lost sight of her as Siblea helped her up the ladder and into the palanquin, but the image of her desperate, hopeful face burned in her mind's eye. Far more than the roaring crowd here or at the confirmation, that woman and her strangely old child made Haly wish that the Redemption was as Gyneth believed it to be, and not just the grab for power that it was.

The palanquin was roughly six feet on a side and lavishly furnished with cushions and rugs. Draperies hung from the canopied roof, nearly disguising the narrow-spaced iron bars.

Siblea climbed in behind her and settled himself on a cushion across from her. He turned and waved a hand through the bars at the front of the palanquin, signaling the elephant's rider to depart.

The beast took its first step and the entire conveyance

lurched forward and to one side, taking Haly's stomach with it. She thought of the seasickness that plagued so many of the characters in the seafaring novels she'd heard and wondered if she would be similarly cursed. Well, it would be no pleasure cruise for Siblea, either, if such were the case. The spaces between the bars of the palanquin were too narrow for her to stick her head through them. She'd have no choice but to throw up in here. She decided to aim for Siblea if it came to that.

But after the first few strides her body became accustomed to the rolling gait, and she gazed out at the city streets, thronged with jubilant members of the Righteous Chorus. It seemed that the entire city planned to accompany them on their pilgrimage to the Libyrinth, and indeed, when they passed through the gates they were accompanied by a mighty procession that dwarfed the contingent of black-garbed priests surrounding the elephant and its holy cargo.

Haly lifted the curtain behind her and peered out at the crowds behind them. At the back of the procession loomed the Horn of Yammon, lurching along on its trolley. It was so large that she had a moment's hope it would be too tall to pass through the gates. But the engineers had measured everything carefully, and there was just enough room beneath the archway for the great steel trumpet. She looked at its implacable curves a moment longer, sighed, and dropped the curtain.

As the domes and spires of the Corvariate Citadel sank beneath the horizon and the roar of the crowd died down to a constant, sibilant murmur, Siblea clasped his hands together and looked at her eagerly. "So," he said, "how shall we amuse ourselves?"

Haly was suddenly reminded of the knife and jar on the table in Siblea's office, and of Gyneth's words: *People don't lie to Censor Siblea.* She tried not to shrink from him, but her shoulders pressed into the fabric-draped bars of the enclosure just the same. She didn't speak. The gleam in his eye choked off her words.

"I know," he said. "I'll sing you a song. You'll like this one. It's about Yammon and Iscarion when they were young, before Iscarion's betrayal." Siblea hummed softly in preparation, and then lifted his clear, tenor voice, and sang: "Like the flower and the seed, like the water and the shore, Yammon and Iscarion were brothers, friends, before. Yammon strong and brave, Iscarion sharp and quick, the one did not have a thought but that the other followed it."

The song told of how Yammon's bold ways made him a target of Hiop, their overseer, who whipped him on any pretext. Hiop would have killed Yammon if Iscarion had not taken the blame for dropping a bale of wood, and after Hiop punished Iscarion, Yammon nursed him back to health. It was Iscarion who first suggested the rebellion, and it was he who devised the songs by which slaves could pass information to one another without being detected.

"Two once one forever parted, Yammon in grief, Iscarion in folly. The Song and the Word shall not meet, 'til Redemption makes the past complete," he finished.

Haly found herself leaning forward. It was a very interesting song. "If Yammon and Iscarion were so close, why did Iscarion refuse to teach Yammon to read?" she asked.

Siblea leaned back, poured a cup of water from a flask, and drank it up. "There is more than one chorus of thought on that matter. Some believe he was seduced by power. Others think that literacy itself poisoned him."

Haly considered that, and another question occurred to her. "You said once that I was a . . . child of Iscarion. Why?"

Siblea gave her a puzzled smile. "Your home was Iscarion's refuge after he fled the citadel. He is the founder of your people. You do not know this?"

"Theselaides discovered the Libyrinth and founded the community of Libyrarians," she countered.

Siblea's pale eyebrows nearly disappeared beyond the crest of his forehead. "Theselaides? No. I've never heard of Theselaides. I assure you, it was Iscarion."

His arrogance made her angry. "How do you know?" she challenged. A part of her couldn't quite believe she was speaking so to Censor Siblea, but the dungeon was far, far away, and he needed her now. "Who among the Singers accompanied Iscarion in order to know *where* he went?"

Siblea put his hands out to his sides. "It is obvious. Where would he go but to a place filled with his beloved books? What else would he do but found an order dedicated to their preservation?"

"You *don't* know," she said.

Siblea shrugged. "No one can know for certain, it is true," he admitted. "But sometimes things really are as they appear."

As the sun brushed the horizon, the procession came to a halt. Haly and Siblea watched priests, subalterns, and common folk alike scramble to make their camps. As the sun set, the Plain of Ayor became a sea of firelight.

Siblea preceded her down the ladder that two of Michander's men held steady against the side of the elephant. Once on the ground, Gyneth's chorus was there to greet them, their faces flickering in the light of the campfire. In the manner that was becoming familiar to her, Siblea stood at her side and Michander came to her other side. Subaltern Chorus Five sang a song about welcoming the Holy One to blessed rest beneath the canopy of Song. Haly watched over her shoulder as the elephant knelt and men of Michander's chorus lowered the palanquin to the ground and positioned it in a place of prominence among the tents that circled the campfire.

If she could get away from the campfire she might be able to lose herself in the darkness. This was her best chance to escape, and they knew it. Even as she spotted the quickest path to the alley of darkness between their camp and the next, the chorus finished its song and Siblea took her elbow. He and Michander steered her toward the palanquin and bundled her through the door. Gyneth appeared with her trunk of clothing and followed her inside.

"Did you like our song, Holy One?" Gyneth murmured, placing the trunk in one corner. Without waiting for her to answer, he went on, "I see you Nod." He looked at her and quite deliberately placed his hand upon the trunk, and patted it once. "Your servant is most gratified that you were pleased with his paltry effort on your behalf."

She had the unmistakable impression that he was trying to tell her something—something that he couldn't just come out and say directly. Gyneth left and returned immediately with a basin of water and a covered necessary pot. He didn't speak again but simply locked the door behind him when he left and lowered the curtains on the palanquin to give her some privacy. Haly crept to the chest and opened it, peeking inside. It was dark in there, but she could just make out the gleam of a tiny pair of eyes, looking up at her from the folds of clothing.

"Story?" asked Nod in a soft voice.

So that's where Nod had gotten to. And Gyneth, who had packed her trunk, knew about it. "Stay quiet, Nod," she said. "Maybe I can tell you a story later, when the others have gone to sleep."

She left the lid of the chest open a crack, though she was not at all certain Nod needed to breathe. She had time to use the necessary pot and splash water on her face and arms before she heard Gyneth at the door of the palanquin. "Holy One? I must lift the curtains again. Are you ready?"

"Yes."

As he lifted the heavy fabric, a rich smell of lamb stew wafted in and she realized how hungry she was. She hadn't eaten since morning.

In addition to Haly's palanquin, four tents sat spaced around the campfire. Censor Siblea's tent was on her left, Orrin and Michander's tents were on her right, and the subaltern's tent sat almost directly opposite hers on the other side of the fire. Each of the censors sat on a stool in front of his tent as the subalterns served bowls of fragrant stew.

Gyneth brought Haly a bowl, handing it to her through the bars of her palanquin. She brushed her hands over his as she took the bowl from him. "Thank you," she said, hoping he would know that she meant it for more than just the food. Gyneth ducked his head and she saw him swallow as he returned to his fellow chorus members, who were gathered in a group near their tent.

Orrin's attendant, Thale, began to beat on a drum, softly at first and then harder. Another boy joined in with a flute, and a third strummed a stringed instrument that Haly could not identify. The others sang and danced. Their arms linked together, they kicked and jumped and spun, their firelit faces full of delight. This was an entirely different form of music than the choruses, and though it was intended as entertainment for Haly and the censors, it was clear that the boys were enjoying themselves immensely.

She realized she recognized the words. "Six-pack, Cadillac, give that god a phone, this cold hand is growing chrome."

It was an Ayorite nonsense rhyme; she didn't know why she was surprised, really. Most of these people were of Ayorite stock. In fact, everyone except the Ilysians and the Thesians were Ayorites, if you went back far enough. But what was really meant, when people said "Ayorite," was "peasant," and Haly simply had not made the connection between these Singer priests and the common folk from which they'd sprung.

They had been slaves. But many Ayorites and Thesians had been slaves of the Ancients, so much the same could be said of the Libyrarians. Haly thought of the song Siblea had sung her today about Iscarion. But if Iscarion had founded the community at the Libyrinth, that meant that Theselaides was a fraud.

On the other side of the fire, Gyneth linked arms with Thale and they spun in an ever-quickening circle. "My tin can, it has holes, it can tear your fancy clothes . . ." His brown hair fell across his face and the firelight gleamed in the sweat running down his neck. His eyes were bright; his smile, for once, unselfconscious. Haly smiled herself, in spite of everything.

It grew late. Haly and the censors finished their meal. The subalterns stopped dancing and fell upon the remains of the stew, eating hastily. Michander, Orrin, and Siblea retired to their tents, and Haly's guards lowered the curtains of her palanquin. She lay down on the soft rugs and tucked a pillow beneath her head. She only meant to lie still and wait until the others fell asleep, but she found herself awakened some indeterminate time later by tiny hands tugging at her hair. "What does she say? What does she say?"

Haly groaned. Who would think sitting in a moving box all day would be so exhausting? She opened her eyes. Nod had shoved the metal case containing Anne Frank's diary to the side of her makeshift bed and now perched upon it. "I'm tired," she complained, but the truth was, she loved listening to Anne go on about life in the Secret Annexe. She closed her eyes again and began to recite somewhere in the middle of the book—the lovely romantic part where Anne keeps meeting Peter in the attic. At some point Haly fell asleep and the

words worked their way into her dream, only it was she and
Gyneth in the attic, and outside the window was the Horn of
Yammon. She felt tiny ants crawling all over her and then she
and Gyneth and the house all dissolved into dust and blew
away across the Plain of Ayor, whispering as they went.

The Plain of Ayor had become one great city on the move.
While Haly slept, people came from every village of the
southern plain to join the pilgrimage of the Redeemer. Now it
was midmorning, and they were on the march, and Haly was
once again ensconced with Siblea atop the elephant.

*Now the time foretold has come, when Song and Word will
be as one. Righteous chorus lift each voice, the Redemption
is at hand, rejoice.*

As the people walked, they sang, and the cadence of their
song rolled in time with their strides and with the slow steady
gait of the elephant. It was a bright day, the vast blue sky as yet
only faintly smudged by the dust of their passage. Haly stared
at the thousands of faces—smiling, toiling, singing—and she
felt ill. They were depending on her for a miracle. Tales save
her.

She shut the curtain and turned to face Siblea. "What they
expect of me . . . I can't do it."

Siblea smiled at her. "And yet it will be done."

"I can't perform a miracle. The Redemption—what does it
even mean? They're expecting some kind of transcendent,
blissful union with the Song. I can't do that."

Siblea kept smiling at her.

"It's impossible," she said.

"That's why it is a miracle. And the wonderful thing about
miracles, my dear, is that they are open to interpretation.

Who is to say that an Egg in every village on the Plain of Ayor is not a miracle? And when their homes are warm this winter, who will lament that they are not one with the Song? The miracle of the Redemption is a beautiful story, of course, but beautiful stories do not keep one from freezing to death."

"But that is next winter, Censor. What about six days from now when I translate that cursed *Book of the Night* for you, and nothing happens? What will you do then, surrounded by your multitudes of faithful?"

Siblea gave her a smile. "Who is to say that a miracle will not occur? After all, you hear the voices of the murdered words. How is such a thing possible? It isn't. It is a miracle. Many things happen for which there is no explanation."

"But—"

"And as far as satisfying the multitudes, if they cannot have a miracle, then the utter destruction of the symbol of all that is evil will more than suffice."

Haly swallowed. "The Libyrinth."

Siblea nodded. "I believe you have seen the Horn of Yammon in operation. Don't worry. We will give your people a chance to leave before we use it."

"And what if I refuse to translate the book for you?"

Siblea sighed. "Then we will make you do it. You know that we can."

Dread filled her. She knew what he said was true. She swallowed and tried to calm herself. Pain, she told herself. It was only pain. Surely, she could endure it again?

A thought occurred to her. There was one way to render the Redemption impossible by anyone's definition. She ran her tongue around the insides of her teeth. A Redeemer without a tongue could not translate anything.

Siblea nodded to the metal box at Haly's side. "Perhaps the Holy One would indulge me with a recitation," he said.

Haly stared at him. "You want to hear more about Anne?"

"I am . . . curious," he admitted.

And if she could bring herself to do the thing she contemplated, this would be her last chance to read to anyone.

Like Gyneth, Siblea had many questions for her concerning Anne's world. She answered them as best she could, and as she made her way through the diary, she saw Siblea's sympathies change. At first he'd been suspicious of Anne because she read and wrote, despite Haly's assertion that such was true of nearly everyone in Anne's time. But by the time her voice gave out that afternoon, Siblea was equating the persecution of the Jews with the enslavement of the Singers, and eagerly suggesting strategies for the survival of Anne and her family. "They have electricity," he observed at one point. "They should electrify the doors so if the Germans come, they will be killed the moment they try to enter. Or perhaps Miep or Mr. Kugler could obtain rifles for them, and Peter and Pim and Mr. van Daan could watch from the attic, and pick off anyone who approaches."

That night when everyone had gone to sleep and her guards had lowered the curtains of her palanquin, Haly stuck her tongue out and clamped her teeth around it, as far back as she could get. She bit down.

Twenty minutes later all she'd accomplished was a sore tongue and the full knowledge of her own cowardice. She simply couldn't do it. She couldn't even break the skin. It was the pain that stopped her. She couldn't both feel the pain and cause the pain.

"Nod," she whispered, creeping to the chest that she left propped open just as she had the day before. "Nod. Are you there?"

"What does she say?" said Nod, crawling out of the chest and into her lap. He poked her knee impatiently. "What does she say?"

"Nod, I need you to do something for me."

Nod folded his arms across his little chest. "Story."

Her voice was hoarse from reciting to Siblea. Haly said, "I'll tell you a story about Mary Morey and now my story's begun. I'll tell another about her brother, and now my story is done."

Nod frowned. "She cheats," he grumbled. "But Nod heard all about the girl in the secret house today. Nod lies in the soft cloths and listens through the keyhole. So what does she want?"

"I need you to help me cut out my tongue, Nod."

The imp recoiled in horror. "Cut out her tongue!" he shrieked and she grabbed him and firmly closed her hand over his face.

"Be quiet," she whispered. "They'll hear you. Do you know what they'll do to you if they find you?"

Nod nodded and Haly released him. "But she must not do this thing," he said, his voice an urgent whisper. "She tells the stories. No tongue, no stories. No, no, no, no . . ."

Haly sighed and tried not to notice how relieved she was by Nod's refusal. If Nod would not help her, who could, or would? Gyneth? Even if she could convince him it needed to be done, when would they have the opportunity to do it?

A re they mad?" Siblea exclaimed. "They have already had how many suspicious break-ins? And now they are frolicking about the kitchen like children at a picnic. I don't like this."

It was the fifth day of the pilgrimage, and Haly had come to the part in Anne Frank's diary where the residents of the Secret Annexe, worn down by two years of hiding, all came downstairs to help wash and prepare an unexpected bounty of strawberries—the first fresh fruit they'd had in many months. "I could stop if you'd like," said Haly.

"No. No. If the Holy One's voice can withstand it, please go on."

She did not smile.

As the sun neared the horizon that afternoon, she finished Anne's last diary entry, and then she recited the afterword, which explained that Anne died in a concentration camp two months before the war ended. It was the second time she saw Siblea cry. "She didn't survive," he whispered.

Anger filled her—on behalf of Anne, on behalf of herself, and most of all, on behalf of the Libyrinth, which this man, who had the gall to be moved by Anne's words, would destroy. "No," she said, a quaver in her voice, "but she left her words behind, and because of them, we know her, and she lives in us. You will never forget her, because of these words," she placed her palm upon the box at her side. "These words that you say are dead, that you *burn* to liberate. How many Anne Franks have you silenced, Censor, because you cannot hear them? Because you are too stubborn to learn how to hear them?"

He appeared to be startled, though by her words or simply her vehemence she could not know. He steepled his fingers and sat for a moment in silence. "You make it sound so very simple," he said at last. "As if we were nothing but recalcitrant children unwilling to learn. We overcame centuries of slavery and oppression, and we did it with song. Why? Because song is what was available to us. You are mistaken. We did not choose song. The Song chose us."

Haly lay awake that night, her thoughts turning and turning in circles, and always coming back to the Libyrinth in ruins, its books burned or buried. She wouldn't do it. They would torture her. They would murder her friends and teachers, but she would not redeem *The Book of the Night* for them.

A vivid memory of Clauda screaming and contorting under the blows of a mind lancet ripped away her resolve the moment she'd formed it.

But if she refused to recite or was unable to recite, the Libyrinth would be safe. Or would it? The secret of making Eggs was all that really mattered to the Eradicants. Once they had *The Book of the Night* in their possession, they could take it and her anywhere they chose, and destroy the Libyrinth anyway. No. She was thinking about this the wrong way around.

For all their talk of miracles, these Singers were practical people. They had the horn, and an Egg to power it. That, as much as this Redemption of theirs, was the reason for this pilgrimage. If only there was a way to destroy the horn, or at least prevent it from working. But she was too closely guarded to try to sabotage it herself, and she could not ask it of Gyneth. Maybe Nod.

She sat up and threw off the blanket, welcoming the night chill and its invigorating effect. "Nod," she whispered, "I'll tell you a story."

Nod crept from the chest and scrambled to her knee. He climbed up and perched himself there and looked up at her with his tiny red face. "What does she say?"

Haly took a breath against the tension that filled her. This had to work. She gazed upon the little creature, wondering how best to reach his tiny, alien mind. She swallowed, and began. "She says, 'Once upon a time there was a Nod, a child of the Libyrinth. But Nod was sad, because the Libyrinth, which was both his mother and his home, was broken.' Do you know why, Nod?"

The homunculus nodded sadly. "Heart is missing."

"Yes. The Libyrinth's heart was stolen by bad singer-beasties who want to destroy Nod's mother-home. They took her heart and put it in the Big Metal Noise Tube."

Nod was scandalized. "What does she say!?"

"They will use the Libyrinth's own heart to destroy her."

Nod stared at her. She could not read what was in the depths of his black eyes, but at length he said, "She still saying story?"

"She is saying Nod's story."

His eyes grew wide and he leaned back, his face filled with wonder. "Nod's story?"

"Yes. Nod can save the Libyrinth by stealing her heart back from the Big Metal Noise Tube."

"She give Nod his own story?" Awe and delight glittered in his black eyes. "She give Nod his own story."

The next thing Haly knew, little hands clutched at her neck and she tried not to flinch as she felt a tiny kiss on her chin. "Nod make great story," he whispered eagerly. "Best story. She be glad she gave Nod this story!"

He scrambled from her lap and to the bars of the palanquin. He was just able to squeeze between them, and then he lifted the bottom edge of the curtain, ducked beneath it, and was gone.

Haly stared though the bars of the palanquin as the elephant lurched along, surrounded by hordes of the Righteous Chorus. It might have been her imagination, but she found the beast's gait labored on this sixth day, and the voices of the people sounded weary instead of joyous. She was searching for Nod, or some evidence of his mission, though she knew how unlikely it was she would find any.

Siblea shut the curtains, plunging the interior of the palanquin into dusty dimness. What now? Her heart beat a little faster and she swallowed against a sudden dryness in her throat. She turned to face him.

His face was pale in the gloom, his mouth tight with agitation, his eyes bright. "There is more than one chorus of thought among us concerning the sin of literacy, you know." His voice was accusatory—no, defensive.

Haly stared at him and said nothing.

"Many, like Michander and his Chorus of Soldiers, believe that text itself is an evil thing, with the power to corrupt those who come into contact with it." He paused.

"And what about you, Censor?" she asked. "Where does the evil of literacy reside for you?"

He studied her a long time before answering. "Where all evil resides, in human frailty."

She blinked. It wasn't what she'd expected.

Siblea continued, "Iscarion's sin was not in writing down the testimony of the last Ancient, but in denying that information to Yammon. It is the human failings of pride and greed that make books dangerous." His gaze strayed to the box at her side. "For one who is disciplined, who has purified his mind through the Song over the course of a lifetime, there is little risk."

Excitement quickened her pulse. Perhaps she'd gotten to him after all. "One such as yourself, Censor?"

His eyes glittered. "I must admit, I am curious."

Haly dared not speak. It was as if a rare bird had suddenly landed upon her hand. Any movement at all might frighten it off.

Siblea's hand went to his neck and pulled free a long chain from which hung a key. He stared at her. "Will you tell anyone, I wonder?"

"If I do, you will deny it. They will believe you if you say I hate you, and wish to get you killed."

He nodded. "Very well," he said, and he unlocked the box. "Ah," he murmured as he lifted the book out and held it in his hands. Gingerly he opened it. For a long time he stared at the pages. "So that is what murdered words look like. In truth, they do look broken."

"I can teach you to read them, Censor."

He glanced at her and smiled. "That, I think, would be going too far." But he stared at the words for some time before finally placing the book back in the box and relocking it.

"What if everyone had access to the knowledge in books?" she asked. "Then there would be no pride or greed in literacy— no sin."

"That is impossible."

She shook her head. "Difficult, maybe, but not impossible."

Siblea lifted the curtain of the palanquin and waved at the multitudes outside. He dropped the curtain again. "You would teach each and every one of them."

"I would teach you and Michander and all the priests and subalterns, and you would teach them."

"But what is the good of reading to those who have no books? Don't tell me the great scholars of the Libyrinth will welcome such as these with open arms. No. You may not believe me, but I sympathize with you. Unfortunately, what you propose is impossible."

He had a point, but if ever there was a time when she could change the Libyrarians' minds on that subject, it would be when she had the entire Singer nation at her back. It was only the faintest whisper of a hope, but it was more than she ever thought she'd feel again. She smiled at Siblea. "That is why it is a miracle," she said.

17

The Other Half of the Plan

Iknow you are doing all you can to help me," Clauda told Adept Ymin Ykobos after their session. She'd had another seizure earlier that day. Despite everything Ymin and Po and Helene did for her, they were coming more frequently.

Ymin looked grim. There were dark circles under her eyes and Clauda wondered if she was getting any sleep at all. She stood and went to the glow warmer and prepared another pot of tea. "Helene, we're out of mint, would you fetch some from the kitchen, please?"

The girl nodded and left.

"Are you sure your queen does not mind you devoting so much time to an Ayorite servant?" Clauda asked Ymin.

That won her a sharp glance over the adept's shoulder. Clauda had been at this for a couple of days now, making little comments about the adept putting her patients' welfare above all else. Saying anything she could think of to make Ymin feel guilty about not using the wing to heal her. She didn't have much time left, though. The army must be almost in position. Soon Jolaz would take the wing and the army to the Corvariate Citadel, along with all of Clauda's hopes. "It's not fair of her, if you ask me," Clauda went on. "The queen, I mean. Asking you to cure me. I'm not dismissing kinesiology, but surely it has its limits. It seems to me she's asking you to do something you were never meant to do." Like spy for her; like be her prison guard.

Ymin's back was to Clauda, but she saw her square her shoulders. "This is ridiculous," she said. She turned around. "I will not stand by while a patient who can be treated slips into decline."

Decline? She was declining? Ykobos's words nearly set off another seizure, but Clauda firmly clamped her mind around the image of Selene in the library, and breathed, and breathed, and the trembling lessened, though it was never altogether gone anymore. She was declining.

". . . not when the means of treatment are at hand," finished Ykobos. She leaned forward. "Clauda, what I am about to propose is . . ." She glanced about the room nervously, then went to the door, shut it, and returned. The adept leaned close to Clauda and spoke in the barest of whispers. "I know of something that might help you, but it must be done in secret."

Clauda's pulse quickened. "It sounds dangerous."

Ymin studied her closely. "It is. I wouldn't even suggest it but we've tried everything else. If my traditional methods of therapy were going to work, they would have by now."

Clauda nodded her understanding, pressing firmly down on the mix of excitement and panic that welled up inside her. It occurred to her that for once, the queen's policy of secrecy might backfire. Ymin probably did not know of the plan for the army to follow the wing. "I would be grateful for anything you can do for me."

Ymin crossed her arms. Her body was rigid with tension. "There is a device of the Ancients. Most consider it a weapon of great power, but it also has great power to heal. I have used it many times to mend those who have been broken by its violent side. But the queen suspects you. She has asked me to report to her anything you say that might relate to state secrets or to your involvement with the chambermaid Scio."

Poor Scio. Clauda did her very best not to react, grateful for once that Ymin's treatments left her too exhausted to move.

Ymin stood and began to pace. "Which you have not done, even when you were unconscious and babbling about *The Book of the Night* and the princess's childhood copy of *Theselaides*."

Clauda pretended to experience a tremor, and said nothing.

"It might be different if you were an enemy of our nation, but you are clearly not," continued Ymin. "And still the queen is content to let you suffer and to make me complicit in your fate. I am not a jailor or an inquisitor, and the wi—the device is not a machine of war. It is much more than that."

"You think this device can help me?"

Ymin's lips compressed into a thin, flat line. "I can make no guarantees to you, Clauda of Ayor, but yes, I believe it can. You more than most.

"Some people's energy systems are more fluid than others. Such people, like yourself, are particularly susceptible to the effects of a mind-lancet attack, and are very difficult to treat with kinesiology. As soon as we balance one part of your system, it starts working overtime to correct the other imbalances in your system, and pretty soon it falls out of balance again from overwork and we're right back where we started again. However, the very fluidity that presents such a problem to us makes you an ideal candidate for this treatment."

"That's wonderful."

Ymin held up a hand. "But there is another danger."

"Other than being caught by the queen and 'transferred to the summer palace'? What is it?"

"When you are within the mantle of the goddess, enmeshed with the device, you will experience a phenomenon we call flow lines. If you leave them be, they will not harm you. But if you try to manipulate them, if you try to operate the device through them, and fail . . . In your condition, they may kill you."

It was done in the dead of night. Ymin and Po put Clauda on a litter and covered her with a blanket. "If anyone stops us, wail for all you're worth, but don't push off the blanket," said Ymin. "We are pretending that you are Sergeant Bilos tonight, you understand?"

Clauda nodded.

They were stopped only once, at the entrance to the cavern. Clauda wailed and moaned for all she was worth. She even threw a few barks in for good measure. "Poor Bilos," she heard the guard mutter as they passed.

Clauda could see a little bit through the weave of the blanket—enough to make out the shape of the wing. She breathed a sigh of relief. She'd been afraid she'd miscalculated, and that the device Ymin spoke of really was something else. She saw Ymin place a hand on the side of the wing and a door appeared. They carried her inside.

Once inside the wing, Po drew the blanket from Clauda's face and she looked about eagerly. It was a small chamber, with curving golden walls. She'd expected to see a pilot's seat, and a steering device of some sort, and a window to look out of, but there was none of that. There was only a life-size statue of a woman in the center of the room made of the same golden-colored metal as the rest of the wing.

Adept Ykobos stood before the statue. "Mighty Queen, mother of Ilysies, blessed, brave Belrea, open for your daughters, bathe us in the light of your righteousness." She leaned forward and kissed the statue on the forehead, lips, and belly.

Clauda gasped as the statue parted before the now-kneeling adept, and brilliant light like a thousand spring mornings dawning all at once flooded forth from inside and inundated the chamber.

Po put a hand to Clauda's shoulder. "You'll need to stand, but only for a moment. Once you are inside, it won't matter to you."

"I-i-inside?"

He nodded. "Don't be afraid. I've seen this done many times. It will help you. You'll feel much better."

Clauda nodded shakily and let him help her to stand. He supported her as she stumbled toward Ymin, who still knelt on the floor. Po positioned Clauda so that she was between Ymin and the statue, facing Ymin.

The adept stood and gripped Clauda's trembling shoulders as Po retreated. "Daughter of the plain," said Ymin, "receive the blessing of the first queen, Belrea, mother of Ilysies." And she shoved Clauda back into the streaming light, into the open statue.

Clauda felt as if a million tiny hands caught her. Warm, tingling fingertips seemed to be everywhere upon her, gentling her free from her initial panic, soothing and surrounding her with ease, with a relaxation so complete and deep that she was barely aware that she had a body at all. She could not recall ever being this comfortable in her entire life. All she saw was the light around her, and in it, perhaps, some rosy shapes not readily made out, patterns or spirals, fleeting and subtle. She was so relieved not to be trembling that she couldn't really be bothered to pursue them.

And then the light faded and the tingling stopped, and large, rough hands pulled at her and jostled her and carried her with jarring, monstrous steps to the litter, then laid her upon its hard, scratchy surface. Wait, that was it? She was supposed to steal the wing! There'd been no time. Where had the flow lines been? She'd been so taken with the pleasure of being free of her symptoms, she'd lost her chance to save her friends. "No!" she cried out, unable to stop herself. "No, put me back in, please!"

"Don't worry," said Po. "We will. This was just the first time. Look. Look how much better you are already."

Clauda flexed her fingers, and her toes. She sat up. She held her hand in front of her face and saw that it was steady.

Ymin examined her from head to toe, tracing the energy pathways up and down her spine and arms and legs that were by now familiar to Clauda. The adept gave a sigh of satisfaction. "Your body has responded well to the therapy," she said. "You should be able to get some sleep now, and I recommend that you do. The relief from the tremors will be temporary at first. I'll do my best to get you back in here again tomorrow."

The next night, as soon as she was inside the statue, surrounded and supported by the wonderful light and warmth, Clauda gave her full attention to the vague shapes that wound through the light like faint wisps of rose-colored smoke. They danced the way light does on the surface of undulating water.

They seemed to sense her presence, gathering around her

like curious children. But every time she tried to get a really good look at one of them, it shied away, only to come closer again when she focused on a different one. Understanding quickened her heart. They wanted to come to her, not the other way around.

As time passed the shapes became more distinct, resolving into curving, swirling lines like the ones on the outside of the wing. In her excitement Clauda reached out with her mind and tried to touch one of them, to see if she could bend it. Pain sliced through her, hot and cold, and the line broke. She suddenly found herself facedown on the floor of the wing's cabin, paralyzed by a full-body muscle cramp.

"What did you do?" Ymin Ykobos scolded her even as she massaged Clauda's limbs. "You tried to manipulate the flow, didn't you? I told you keep your eyes closed. Don't interfere with the flow lines. Stronger minds than yours have tried to master them, and failed, and always with the same result. Even the heir had difficulty at first. Many a time I had to treat her for going too far too quickly with the flow lines. They are not tools to be operated, nor powers to command. They command us. We are their tools. Remember that the next time."

Clauda managed a nod and a hoarse croak of assent. Ymin and Po worked on her for another half an hour or so, and then Ymin asked the statue for permission for Clauda to enter once again. The statue opened.

"Now remember, leave the lines alone," admonished the adept as she pushed Clauda backward into the all-welcoming warmth.

Immediately her tremors stopped. Comfort and warmth spread through her exhausted body and the flow lines appeared, more vivid than ever. But this time, instead of imagining herself reaching out to touch them, she imagined letting them touch her. The swirling, curling threads wound around and into her, meeting her nerve endings and melding with them. Ecstasy consumed her like a replenishing fire, awakening an almost unbearable awareness. She was no longer Clauda, kitchen scrub of the Libyrinth. She was a great golden curve of living metal, a wing poised for flight. She'd known pleasure before, but never anything like this.

The experience was all-consuming. She did not know how long she remained in contact with the flow lines; she was only aware of a time during which gravity was a small, inconsequential thing, and she yearned for the sky. And then, too soon, it was over and it wasn't until she was back in the litter and being carried out by Po and Ymin that she remembered her mission.

"You are so much better now," said Ymin the following morning after examining her. Clauda didn't need to be told. She felt better. Worlds better. She could sit up, as she was now, in her bed, with her robe on. She could also stand, even walk a few paces about the room, all on her own. She was free from pain and all but the most minor tremors. It was almost enough to overcome her fear for Selene and Haly, her guilt over Scio, and her grief at having missed her second opportunity to steal the wing.

Ymin smiled happily as she set the kettle on the glow warmer for tea. "I think we can go back to traditional treatment methods for you now," she said.

Anxiety spiked through Clauda, causing her to gasp. But she really was better; she didn't have to fight off a seizure at those words. Still, she felt hollow with dread. "Are you sure? So soon?"

"Yes, unless you have another relapse. It is as I suspected. You have a very sensitive nervous system. It responded quickly. It's really just a matter of retraining your energy pathways now. They're no longer in trauma—just out of practice."

Clauda fought back tears and reminded herself that she was supposed to be happy about this news. Belatedly, she replaced her stricken expression with a smile. "That's wonderful," she said. Her voice was faint.

Ymin frowned. "Aren't you pleased?"

"Of course I am. I just . . . I . . ." Her mind raced. "I can't help but wonder what will happen to me now."

Ymin drew herself up and nodded, her frown deepening. "Oh, that. Don't worry. I've told the queen that even in the greatest extremity, you never once revealed anything suspicious. Whatever Scio's activities were, you were not involved and now she knows that."

Clauda, her stomach in knots, nodded. "Oh. That's good."

Ymin smiled at her and nodded. Her expression took on a sad quality. "In any event, the device won't be available to me anymore after tomorrow, so your recovery is timely."

Clauda fought to breathe against the weight of grief and guilt that was pressing down on her. She'd failed everyone. She slid down on the bed and put her head on her pillow. "I'm tired," she said. She stared at the books on the bedside table: Volume I of *Queen Belrea and the Wing of Tarsus* and *The Book of the Night* in disguise. She'd failed. She took *Theselaides* from the table and held it to her, then turned to face the wall so Ymin couldn't see her face. Scio was probably dead because of her. Selene soon would be, and Tales only know what was happening with Haly. What was wrong with her? She'd been in the wing twice! She'd failed.

She trembled and felt that familiar pins-and-needles feeling in her hands and her feet. For once she welcomed the pain. Maybe it wasn't too late. Clauda closed her eyes and let all the thoughts she had not permitted herself rush to the front of her mind at once.

Haly is being tortured, she thought. *All of this time, while I*

*loll about the palace, my best friend is enduring horrible
agony—everything that happened to us in the vault and more.
Things I can't even imagine. Not to mention that she's probably been raped any number of times by now.*

And Selene. Selene will die. In her mind's eye Clauda saw
her lying on the floor of the Great Hall, blood spreading in a
pool all around her, her great dark eyes staring up, vacant and
dead.

The tingling in her hands and feet grew stronger. It was
working, but she couldn't afford to stop now.

*Selene will die because I was unable to help her. I was
supposed to come up with the other half of the plan and I've
failed. And Scio. Scio is dead because of me. And who knows
what Thela did to her before executing her. Surely she was
questioned and tortured, and it's my fault.*

*Even what I'm doing right now; it's half-assed. How is
Ymin going to get me into the wing tonight? What if Sergeant
Bilos has recovered? What will she tell the guards? It's a
guess. That's the best I can do for my friends; a lousy guess.
And what if I'm wrong?*

Fire raced from Clauda's fingertips to her spine and back
again. Even with her eyes closed, she saw the gray flies clus-
tering around her.

*I'm never going to see Haly or Selene again. And the
Libyrinth will be destroyed, and it's all my fault. I pride
myself on being such an accomplished gossip, and yet I did
nothing while my friends suffered and died.*

She heard someone approaching the bed and she smelled
the familiar lavender and camphor smell of Adept Ykobos,
but she couldn't open her eyes. The fire in her limbs was
replaced by numbness as her muscles started to lock up.

*And if I hadn't opened my big fat mouth and put ideas in
Haly's head, none of us would have ever left the Libyrinth in*

the first place. Haly wouldn't have been captured by the Eradicants, Selene wouldn't have been sent to her death. My uncle and my father and my mother wouldn't die in the destruction of the Libyrinth. Everyone I've ever known and loved is going to die and it's all my fault.

The next thing Clauda was aware of was the jostling of the litter as she was carried on it, covered by a blanket. The disguised *Book of the Night* was still clutched in her arms. They'd been unable to pry it from her grip. Good.

"Will we be able to get in, Adept?" It was Po's voice.

"I don't know," said Ymin. "We'll say it's Sergeant Bilos again and hope for the best."

They came at last to the cavern entrance. "Are you awake?" Ymin asked, leaning over the litter.

"Yes," Clauda's whisper was hoarse.

"Make a lot of noise, as awful as you can make it."

Clauda moaned and wailed and thrashed about, careful not to dislodge the blanket or lose her grip on the book. She arched her back and threw back her head and made the grunting, barking noises that had so humiliated her when she'd been aware of them in the past.

Ymin knocked on the door.

"Who's there?" said a voice on the other side.

"Adept Ykobos, with Sergeant Bilos, for treatment," said Ymin.

The door opened. Clauda saw the vague form of a woman in the white tunic of a soldier. Ymin took a step back. "Sergeant Bilos!" she cried, and Clauda knew she was not describing her, but addressing the soldier.

"Who's that?" said Sergeant Bilos.

Clauda threw off the blanket, leaped from the litter, and ran headlong through the door. She swept past the guard before the woman could react. Behind her she heard the clatter of the litter hitting the floor and more footsteps, but she didn't dare look to see if Po and Ymin followed her or if the guard was giving pursuit.

She reached the wing unimpeded. She placed her hand on its side and risked a look behind her. Po was almost upon her, followed by Ymin, and then Sergeant Bilos, disentangling herself from the litter as she ran.

The door to the wing irised open and Clauda leaped through. She went to the statue, rushing through the incantation she'd heard Ymin make: "Mighty Queen, mother of Ilysies, blessed, brave Belrea, open for your daughter, bathe me in the light of your righteousness." She kissed the statue on the forehead, lips, and belly.

Po climbed inside the wing just as the statue was opening. Clauda turned so that her back was to the streaming light. He didn't try to stop her or pull her away. He reached through the doorway and as Clauda fell backward into the light she caught a glimpse of Ymin, climbing into the cabin.

Now all Clauda was aware of was a warm glow surrounding her. The fear, tension, the rush of the chase were gone and she was in a space of light, supported effortlessly by the millions of tiny tendrils of illumination inside the statue in the wing.

The waving lines and spirals appeared to her, and she let them in. It was even easier than it had been before. They soaked in and wound through her and she became one with the wing.

It wanted to fly, and so did she. Together they heard the mouth of the cave like the call of infinity. Gravity let go and they rose smoothly off the floor of the cave and glided through the mouth, out over the ocean which was now an undulating mass whose crests were the taste of salt, and whose hollows were the bite of wind, and all of it blue with the ebb and flow of life. And above was the sky; a great emptiness that smelled like joy and sounded like freedom. And it was blue, too—the blue of flying.

18

The First Redemption

They reached the Libyrinth at dawn on the seventh day of their journey. The sun tinged the dome and spires of the ancient library with pink and gold, and Haly remembered the morning of the Eradication. The banners atop the spires fluttered in the wind like the flames that had devoured Charlotte and Wilbur. How solid those curving sandstone walls had seemed to her then, but now she knew they could be disintegrated by a single blast from the Horn of Yammon, which loomed at the back of the procession. The Libyrinth, which had been her whole world, was not even as big as the Temple of Yammon, a small, frail thing compared to the great fortress of the Corvariate Citadel.

The Singers and their entourage circled the domed structure. Haly and Siblea got down from the elephant and the palanquin was lowered to the ground. Orrin stood at the front gate, waiting for them. Siblea and Michander led her to him.

The old man looked her over critically. "Mmm," he said and looked at Siblea. "Where is her hood?"

The Redemption hood. It was a black head covering, trimmed with gold ribbon around the edges. She had seen Gyneth pack it before they left the citadel.

Siblea went into the palanquin and opened the clothes chest. Fearing he would discover Nod, Haly held her breath. But Nod was not there. Neither was the hood.

"I am sorry, High Censor," said Siblea. "It is not here. He turned to the subalterns, gathered nearby. "Gyneth, did you pack it?"

"Yes, Censor."

"Maybe it is at the bottom," said Michander, and he joined Siblea in rummaging through the chest. Haly bit her lips to keep from laughing at the spectacle.

"Enough!" said Orrin. "Forget about the hood. We will do without it."

Siblea and Michander shut the chest, straightened their robes, and led Haly to the front gate. For a moment there, she'd had the mad hope that they wouldn't go through with this—that they'd turn back due to insufficient headgear. But no, of course not. Orrin himself raised the great ring on the door and let it fall. It made a sound like the earth cracking in half.

Though the Libyrarians must have spotted them a long way off, it was some time before the window in the door opened. Haly could just make out Griome's face as he shouted, his voice thin on the ever-present wind of the plain. "What do you want? You were just here three weeks ago!"

Three weeks? Was that all it had been?

"We are here for *The Book of the Night*, borne here by your Libyrarian Selene," said Michander. "The time of the Redemption has come, and we will not be turned away."

"There is no *Book of the Night*," countered Griome. "I

gave you the map to the vault. If you did not find it there, then it does not exist."

"Do not lie, Griome," said Orrin. "We know the book was recovered by the Libyrarian Selene. We know she has brought it here. If you do not admit us, we will unleash this multitude upon you, and if they cannot overwhelm your battlements, the Horn of Yammon will turn the Libyrinth to dust and we will sort through the rubble to get what we want."

There was a pause as Griome looked out upon the sea of humanity that surrounded the Libyrinth in every direction, and upon the vaulting curve of the horn. His eyes flicked to Haly's with an unreadable look, and he opened the gate and let them enter.

"The first hour of the war between Kalgan and Foundation"; "The calm of the night was broken by a roar of thunder, and something smote the water"; "The courtship display of the male Common Goldeneye looks much like an avian slapstick routine." The voices of the books flooded in upon her, a multitude even greater than that which surrounded the Libyrinth. Only these were voices without bodies—defenseless.

Led by Orrin and Siblea, Haly stepped inside the Great Hall. All around the edges of the hall Libyrarians stood with their backs to the shelves, a human barricade between the Eradicants and the books. Haly spotted Palla, Jan, Peliac, and Selene. Everyone but Clauda. Even Kitchenmaster Sakal was there, holding a cast-iron cooking spit in his meaty hands. If it was possible, she missed every one of these people more in this moment than she had the entire time she'd been gone. A sob broke through Haly's reserve and she wanted to run to Palla and hide in her robes, but she stayed where she was, and though the room wavered from the tears she could not stop, she allowed herself to be maneuvered to a position directly in front of the console and facing the main gate.

Haly, Siblea, and Orrin were followed by Gyneth's chorus

carrying the palanquin. Behind them came Michander and a chorus of twenty soldiers, and then a chorus of twenty memorizers. Gyneth's group set the palanquin down midway between the central console and the southern alcove, to Haly's right. The Chorus of Memorizers bolted the gate shut once again and stood before it in rows three deep, ready for her recitation. Michander and his men took up positions in a loose ring about the hall, their rifles trained upon the Libyrarians and servants.

"Where is the Libyrarian Selene?" demanded Orrin.

"I am here," said Selene, stepping forward with a book in her hands—a book with a green cover. "I am Theselaides, and these are my words," it said. In spite of everything, a wave of relief swept over Haly. Selene had switched the books. Oh, clever Selene.

Selene gave her a reassuring smile as she stepped up to Orrin and handed him the book. He turned to Haly, a bright smile taking ten years from his face. "The Redemption can begin," he said.

They all stared at her. The Singers were waiting for her to recite *The Book of the Night*. Only this wasn't *The Book of the Night*. What would they do when she began to recite Theselaides to them? Well, and they had never read *The Book of the Night*, so how would they know the difference?

In fact, she could say anything she wanted to. She could just make it all up. Did she dare? She'd dared a great deal already. Why stop now? She took a deep breath, opened her mouth, and said, "I am the Literate Iscarion, and these are my words: We have overthrown our masters. On this day, the first day of our nation, my brother Yammon has led us to victory and the Corvariate Citadel is ours. Our time of darkness is over. Everywhere, the Righteous Chorus celebrates. All but I, who labor here to bring the light of this day into the future, for you who are waiting."

She paused as the first tier of memorizers moved to the back, muttering her words and casting them into song, and a fresh row of Singers faced her, awaiting the rest of her fabrication. Selene stared at her, mystified. Orrin looked expectant; Siblea, of all things, looked proud. And she caught sight of Gyneth, standing with Thale beside the palanquin, his eyes shining. She swallowed and plunged on, wondering how long she could keep this up. "I know this time will not last. Our people embrace in the streets as one, but it is the fate of all lasting joy to become commonplace, and soon the old enmities will rise again. Already there are those who whisper to my brother against me, painting me a would-be master, greedy and hoarding of knowledge. I would have taught reading to Yammon and all the others long ago if time and the Ancients had permitted it."

Orrin grew restless. He exchanged glances with Michander, who readjusted his grip on his rifle.

"But now all will learn. I will seize this peace, temporary as it might be, and I will make of it all that I and Yammon and the Song and the Word can. We have some Ancients still alive in the building that will become our new temple, and I have volunteered to question them. Much as the thought of taking up the masters' tools sickens me, I insisted I be the one to do it, and do it alone. I will write down what they tell me. But I will not speak their words, for if the secrets of the Ancients can only be known by reading, then surely all will eagerly learn to read."

The Great Hall was silent. Presumably the Libyrarians, who knew *The Book of the Night* was a fake, were just as stunned by the scope of her fabrication as the Singers were shocked by its content.

"The sudden appearance of a tiger is arresting in any environment," said a book.

Haly met Selene's gaze, her mistress desperately searching

her face, trying to determine what she was about. Next to her, Censor Orrin frowned deeply. "Skip to where he talks about the Eggs," he whispered.

Haly's already rapid pulse sped up even more. Skip to the part about the Eggs. She couldn't do that, and Selene knew it. Haly looked at her mistress, pleading silently for her to have a plan. Anything. Selene blinked once, then looked to a woman among the kitchen folk who was unfamiliar to Haly. She was tall and broad, with a red kerchief tied about her head. It seemed unlikely she was a new addition to the staff. Was she one of Selene's women?

Selene's nod was nearly imperceptible, but Haly saw the woman acknowledge it, and slowly lift her hand to adjust her kerchief.

It must have been a signal. From the balcony behind Haly there came a loud bang, like a heavy piece of metal striking stone. With a cry, Orrin twisted and fell. There was a red hole in his temple, and more blood flowed out from the other side of his head, pooling on the marble floor. All the Libyrarians had turned to the shelves the moment the sound was heard, and now they turned around again, holding rifles. People dressed in white ran along the balcony, also carrying rifles.

More sharp, loud bangs sounded as the Libyrarians opened fire upon the Singers. People screamed and ran. Groil and Yabir, two men who had been with Michander when he came to the vault, fell under the hail of bullets, and others were wounded.

The Chorus of Memorizers, unarmed, turned and ran for the front gate, but they were blocked by the Libyrinth servants, who met them with frying pans, pitchforks, and fists. Haly saw Sakal laying about with his cooking spit. Hephaestus wrenched it from his grasp and dealt Sakal a staggering blow to the side of his head.

By now, the soldiers were firing back at the Libyrarians.

The sound was deafening. Haly saw Frise fall because of a shot to her chest, and beside her, Breal dropped his weapon and knelt at her side. An instant later, a bullet struck him in the neck and he fell on top of her.

"S-stop it," said Haly, but her voice was no more than a whisper. She was shaking. "Stop it!" she shouted, but her voice couldn't be heard over the screams and the gunfire. She turned to Selene and Siblea. She grabbed both of them by the arms. "Tell them to stop it!"

They both looked at her, and then each tried to push her down and cover her at the same time. "Leave her alone!" shouted Selene.

"I'm trying to save her life, you ignorant lit!" he yelled back.

Haly twisted free of both of them and crouched beside the console. She scanned the Great Hall for Gyneth, and could not see him, but everywhere she looked, people were killing and dying. From the balcony, figures in white fired down upon the Singer soldiers with weapons that shot blue arcs of fire. Who were those people?

At the main gate the memorizers were trying to get past the Libyrinth servants to open the doors, but were being repelled.

"The doors! We have to take the doors!" Michander shouted to his men. "Golray, you and your tenors cover the rest of us." They did, firing at the people on the balcony as the others advanced on the Libyrarians. The soldiers were outnumbered, but they were more experienced fighters. In the vanguard, Michander swung his mind lancet and people scattered.

"Night was striding across nothingness with the whole round world in his hands," added the same book.

Finally Haly spotted Gyneth near the palanquin, retrieving a rifle from a fallen soldier. Thale reached for the soldier's mind lancet and then fell back as he was shot. He clutched at his belly, red blood streaming around his hands as he sank to the floor. She saw Gyneth's mouth move as he watched his friend fall, but she couldn't hear what he said in the din of gunfire and screaming. Gyneth raised the rifle and aimed it at Selene, who was still wrestling with Siblea and spitting epithets at him.

"Get down!" Haly screamed. She leaped up, pushed Selene to the floor, and then fell on top of her. Beside them, Siblea muttered a curse and attempted to shield Haly with his own body.

Near as she could tell, Gyneth missed all three of them. Beneath her, Selene grunted and then gasped as she saw Siblea draped over Haly's back. "Get off of her!" she shouted, scrabbling for the knife at her belt.

"It's okay," said Haly. "He's just trying to keep me from getting shot."

But the sounds of fighting had stopped. Siblea got off her, brushing off his robes. Haly and Selene untangled themselves from each other and Selene immediately drew her knife and turned toward Siblea. Haly leaped between them. "No," she said. "We may need him."

Someone ran up and the three of them very nearly threw themselves on the floor again. It was the woman in the red kerchief. She lowered her rifle when she spotted Selene. "Your Grace, we have the survivors surrounded." Though she spoke to Selene she kept a watchful eye on Siblea.

Siblea gave a deep sigh. "It would seem you have won, for now," he observed.

It was quiet but for some sporadic moaning and crying. Black-clad bodies lay scattered on the floor of the Great Hall. In most cases it was impossible to tell which were Libyrarians and which Singers, but Haly did spot Michander on his back five feet from the console, his empty blue eyes fixed on the dome above.

"What is the purpose of reason, Richard Parker?" asked a book.

Selene reluctantly resheathed her knife and took Haly by the shoulders, holding her at arm's length and scanning her anxiously. "Are you all right?" she asked, lifting one hand to trace a finger along the scar on Haly's cheek.

Haly blinked and shifted away from the touch. "I'm fine. Selene, who are all those people in white? Where did the Libyrarians get all these rifles? And where's Clauda? Is she okay?"

"Clauda is in Ilysies. The women in white are Ilysian soldiers. I brought the rifles along with the soldiers." Selene still stared at Haly, her jaw working. Suddenly she pulled her into a fierce hug that forced the breath from Haly's lungs. "We were always trying to get you back," said Selene. "You have to know that."

Tears threatened to overwhelm Haly. She tucked her face into Selene's shoulder and breathed in the comforting, familiar smell of wool, sweat, and old paper. In spite of everything that had happened and would happen, she was home again. Haly would have liked to stay wrapped in those arms forever, encircled, protected, safe. But it was an illusion. None of them was safe.

The Ilysians and the Libyrarians had herded the remaining Singers into a tight knot midway between the console and the main gate and now stood around them in a ring, their rifles at the ready. There were no more than twenty Singers left standing. "What do you wish done with the survivors, Your Grace?" asked the woman in the red kerchief.

Haly looked to Selene. "Tell her to keep them under guard," said Haly, afraid Selene might order them to be executed.

"How? Where will we keep them?" Selene scanned the Great Hall, doing her own tally of the dead.

Haly had not yet spotted Gyneth, but she had spotted Jan among the Libyrarians on guard. Her gaze fell on the palanquin, which was still standing. It would be very tight quarters indeed, but they'd be alive, at least, and it would be easy to guard them there. "Put them in the palanquin," she said.

"That cage?" said Selene. "Is that what they kept you in?"

"It's a palanquin," said Haly. "It went on top of an elephant."

"It looks like a cage."

Haly stared at Selene. Suddenly she wanted to smack the look of pity right off her face. She didn't want Selene's pity or protection or righteous anger. She'd done just fine up to now not thinking about certain things, and right now there were much more important things to think about than scars and cages. "Then use it," she said.

Selene blinked, and then looked at the woman in the red kerchief and nodded.

The Singers, though vastly outnumbered, had put up a fierce struggle. Ten Libyrarians were dead, among them Frise and Breal. The servants had fared somewhat better—six of them had died, including Sakal. Twenty or more folk of the Libyrinth were wounded, some mortally. No Ilysians were killed, but three were wounded. Of the Chorus of Memorizers, only two had survived. Ten of Michander's soldiers still lived, though two of them were not expected to see another sunrise. And of Subaltern Chorus Five nine remained, including Gyneth.

The combined smells of blood, gunpowder, and electricity coated the back of Haly's throat as she made her way to the palanquin, which was now packed with Singers. Her clothes chest sat a little distance from it, having been moved to make room for the prisoners. It looked odd and forlorn, sitting there amid the wreckage of the battle. She should carry it upstairs to Selene's room, but the mundane task seemed irrelevant now.

The Singers had been given water and bread, but there was no other comfort for them. There wasn't even room for them to sit down. She had ordered this, but it was either this or let them be executed. *It's only temporary,* she told herself as she scanned the haunted, anxious faces on the other side of the bars. "Gyneth?"

"He's over here," said a voice from the other side of the cage. Haly walked around, and inside the cage bodies shifted until Gyneth stood there at the bars, looking at her with hollow eyes. His hands were covered in blood from Thale, who had died from his wound before the battle ended. But Gyneth himself was unharmed. No, not true, she thought, taking in his blank expression, with just the faintest hint of dull anger at the bottom of his dark eyes. He would never again be that boy who had danced in the firelight. She opened her mouth to speak, but no words came.

"Are we Redeemed, Holy One?" he asked hoarsely.

She shook her head, deciding in that moment that she *would* bring about a redemption, for all of them—Singer and Libyrarian both. Somehow. The nascent idea that had been forming in the back of her mind kicked again, and she began to see how there might be a way. She put her hands through the bars and grabbed Gyneth's arms. He flinched, but she hung on anyway. "Not yet," she said. "But we will be."

19

Siblea's Redemption

S elene, you must order your soldiers to execute the rest of the Eradicants immediately," said Griome. Even with the flames of anger in his sunken brown cheeks, he looked like he had aged ten years since Haly had left home. He'd lost a lot of weight to sorrow or illness or both, and as he stood beside Peliac at the hearth in his tower office, he gripped the younger Libyrarian's arm with a trembling hand. The room smelled of wood smoke and ink, and it was overly warm from the fire blazing in the hearth.

"The rest of the Eradicants?" Selene barked with open laughter. "Have you looked outside the window, Head Libyrarian?"

Haly shifted uncomfortably. Selene was right, of course, but it was strange to see this man she had feared all her life mocked by a junior Libyrarian.

" 'Fortune repays an ungrateful tyrant's oppressive ways

with the just punishment he duly deserves,' " said a book on
Griome's desk.

Beside Griome, Peliac tightened her jaw and said, "If we
are doomed, we must take as many of them with us as we
can." She focused the full power of her glare upon Haly, and
she remembered she'd been afraid of Peliac, too. "What are
you doing here? This is none of your concern. Why don't you
go help Arche with the wounded?"

And leave her and Selene, and to a lesser extent, Griome,
to make the decisions.

Ever since talking to Gyneth after the battle, an idea had
been forming in Haly's mind. She had just about all of it now,
if only she could get them to listen to her. Haly struggled to
find her voice. "I'm staying," she said. "I—"

She was about to say, *I have an idea how we can all get out
of this,* but Selene put an arm around her shoulders and pulled
her close, saying, "She's my clerk. It's not for you to order her
about."

Peliac narrowed her eyes, taking a closer look at both of
them. Her long face was deeply lined with bitterness and
exhaustion, her black robes torn and stained with blood. "I
suppose we can use her as a messenger. They will not harm
her, I think. We'll keep their censor alive and she can tell whoever is in charge out there that Siblea will die if they attack us.
But is it enough leverage?" She looked at Griome, who stared
at the flames in the fireplace and did not answer.

"It is enough to stall them," said Selene. "And I am expecting reinforcements from Ilysies. But we can find someone else
to take the message. She's been through enough."

Peliac sneered at her. "You've been expecting reinforcements from Ilysies ever since you got here! They're not coming! You know it very well. Your mother has betrayed you and
left you out for the buzzards."

Selene nodded her head, glaring at Peliac, her face stiff and pale. "But I have not relied on my mother. Our own Clauda is a great weaver of webs. She will find a way."

"Clauda?" said Haly and Peliac in unison. Haly extricated herself from Selene's arm and turned to face her.

Selene looked at her and nodded, a smile warming her face. "Did you know how smart she is?"

"All persons are doomed to be in love once in their lives," said a book on the shelf behind Griome's desk.

Haly blinked. "Oh that, yeah. Yeah, she's very smart."

"The pot girl? Our survival hinges on the pot girl?" Peliac gave a bitter laugh. "Then we have nothing to worry about," she said sarcastically. Peliac grabbed a decanter and glass from the mantelpiece and poured herself a generous portion of brandy, which she downed in one gulp. "Let's start celebrating, by all means," she said, her voice thick with emotion. She offered the bottle to Selene, her eyebrows raised in question.

Selene shook her head, her cheeks flushed. "As long as she's out there, being Clauda, I'm not ready to give up."

Peliac put the decanter back on the tray. "Then while you are waiting for the exalted ladle to pour blessings upon us all, pray have your soldiers finish at least part of the job!" she hissed.

"Make up your mind. Do you want them dead, or do you want bargaining chips?" yelled Selene.

"One will suffice," said Peliac. "Siblea. The rest—"

"Stop!" Haly raised her voice, using the practice she'd had declaiming at Singers for the past several days. Peliac, Griome, and Selene stared at her in momentary silence and she took the opening. "There is a surer way. Give them the Redemption."

Peliac sighed. "They've gotten to her. How sad. Have you ever read *The International Handbook of Traumatic Stress Syndromes*?" she asked Selene, who shook her head. "Interesting book. The author uses a term for people sympathizing with their own kidnappers. Stockholm syndrome, he calls it. Apparently it's quite common."

Concerned, Selene looked at Haly as if she thought it was true. She put a hand on Haly's shoulder. "Perhaps you should rest. Why don't you go to my chambers? I'll have Jan bring you something to eat."

"Isolation of patients who are suffering from a contagious disease," said another book on Griome's desk.

Frustration filled Haly. It was her turn to flaunt tradition. She could not contain the incredulous glare that shot from her eyes and actually made Selene take a step back. "Are you insane? There is a *nation* out there"—she pointed at the window— "waiting for a miracle. And if they don't get their miracle, they're going to use the Horn of Yammon to destroy the Libyrinth and call that their miracle. I say let's give them the goat-fuck miracle!"

"She's out of control," Peliac murmured to Griome, but they both watched in fascination as Selene's clerk dressed her down.

For her part Selene blinked and said, "What are you talking about?"

"We have the highest surviving member of the Singer hierarchy downstairs locked in a box, and we have their messiah, me. Yes," she said, pausing for a moment for that to sink in. "They really think I'm the prophesied messiah, the Redeemer. If we can't make a miracle to satisfy them with those ingredients, we don't deserve to survive. We're going to bring Siblea up on top of the battlements, and he's going to announce the Redemption, and then I'm going to tell them that the Word is united with the Song, and in proof of this, I will be choosing novitiates for the Chorus of the Word. We'll take a few at a time, bring them inside and teach them to read, then they'll go out and teach others."

"This is madness," blurted Peliac. "Selene, don't listen to the poor girl. Even if it weren't for the fact that there are too many of them, they are illiterate rabble."

Griome at last roused himself. "The knowledge we of the Libyrinth have dedicated our lives to preserving is not for peasants and book burners," he said. "Even if they can learn, they don't want to learn, and even if they wanted to learn, they would not understand. They would take the first opportunity to destroy us and our sacred charge. Better we should all die than betray our trust."

Siblea had been right. The Libyrarians did not want to share their knowledge. Haly wasn't surprised. But how could she get them to accept what needed to be done? Maybe she didn't have to. She took another look at Griome and Peliac. What were they going to do, glare her to death? She'd been through torture, for Tales' sake. Neither of them was even remotely as scary as Ithaster with that little knife and jar.

Haly glanced at Selene. Selene controlled the soldiers downstairs, and Selene was listening. "You know, that is exactly the attitude that got us into this mess in the first place," said Haly. "The Ancients did not permit their slaves to read. Then Iscarion refused to share *The Book of the Night* with Yammon. Throughout history, the literate have kept their knowledge from the illiterate. Is it any wonder the Singers regard us as a threat? But now we have a chance to make things right. Not all of the Singers are bent on destroying the written word. One of them, my friend Gyneth, has learned to read. And Censor Siblea is sympathetic to the books. Selene," she said, putting her hand out. "It is the right thing, besides being our best chance for survival."

"Selene, listen here—"

"You must control your clerk!"

Peliac and Griome clamored for Selene's attention. Haly was right. It all depended on what Selene told the Ilysians to do, and they knew it well. Selene ignored them and continued to stare at Haly for a long time. "I don't know if I'll ever think of them as anything but Eradicants," she said, "but you're right about the second part. It's a good plan."

Haly and Selene came downstairs to discover that one-quarter of the Great Hall—from the Alcove of the Fish to the Alcove of the Cow—had been converted into a makeshift hospital. About twenty wounded Libyrarians and servants lay on pallets on the floor, tended to by Libyrarian Burke, who had dedicated herself to the study of medicine. She supervised three clerks—Kia, Clae, and Issic—as they changed bandages and gave their patients water.

"Winter comes to water as well as land, though there are no leaves to fall," said a book.

The stench of death emanated from the Alcove of the Dog, where the corpses had been gathered. Hearthmistress Hepsebah, herself nursing a bandaged arm, oversaw servants in the process of carrying the bodies up to the top of the sixth tower where they could be decently burned.

"The weight of the odors was heavy on his soul, like chains, like old burdens reassumed," said another book.

Between the dead and the Libyrinth wounded lay the wounded Singers, no more than ten of them, languishing on the hard stone floor. "We can't have that," said Selene, and she broke away from Haly.

Haly watched, expecting Selene to confront Burke about the Singer wounded. Instead she went up to Hepsebah. "They can't be burned yet," she said, pointing to the body of a Singer soldier that was being hoisted up the stairs by Jan and Bessa.

"Oh, don't worry, Mistress Selene," said Hepsebah, "we won't be burning them, just our own dead. Them we can pitch over the walls and let that rabble out there take care of them."

Selene shook her head. "You can't do that, either. There's

a chance that those outside don't know yet about what happened in here. We need to keep it that way for as long as possible. So no burning, of anyone, and definitely no throwing the bodies over the walls."

Hebsebah nodded. "I see, Mistress. Yes, of course. But let us take them to the top of the Dog's Tower all the same, won't you? They're stinking the place up something fierce."

Selene nodded.

Haly caught up with Selene and tugged her sleeve. "What about them?" she asked, pointing to the Singer wounded.

Selene frowned. "What about them?"

"Something should be done for them."

Selene sighed and gazed past the Singers to the orderly pallets where the Libyrinth wounded lay. "It looks to me like Burke has her hands full with our own people."

"But—"

"They'll die soon anyway, Haly."

Haly looked at the nearest of the Singer wounded. He was a soldier with a broken leg. There was no need for him to die, but he would if he didn't get any medical attention and gangrene set in. "Selene—"

Just then screams came from the far end of the Great Hall, where the rest of the surviving Singers were penned up inside the palanquin. Haly saw a number of Libyrarians standing close to the bars of the enclosure, but from where she stood she couldn't make out what they were doing. Whatever it was, the Singers didn't like it. She ran toward the cage.

Arche, along with the Libyrarians Talian, Micah, and Noil, stood clustered at one end of the enclosure. They had all lost loved ones in the battle. The four of them were surrounded by a larger group of Libyrarians and clerks, who were shouting things like "Book burners!" and "Eradicant savages!" The Ilysian guards, standing in a loose ring about ten feet from the cage, looked on placidly.

Talian and Micah, both large, strong men, had one of the Singers by the wrists and had pulled his arms through the bars of the palanquin, stretching them tight. The Singer's face was wedged into one of the spaces between the bars. Haly recognized him. He was a member of the Chorus of Medicine, and he was screaming.

"Maybe only a god could bear it," suggested a book.

In the space between his outstretched arms stood Arche and Noil. Arche's hair was matted with sweat and blood, and there was a streak of scarlet across her cheek. Beside her stood Noil, who had been Frise's master. The older man was of primarily Ilysian stock, with dark hair gone to gray; a tall, slender build; and a prominent nose. Arche held a book open in front of the Singer while Noil pried his eyelids open, forcing him to look at the words.

"The question of fragmentation and wholeness is a subtle and difficult one," said the book.

The rest of the Singers were in an uproar, all except for Siblea and Gyneth. Siblea leaned down, his face close to the man's ear, speaking quietly to him. They were packed so tightly into the cage that Gyneth, though only three feet away and on the same side of the cage, was separated from them by five people or more. He stood up on his toes to shout over the panicking Singers. "It's okay, Rossiter, you can look. The words won't hurt you."

"Stop it! Release him!" yelled Haly. The Libyrarians merely looked at her and snorted in derision. "You were the one who wanted them left alive," said Arche.

By now Selene had caught up. Haly turned to her. "Selene, make them stop this, now. This isn't the way."

Selene eyed her. "They aren't actually hurting him. If what you say is true, if the Eradicants are willing to learn to read, then let's start with him. Let him prove it."

Haly swallowed. She had a point. Though what the Libyrarians were doing amounted to torture, that was only because the Singers clung to a belief that had to be cast aside.

Haly stepped up beside Arche. This close, she could hear Siblea's voice underneath Rossiter's screaming. "I tell you there is nothing to fear, Rossiter. Stop screaming. Don't struggle. You are only doing what they want."

"I am damned," Rossiter cried. "I won't hear the Song."

"You will," shouted Gyneth. "No harm will come to you!"

Beside Gyneth stood Baris, the heavyset subaltern who had been horsing around with Gyneth and Thale on the day she'd visited Subaltern Chorus Five. She remembered him laughing as he tried to climb on Gyneth's back. Now his face was dirty, and a gash on his forehead slowly oozed blood. He was pressed up against the bars of the cage. "How do you know?" he accused, grabbing Gyneth by the shoulders. "You spent a lot of time with that lit. What did she do to you?"

Gyneth tried to take Baris's hands, tried to calm him, but the other boy's fists curled tighter into the fabric of his robe. "She didn't do anything to me," said Gyneth. "She did me no harm! Our Redeemer showed me the error of that teaching when she was our guest at the citadel. Written words are nothing more than symbols on paper. She taught me how to read them and I have heard the Song many times since then! Do you hear that, Rossiter? You are not damned!"

Baris's lips contorted with outrage. "Blasphemer!" he screamed and grabbed Gyneth around the neck, choking him.

"Stop!" cried Haly, but Baris did not let go. Others in the cage urged him on, and joined in as best as the cramped conditions would allow, clawing and jabbing at Gyneth. Haly's heart hammered in panic.

Meanwhile, the rest of the Libyrarians had grabbed books from the shelves and rushed to the bars of the cage, holding them open and jeering.

The books clamored, "He had the most astounding collection of teeth"; "To oppose something is to maintain it"; "The essence of strategy on these occasions is to be as near the door as possible."

All of the Singers except for Siblea, Gyneth, Rossiter, and Baris screamed and clapped their hands over their eyes. Rossiter's voice gave out and he subsided into muffled sobs. "Baris!" shouted Siblea. "Let him go." But Baris simply closed his eyes and continued strangling Gyneth.

Haly looked around frantically. One of the Ilysian guards had a Singer mind lancet slung through the sash of her tunic. Haly went right up and wrested it from the cloth. Before the guard could retaliate, Haly twisted the spiral-engraved sleeve midway along the shaft and activated the mind lancet. The orb at the end of the lancet glowed blue.

The look Haly gave the guard left no doubt as to her willingness to use the weapon, and the woman made no attempt to stop her or retake it.

Haly turned and shoved the mind lancet through the bars of the palanquin into Baris's side. He screamed and went limp, sagging forward onto Gyneth, his hands falling away from Gyneth's neck.

Gyneth coughed and gasped for air. Thank the Tales, he was still alive. She whirled on the Libyrarians surrounding the cage, brandishing the mind lancet at them. "Back off!" she shouted. Those nearest her blinked and stepped away, lowering their texts. She stalked around the sides of the cage and the others followed their example, until she reached the group surrounding Rossiter. Arche looked up at her, her nostrils flaring. "What are you going to do? Attack us? Your own people?"

If she had to, Haly thought. Out of the corner of her eye she saw Selene reaching out to stop her, but before either of them could act, Siblea shot his hand through the bars of the cage and snatched the book from Arche's hands. Surprise registered on the faces of those who saw it happen.

"Enough!" Siblea roared. "Members of the devout chorus, collect yourselves! We are not children to be cowed by superstition. *We* are the learned ones. What Gyneth says is true—there is no harm in the written word. Look!" Casting a defiant look at Arche, he opened the book and leafed through it, his eyes scanning the pages.

"Knowledge, too, is a process," said the book *Wholeness and the Implicate Order*, which had a large orange butterfly on the cover.

One by one, the Singers peeped through their fingers and beheld their last living leader gazing upon the pages of a book. Everyone, Libyrarian and Singer alike, fell silent, staring in amazement. Talian and Micah released Rossiter's arms and stepped away from the cage. Noil put an arm around Arche and drew her back.

Siblea looked up from the book, his piercing eyes meeting those of the Singers and the Libyrarians, one by one. "Behold the first miracle of the Redemption," he said.

Rossiter alone did not watch Siblea. Once released, he sank down upon his haunches as best as the cramped quarters would allow, and covered his face in his hands. He was crying and muttering, "I saw them . . . I saw the murdered words."

Haly reluctantly glanced at Gyneth, who now rubbed his reddened neck and swallowed, his gaze exultant as he watched Siblea. How she wanted to go to him, but she crouched down beside Rossiter instead, twisting the carved sleeve on the mind lancet as she did, powering it down. She tucked the weapon under her arm and reached her hands through the bars of the cage. She stroked his head, then took his hands and firmly pulled them down. "Rossiter," she said. "Brother, open your eyes."

"R-r-redeemer?"

"Yes. Open your eyes, Rossiter."

He swallowed and at last opened his eyes. They were blue. He stared at her. "I . . . I can see."

Haly smiled at him, and nodded. "You are not blind, and you are not damned," she told him, and then turned her head and nodded toward Siblea. "Look."

Rossiter gaped openly. "B-but, the murdered words—"

"Are dead no longer," Haly finished, her voice rising in volume, pitched now to carry. As she spoke she stood, and pulled Rossiter up with her. "They speak to those chosen to hear them, and you, and Censor Siblea, and Subaltern Gyneth are the first of my chosen. The first three members of the Chorus of the Word." She released Rossiter's hands and took the mind lancet in her right hand, holding it at her side. She turned to look at Selene. "Three have embraced the Word," she told her, "and they will be released from bondage."

Selene's eyes traveled from Haly's determined face to the mind lancet in her hand, and then to the Libyrarians and Ilysians who were looking on. Haly watched her calculate what the others would do if she released them against what Haly would do if she didn't. She couldn't be certain what sum Selene came up with, of course, but Haly was pretty sure it involved herself going berserk with the mind lancet and ultimately getting torn apart by a mob of angry Libyrarians. And Selene had gone through a great deal—too much—on Haly's behalf to let that happen now. Selene looked profoundly unhappy, but she nodded, and gave the order.

How vast was the sky, and how small and inconsequential the world and its people and their problems. A little snarl of matter compared to the clear pure blue above.

Clauda had no way of knowing whether she could get to her friends in time, but then there was very little left of Clauda to worry about it. She was doing what she was made for: flying, soaring, coasting on the currents of air that wound about her like the curving lines she saw in her mind when she entered the statue. Below her the mountains were sharp, jagged exclamations of matter, like the earth shouting, but she was too high up to listen to the whiteness of their icy voices. And then they were behind her and all the earth below sloped down into the vast brown Plain of Ayor. *Home,* she thought, and she felt it was the Clauda part of herself that thought it.

And that was when she remembered she had someplace in particular to go, and an army to bring with her. She could sense them below, a great encampment dwarfed by the breadth of the plain where they awaited her. *Follow the wing,* the queen of Ilysies had told her general. The queen had intended the wing to lead them to the last home of the Makers, the Corvariate Citadel, but that was not what Clauda-in-the-Wing intended to do.

Something in her metal skin tingled and spoke with something vast far to the south—a milling roil of voices whose words were indistinct, though she felt them like a rippling on her skin. The Libyrinth called to her.

She climbed higher and higher, up until no birds flew near her, until the clouds were far below and she saw the great curve of the world, stretching down and out against the lip of the blackness that would someday consume everything.

From here she saw the whole Plain of Ayor and the Lian Mountains and bright Ilysies near the sea—the sea that remembered the blackness beyond and did its best to be like it. She saw the Corvariate Citadel in the north, a humped mass of steel no larger than a pebble, and she saw the Libyrinth, surrounded by its own devouring cloud of blackness. When she saw that, her rage knew the color of righteousness, white hot and electric blue, and it built inside her, and she gathered herself for war.

She dove, down and down, reveling in the wind and the

velocity, pulling out of her headlong plummet just before gravity would have made her its prisoner. She swooped over the tents of the Ilysian army's camp, low and fast enough to make the fabric flutter, to make the women's hair lift and the dust rise. She banked and turned. As she passed over them again, they were already mustering to follow her.

Rossiter, under guard, was set to tending the Singer wounded, while Haly, Selene, Siblea, and Gyneth all went to Selene's chamber to discuss the Redemption.

"The middle of the Atlantic Ocean"; "balance is necessary"; "challenge the rule"; "her thoughts strangely torn"; "a cataclysm of love"; "friend."

Haly was tired, and her cot in the corner called to her with a tale of sleep more compelling at the moment than any book in the Libyrinth. She led Gyneth to her cot and sat down beside him. She pulled back the collar of his robe and saw the red marks of Baris's fingers on his neck. "Are you all right?" she asked him, and he nodded, but he was still swallowing a lot, and there was a glassiness in his eyes, a mix of exhaustion and fear.

Selene pulled the chair from her desk and stood it next to the fire, across from her own customary seat. "Siblea, isn't it?"

Siblea inclined his head.

"Please sit down." She rummaged around in the scroll case beside the desk for a moment and then pulled out a dusty bottle. The Pavanian whisky. In the time that Haly had been her clerk, she'd only seen Selene open that bottle once before. But Selene opened it now. She looked around the room for glasses or something like them, and found only a mug with the mostly evaporated dregs of three-week-old tea inside it. She grimaced and threw the dregs into the fire, looked back into the cup, and grimaced again. She set it back on the desk and said, "Let the Lion gnaw it." She put the bottle to her lips and took a healthy glug, then handed the bottle to Siblea.

They all had a drink. The whisky filled Haly's mouth with fire and a taste like burned moss.

For a moment nobody said anything and Haly realized they must all be as tired as she was.

"The beginning is hearing," said a book.

Selene had taken her seat beside the fire and now stared at Siblea. At length she said, "Why did you do that, down there?"

"You mean when I looked at the book?" said Siblea.

She nodded.

Siblea opened his hands. "It struck me that the time had come to abandon what was no longer useful."

Beside Haly, Gyneth took a sharp intake of breath and sat up straighter. Selene narrowed her eyes and said, "What is that supposed to mean?"

"We find ourselves in an interesting situation," said Siblea. "Those of us within the Libyrinth are in your power, and yet you are surrounded by us and we possess a weapon that can destroy the Libyrinth and all within it. First and foremost, I wish to live, and therefore, it is my fervent desire that those of my brethren outside do not use the horn while I am still in here. But there is more. That young woman, your colleague, the Thesian—"

"Arche," supplied Selene.

"Yes," said Siblea. "Before she got the idea of forcing poor Rossiter to look upon the words, she read aloud to us. It did not terrify us as much as she'd hoped it would, and that is when she became more inventive. However, what she read was this." He sang,

Active immunization,
describes the administration,
of all or pa-a-a-rt

of a biologic agent
in
an
ef-
fort
to
evoke
a defensive response
in the host.

Gyneth's eyes widened and he leaned toward Siblea. "Oh! Oh that makes sense!" he said.

Siblea nodded happily, then looked at Haly and Selene. "We've always known that the mark of Yammon protected children against certain diseases. And we knew how to make the patches that bear the mark, but we didn't know *why* they worked. You see? We know the how, but you know the why. And that is why, even though *The Book of the Night* is a fake, I think we'll be well-served to stay here with you and learn to read. At least for now."

"What? *The Book of the Night* is a fake?" blurted Gyneth.

Siblea looked at him and nodded. "I'm sorry, Gyneth. We've been tricked. *The Book of the Night*, if it ever existed, is not here."

Haly and Selene stared at each other and then at Siblea. Maybe he was bluffing. Haly said, "But I recited—"

Siblea laughed, not unkindly. "You made it up. You did quite a credible job, too, for the most part, but you said that the Ancients were held in the temple. They were not. The temple had not been built at that time. Frankly, I'm surprised Orrin didn't catch it, but then I think he was rather focused on learning how to make Eggs. At any rate, he is dead now and I, the highest-ranking official left alive, must choose the course for my nation.

"Holy One, you once told me that you would teach every member of the devout chorus to read, and call that the Redemption. I think we need a miracle now, don't you?"

They were all silent. Haly stared at Siblea, who regarded her with a happy smile. This is what she had worked for since the moment Anne spoke to her from the iron box. But something about the self-satisfied curve at the corners of Siblea's mouth made her queasy. There were so many more of them than there were Libyrarians. What was to stop them from doing everything their way and totally subsuming the Libyrarians?

"Now," said Siblea, clapping his hands and standing up, "is there a song for learning how to read?"

A-B-C-D-E-F-G, H-I-J-K-L-M-N-O-P, Q-R-S, T-U-V, W-X, Y and Z. Now I know my A-B-Cs, all the books are mine to read."

Haly stood in the archway to the seventh tower and watched as Siblea led the imprisoned Singers in a new song. He stood outside the cage in the Great Hall, singing with great force and waving his arms energetically in patterns that probably meant something to them. He had a big grin on his face.

"He inspired uneasiness," said a book.

The other Singers sang along with varying degrees of enthusiasm. Some lifted their voices in rapture, jubilant that the Redemption was nigh; others, like Baris, mouthed the words while staring around with wide, fearful eyes, as if expecting the wrath of Yammon to come crashing down upon them at any moment.

Siblea abruptly dropped his arms and the singing stopped. In an eyeblink his expression had turned from energetic delight to menacing wrath. He stepped forward quickly and reached through the bars of the cage, wrapping his fingers into the collar of Baris's robes. He pulled the hapless boy against the bars of the cage. "Do not think you can fool me by simply mouthing the words. I can hear that you are not singing." Still keeping a firm grip on Baris, Siblea looked among the others, picking out several more who had appeared unenthusiastic and pinning each of them with a glare that made Haly shiver. "As I can hear all of you who are not singing." He released Baris at last and the boy fell back against two of his fellows, gasping. "You will all learn this song, and you will all learn to read. Because it is the will of Yammon!"

And of Censor Siblea, thought Haly, finding herself grateful that he had never felt the need to go beyond unspoken threats in his interrogation of her.

"Now, again from the beginning." Siblea stepped back, lifted his arms, and began to sing. "A-B-C-D-E-F-G . . ."

A few feet away, Gyneth knelt beside a bedsheet that had been laid out upon the floor. He dipped the feather end of a quill into the pot of ink at his side and painted an *S* on the fabric. As she approached he looked over his shoulder. When he spotted her, he broke out in a grin and sat back on his haunches. "Holy One! Look!"

Haly returned his smile and quickened her steps, wondering as she did if his evident pleasure at the sight of her was no more than religious zeal. She pushed the thought aside and surveyed Gyneth's handiwork. He had written the letters of the alphabet out large, in a painstaking and rather jagged hand. But it was readable.

"I thought we could hang it from the shelves," he said. "If they can see the letters while they sing the song, they will learn quickly."

Haly nodded. "It's a great idea."

Siblea smiled happily and looked as if he was about to say something else, but someone called to her from the part of the hall where the wounded were being cared for. She glanced over and saw Rossiter, standing beside the Singer wounded, on the side closest to the Libyrarian wounded. He looked down at Palla, the crèche nurse, who had been shot in the leg. It was a flesh wound, but she was not recovering. She had a high fever and was weakening rapidly.

Haly started toward him. The dead had been removed to the top of the sixth tower to await cremation. And the Singer soldier whose leg was broken was sitting up now, his leg in a splint. Among the Libyrarian wounded, many were up and helping Libyrarian Burke with the others. Those who had not recovered were, however, in grave condition. As Haly reached him, he looked over at Burke, biting his lip. "Holy One," he said, "I have something that might help these people." He took a pouch from around his neck and opened it. Inside were small, oval, shiny objects. Haly stared at them. "Are . . . are those pills?" she asked. She'd heard descriptions of pills, but she'd never seen any before now.

He nodded. "The song for making them comes directly from the Ancients themselves and is one of the most prized of the medical chorus. They're a broad-spectrum antibiotic. With just one dose they destroy infections of all kinds. Those of your people who have not either recovered or died from their wounds are suffering from infection. This could save them."

Haly nodded. She turned and called Burke over. "Rossiter, tell her what you just told me."

When he finished, Burke pursed her lips. "I don't know," she said, staring warily at Rossiter. "It could be a trick."

" 'Don't trust that dingblasted old Cat neither,' " said a book.

"Libyrarian Burke . . ." Before Haly went on she pulled Burke and Rossiter with her some distance from the wounded. "What would be the purpose of poisoning them? They're already dying."

She shrugged. "How should I know the purpose of anything these people do?" She hesitated, then looked closer at the pills in Rossiter's hand. "Let me see one."

Rossiter handed her a pill and she scrutinized it. "The books tell of such medicines," she admitted. She looked back at the Libyrinth wounded and was silent a moment. At last she nodded. "All right," she said. "But I will administer the pills."

As she watched Burke giving out the medication, Haly remembered she'd meant to see about getting the imprisoned Singers something to eat. She turned toward the kitchen, but on her way there she ran into Selene. "I've just been talking with Peliac and Griome. They're not happy, and for that matter neither am I, but we all agree this is the best chance for the books to survive."

Haly nodded. "Look what Gyneth is doing," she said, dragging Selene over to where Gyneth was just finishing the Z. He looked up, smiled at her, and gave Selene a strained, polite nod.

Selene opened her mouth to speak but her reply was cut off when Jan came running headlong from the second tower as if the Lion itself were after him. "Haly! Selene! You know that big horn thing they have out there? It's moving!"

Haly, Selene, and Gyneth exchanged glances. As one they ran to Selene's chamber. They went to the window and looked out upon the multitude of the Righteous Chorus. What Haly saw sent a shudder through her. *No. Oh, no.*

"The true parasites of Pern were Threads," said a book, one Haly knew, but there were no dragons here to save them.

The sun was setting, but the horn was clearly visible, a black disk rising up out of the mass of people outside like a new and terrible dawn. Tiny figures swarmed over the lowest curve of the spiraling horn as it gradually turned to face the Libyrinth. "It's too late," she whispered. All their work, all the difficult, miraculous work they had all done over the past day was wasted. "They're going to use it," she said.

20

The Libyrinth

Haly strained for the first vibrations of the horn's sound wave. Gyneth and Selene stood on either side of her and she took their hands, gripping them tightly as she waited for the antlike, crawling sensations to creep over them.

"It hushed the eloquent, struck down the powerful, abolished the beautiful and good," said a book.

Someone pounded at the door. "Princess Selene, you must come at once. We have a . . . situation," shouted a voice.

Selene spun from the window and opened the door. Haly turned to see Vorain, the woman who had worn the red kerchief, now dressed in the uniform of the Ilysian army. Her cheeks flushed vividly and she sweated a little. "I've never seen the likes of it, Selene," she said. "A little red man!"

"Nod!" shouted Haly, and her heart lifted with hope. *If he's managed to steal the Egg from the horn . . .* Dragging

Gyneth by the hand, she shouldered past Selene and the soldier and ran down the stairs, following the sounds of commotion to the Great Hall.

"The most frightening thing was probably the tenacity of his continued existence against all the physical odds," said a book as Haly arrived in the Great Hall.

The ring of Ilysian guards around the prisoners shouted and brandished their weapons toward the top of the palanquin while the Singers inside wailed with terror, and above it all shrieked Nod, squatting atop the peak of the roof with a bundle of black cloth clutched to his chest. Haly couldn't be sure, but she thought the bundle glowed ever so slightly. Gyneth opened his mouth as if he would say something, but couldn't seem to find the right words.

"Everyone calm down!" shouted Siblea, an edge of hysteria to his own voice.

The Singer wounded, those well enough to move, were huddled together behind Rossiter, who stared wild-eyed at the imp. Meanwhile, Libyrarian Burke, her attendants, and those Libyrinth wounded who were well enough to sit up and look around were watching with amazement. As Haly looked on, Burke approached Rossiter, put a hand to his sleeve, and said something to him.

Selene skidded to a halt beside Haly. "It's Nod," she said.

Haly nodded and turned to her, grinning. "I think he's got the Egg from the horn."

Selene's eyes widened. "Are you sure?"

"No, but on the way here I tried to get him to steal it. And just now, they tried to use the horn and nothing happened."

Just then a shot was fired and they both turned in horror to the palanquin. Fortunately the nervous soldier had missed both Nod and his mysterious bundle. Nod screeched in further indignation and spat at her. "Selene, would you tell your women to stand down, please?" asked Haly.

Selene nodded. "Everyone lower your weapons, there is nothing to fear," she said, striding forward. The women looked uncertain, but they brought their rifles to their sides and backed off a trifle, allowing Haly to pass between them.

Haly approached the palanquin, tilted her head back, and lifted her hands to the edge of its roof. "She says Nod is the hero of the Libyrinth. She says come to her now. There is still more to his story."

Everyone waited in silence as Nod, still clutching his bundle, crawled to the edge of the palanquin and peered at her. "Story?" he said.

She smiled and nodded. "Nod's story. Best story. Come now."

The imp permitted her to wrap her hands around his ribs and lift him down. She held him close, cradled against her chest much as he cradled the bundle. "Thank you, Nod."

"What is that thing?" said Siblea, more unnerved than Haly had ever seen him. "It crawled through one of the skylights above"—he pointed up at the dome—"and then it dropped. It landed on top of the palanquin, unharmed. How did it do that? And why does it have your Redemption hood?"

Haly ran her finger along a ribbon of gold that was sewn into the cloth Nod held. So that was what had happened to her hood. Gently, making no attempt to remove the object beneath from Nod's grasp, she pushed the fabric aside to reveal an Egg. Glowing amber and traced with copper veins, it shone forth in all its glory and everyone, including Siblea, gasped. Haly grinned.

"This," she said, nodding at the little red man in her arms, "is Nod, my traveling companion."

"Your traveling companion?" Siblea glanced at Gyneth and narrowed his eyes in speculation. Gyneth swallowed.

"Yes," said Haly. "And he stole this Egg from the Horn of Yammon and saved us all. They were about to use it to bring the Libyrinth down around us all, but it is powerless now. Now we have time to prepare for the true Redemption."

Nod tugged at her hair. She looked down at him. "Nod give Libyrinth her heart back now?"

"Yes," said Haly. "She says, 'Does Nod know where the Libyrinth's heart goes?'"

He nodded his head vigorously and squirmed. "She must put Nod down!"

Haly set him on the floor and he raced with the Egg across the Great Hall to the console. The hood, no longer needed, fell to the floor and was left behind.

Haly ran after Nod and found him inside the curved wooden counter, splaying his hands upon the seal on the floor. The Egg rested at his side.

In the center of the floor inside the console was a round seal of brass, engraved with the seven guardians. "Must open," said Nod.

Haly remembered the vault and the constellations on the rim of the hatch and the simple scale she and Clauda and Selene had sung to open it. Here, they had a voice for every Tale. More than one. And they might need them, because the vault had an Egg and was fully functional. The Libyrinth had not had an Egg in all the centuries that its people had lived there. *This might not work at all*, Haly thought.

But if they were going to perform a Redemption for those waiting outside, then singing would need to be part of it. And if the Singers were going to learn to read, hadn't the Libyrarians better learn to sing, just in order to keep up? "All life is a form of cooperation, an expression of feedback arising out of the flux of chaos," said a book.

Haly turned to face all of those who now gathered expectantly around the console. "It's time for voice practice," she told them.

She had expected resistance, but the possibility that singing might allow the Libyrinth to at last have its Egg had the whole population of the Libyrinth sorting itself into Tales almost before Haly had finished telling them what to do. Now standing on top of the console to make herself heard, she watched in amazement as each group assembled itself behind its respective guardian in a wedge. Peliac stood at the head of the Mice, Micah the Goats, Arche the Lions, Burke the Fish, Talian the Cows, Noil the Dogs, and Selene herself motioned to Haly to jump down and take the place before her, at the head of the Flies.

It was no easy task to get this many people in key at the same time, and in the end Siblea—perhaps in self-defense— pushed through the crowd and began to direct them, Tale by Tale.

At last, some hours later, they were ready to sing. As their voices filled the Great Hall, Haly, standing before the gap in the console, stared at the seal in the floor. Nothing happened.

"Louder," cried Siblea. "Sing louder!"

They did. Their voices doubled in volume. It was not the most beautiful chorus, but it was amazingly good considering how bad they had been when they'd begun. They drew their breath deep and belted forth their notes with all the power they could muster. Sparks appeared, faintly, around the edge of the seal. Haly and Siblea both nodded and waved their arms in encouragement and somehow, the Libyrarians sang even stronger. Haly's ears rang with the sound. It thrummed in her bones. Nod rolled the Egg into the center of the seal and suddenly the figures of the guardians came alive with light. It was different than it had been at the vault; this was smaller and less showy, and instead of erupting with intertwining lines, the animals themselves flowed and moved with light, and chased one another around and around in a circle. The seal began to open, and Nod barely caught the Egg before it fell through the hole. He danced around the widening circle with it in the same direction in which the animals ran, until there was no place left for him to stand and he had to leap outside the circle.

The light went out. Silence rang in Haly's ears in the wake of the sound they had made, and she found herself overwhelmed with pride for her people and what they had just done. No, it was not like the Song, or even like any song, but it was their sound, and a good one.

Beneath the seal was a round tunnel leading straight down. A narrow metal staircase clung to the walls of the tunnel and spiraled down into the darkness. Nod, still holding the Egg, began to climb down the steps, and Haly stepped past the console and followed. Behind her she heard a scuffle as several people tried to access the steps at once.

"No," said Selene, "we can't all get down there."

"And let's not waste more time arguing over who goes," Peliac amazed Haly by saying. "Besides," she noted, "it could be dangerous. We've lost enough people already."

Haly might need someone who could repair the ravages of time upon the Ancient technology, but Libyrarian Grath was dead. But there was someone else, who might know even more. "Gyneth," she said, craning her head about. She'd lost track of him in all the excitement. "Where is Gyneth?"

Haly and Gyneth followed Nod down the steps. The walls of the tube were covered with waving lines that glowed gold as they neared them and then faded back into obscurity once they'd passed. The lines curled and eddied around each other, sometimes in ever-tightening spirals; sometimes in long, graceful arcs that swooped around the entire tunnel. "It's the Egg that's doing it, isn't it? It's making them glow."

Gyneth nodded. "Songlines glow in the presence of an Egg, and that's probably why we were able to open the seal."

Some time later Haly said, "I wonder how far down this

goes." They had been descending for what seemed like a very long time. The opening of the tube above them had dwindled into a tiny circle and then disappeared.

"Well, we fell on those books with even more appetite than on the food, and in the end, we moved into the house and stayed all winter," said a book.

And another: "Everybody wants programmable animals."

"One meaning of the term *labyrinth* is 'the internal ear,' " noted a third.

In addition to the book voices and the ring of their footsteps on the metal grating of the steps, there was a faint hum. "What is that? That hum?" she asked.

"That's the sound of the songlines," said Gyneth.

As they descended, Haly concentrated on the sound. It wasn't as constant as she'd thought; or rather, there were modulations within the sound; a soft rise and fall in pitch. The more attention she paid to it, the more detail it seemed to have. "Do you hear that?" she asked.

"The hum? Yeah," said Gyneth, giving her a funny look.

"I mean inside the hum, the different notes. It sounds . . . It sounds like a chorus."

Gyneth looked at her blankly. "You mean like voices? No. Just the hum."

Haly swallowed. She heard the music more strongly now than ever, as if her ears were learning to hear it. It was the Song.

At last the tunnel came to an end and they found themselves at the top of an enormous cavern that stretched in every direction as far as the eye could see. Like the walls of the tunnel, the cavern ceiling was covered with songlines that blazed to light in the presence of the Egg, illuminating what lay below them.

"Who is she, staring down like the dawn's eye, bright as the white moon, pure as the hot sun, frightening as visions!" said a book.

Directly beneath the tunnel opening was a great, golden face.

Like the Devouring Silence, it lay flush with the floor and was covered also with songlines. Surrounding it, and going on for as far as the eye could see, were the curving, twisting shelves of the Libyrinth stacks.

Haly had never seen the stacks from this angle. She was pretty sure no one ever had. Certainly if anyone had come back from a long sojourn and reported seeing this, word would have gotten around.

Before, Haly had always been in the stacks, pressed close in the narrow spaces between the shelves, unable to discern any sort of overall layout. As it turned out, they formed a true labyrinth, trailing away from the face in all directions. They looked like nothing so much as kinky, wiry gray hair.

They descended the rest of the staircase, which was nerve-wracking, since now there was nothing between them and the floor except a slender handrail.

When they finally reached the floor, Haly immediately went to investigate the face. It was rather larger than the Devouring Silence had been, and it was a coppery color similar in hue to the glow of the Egg and the songlines. Its eyes were closed, its lips slightly parted. The curving lines on its face flickered and glowed in the presence of the Egg.

"The Library is unlimited and cyclical," said a book.

Haly looked at Nod. "Where does the Egg go? Does it go in the face?"

"On her tongue, her tongue," he said, but then he shook his head and scrambled to the face, crouching beside the chin. He pointed to a discolored patch at the corner of the mouth. It was a whitish, pebbly residue.

"Corrosion," said Gyneth. "I don't think it's safe to put the Egg in yet."

Nod shoved the Egg into Haly's hands and began to lick at the streaks on the face. As he did this, Haly caught sight of movement at the edge of the clearing. It was the shelves—

they were moving. No, not moving; covered with something that was moving.

Nods, thousands of them, crawling, leaping, and hopping from shelf to shelf. "What does she say? What does she say?" they said in unison. The sound was deafening.

"Shit," Gyneth murmured, gripping her hand tightly. "I thought there was just the one."

As the Nods swarmed toward them, Haly and Gyneth turned to each other and held on tight, burying their faces in each other's shoulders. Haly expected to be suffocated by them, perhaps devoured, but that wasn't what happened. The Nods swept past them and crawled all over the face in the floor, licking and cleaning it.

Haly released a breathy laugh and looked up at Gyneth. He stared at her. "I guess we're okay," he said.

She nodded. She hadn't pulled back and he hadn't, either. She stood up on her tiptoes, and at the same time he bent forward and their lips met. His mouth was warm and it tasted a little like the oatmeal the Singers had been given. She liked it.

They separated, only to hug each other tightly and then kiss again. *This can't be the right time for this*, she thought, but she didn't care. Gyneth was so warm, and the fuzz on his upper lip felt nice against her skin. This time when they separated she said, "You said you wouldn't break the rule."

"The one I'd break the rule for was out of my reach. I thought so, anyway."

"I'm not. I'm right here."

"But you're my Redeemer."

She nodded. "And you're mine."

They kissed again and he held her close again. She peeped over his shoulder at the face in the floor. It was still covered with Nods, cleaning away. So many things had happened so quickly. She felt like she'd been fighting one battle after another for days, and she supposed she had. And now, here in this strange place, with Gyneth beside her, it finally came to her how tired she was. "Let's . . . let's find someplace to sit down."

They wandered hand in hand around the little clearing between the face and the bookshelves. "I never realized there were so many books," said Gyneth.

Haly nodded. She was about to tell him about one of her favorites when she spotted a pair of figures huddled against one of the shelves. They wore black robes. "Hello?" Haly said, stepping toward them. Their faces were hidden by the hoods of their robes. They appeared to be sleeping, but who could sleep through the light and noise of their arrival? More to the point, what were they doing here in the first place? A dry, acrid smell filled her nose as she crouched down beside them and put a hand out to touch the shoulder of the nearest one. "Hello?"

The wool of the figure's robe was dry and rough. It rasped against something hard beneath it. At Haly's gentle pressure, the figure shifted and then collapsed. A cloud of dust rose up and she sneezed. When she opened her eyes again, it was to behold a fleshless skull grinning up at her from the shroud of the Libyrarian's robe. The other figure, too, had collapsed. She saw finger bones protruding from the folds of a sleeve.

She screamed. Instantly Gyneth was at her side. Backing up swiftly, Haly stumbled. Gyneth helped her to sit down on the floor. She was shaking. She'd heard the stories since childhood: overambitious Libyrarians lost in the stacks, never to return. But it was another thing to see it for herself. "They're dead. Who are they?" she babbled.

"Her mommy and daddy," the Nods muttered absently as they worked away at cleaning the face in the floor.

"What?" Haly sprang to her feet, grabbed one of the Nods with both hands, and held it before her face at arm's length to avoid the flailing arms and kicking legs.

"Put Nod down! She must put Nod down!"

"No. Not until you explain. These are my parents you say? Then how was I born?"

The creature squirmed. "Nod helped! Nod didn't mean for the beasties to die. Not Nod's fault they had no food! Not Nod's fault they ran out of water! If Nod hadn't helped, she would have died, too! Nod saved her life! Nod made her better than beastie parents could. Nod wanted to hear the stories. Nod always cleans books, keeps everything neat and in good repair, but Nod never hears the stories! Is that fair?"

Haly felt cold. "What did you do?"

"Mother beastie was dying. Other beastie was already dead. Nod has always wished for a beastie that was at least a little bit like Nod. So Nod took the protobeastie out of the mother beastie. She was very small. She was dying, too. Nod gave her some of Nod's own code. That made her strong. Nod surrounded her, kept her warm, fed her on Nod's own bodies so she would grow and live, and hear the stories and then tell them to Nod. When she got big enough, Nod took her to the crèche."

Haly dropped the creature, sank to her knees, and vomited. She wasn't even human. She retched until she could bring up nothing but bile and mucus. It stank. Some of the Nods twittered in consternation and left the face to clean up her mess. Dully she watched them wiping and licking, feeling nothing, gratefully sinking into shock.

"My mother is a fish," said a book with a small boy's voice.

She felt a hand on her shoulder. A human hand.

Gyneth peered at her. "Haly . . ."

She looked up at him, not knowing what to say. Some part of her brain noticed that he had used her name, but the rest of her just felt ashamed. He hadn't known, when he kissed her. She hadn't known. What was she? "I-I'm sorry," she managed.

He knitted his brows and shook his head. "Sorry? For what?"

"I didn't know. You didn't know. What I am. What am I?"

Gyneth shrugged. "I don't care what you are. I'm glad. I'm glad they did it, if it was the only way for you to live."

"B-but I'm not human."

"You're the Redeemer; of course you're not entirely human. How could you be?"

Haly stared at him. Gyneth looked calmly back at her as if it were nothing to be ashamed of. Haly blinked, trying to think of how to get through to him. "But surely this proves I'm not divine," she said, and suddenly realized there was some tiny part of her that had thought she might be. Now that part was both relieved and disappointed.

"The sight once seen can never be forgotten, but we turn from it and pursue our way," said a book.

Gyneth nodded, biting his lip and looking like he was trying very hard to think of the right thing to say. "I don't think it matters. I don't think the Song cares who sings it. Besides, maybe you can do more as a person than as a god. A god is all. A person is change."

A person, was she even that? "But . . . little red men?"

Gyneth laughed sheepishly and hung his head. "I'll admit it's a bit embarrassing, especially for people like Censor Siblea, but . . ." A mischievous smile curled the corners of his mouth. "They've obviously got it all wrong. You opened my ears to the truth. And I do believe that the divine runs through you, but if it turns out that the divine is a bunch of tiny red demons, well then I think it serves some people right."

All of a sudden Haly felt a bit better. She blinked. Gyneth reached for her and she let him wrap her in his arms and for a while they just sat like that, two robed figures huddled together against the bookshelves.

The Nods finished cleaning the face in the floor, and then one of them unhooked a latch at the side of the face and the rest scrambled to his side and lifted up the face to reveal the machinery inside. It looked like a lot of wires and there was a large copper-colored cup that looked like it might be where the Egg was supposed to go.

The Nods were busy there a few moments more, and then at last they retreated, muttering sadly as they went. Only one Nod remained, looking up at Haly and Gyneth mournfully. "Heart face clean, still no good. Heart place broken. Beasties must fix."

Haly looked at Gyneth. "Can you do it?"

He looked back at her, wide-eyed. "I don't know. I haven't even completed my Circuits yet." After a thorough examination, Gyneth stood up again. "I think I can fix it, but it will take time. I can start on the tone capacitors right now, but after that I'll need tools," he said, "a hand harp, pliers and cutters, and copper chording."

Haly frowned. "I don't know if we have those things."

"Gilleach will, and Javer did. If you can get them to send Gilleach down here with anything he can find, and one your own people, too, someone with experience with electronics . . . Do you have anyone like that?"

"Grath, but he's dead. His clerk, Thotis . . . I think she's still alive."

Gyneth nodded. "Send them both if you can."

"I will. I'll be back as soon as I can."

He was already kneeling over the copper innards of the face in the floor, but he looked up suddenly. "No. You stay up there. You have to do the Redemption."

"I'll wait until you finish."

He shook his head. "We don't know how much time we have. They could get another Egg for the horn. You need to do the Redemption as soon as you can."

She saw the sense in this. "I'm sorry you'll miss it."

He smiled. "If it's a real Redemption, I won't."

Around the outside of the Libyrinth's dome ran a terrace some ten feet wide. It was bordered on its outer edge by

a parapet three feet high. The ever-present wind of the Plain
of Ayor whipped Haly's hair around as she stepped onto the
terrace from a door in the side of the seventh tower. She went
to the parapet and looked down. She was directly above the
front gate, and more than fifty feet above the plain. She had
that same dizzy feeling she'd had in the amphitheater in the
Temple of Yammon, and she stepped back a little.

"He had felt nothing but fear, sheer naked fear, when he
thought about the parachute jump."

It was dawn. She had been beneath the Libyrinth for most
of the night, and when she resurfaced, it was to find Censor
Siblea and Selene and the other Libyrarians waiting for her.
Waiting for the Redemption.

Rossiter's pills had helped all but two of the Libyrinth
wounded, and Burke, her assistants, and those recovered
patients who were strong enough to stand had joined the Chorus of the Word. They all stood behind her now, arrayed in the
same formation they would have used in a recital hall at the
Corvariate Citadel, though there were no steps for them to
stand on, and so they arranged themselves with the tallest
members in the back and the shortest in the front. Censor
Siblea stood beside her.

Haly looked again at the waking multitude below them.
"How can we make ourselves heard?" she wondered aloud.

"That may be our greatest obstacle," Siblea admitted.

Haly turned to face him. "But what did you plan to do? If
the Redemption had gone as you expected it to, how did you
plan to address the multitudes?"

Siblea looked chagrined. "If the Redemption had gone as
planned you would have translated *The Book of the Night* for
us, we would have memorized it, and then Michander, Orrin,
and I would have gone back out to the camp and declared the
Redemption accomplished. The horn would have been used,
the Chorus of Yammon would have sung the Song to all those

near enough to hear it, and then everyone would have gone home. We never had any intention of addressing the multitudes from up here."

"Then maybe we'd better go down there ourselves."

"That would be dangerous in the extreme. They have already attempted to use the horn; I do not think that any of us would be safe among the multitudes now. No. Yammon smiles upon us. The wind is at our backs. It will carry our voices to the Righteous Chorus. Look, even now they are gathering."

People had spotted them standing up here and begun moving toward the front gate where they stood shoulder to shoulder, waiting.

Haly's mouth went dry. She felt as if she could barely whisper, let alone make herself heard by those below. In her hand she held the diary of Anne Frank. She was about to attempt a Redemption without *The Book of the Night*, with the alphabet song instead of the Song, without anything but the wind to carry her voice, and she herself was not even truly human. This was probably about as far from anyone's idea of a Redemption as you could get. But they were waiting.

"The present moment is the only moment when life is available to us."

Haly swallowed and held her hand aloft, brandishing the book. "Members of the Righteous Chorus, welcome to the new day!" she shouted. Her words were greeted by a smattering of applause that soon died off. "The first day of the union of the Song and the Word. The errors of the past are cast off, and a new chorus is born"—she turned and lifted her hands to those assembled behind her, and then faced the multitude once more—"the Chorus of the Word, whose members will teach us all a new song, and through the blessing of the Redemption, the Word and the Song will be reunited, to be heard by all and sung by all together, so that none will ever forget the sacred words!"

Below people were milling about and talking to one another. Haly got the distinct impression that they had heard some of what she'd said, but not all of it, and were now turning to their neighbors in an effort to fill in the gaps. Those further away from the front gate were not even listening. Haly watched as a farmer poured water into a trough for his ox. No matter what Siblea said, they would have to go out among them. There was no way this could be adequate.

But it was a start. She turned to the chorus and motioned them to begin singing. She and Siblea joined in. "A-B-C-D-E-F-G . . ."

By the second time through, a few people had started singing along. By the third there were more, and then something amazing happened. The wind picked up, and all at once, all throughout the encampment, everyone turned and looked at Haly. They were all staring up at her, some still singing, others agape in awe.

"And the wind blows right through us."

The wind grew stronger still, and with it came a roar the likes of which she'd never heard before. She turned and looked up and saw what everyone on the ground had already seen: a golden crescent, flying overhead like a swift and errant moon. As it barreled past them the noise became unbearable. Reflexively, Haly ducked. The flying machine swooped and banked over the gathered multitude and she found herself gaping along with everyone else. It turned again and flew straight for the Horn of Yammon. From the underside of the flying machine burst a beam of blue light that struck the bell of the horn. With an ear-splitting crack, the horn shattered.

21

Clauda's Redemption

Clauda-in-the-Wing waited until the Ilysian army was near the Libyrinth, but still on the other side of the low hills facing the front gates of the library. While they were still hidden from view of the Eradicants, she flew to the back of the Libyrinth in a high, wide circle, being careful to remain out of the enemy's sight. And then she descended upon them.

There was a thing they had: a great iron horn. The part of her that was the Wing of Tarsus smelled it as evil and the part of her that was Clauda of Ayor knew that it was their greatest weapon. So she struck that first.

It was a simple matter to unleash the Sword of the Mother. Every speck of anger and fear that she had felt—from the first Eradication she'd witnessed at the age of three to the atrocities that had occurred in the vault—was already burning bright white and hot blue within her. All she had to do was let them go. And she did and they flew out of her in a concentrated beam of rage that sliced through the air, burning dust particles as it went. It struck and the iron horn shattered with a satisfying crack. Her soul gloated over the great spinning chunks of metal and the black-clad figures scattering to avoid them.

Clauda-in-the-Wing climbed higher, saw that the Ilysian army was almost at the top of the ring of low hills surrounding the Libyrinth, and wheeled and darted down to strike a wagon that was full of the jagged smell of gunpowder. It exploded, too, and she found another, and another. Righteous anger raced along her veins and brought a glow to her metal skin. She felt something akin to joy.

In a vast white wedge, the Ilysians descended upon the crowd gathered around the Libyrinth. And the Eradicants, caught unprepared, struggled to form ranks and meet them. They were only partially successful. While Clauda-in-the-Wing wheeled and banked and struck another ammunition wagon, the Ilysians broke through the Eradicants' hastily formed line. The sounds of rifle fire, the crackle of mind lancets, and the screams of humans and horses prickled on her skin and she twitched at the sting of it.

Clauda-in-the-Wing swooped and fired at another wagonload of ammunition. It went up like the others had, in a triumphant blaze, but this time a man ran from the burning wreckage. He was on fire. His screams raked her golden skin and the feeling might have been horror and it might have been sharp delight at the downfall of an enemy. But the Clauda part of her knew that it was horrible. He ran as if he could escape the burning flames but they were all around him. He twisted and fell and rolled but he just kept on burning. His screams dwindled as she flew away, but the image of his contorted body, twisting in the orange fire, stayed with her.

On the ground all was chaos as Ayorites ran in every direction, screaming, trying to avoid the Ilysians, who now focused their wrath upon the Eradicant soldiers, pressing them back and back, toward the walls of the Libyrinth.

A man driving a cart full of roasted corn found himself suddenly in the midst of the Eradicants' retreat. As the black-garbed soldiers melted away around him, he came face-to-face with the bulk of the Ilysian force. He lashed frantically at his ox, but the animal balked, terrified by the noise and the smell of the fighting. A young boy sprang from the back of the cart, wielding a pitchfork. A woman ran after him, crying out for him to stop. But the boy threw himself at the nearest Ilysian, who cut him down with a sweep of holyfire from her weapon. The woman ran to his fallen body and fell beneath the hooves of the Ilysians' horses as the unit parted and flowed around the wagon.

This was what she had intended. These Eradicants and their Ayorite followers were enemies of the Libyrinth. The wing wanted to strike at them. They were a black mass of Enemies, but Clauda didn't want to see another person burning. She didn't want any more to die. She fought against the urge to bank and turn and strafe the man in the wagon. The wing's will to do so was a tangle of black twisting threads all around her and she fought against them. The lines lashed her with fire and the horizon tilted and she realized that she was falling.

In reflex she swerved and swooped, righting herself as she targeted a family desperately trying to get out of the way of the advancing Ilysians. She watched them as they fled, but she managed not to fire on them. It was the wing. The wing was a machine of war and it wanted to kill. She couldn't let it.

The curving lines wrapped around her and she tried to twist free of them, but the more she struggled the deeper they dug into her, searing her with white-hot fire. She was no longer one with the wing. It wobbled and started to fall.

Where there had been song, there was now screaming. From the parapet of the Libyrinth, Haly watched

Singers and Ayorites run from the falling shards of the ruined horn. The gold crescent flying machine darted back and forth while several wagons filled with rifles and ammunition exploded. Beyond the chaos, a thin line of white appeared on the horizon and grew with tremendous speed, like a second dawn. Banners waved above them, emblazoned with the red bull of Ilysies.

Haly turned to Selene, who stood a little bit away from the chorus. A feral grin lit Selene's face as she met Haly's eyes. "Clauda," she said. "I knew she'd think of something. I wonder how she managed it? But that doesn't matter now. The important thing is that we're saved. Look!" She pointed to where more Ilysians converged upon the Singers and Ayorites who were massed before the front gates. "There's no escape for them."

"No!" shouted Haly. "This is *not* good news!"

Siblea was at the parapet beside her, looking down on the battle now raging. "They did not go to the Corvariate Citadel," he said, and looked up at Selene. "You knew they had not gone to the citadel."

"I knew nothing of the kind, but I believed," said Selene.

Siblea's lip curled and he shoved Haly to one side and lunged at Selene, reaching for her neck with those long arms of his. "You Ilysian bitch!"

Selene stepped to one side and drew her knife, and the next instant the two of them were rolling around on the ground, an undifferentiated mass of black robes, punctuated occasionally by a hand or an ear or the bright silver gleam of Selene's knife.

"Stop it!" yelled Haly, but they didn't pay any attention to her.

Behind her, the Chorus of the Word was breaking up as Baris tried to go to Siblea's aid and Burke tried to stop him, and Jan tried to go to Selene's aid and Rossiter tried to stop him. Everyone was shouting words like "Eradicant" and "lit."

"The horrible words, mocking looks, and accusations which are leveled at me repeatedly every day, and find their mark, like shafts from a tightly strung bow," said the diary of Anne Frank.

If this kept up, they were all going to kill one another. "Stop! Everyone! Stop this now!" Haly yelled, but it didn't do any good. No one was listening.

Everything she had worked so hard for, all the good that she'd been so determined to see in the people around her, that she'd needed to see in order to survive—in order for all of them to survive—it was all being destroyed. They were destroying themselves. Haly felt as if her heart would explode with the agony of it.

"I want to bring out all kinds of things that lie buried deep in my heart," the diary of Anne Frank told her. Haly opened her mouth and a sound came out. It was partway between a wail and a shout and it sounded like the first thin strains of the Song. Realizing this, she kept it up. Maybe if they heard the Song . . .

Burke looked at her, and so did Rossiter. They seemed to collect themselves as they looked around and tried, in turn, to get the others to stop fighting. Haly kept singing, but the Song was not for one voice alone. Burke and Rossiter seemed to realize this, and they joined her, but three were not enough, either.

Baris straddled Jan, punching him hard in the face. Selene got her knife free at last and raised it high above her, poised to stab Siblea in the chest. Burke and Rossiter and Haly stared at each other in dismay and their voices faltered.

And then something changed. Every book, every voice that had whispered, murmured, spoken to Haly her whole life, suddenly began to sing. She knew at once that Gyneth had finished his repairs and powered up the Libyrinth. At first she nearly fell from the force of it as the voices of the Libyrinth's books combined to form a harmony she knew very well—a harmony that united the ocean tides and her beating heart. It was the Song, and it was inside her and outside her and she opened her mouth and it poured forth from her.

Just as she had discovered at the citadel, one did not need to know the Song in order to be affected by it. Baris and Jan looked up at her, their faces full of awe at the sound issuing from her mouth. She knew what they were feeling. She felt it herself, that sense of union with all things—including one's enemies.

Baris and Jan stared at each other. Did they see themselves? They appeared to be surprised to find their hands around each other's throats and they let go. They helped each other up and they joined Burke and Rossiter as they sang along.

Soon everyone on the rooftop had abandoned fighting and taken up the Song. Haly could do nothing but let the sound pour through her, but Selene and Siblea came to her and turned her to face the parapet. They guided her forward and the others came, too, and they all sang with everything they had, in hopes that it would reach those who were in battle on the ground.

But with despair, Haly saw that they were not heard, and the battle raged on.

*B*reathe, Clauda told herself. *Breathe*. She stopped struggling against the lines that enwrapped her. She took deep breaths and she thought of Selene standing in the library. *We want to live,* she thought, and she felt the wing trying to pull out of the spiraling dive they were in. *The sky,* she thought. *We love the sky and we love to fly in it.* And that was something that she and the wing definitely agreed upon. Together they strained for the sky.

Clauda-in-the-Wing felt as if the effort would pull her apart, tear her wings off, and buckle her spine. The ground was approaching faster every second but at last she was able to force her way through the momentum of the dive and pull up. She grazed the tops of a cluster of abandoned tents as she did so, but her metal hide was strong. And then she was soaring up again, up into the sky. She flew high, and the farther from the battle she got, the less impulse she felt to use the sword. She looked down, taking a survey of the battlefield. The Eradicants had rallied and reformed in a defensive line behind which chaos reigned as Ayorite peasants sought to flee the battle. They were protected for now, but if the Ilysians broke the Eradicant line again, they would be trapped between the advancing army and the walls of the Libyrinth. Clauda did not think the Ilysian soldiers would differentiate much between Eradicant soldier-priests and their untrained followers.

But what could she do? Was not the wing a machine of war? At the thought, the part of her that was the wing quickened with purpose and it took all the willpower Clauda had not to dive and launch another attack. She flew higher still and turned her attention to the limitless dark above the blue sky, hoping that in that void, and far from the smell of fear and death below, she might be able to think.

Adept Ykobos had said that the wing had many uses. For example, it could heal her seizures and hear the books in the Libyrinth. What else could it do?

As she thought about that, banking around and around the Libyrinth and trying to figure out how to stop this war that she'd started, something changed. What she had been hearing from the Libyrinth, the multitude of voices, all speaking at once over and around one another in a great babble— suddenly the voices merged and became one great voice lifted in the most beautiful sound Clauda had ever heard. If the sensation of being inside the wing had a sound, this would be it. Clauda didn't understand it, but the part of her that knew the spiral language of the wing recognized this song as the ocean from which those curving lines and peaks of intention sprang. This was the source; all-nourishing, all-loving, whole, and able to make whole all who heard it.

Integration. That was what this was. It was integration on a grand scale. The ultimate goal of the teachings of kinesiology was to bring the individual mind into alignment with the body and thus with the world around it. When all was in synch, when communication flowed effortlessly from mind to heart and from brain to eye, then nothing could be wanted, nothing could be feared, because all was together. And in that awareness of the unity of all things, desire and fear and pain became meaningless and fell away. There was no need for worry ever, because moment to moment, everything needed was present either in oneself or in the environment—self and environment being one and the same.

Clauda scanned once more the ground below her, half expecting to see the Eradicants and the Ilysians dropping their weapons. But no. The battle raged on and then she understood why. They couldn't hear it.

The wing has many uses. The wing has many uses. The words repeated themselves over and over again in her mind. Was there a way for the wing to let everyone hear what Clauda heard? She had no idea. The wing's powers were based on light, not on sound. And yet she heard . . .

The Sword of the Mother was a concentrated beam of light. Could it be made diffuse instead? Could it be modulated to carry a signal, instead of concentrated to bring death?

She banked and rolled and thought about a great canopy of light; soft, lambent light like that which bathed her inside the statue. She rolled onto her back and released the light up into the sky.

The first time, the sword shot out and up into the air and she was glad she had thought to turn over. She tried again, concentrating on the idea of a fierce, narrow river flowing out from its canyon into a wide and placid lake.

As Clauda-in-the-Wing released the light once more, it was at first the raging torrent of killing energy, but then it broadened and softened until it was a dome of luminescence emanating from the belly of the wing. Light like the kind that surrounded her in the statue. Her joy tripled with the rush of rediscovering more of who and what she was. The wing was. She and the wing were.

When she had held the dome of light for some time, when she was sure it would not revert to the sword, she rolled back over and the light streamed down over the Libyrinth and all those who surrounded it.

The fighting stopped. Everywhere, people were dropping their weapons and reaching out to each other, helping those whom a moment ago they had sought to kill. Clauda-in-the-Wing felt relief and a growing sense of pleasure at having remembered her ancient ways.

But the fact that the light was now also encompassing the Libyrinth had unexpected consequences. The song went on, flooding through all her energy pathways. She felt as if she were being rocked on the ocean, enwrapped in the wing's light, floating, dreaming, singing. She was singing. Everyone was. Below, everyone was looking up at the sky with open mouths, their voices taking flight. Everyone was singing the same song at the same time, and though Clauda did not know this song, she did not need to. It was as if her body knew it, as if the air around her and the soil below her knew this song, had known it all along, but until now had been unable to voice it.

The song came stronger and stronger and the air filled with the curving tendrils of its notes, like the lines of light inside the statue of the wing. These new lines in the sky grew brighter and brighter and the song grew louder and louder and more joyous.

Clauda realized they were caught in a feedback loop between the Libyrinth and the wing.

The energy was ramping higher and higher and soon it would overwhelm them all and incinerate everyone in a bonfire of ecstasy.

In panic Clauda reached out for something she knew, and what she found was the voice of one book, her most favorite. "And for those few minutes, while the song lasted, Times Square was as still as a meadow in evening, with the sun streaming in on the people there and the wind moving among them as if they were only tall blades of grass," said *The Cricket in Times Square.*

D ovrik had an Ilysian pinned to the ground and was about to smite her with his mind lancet when he heard the Song. He glanced up and what he saw took his breath away. The sky was filled with streaming, curling, curving rays of light. It was the Song made visible. He dropped his mind lancet and stood. It was the Redemption.

G alatea struggled for the knife at her belt as the Singer reared back, his mind lancet poised to strike. And then came a sound unlike any she had ever heard before. It came from the earth and the sky, and in the sky was written the name of the ocean in golden, swirling lines. The man on top of her dropped his weapon and stood, and she knew this was her chance to drive her knife into his belly but this sound she heard stopped her. They were all one in this sound. It would be her own belly she opened.

O ck huddled beneath the overturned cart and cursed his greed for bringing him here. Tala had been all for it. She had insisted that they come for the Redemption, and that they bring the boy, too. Now his wife and son were both dead.

Ock's only reason for joining the pilgrimage was to sell roasted corn to the faithful, yet here he was, still alive.

When the first few notes of the music reached his ears he thought this was some new weapon of devastation. But then the sound seeped into him and he knew that it was the Song. The one the Singers taught the villagers about, those who came to their services. He had never believed. As the music swelled, the sounds of fighting died out. Cautiously he poked his head out from beneath the wagon and beheld lights in the sky, like golden serpents flying through the air, twirling and undulating as they went. The sight brought tears to his eyes. The Redemption. It was real.

He hadn't really believed it was true, but Tala and the boy had. Why had he been spared to witness the Redemption when they, who believed, had died? They were his past and his future and they were gone now.

Nothing could take away his sorrow. If anything, the beauty of the Song only made him feel it more deeply, and to feel also the loss of all the others whose loved ones had perished in the battle. This was not like the previous year, when his prize cow had been lost to the disease of his neighbor's herd and he had wanted to go over there and kill Gormak's bull. Tala had barely been able to stop him.

No. He could not even contemplate revenge for the deaths of his wife and child, because all that would bring was more death, more loss, more heartache. No. He wanted to make sure no one ever lost another loved one to violence. No Ayorite, no Singer, no Ilysian, no Libyrarian.

This was what Tala had tried to tell him about the Song, but he hadn't listened. The Song united all as one. His sorrow was the world's sorrow. He did not have to bear it alone.

Ock crawled out from beneath the wagon and stood. He lifted his hands to the swirling sky and raised his voice in Song, tears of grief mingling with those of gratitude that he had the opportunity now to do differently. That they all did. They could all work together to make sure that nothing like this ever happened again.

He watched as the snakes in the sky grew brighter and brighter and twisted faster and faster and then, just when he thought the beauty of it would blind him, they all shot down into the ground. One landed very near him and he felt the earth vibrate with its passing. Then he heard a voice say, "And on either side of the river was there a tree of life, which bare twelve manner of fruits, and yielded her fruit every month; And the leaves of the tree were for the healing of the nations."

22

The Holy Ones

I am grateful to God for this gift."

The words were Anne Frank's, but Haly felt as if they could be her own. She was grateful. Looking down upon what had been a battlefield, where now former enemies embraced, she was grateful for the Redemption, and that meant being grateful that she was the way she was. Her ability to hear the voices of the books, the gift that she had so long cursed and hidden, was a blessing, and she cherished it.

But that ability had changed. With the Libyrinth powered up, she heard all the voices together in Song. It thrummed through her like her own heartbeat, and like her own heartbeat it faded into the background. The voices no longer intruded upon her thoughts, but she could concentrate, and hear them, and ask for one in particular to speak to her when she wished it.

Through her connection to the Libyrinth, Haly understood

that for a moment everyone had been as she was, and each person had heard the book they most needed to know. That had been Clauda's idea, and Haly had felt her having it, up there in her golden flying machine. Haly scanned the sky and for a moment her heart lurched, for she did not see Clauda's crescent ship. But there, on the ground just before the gates, it rested. Haly ran to the stairs, suddenly overwhelmed by the need to see her old friend again.

When she got to the main hall, it was to discover yet another miracle. A part of the console had lifted up to reveal a face, just as had happened in the vault. Libyrarians ran from the console to the shelves—the shelves that were moving.

"Isn't it wonderful, Haly?" enthused Noil, running from shelf to shelf, his arms full of books. "We can find anything now! Anything at all!"

"Except for *The Book of the Night*," said Peliac, whose stack of books was even taller than Noil's. "That was the first thing we tried. But still, look!" She nudged the top volume on her stack with her chin. "Volume two of the *Principia Galactica*! Volume two! I've been searching for this for the past forty years!"

It was a strange feeling, being just herself again. Clauda leaned against the outside of the golden statue in the wing and looked at the book in her hands. Her vision, still adjusting, was blurry at first but quickly cleared. She tucked the book under her arm and flexed her fingers, then ran her hands over her arms. She felt both small and large at the same time.

She looked down at her feet. They were her ordinary, every-day feet, standing upon the floor of the cabin. She blinked and for a moment she felt as if her feet were far, far below her, as far as the ground had been, when she was flying, but then she blinked again and they were right at the ends of her legs where they were supposed to be.

She took a deep breath, and as she exhaled she felt more like herself and less like the wing, and a little bit sad about it. But she felt good—tired, but good. In fact, for the first time since the mind-lancet attack in the vault, she felt completely fine. All trace of the tremors, the unsteadiness, the not-quite-put-together-right feeling—it was all gone.

She turned around to find Ymin and Po sitting sprawled against the hull of the ship, bruised, bleeding, and wearing identical expressions of transcendent wonder.

Po bled from a contusion on his forehead, and Ymin cradled her right arm in such a way that Clauda thought it might be broken.

"That . . . that was integration," said Ymin. "I always knew it would be like that." She smiled and looked at Po.

He grinned. "You heard it, too? That song? And then there was a voice telling me the most amazing story. I want to hear the rest of it."

Ymin nodded and tried to take his hand, but stopped, wincing. "My arm . . ."

Clauda went to her side and knelt beside her.

Ymin's lips compressed into a thin, pale line. "A simple fracture," she said, examining her broken limb with professional detachment. "Not difficult to heal, though it will take some time."

"I'm sorry," said Clauda.

"I think I landed on you, Adept," said Po, rubbing his forehead, "the first time we flipped over. Then it happened again, and then we heard that song . . ."

"Integration," said Ymin. She looked at Clauda. "But I never expected to experience it in this manner. You've taken the wing," she said. "Where are we?"

"The Libyrinth," said Clauda, and she told them all about the battle and what she had done.

When she finished, Ymin nodded gravely. "I knew it. I knew the wing was much more than a killing machine. And now no one can deny it. The wing is yours, Clauda of Ayor. You are the one who taught it to remember its true nature. You must keep it, even if Queen Thela herself comes to reclaim it."

Clauda did not know what to say to that, so she pressed her hand to the panel next to the door.

The wing's nose pointed directly away from the Libyrinth, whose gates were no more than twenty feet away. On every other side they were surrounded by people: Ayorites, Eradicants, Ilysians, and Libyrarians. Some of them were wounded, and those nearest them assisted them as best they could. An Ayorite gave an Ilysian water; an Ilysian helped a Singer to stand. There were dead, too, though not anything like as many as there nearly were. The faces of the living, which turned to her as she stepped away from the wing, were streaked with tears of sorrow as well as joy.

They all stared at her. "The Redeemer," somebody murmured, and then to her utter shock, others took up a chant: "Redeemer, Redeemer."

Clauda panicked. "No, you don't understand. It's not me. It's Haly, she's the one . . ." Clauda turned, and pointed at the gates of the Libyrinth with the hand that held *The Book of the Night* in it.

"Redeemer! Thank you! Thank you for bringing the sacred book," said a peasant, a man with a soot-smeared face.

"Read it to us, please," cried an Ilysian soldier.

Frightened, Clauda shook her head. "No. I'm not the Redeemer," she said. "It's my friend, it's not me."

And then the gates of the Libyrinth opened and Haly stepped out. The scar on her cheek curved from her left ear through the hollow of her cheek and curled up, ending just below her left eye. She was surrounded by people in black and brown robes. Some of them Clauda recognized, such as Peliac and Burke. Others she didn't; Eradi— She stopped herself. Singers. Haly held hands with one of them, a boy her own age who wore a brown robe.

Haly caught sight of her and grinned. She let go of the boy's hand and ran. The next thing Clauda knew, Haly's wiry arms were around her and her face was buried in Haly's thick, curly hair. Clauda breathed deep, taking in the smell of Haly, of home.

"Are you all right?" Haly asked her.

Clauda nodded and pulled back to peer up into Haly's face. Her eyes strayed to the scar on Haly's cheek. "And you?"

Haly smiled and nodded, and they hugged again. "We tried, we were always trying to get you back. You have to know that," said Clauda.

She felt Haly nodding and those arms gripped her tighter. "You know, Selene told me exactly the same thing."

"Selene? Is she here? Is she all right?"

"Yes," said Haly. "I have so much to tell you. There were so many times I wished I could talk to you, and now you're here . . ." Her voice broke at the end and dampness seeped through the thin cloth of Clauda's tunic where Haly rested her face.

Clauda found her own tears answering her. There were plenty of things she'd done in the last month that she didn't like. And so many times that she'd been afraid, and had to keep going anyway, and now—it was as if now, reunited with her old friend, the true enormity of it came to her all at once. Clauda didn't know what would happen next, but one thing was certain. They'd never again be just a clerk and a pot girl, sneaking food and hiding in the laundry yard to gossip. "The Libyrinth is safe?" she asked Haly.

"Yes," said Haly, who took a deep breath and steadied herself. She released Clauda and stood back, looking at her. "Thanks to you. What did you do? One minute I was struggling to make myself heard, and the next the Song was everywhere, everyone heard it. It was the Redemption, Clauda. The real Redemption, and it has made the Singers Libyrarians, and the Libyrarians Singers."

"Holy One, read us the book!" cried the Ayorite man who had thanked her for bringing *The Book of the Night*. He was kneeling and he lifted his hands to Clauda in supplication.

"They think it's me," said Clauda. "I'm sorry. Because of the wing, I guess . . ."

Haly shook her head. "They're not wrong. At least, no more wrong than they are about me."

The crowd around them parted and Selene appeared. "Clauda!" she shouted and charged forward, seizing her in a hug that would have been terrifying for its strength if it were not so welcome. Clauda buried her face in Selene's robes and hugged her back for all she was worth.

Their reunion was disrupted by a commotion at the outer edges of the surrounding throng. People were pointing at the crest of one of the low hills that surrounded the Libyrinth, and someone muttered, "Queen Thela."

Clauda and Selene stared at each other and then Clauda scrambled up onto the wing for a better view. There, just descending from the hilltop, were a chariot and two outriders. The golden chariot glinted in the sunlight. It was drawn by two white horses and the figure driving them wore white. One of the outriders carried a standard flying the flag of Ilysies: a red bull upon a green field. Clauda swallowed against the sudden dryness in her mouth.

Selene and Haly climbed up and stood beside her. "Oh, shit," said Selene.

Clauda nodded, frightened all out of proportion to the

apparent situation. Thela had two escorts, nothing more. What could she do? Anything.

"What in the Seven Tales is she planning?" said Haly.

Selene shook her head. "I don't know. She meant to send her army to the Corvariate Citadel, to conquer it once the Singers had left for the Redemption."

An Ilysian woman holding a helmet with a brilliant red crest on its crown looked up at them from the ground and said, "But rather than disclose to me her true intention, she ordered me to take the army and follow the wing." Clauda recognized the woman's voice. It was General Tadakis.

"And I stole the wing and flew here," said Clauda, meeting the general's eyes.

Tadakis smiled and tilted her head to one side. "And so here we are."

"She can't be pleased," observed Adept Ykobos, who stood near the door of the wing, Po beside her.

"No. I don't imagine so," said Selene.

"I suppose she'll want the wing back," said Haly.

"Unless she means to carry it away on her back, there is nothing she can do about that," said Clauda. "She can't fly it." She looked at Adept Ykobos, and then at Tadakis. "If she could, she never would have sought another pilot."

Adept Ykobos and General Tadakis both nodded their heads. "That's right," said Ykobos.

"Well, her army, anyway," said Haly. "Surely she'll take that back."

Tadakis shook her head and threw her helmet on the ground. She unsheathed her sword and unslung her rifle and laid them on the ground as well. "I cannot speak for all my country-women. But I am a soldier no more."

Around her, those Ilysians who had not already abandoned their weapons dropped them.

Thela and her retinue rode right up to the throng surrounding the front gates and halted. From her elevated position in the chariot—a beautiful thing of gold and mother of pearl—she surveyed the crowd surrounding the wing. "My sincerest congratulations to all of you who have received the blessing of Redemption today," she said, her voice pitched to carry far and wide. "This is truly a moment that will live in the memories of all those who have witnessed it."

Her outriders applauded and many others joined in.

Thela put one hand to her breast and swept the other before her as if to encompass the crowd. "I myself saw the lights in the sky and hastened to be the first to congratulate you, the Redeemed. Now we are all one, embraced by the Mother, bathed clean by the ocean. Our families will rejoice for us, and though not privileged to experience such rapture for themselves, will take comfort in the knowledge that their mothers, their sisters and daughters, are now more committed than ever to do their duty, to protect not just their beloved home, Ilysies, but also the incalculable treasures left to us by the Ancients. Treasures such as the Libyrinth."

A good number of Ilysians cheered and clapped.

Thela acknowledged them with a nod. "I am grateful that this irreplaceable resource still stands, thanks to the efforts of my honored countrywomen and to my foresight in sending you here. It is an honor even more precious than Redemption itself to be the protector of this jewel of knowledge. Preserving it for all is a sacred duty that nothing can transcend."

This time the Ayorites and even some Libyrarians joined the Ilysians in the cheering.

Clauda, Haly, and Selene looked at one another with concern. "You see what she's doing, right?" said Haly.

Clauda nodded. "Yeah, taking credit and twisting the situation so that she's in charge. But what do we do about it?" She was so tired.

Suddenly she saw how tired Haly was, too—she had dark

smudges underneath her eyes and a bit of a tremor in her arms and legs. "I don't know," said Haly. "I think I'm all out of ideas."

"It's okay," said Selene, touching them each on the shoulder. "I'll deal with her."

Clauda and Haly gave each other surprised looks as Selene stepped past them to the front of the wing.

Thela continued. "And so let us be united in defense of the Libyrinth, so that its gifts can be pre—"

"Queen Thela," said Selene, demonstrating that she could project every bit as well as her mother, when she chose to. Her voice rang out clear and true over the assembled crowd. "You intended for the Libyrinth to fall."

The people murmured and looked between Thela and Selene in confusion.

"You did not send the Ilysian army to our rescue," said Selene. "You meant for them to go to the Corvariate Citadel and attack it while the Singers were on holy pilgrimage."

This sent the Singers and most of the Ayorites into an uproar and it was several moments before the noise died down enough for anyone to be heard.

"And yet my army is here in full strength. They cannot be in two places at once, my daughter," said Queen Thela.

General Tadakis jumped onto the wing and joined Selene. "My orders were to follow the wing, and attack what it attacked."

The Ilysian soldiers in the crowd nodded. "Yes, that's true," Clauda heard one of them say. "We didn't know where we would wind up, remember?"

Selene took advantage of the lull. "You told General Tadakis to follow the wing, and then you told Jolaz to fly the wing to the citadel. But before she could carry out her mission, Clauda of Ayor stole the wing and flew it to the Libyrinth. Clauda of Ayor is the savior of the Libyrinth."

Haly pushed Clauda to stand between Selene and Tadakis as the crowd erupted into more cheering. As an afterthought, Clauda lifted her hands, still holding *The Book of the Night*, displaying it to the crowd.

"Clauda of Ayor! Clauda of Ayor!" the crowd began to chant.

Panic gripped Clauda. What was she going to do now? She looked at Haly, who was every bit as reluctant to take over as she was. But someone needed to lead the people, or Thela would take charge.

"Read us the book, Holy One!" cried the Ayorite man who'd made the same request before Thela's arrival. "Reveal to us the secrets of the Ancients!"

Hoping Haly would forgive her, but also knowing that she could guide them far better than herself, Clauda reached behind her and grabbed Haly by the sleeve, tugging her forward. "I cannot!" said Clauda. "I am no Holy One. I am only the pilot of the wing. This"—Clauda thrust Haly forward—"is your true Redeemer. She is the one who can reveal to us all the words of the last Ancient."

"Holy One! Holy One! Read us the book! Holy One!" Amid the joyous throng, Thela stood forgotten. She looked around her and Clauda saw resignation in her face. She flicked the reins of her chariot and inched her way forward. Her outriders, appearing concerned, stayed by her side. The crowd quieted as she approached the wing.

Clauda tensed and looked at Haly, Selene, and Tadakis. "Now what?"

Selene shook her head. "I don't know."

Queen Thela came close enough for them to speak in ordinary conversational tones. In the chariot, she stood just a bit lower than them, but nevertheless inclined her head as if she condescended to speak intimately with them. "Very well," she said, and the sly, sad smile she gave was so winning, Clauda could not help but be a little affected by it. "It was worth a try."

She focused on Clauda. "You have bested me, my dear. If you were Ilysian I would throw Jolaz off a cliff and make you my heir. Alas." She twitched the reins of her chariot and turned away. But as she reached the outer edges of the gathered throng, she turned once more. She raised her hands to the multitude, her voice again pitched to carry. "Remember this, all you Redeemed: Through circumstance or intent, Ilysies is the friend of the Libyrinth. Any Ilysian here who wishes to return to their beloved families may do so, as a soldier or as a civilian. And as for you, honored Libyrarians and Singers, Ilysies stands ready to assist you in any way she can." She flicked the reins of her chariot, gave a sharp cluck of her tongue, and drove off, her outriders following behind her.

Haly sat on top of the wing with *The Book of the Night* in her hands. She was tired and she knew there was no way she could read all of the book to those gathered around. Not all at once. What they wanted to hear most, of course, was how to make Eggs. So she focused on the book in her hands and she silently asked it to tell her.

"I have failed. The secret of making Eggs remains a mystery. No matter what I do to Endymion, she will not tell me. I begin to think she cannot, even though she is the last Ancient. I loathe myself for all that I have done in pursuit of this knowledge. The futility of it all will surely destroy my soul.

"Now I must tell Yammon that those treasures he fought so long and so hard for remain outside his grasp, and we will forever live as strangers in this world. I do not know how I will face him."

Haly finished. Stunned silence greeted her from all sides. "He failed?" said an Ayorite man in the rough-spun tunic and pants of a peasant. His face was streaked with soot.

The crowd muttered uncertainly.

"He failed," said Peliac. Even from up on the wing, Haly could see the tears in her eyes.

Beside her stood Selene, her face ashen. Her arms hung listlessly at her sides. "Then all of this was for nothing."

"No!" shouted the Ayorite peasant. "Not for nothing. We've been Redeemed! How can that be nothing?"

"He's right," said an Ilysian soldier who was standing next to the Singer. Haly noticed she was holding his hand. "We have each other now. Plus all the knowledge in the Libyrinth and all the knowledge in your songs."

"That's right," Haly said, her voice pitched to carry. "Theselaides was only one person, but we are thousands, and we all have our own unique knowledge. If we pool all of those resources together, who knows what we may be able to discover?"

"Theselaides, or Iscarion?" asked Selene.

"Both," said Haly. "It's something I've suspected for some time. The Singers believe that Iscarion founded the community of Libyrarians. They're right. It is also true that the Libyrinth was founded by Theselaides. They were the same person. And he founded this community," said Haly. "I don't think he did that just for the literate. I think he made it for all of us."

For a moment those nearest the wing all stood looking at one another. At last the Ayorite man spoke again. "So now what?"

Haly looked around at all of them. She knew what she wanted to suggest, but could it work? Redemption or no, they were so different from one another. But then, many things had occurred that she would not have thought likely or even possible. "Stay here," she said. "Build a city here, and stay. Study in the Libyrinth. Share what you know. Bend your minds and your hearts to the mysteries of the Ancients, to all the mysteries that surround us. If we can understand each other, then is anything really beyond our reach?"

For a moment silence hung over the plain and then, as one, the crowd erupted in cheering. The sound of it buffeted Haly and uplifted her and terrified her. It was not going to be easy to make this work, but it was too late now. She was committed. She remembered how she'd felt in the Temple of Yammon when she'd been proclaimed Redeemer. This was something like that, only infinitely better. This was of her choosing.

"For the Redeemed city of the Libyrinth!" shouted the Ayorite man, and the cry was taken up and spread until it seemed that the whole of the Plain of Ayor echoed with hope.

H aly woke from the first full night's rest she'd had since they'd arrived at the Libyrinth. As she came to consciousness she felt inside herself the Song that was now as much a part of her as her flowing blood. The voices of the books of the Libyrinth combined to form a chorus so ubiquitous that for the most part, no single voice stood out, but still in moments of distraction individual voices broke through and she could always pick out books to listen to at will. She opened her eyes and saw Gyneth at Selene's desk, writing. "There were three Redemptions. The first was disrupted by rifles, the second by war, but the third Redemption was the true Redemption of the Word, and it came in the midst of death and hatred, and it turned them to hope and love. Those who heard the Song that day were truly Redeemed, and those who listened learned the Word, and knew Word and Song together. At last it was understood that what appear to be opposites are only different aspects of one whole, and that when we unite, not even the power of the Ancients can stop us from making of this life a blessing for all."

She smiled. She should get up, she thought. She had to meet with Burke and Rossiter about setting up an infirmary, and with Galatea and Ock about the drainage ditch in the eastern quarter of their new city. And then there was a meeting with

Peliac and Siblea about their research on suitable crops for the region. She would get up in a moment, but just then she stretched instead, and listened as Gyneth's soft, strong voice wound through all the other voices of those she loved.

Where to Find What the Books Said

A Guide to the Quotations

CHAPTER I

"Wilbur liked Charlotte better and better each day."
E. B. White. *Charlotte's Web*. New York: Harper and Row, 1980.

"Two houses, both alike in dignity."
William Shakespeare. *The Complete Works of William Shakespeare, Romeo and Juliet*. New York: Avon Books, 1975.

"He was just a country boy."
Isaac Asimov. *The Foundation Trilogy*. New York: Doubleday, 1951.

"In a hole in the ground there lived a hobbit."
J. R. R. Tolkien. *The Hobbit*. New York: Ballantine Books, 1966.

"The heart of the young Gasçon throbbed violently, not with fear, but with eagerness."
Alexandre Dumas. *The Three Musketeers.* Oxford, UK: Oxford University Press, 1991.

CHAPTER 3

"Heat to the boiling point in a double boiler over, not in, boiling water, one-half cup dark molasses."
Irma S. Rombauer and Marion Rombauer Becker. *The Joy of Cooking.* Indianapolis: Bobbs-Merrill, 1975.

" 'How is he?' 'Weak. They are quite pitiless.' "
Patrick O'Brian. *H.M.S. Surprise.* New York and London: W. W. Norton, 1973.

"I was awakened by the waves dragging at my feet."
Scott O'Dell. *Island of the Blue Dolphins.* New York: Dell Publishing, 1960.

"All that is told here happened some time before Mowgli was turned out of the Seeonee Wolf Pack."
Rudyard Kipling. *The Jungle Book.* New York: Grosset & Dunlap, 1963.

"Route the wiring from the front light along the frame members to the area of the generator-mounting bracket."
Clarence W. Coles and Harold T. Glenn. *Glenn's Complete Bicycle Manual.* New York: Crown Publishers, 1973.

"When tweetle beetles fight it's called a tweetle beetle battle."
Dr. Seuss. *Fox in Socks.* New York: Random House, 1965.

CHAPTER 6

"It is far better to be feared than loved if you cannot be both."
Niccolò Machiavelli. *The Prince.* New York: Penguin Books,
1981.

"Little boys squash ants in fun, but the ants die in earnest."
Lars Eighner. *Travels with Lizbeth.* New York: Fawcett
Columbine, 1993.

"Samuel Spade's jaw was long and bony."
Dashiell Hammett. *The Maltese Falcon.* New York: Alfred A.
Knopf, 1930.

"Simon was inside the mouth."
William Golding. *The Lord of the Flies.* New York: Putnam
Publishing Group, 1954.

"I saw death rising from the earth."
Philip K. Dick. *A Scanner Darkly.* New York: Doubleday, 1977.

"Never live in the village again."
Scott O'Dell. *Island of the Blue Dolphins.* New York: Dell
Publishing, 1960.

CHAPTER 12

"I hope I shall be able to confide in you completely, as I have
never been able to do in anyone before."
Anne Frank. *The Diary of a Young Girl.* New York: Double-
day, 1952.

"In spite of everything, I still believe that people are really
good at heart."
Ibid.

"Sunday, 14 June, 1942. On Friday, June 12, I woke up at six
o'clock and no wonder; it was my birthday."
Ibid.

"There is a saying that paper is more patient than Man."
Ibid.

"Anti-Jewish decrees followed each other in quick succession."
Ibid.

"And I firmly believe that nature brings solace in all troubles."
Ibid.

"Who besides me will ever read these letters?"
Ibid.

CHAPTER 18

"The first hour of the war between Kalgan and Foundation."
Isaac Asimov. *The Foundation Trilogy*. New York: Double-day, 1951.

"The calm of the night was broken by a roar of thunder, and something smote the water."
Rafael Sabatini. *The Seahawk*. New York and London: W. W. Norton, 1915.

"The courtship display of the male Common Goldeneye looks much like an avian slapstick routine."
Ted Black and Gregory Kennedy. *Birds of Michigan*. Auburn and Edmonton, Alberta, Canada: Lone Pine Publishing, 2003.

"The sudden appearance of a tiger is arresting in any environment."
Yann Martel. *Life of Pi*. New York: Harcourt, 2001.

"Night was striding across nothingness with the whole round world in his hands."
Zora Neale Hurston. *Their Eyes Were Watching God*. New York: Harper & Row, 1937.

"What is the purpose of reason, Richard Parker?"
Yann Martel. *Life of Pi*. New York: Harcourt, 2001.

CHAPTER 19

"Fortune repays an ungrateful tyrant's oppressive ways with the just punishment he duly deserves."
Richard F. Burton, trans. Adapted by Jack Zipes. *Arabian Nights*. New York: Penguin Group, 1991.

"All persons are doomed to be in love once in their lives."
Henry Fielding. *Tom Jones*. London: Everyman's Library, 1909.

"Isolation of patients who are suffering from a contagious disease."
Sir Thomas More. Peter K. Marshall, trans. *Utopia*. New York: Washington Square Press, 1965.

"Winter comes to water as well as land, though there are no leaves to fall."
Gene Wolfe. "The Island of Dr. Death and Other Stories," from *The Island of Dr. Death and Other Stories and Other Stories*. New York: Pocket Books, 1980.

"The weight of the odors was heavy on his soul, like chains, like old burdens reassumed."
John Crowley. *Little, Big*. New York: Bantam Books, 1981.

"Maybe only a god could bear it."
Sean Stewart. *Galveston*. New York: Ace Books, 2000.

"The question of fragmentation and wholeness is a subtle and difficult one."
David Bohm. *Wholeness and the Implicate Order*. London and New York: Routledge, 1980.

"He had the most astounding collection of teeth."
Douglas Adams. *The Hitchhiker's Guide to the Galaxy*. New York: Harmony Books, 1979.

"To oppose something is to maintain it."
Ursula K. Le Guin. *The Left Hand of Darkness*. New York: Ace Books, 1969.

"The essence of strategy on these occasions is to be as near the door as possible."
P. G. Wodehouse. *Right Ho, Jeeves*. London: Herbert Jenkins, 1934.

"Knowledge, too, is a process."
David Bohm. *Wholeness and the Implicate Order*. London and New York: Routledge, 1980.

"The middle of the Atlantic Ocean."
Lincoln Barnett and the Editorial Staff, *Life*. *The World We Live In*, New York: Golden Press, 1956.

"Balance is necessary."
Starhawk. *The Spiral Dance*. New York, Hagerstown, San Francisco, and London: Harper & Row, 1979.

"Challenge the rule."
Abbie Hoffman. *Steal This Book*. New York: Pirate Editions, 1971.

"Her thoughts strangely torn."
Arnette Lamb. *Border Lord*. New York: Pocket Books, 1993.

"A cataclysm of love."
Gabriel García Márquez. *Love in the Time of Cholera*. New York: Alfred A. Knopf, 1985.

"Friend."
Ramsay Wood. *Kalila and Dimna*. Rochester, VT: Inner Traditions International, 1980.

"The beginning is hearing."
Mary Daly. *Gyn/Ecology*. Boston: Beacon Press, 1978.

"Active immunization describes the administration of all or part of a biologic agent in an effort to evoke a defensive response in the host."
Sybil P. Parker, ed. *Concise Encyclopedia of Science and Technology, Second Edition*. New York: McGraw-Hill, 1984.

"He inspired uneasiness."
Joseph Conrad. *Heart of Darkness*. Oxford and New York: Oxford University Press, 1899.

"Don't trust that dingblasted old Cat neither."
Robert Lawson. *Rabbit Hill*. New York: Dell Publishing, 1944.

"The true parasites of Pern were Threads."
Anne McCaffrey. *Dragonflight*. New York: Del Rey, 1977.

CHAPTER 20

"It hushed the eloquent, struck down the powerful, abolished the beautiful and good."
Charles Dickens. *A Tale of Two Cities*. New York: New American Library, 2007.

"The most frightening thing was probably the tenacity of his continued existence against all the physical odds."
Douglas Adams. *The Hitchiker's Guide to the Galaxy*. New York: Harmony Books, 1979.

"All life is a form of cooperation, an expression of feedback arising out of the flux of chaos."
John Briggs and David F. Peat. *Turbulent Mirror*. New York: Harper & Row, 1989.

"Well, we fell on those books with even more appetite than on the food, and in the end we moved into the house and stayed all winter."
Robert C. O'Brien. *Mrs. Frisby and the Rats of NIMH.* New York: Scholastic Book Services, 1971.

"Everybody wants programmable animals."
Kevin Kelly. *Out of Control.* New York: Addison-Wesley, 1994.

"One meaning of the term *labyrinth* is 'the internal ear.'"
Mary Daly. *Gyn/Ecology.* Boston: Beacon Press, 1978.

"Who is she, staring down like the dawn's eye, bright as the white moon, pure as the hot sun, frightening as visions!"
Marcia Falk, trans. *The Song of Songs: A New Translation.* New York: HarperCollins, 1973.

"The Library is unlimited and cyclical."
Jorge Luis Borges. *Labyrinths, The Library of Babel.* New York: Modern Library, 1962.

"My mother is a fish."
William Faulkner. *As I Lay Dying.* New York: Random House, 1930.

"The sight once seen can never be forgotten, but we turn from it and pursue our way."
Sir James George Frazer. *The Golden Bough.* New York: Macmillan, 1922.

"He had felt nothing but fear, sheer naked fear, when he thought about the parachute jump."
Alexander McCall Smith. *The Full Cupboard of Life.* New York: Random House, 2003.